# THE POWER OF THE WEREKIND

The boar, the bear, and the wolf turned grimly to advance upon him, their eyes gleaming, no recognition in their depths.

"Stop!" he shouted to the Wereriders. "Brothers in blood, bloodkin! Look upon me, and fight the Darkness that makes you worse than beasts! By the Light, by the Cold Steel, by the Rowan, by the Candle of the Weres! Stand as *men* once more!"

He flung his arm aloft, the crimson-dyed amulet dangling from his fingers. "I conjure you, by the blood we share, by the blood I have shed, stand as *men* once more!"

A green mist swirled between him and them, doubly bright in the westering rays of sunset. When it cleared, the Pack stood two-legged.

*You may cease your efforts, young Rider,* echoed a voice inside his head. *We have removed the ensorcelment.*

## Tor Books by Andre Norton

# Tales of the Witch World

Created
by

Andre Norton

A TOM DOHERTY ASSOCIATES BOOK
NEW YORK

TALES OF THE WITCH WORLD

Copyright © 1987 by Andre Norton

All rights reserved, including the right to reproduce this book, or portions thereof, in any form.

Cover art by Victoria Poyser
Map by John M. Ford

A Tor Book
Published by Tom Doherty Associates, LLC
175 Fifth Avenue
New York, NY 10010

www.tor.com

Tor® is a registered trademark of Tom Doherty Associates, LLC.

ISBN: 0-812-54757-8        Can. ISBN: 0-812-54756-X

First edition: September 1987
First mass market edition: February 1989

Printed in the United States of America

0  9  8  7  6  5  4  3  2

# CONTENTS

# INTRODUCTION

*Witch World* was never planned—it grew more or less by itself. I once intended a small portion of the first volume to be part of an historical novel about the knights who settled in Outremer during the Crusades and built up small kingdoms and holdings for themselves. The jump into *Witch World* came almost by chance. However, it seems to be a very demanding place nowadays and I find myself visited with more and more ideas for a new venture into Escore or some derring-do in the hills of High Hallack. Though the stories are not written chronologically, they have, during the years, developed a skeleton framework for two sections of that world—Estcarp and Escore in the East, and High Hallack and Arvon in the West.

I have had so many requests for more stories and suggestions from other writers as to good plot material that this anthology, *Tales from the Witch World,* was born. It has been an exciting experience for me to see how other writers use my backgrounds and react to the various customs and histories which have grown over the years. It has been an illuminating experience for me to watch my world stretching out and growing deeper, under the pens (or word processors) of others, one which makes me both humble and proud.

—Andre Norton

# OF THE SHAPING OF ULM'S HEIR

## by

## Andre Norton

When my Lord Ulric put aside his wife, the Lady Elva, because within two years she had borne naught but dead babes and those far ahead of the time of normal birthing, there was much whispering in the Dale—both of keep folk and of those who dwelt on the land. Yet the majority of those who spoke behind one hand and kept an eye out for any talebearers were inclined to agree with their lord's action. Ulmsdale must have an heir, all knew that. For a Dale where there was no one of the right blood to sit on the High Seat of the hall had wretched times of quarrels, and sometimes its folk were forced to live under a strange banner of some invading lord. Evil and danger one knew was better than what might lie ahead.

Not that Ulric was either an evil or a danger to his own people. He was a man soured by what he considered a major misfortune and which others muttered was the curse of his house. That, since the days of his father Ulm, and that one's impetuous despoiling of a treasure house in the waste, there had been born no living children to the blood of his line—Lord Ulric himself being fathered before that venture. One did not steal from the Old Ones, even though they be gone, without some harsh payment in return.

My lord's first wife had died in childbed—though that was not too uncommon a thing. However, even then the

3

whispers began, for no follower of Gunnora tended her, and all knew that when things go amiss in the ways of womankind the Lady of Fruitfulness can well move to set them aright.

My lord did not even wait the full year of mourning before he was a-wooing again and this time his selection was my dear lady. It was my pride that her choice of first chamberwoman fell upon me who am also accursed in my own small way and live in the keep only by sufferance. For my father was marshal on that fateful trip into the Waste under Lord Ulm, and, in his sin and folly, also wrought ill for his blood. For I was born with a beast one's face—my upper lip split like that of the free running hare. So that people ever turned from me in disgust, from the time I was able to understand my deformity.

Only the Lady Elva never showed such aversion to me. Instead spoke me fair and praised my skill with my needle and my soft touch when putting to order her long hair. Long and beautiful was that hair—lighter than any I have ever seen—closer to the sheen of gold—waving of itself when it was loosed from the formal loops of a matron's styling. Hidden now beneath a dark veil yet she is content to have it so.

For after my lord, speaking in a strange high voice unlike himself and looking everywhere but at her whom he addressed, had said the words of dismissal, she made no plaint but withdrew to the Abbey at Norsdale and there took the secondary vows of one who comes from the world, having been a wife. Though before her all such were widows ready to find a safe refuge from the world.

I begged her to let me go with her, and that was when I first learned that, though she was of pure Dale's blood, she had the Seeing, or some portion of such power. For, even as Lord Urlic's eyes had turned from her as he had ordered her forth from his household, so now did she look beyond my shoulder as if she saw no wall of stone but that which was alive.

"Ylas, there is that ahead in time which will concern you, and more than you. Here you must abide until that hour when what you shall do will be greater than you know and will change much for others." Then she took from around her neck the chain which held an ancient carving which she had worn ever under her robe so that none save me had ever marked it. Worn by years and handling it was, still there was no mistaking its shape—for it was an amulet of the Great Lady Gunnora who smiles on womankind. And this the Lady Elva put around my own neck and then laid her hand upon it, pressing it against me so that I felt its weight even through robe and under smock, and she said, "This will be shield to you, dear heart, when the time is here. Think often upon her whose sign this is and when the evil creeps upon this dale call to her."

Thus she went from us, to be swallowed by the abbey walls and no more have any touch with our world. Sore was that parting for me, very sore—once more I was the outcast one. But I think that my lord might have had second thoughts concerning his act—though the need for an heir ruled him so straightly—for he gave me freely the foretower top chamber and said that I was no longer to be the butt of other's foul humors and laughter. Clever with my needle I remained, and thus I felt that I earned my bread, for I made clothing and worked upon hangings for the walls.

My lord did not remain long without a lady. Save this time he needs must go far afield, since the whispers had run beyond the valley walls and he was looked upon by the neighbors as a cursed man. His new wedding brought us the Lady Tephana out of the north.

She had no right to stand against any curse, for men said—or their wives whispered—that she, too, was from an uncanny House and that her kin had had dealings with some of the remaining Old Ones of the Waste so that strange blood flowed even within her own body.

As my own dear lady had been fair, so this one was dark with a pale skin which seemed more of the moon's giving than any healthy sun-touched flesh. She was small, and quick but graceful in her movements, and she laughed much, though it seemed to me that good humor never touched her dark gray eyes.

Though I was no longer chamberwoman she sought me out and gave into my hands various lengths of fine stuff which my lord had gifted her for her bridal, showing me with well-drawn pictures what she wanted made for her adorning. Though she would have her own maid do the measurements, as if she would not have upon her my touch. Though I did not care, for it seemed to me that there was that about her which was like a thin grayish mist. And always, I noted from the first, when she was nearby, the amulet my dear lady had given me seemed to chill, as if in some queer warning.

Her own chamberwoman she had brought with her from the North. She was a dour, sour-faced creature, much older than her mistress. They said that she had been the lady's nurse and that the lady had grown up always with her tending.

Her name was Maug and she made no friends in the keep, though she had presence even as if she were of the high blood, for people moved quickly to do her bidding. She need only to look sharply at any of the folk and straightway they were eager to do as she wished to get rid of her.

But to me she did not use whatever small power she brought to bear upon the others. Though I was aware that she watched me whenever I was in her lady's presence, almost as if I were some bold raider and she was a loyal guard.

The Lady Tephana was not a bride more than a month

before she went forth from Ulmsdale saying that she would consult with a wise woman who had settled near Gunnora's hill shrine that she might do her duty according to my lord's great desires.

She had already borne one child yet he was not with her but dwelt in her people's keep for a while. So it would seem that the lady had already favored her, and my lord had done well for himself in finding a fruitful lady. Still, when she rode forth with Maug and two of the guards, I noted from my tower window that she did not make the turn to the path which led to Gunnora's shrine but passed that by. Then curiosity moved in me and I changed house robe for a shorter tunic and put stout climbing boots on. Taking a shoulder bag with food for a double day's journey, I slipped out of the keep at twilight and made my own way over the women's road.

Why I thought thus to spy upon my new mistress I could not even understand myself, save that the need for my going gnawed in me like a hunger and would not be appeased.

It was close to midsummer and the moon was new, thus I felt that I had naught to fear for myself, still I took with me a stout staff of ash over which I had rubbed my amulet along with the crushed leaves of illbane. Although I knew no spells, I called with my heart and mind upon the favor of Gunnora, trusting that one so much the greater would know that I meant no harm but that there was that which I must know.

The track was a winding one, for it had never been laid or cut by men but patterned so by the feet of women who sought the care and favor of The Lady. I had taken it many times before since I had sworn service to the Lady Elva seeking with my own petitions to bring her the wish of her heart. Thus, even in the half dark, I trusted to my feet, which seemed of themselves to know each dip and straightway.

None in Ulm had a part in the building of the shrine toward which I traveled. Like much within the Dales THOSE WHO HAD BEEN BEFORE had laid the stone of its walls and planted about its doorway the sweet-smelling herbs which carried in their scent something which would lighten even the most dour heart for a space. But at the coming of our people to this land women were drawn to the place, and, within a generation of our people's lives in the dale below, the power which dwelt here was recognized.

I came out upon the hillside at the top of which stood the place I sought. But there were no horses in pickets, no sign of the two guards, and I needed not even that to tell me that the Lady Tephana had not come this way.

Yet I went to the door and set my hand upon a place where the ancient wood was rubbed smooth and bare by the countless fingers which had touched there before me. There was the clear sound of a chime and the door opened, though none stood within. However, there was light, soft and golden as always, and into my face puffed the air which was deep scented with all the odors of the harvest time.

I came into the first room, laying my staff and my pouch of food upon the floor. Then, daring as I did only in time wherein my heart was sore, I brought forth the amulet and held it out so that which waited could know me for a daughter come for council, and went on into the inner shrine where shafts of light stood as towers on either side of a block of golden stone. In the center of that was a hollow which perhaps would hold as much liquid as I could scoop up in my two hands. By that hollow was a pitcher wrought of gold and bearing Gunnora's pattern of harvest sheath bound with a cording of vine, the fruit ripe upon it—all winking in the light with the glory of gems.

Going to that table I twice advanced my hand to that pitcher, twice withdrew it, as the force of what I would do brought with it fear. Yet I could not now turn aside. Thus on the third try I picked up that flagon and dribbled from it a clear bluish liquid which gathered into the pool. Just to the brim and no more was I careful to pour. Then I took from off my neck the chain of my amulet and that I laid by the pool. To me came words not of my choosing but as if something had stirred within me and spoke now through my lips.

"Lady—this one asks with all humbleness—to know—"

There was a swirl across the water which came of itself and not from any troubling of my doing. It grew dark —dark as a shadow of the midnight. Something moved through that darkness and then it cleared because a smoking torch shown within.

There were two cloaked and hooded figures, very small as if I gazed at them from a far distance. One raised herself even as I watched and laid her body upon a stone. That stone had to it a reddish look almost as if it had once been dipped in blood.

The other one therein the pool stepped forward and pulled at the cloak of she who lay and I saw the Lady Tephana and I did not doubt that that other was Maug. From beneath her cloak Maug brought forth a short rod or wand and holding this above her lady she drew it back and forth in patterns. Also I was sure that I saw come out of the dark where that torch did not light, faces and forms which appeared and disappeared so quickly I could not be sure of them, yet I knew that they were wholly evil, so much so that I quaked with the dread of what I watched.

Then the torch was gone, the water in the pool no longer murky, and somehow the bridle on my tongue was loosened once more and I cried aloud to the lights, the stone, the very walls about me: "What would you have me do, Great One? What evil is being wrought this night and where?"

"When the moment comes you shall know—" Did that

answer come out of the air itself, or was it in my head, a thought from another? I did not know but I was also aware that there would be no other answer.

That the Lady Tephana dealt with evil was plain. That I was to have a hand in some great matter, that was also clear to me. As I took up my amulet and put it about my throat once again it seemed to me that the ancient bit of carving had grown heavier and that I was ever aware of a kind of warmth which comes before a full fury of flame.

I rested that night in the outer room of the shrine and I dreamed, that I knew. But on my waking I could not remember the stuff of my dream save there had been some great peril and there was a need to prevent some act—and that prevention was mine.

I left upon the table in the outer room my offering: a ribbon of fine weaving ornamented with the best my needle could picture. And with the sun's rising I went from that shrine bearing not the comfort I had hoped but rather a sense of purpose I did not yet understand.

The lady was already returned when I came back to the keep. And I heard that she had indeed visited the shrine and prayed the night through that she might give her new lord the gift he wished—a son of his body.

Yet what shrine—not Gunnora's. Though the two guards swore that they had stood their watch apart from that—no man going within that gate. Whoever she had sought it had not been The Lady and had she set dreams upon the guards to hide that?

I had chance to meet Maug that eve as I sought my own tower room and it seemed to me that she hesitated as if she wished to speak with me and then thought the better of it. But I did not like the look which she gave me—as if she knew well that I had spied and how I had done so.

Again I dreamed and this time I remembered after I awoke, while the moonlight still shone full upon my bed. I had been somewhere else, and the feeling of that carried so fully with me that for more than a quick breath or two I looked about my tower room expecting fully to see that other place—a long hall with tall pillars and in the distance a white light—a moon silver one toward which I was drawn. There at the heart of that lay what I sought, a chest of crystal in which lay— But the light burst forth as I tried to see who or what was within. Yet I knew that it was needful that I should do this.

I put forth my hand into the blazing light. It did not sear my skin as I thought it might. Rather my flesh prickled and I felt that into it entered some power which it was needful that I retain—even though I was no wise woman nor one of the Old Ones.

Now as my dream released me I looked down at my hand and it appeared even in the full of the moonlight to have a broad band like unto a burnished ring encircling each of my fingers. Though even as I watched in wonder, those faded from sight but not from touch, for I felt a constraint and weight on each as I moved them, curled and uncurled bone and flesh.

As I lay back again upon my narrow bed I rested that hand on my breast when it chanced to cup to my body the amulet of The Lady. And that warmed from the power, sending through me now a strength such as I had never before known, while in my mind I shaped words and spun them into phrases, though they were strange to me and it was as if I were repeating a ritual which I did not understand but which had been so drilled into my memory that I would never lose it again.

Nor did I sleep the rest of the night, though I lay quietly, wrapped rather in the warmth of what was now within me more than the covers I had pulled up against the chill of that stone-walled chamber. And I strove to remember each small portion of the dream while I wondered at what had lain within the crystal chest and why some great one made use of such a one as I.

It was a strange day which followed. I was uneasy and could not sit still at my stitchery for long at a time, but paced now and then my chamber. When I went down into the kitchen I heard the snickering of the maids and saw them watching from the corners of their eyes now and then a tall figure tending a brew pot on the hearth.

Maug who seldom left her mistress's chamber was there, and to that which bubbled before her she added now and then a pinch of this, a dried leaf of that. While the scent of it was rich but sickly, liken to the smell of meat which is near spoiled and yet covered with spices to hide its nastiness. While she measured and tended so she was humming—not any tune such as might be sung as one went about one's work, but rather a mumble of sound which seemed to pierce into one's head and yet carry no meaning. And I saw that those gathered there made a wide circle about her, even the cook, all powerful here, keeping a good distance.

But not such a distance as I myself chose. For upon seeing her back I thrust under the edge of my upper jerkin my strangely weighted hand and ate bread and cheese awkwardly with my left. For that feeling of cold evil gathered about me and dulled all the pleasure one could take in this homey place before.

Also I hurried away from the kitchen as soon as I had choked down a few mouthfuls and came again into my chamber. For now there settled upon me a feverish need to be about a certain piece of work over which I had dawdled earlier. This was a scarf of that same brave color sun's setting left upon the sky. This was to be patterned with birds the like of which I had never seen. However, Maug had brought to me two days earlier a picture of such, lined out on a thick shaving of wood. They shone bravely in shades of red, but where one might have set gold to give them majesty the pattern had black lines, providing them with feet, bills and crests of that murky hue. Nor did I like to work upon them for I had a queer feeling now and then that when I finished a crested head it would turn a fraction and the eye I had set therein fastened upon me. I had never had such fancies before and I pushed these sternly out of mind. It also seemed, now that my hand was weighted by those rings I could not see, that the stitches I was setting precisely came very slowly into line. Yet also there was driving me this need to be done with the thing and have it off and away, back to she who would wear it.

So doggedly did I labor that the sun was still above the hill crest when I set the last stitch, shaking out the folds to inspect them carefully, making sure that I had not skimped the pattern in any place. Then I folded it over my arm and took up also the pattern chip from which I had worked and went forth to deliver my handiwork.

Lady Tephana had been given the west tower for her own biding place and I hurried along the outer defense wall rather than take the longer way of descent to the courtyard and up again. There were no sentries about since Ulmsdale, to our knowledge, had no enemies to try our strength and I saw a wink of light from a window ahead where that portion of the keep was in the beginning of twilight.

I raised a hand to knock, but instantly, as if she had foreseen my coming, Maug opened the door and beckoned me within. So I entered the scented warmth of the inner chamber where the lord's new lady sat before a mirror gazing steadily into it, not seeming in pleasure at her own features, but as if she saw there something of vast importance. Such strange fancies did fill my mind that day.

"Ylas." She said my name without turning. "Lay it about me—carefully now!" Her voice was sharp as if the placing of the scarf were some weighty matter which occupied all her thought for the moment.

I had expected Maug to take the wispy stuff from me but now I obediently laid the picture from which I had worked down on a table nearby and shook out the scarf, letting it fall gently even as she said, about her shoulders. There was a movement to one side and I caught a glimpse of Maug taking up the wooden plaque I had put down and tossing it into a brazier.

But what was much more important to me was that as soon as I arranged the scarf to the Lady Tephana's liking those weights on my fingers vanished, and it was only when I backed away a step or so that the sensation returned again.

The lady gathered up the scarf, wrapping it tighter about her with small quick tugs which again made those ill-omened birds seem to move. But the color became her darkness very well and she appeared in that moment more beautiful than I had ever thought. Now she smiled into the mirror and laughed.

"You have done well, Ylas. My lord will be pleased. We shall deal together again, you and I."

That sounded with too much emphasis, as if it was more than work with the needle she had in mind. However, I curtseyed and somehow found the words to say that I was glad to have pleased her. She dismissed me with a wave of her hand and Maug moved in with a comb to deal with her long locks which were as black as the bills and legs of those uncanny birds.

So it was that they were both occupied as I turned to go. Only my eyes lit upon what sat on the edge of the table—a small tray of copper well burnished bearing a goblet of gold. And from that stemmed cup, which was fancifully wrought with strange faces of beasts such as no man has seen, there came a whiff of the scent given off by the mixture Maug had been a-brewing earlier that day.

My hand jerked out as if fingers had closed about my wrist to twist it so that my fingers fluttered over the brim. And—I was aware of that as much as if I had seen it happen—from those fingers had slid those rings of power.

There was a moment's troubling of the substance in the cup.

Then I knew fear such as I had never felt before in my life, maimed and kinless though I was. And I sped from that chamber out into the rising night wind on the wall, to hasten back into my own small room.

What sorcery had made me a part of it I could not know, but that I had been used for another's purpose as one might use a goose wing to sweep an ashy hearthstone, that was a truth I did not deny. Thus I ran then until I was within my own room, the door closed tight behind me, both of my hands to my mouth where my breath came fast. My heart pounded and I gasped, at last sinking upon my bed, rubbing that ringless hand with my other one, for it seemed that with the going of those invisible rings my flesh was icy cold and must be brought back to warmth again.

I did not dream that night, nor the next, though I dreaded what sleep might bring me. Nor were there any more strange happenings to make me wish I had some safe person in whom I might confide. However, as the days passed dully one upon another I did not forget, and often, when I was sewing, I would stop and look upon my hand, spreading wide fingers, striving to understand what had happened to me on that one day.

It was not long until we heard that our lord's hopes had again risen—that the Lady Tephana was quick with child. As a favor to her he had brought her son Hylmer to the Keep and made much of him. He was a child in which there was little to admire or please, being large for his age and swift to tattle or hinder one. But in my own place I saw little of him and I heard that my lord took pleasure in noting his sturdy health, foreseeing that as a promise for his own coming heir.

He also urged upon the Lady Tephana the calling of one of the wise women from a neighboring Dale, one who was reputed to be a Handmaid to Gunnora. However, his lady refused, saying that Maug had been at her own birthing and knew more than any strange woman, no matter how high the art she claimed. Had she not successfully seen Tephana through the first birth of her son and as all living might now see—was he not a sturdy manchild?

It was in the eighth month after the lady had given her joyful news that once more I dreamed. Again I was in that hall where lay the chest of clouded light. I stood by it and, at an order I did not hear nor fully comprehend, I stretched both hands into its gleam.

This time I brought back no rings from that meeting, rather did I have always with me the sensation that over each finger, across each palm, was drawn taut the thinnest and finest of gauzy cloth. At first I hesitated to take up my needle again lest in some manner that coating I bore would be loosened upon the cloth to betray me to those to whom I was naught but a maimed one dwelling apart. But when I tried that did not happen, and it was the very day I discovered that with growing confidence that Maug summoned me to the Lady Tephana.

She was lying back upon cushions, her swollen belly now giving her no ease. But by her was a pile of cloth—pieces of two colors—one shining white which was usual for the receiving cloth which was any babe's first garment in the world, and the other of a filmy red.

"Ylas, once more the best of your needle skill is needed," she told me, stroking with both her hands the burden beneath her flesh. "It is to you that I give this that you may make a birthing cloth which will be the finest ever seen in this or any other dale. And with this," she put forward one hand to touch the red length, "you shall skillfully line with certain patterns Maug shall give you. For it is the custom of my House to so ask the protection of High Powers, that the sons we bear shall be straight and strong of body and fair of countenance."

Nor could I say no for in me arose that compulsion which had moved me before. I accepted the cloth and the piece of painted parchment which Maug had ready. Thus burdened, I returned to my chamber. I say burdened, for that I was. The parchment which I had not yet unfolded to look upon I could not carry easily. Light and thin it seemed still it weighed as if it were a block of sword steel.

I threw it on the table in my chamber with the feeling that I had handled filth. Even yet I did not open it but rather sat for a space nursing one hand within the other, feeling still upon the both of them that coating as if I went gloved. At length I brought out my threads and the packet which held my finest needles. And I laid the cloth out, finding it twice as long as was the custom, guessing then that it was to be folded about the red stuff so that would pass unseen.

It was when I at last made myself unfold the parchment that the full blow of unknown power struck at me. That feeling of handling filth was strong. It seemed to me that I breathed in rank odor as I leaned the closer holding a lamp to see. For though it was day without, here the shadows crept from the corners and there was a murk like drifting smoke to hide those lines of red and direst black.

That this was a thing of the Dark I now had no doubt and I wondered that they had so revealed their purposes even to me who had no place among the keep folk. It was as if they thought of me as someone beneath their need to consider.

But that I would stitch such with any needle unto a birthing cloth! What did they think of me—or (and cold spread through me) did they also have a plan in which I would be silenced once my work was done?

I have since many times thought that I was controlled by one greater than myself and that Maug or perhaps even the

Lady Tephana had taken care to bespell me into this labor and were not aware that I had not fallen helpless into their trap.

Now I pushed the parchment back into its folds and sat on my stool considering for a long moment what I would do. That I must stitch the red cloth between the layers of white was plain, for when I experimented, putting one over the other, there was a rosy sheen to the upper layer. But that I would use the symbols of the dark—NO!

Then I marked out for myself with a charred end of ash (which in itself was a powerful talisman against all evil) two other patterns. There was that borne by the amulet of Gunnora and the other—why, the gryphon which was my lord's own sign and under the banner of which we lived.

Looking upon these I set about with my stitchery and my needle flew with such speed and ease that it might have wrought of itself without my urging. The length had room only for four symbols, the two repeated, but they grew out of my best work and I wrought them in silver thread —moonglow such as is blessed by The Lady in her own shrine. Then quickly I laid the cloth within the other and sealed the sides with stitches so small that my eyes should have ached when I made them—yet I suffered neither that nor any fatigue as I worked, upheld by an inner strength which was new to me.

When I was done I folded it with care, making sure that the rose shine was visible, but I wondered if those symbols I had not used might have been visible too. That was a risk I must take.

I had worked the night through, still my head was clear, I had no aching of back, no redness and pain of eye. Not yet would I return it, I thought, let them think that the task was such a labor that I was kept to my needle for hours yet.

Opening my casement to the brightness of the morning I drew a deep breath of the freshness of the air before I turned again to where my work lay and performed one last task—that of passing above the folded cloth the amulet I wore. In my hand as I did so there was a pleasant warmth. Then all at once all the weariness I had earned came upon me and I stumbled to my bed, not taking off my jerkin or skirt, and fell upon it, sleep already sealing my eyes.

It was late afternoon that I awoke to another's shaking and saw above me Maug's lean, ill visage and smelled that sourish, bitter odor which she carried always with her.

"Fool—where is the work!" She raised her hand as if to slap me and then dropped it as one who would bide her time a little to deliver punishment.

"There—" I said, and pointed to the table.

She turned swiftly and snatched up first the parchment, tucking it into some pocket hidden within her fusty robe. Then her greyish-skinned fingers came to the folds of cloth. But she did not quite touch it. Instead she now shook forth another fold of material and gestured for me to place my handiwork upon that and cover it well.

With this she left me, but at the door she turned her head a little and I saw on her face a smile which was more the grimace of one steeped in malice. Again I suspicioned that those two meant me no good. Yet that suspicion did not really trouble me. It was as if I were sure that I wore armor against the worst they could attempt, and I gave thanks to Gunnora. For I truly believed that it was her amulet which had so hearted me. That and what still clung gloved tightly to my hands and which tingled a little now.

It was three days later that the news spread through the Keep that the Lady Tephana, wishing to make sure that her lord not be disappointed again, would go for the birthing to the very shrine of Gunnora where she could be sure that The Lady's favor would be hers. My lord was quick to give in to this plea of hers. But it was unexpected that she also asked for me to accompany them, her plea being that I was a devout follower of The Lady and was known to have her favor.

Thus, though there were clouds hanging over the crown of the not too distant hills we set out, the Lady Tephana in a horse litter, the mares it was slung between being hand-led by my lord's men, Maug striding on foot by her side, while I rode behind with two of the castle maids who were experienced somewhat in the mysteries of birthing.

We went at a slow pace in spite of the gathering of storm warnings, and I was not surprised that we did not turn aside at the hillside path leading to the shrine, for no horses, even the most surefooted, could make that climb. Instead we were to go around, to approach from the other side taking the slight risk of traveling on one of the Old One's roads which for the most part the Dalesmen avoided.

Our snail's pace brought us but barely on that road when the threatening storm broke and Lady Tephana cried out that she could not travel through its fury. The only shelter nearby was one of those half ruins which the Old Ones had erected at places along their roads. Into this we reluctantly crowded.

Luckily there were two half chambers left, and, having loosened the litter, the men bore Lady Tephana into the inner one whereupon we who had been chosen to serve her crowded.

It was then that she began to writhe on her resting place and cried out that the babe was coming too soon and in an evil place and she misdoubted that anything would be well. Maug held her hands and spoke to her softly but still she uttered cries and it was plain that her time was indeed upon her.

Thus we made ready to do what we might for the babe and I prayed to Gunnora that it would come alive and well. For—though I believed its mother to be tainted by some shadow I could not understand—the small new one would come sinless into the world.

Come it did and it was a son, squalling lustily. It was I

who received him upon the birthing cloth while Maug tended her mistress. And when I looked down at what I held I near dropped the child. For the well-formed small legs ended not in feet but in hooves such as one sees upon a kid, and the eyes which opened wide when I rolled the cloth about him were as gold as the glint of that metal in the sun!

Maug swung about as I uttered a cry of my own and reached for the babe. Only at that moment there was a sound which rose above the fury of the storm and the faint moans of the lady. It was like the passage of wings through the air, and so did I indeed see what seemed to be a great wing, larger than anything living could weld, and this swept down between Maug and me. At the same time there was a voice—though whether it spoke aloud or in my head I could never afterward decide.

"Son sealed to me!" There was triumph in it and I saw Maug cower backward with both hands over her eyes and I heard a sharp cry of fear from the lady. But to me came peace and I knew that this was well and good and what I held was no demon's brat but only one marked by nature with a brand even as the one I wore. And there was in me a vast pity as I cuddled him tight against a breast which would never know the weight of a child of my own.

The wing was gone and I heard sounds from the two maids who were crowded back against the wall shaking, their eyes squeezed shut as if they had been near struck blind. As I turned to give the child unto his mother as custom demanded that I should so that she could have the naming of him, Maug threw herself between us.

"Demon's get!" she mouthed and would perhaps have struck the babe out of my hold, and the Lady Tephana screamed full voice and thrust also outward, warning me off.

That was the way of it. They brought us back to Ulmsdale but the lady would not look upon the child and those who had been with us were quick to blame it on both the curse of the house and the fact that he had been birthed in a place of the Old Ones.

Since she would not feed it or even look upon him, the babe was mine for a measure of days and I was forced to allow him to suck warm milk from my finger. Yet he throve, and despite his eyes and those hooves he was a child good to look upon, and I came to cherish him.

But the Lord Ulric was determined that, having gotten his heir, he was fane to raise him. So he called in a forester with whom he had himself been fostered for a space when he was a child—the two of them being as brothers. To him the babe Kerovan was given and thus disappeared into the far reaches of the Dale. It was quickly made known by the will of my lord that no one was to speak of his son's deformity. While the maids who had been present at the birthing were sent with him. As for me I asked for speech with Lord Ulric and spoke of what had long been close to my heart, that I go unto Norseby and be with my lady there. He made me swear upon the mighty amulet which guarded the keep that I would not speak concerning Kerovan and this I agreed to very willingly.

There was only a small glimmering thereafter of all which had been my lot. For the tingling invisible gloves were gone from me when I gave the babe to his foster mother. I could not forget but neither could I speak. And, when I reached Norseby, I had much else to occupy my mind, for I found my lady ill of a deep cough and saw well that death was not far away. Out of their kindness they allowed me to nurse her. And there was one summer night when the moon was full that she spoke to me alone, for the Lady Sister who helped her with potions had gone to get more of a cordial which stifled the cough.

"Ylas—"

I had to bend very close to hear her faintest of whispers.

"The foreseeing—you have done what the Powers would

have of you. He—he—" she sucked in air as if she could not get enough to hold her with us—"he who—was—so —born—has his heritage. No demon as those two tried —no demon—" and so saying she crumpled back a little into the pillows about her and I knew that she had gone.

For me thereafter there was no more ensorcelment. I was given charge of the linens and the robes. Only in my dreams did I seek other places—which were always just a little beyond my reach. Yet never did I forget that great voice which greeted Kerovan at his birthing and thereafter my own dear lady's words concerning his destiny.

# HEIR APPARENT

## by

## Robert Bloch

Truth is a weapon which cuts both ways, and its blade is often bent in the telling.

Let not my words mislead you, for I am neither a swordsman nor any other kind of man. My name is Maug, and my station is that of first chamberwoman to the Lady Tephana.

It is for her that I must tell the truth, lest others twist the tale.

Hear me now, for this was the way of it . . .

It is whispered that we of the North have long had dealings with powers of the Dark and that we bear the taint of their blood. This I shall not deny. To live in a land where once demons held domain is difficult at best, for their power is still strong and we have learned their ways in order to survive. We who wish to dwell in peace under their sufferance must bargain for it. And if, at times, that bargain entails the mingling of bloodlines, so be it.

That my own mother entered into such an alliance has been hinted, but of this I cannot surely say, since she died at my birthing, without revealing my father's name. I was taken into the House of Paltendale as an orphan babe and in its service I grew to womanhood, learning the arts of chamberwoman to earn my keep.

I know also—and freely admit—that from childhood on I possessed certain powers greater than those of ordinary folk around me, and came easily to the study of spells and the distillation of potions employing the lore of the Dark. While other maidens of my years yearned for love, my interest lay only in learning, and I knew naught of womanly wiles and ways. And when at last love came into my life it was not the love of maid for man but the maternal affection of a mother for her child.

The child was she who became Lady Tephana, and I was not her true mother. She, like myself, was born into the House of Paltendale without living parents, both her noble sire and lady mother perishing of a plague which swept the land shortly after her birth. Some called it a curse brought down upon them for trafficking with dwellers from the Dark. Again I know nothing of this save rumor. And all I knew at the time was that a tiny infant lay helpless and unprotected, mewling for a mother's milk and starved for the succor of a tender touch and caring caresses.

Milk was secured through the services of a wet nurse, but it was I, assigned to duties in the nursery, who gave her loving care. And as the years went by it was I who became not only nurse but teacher, I who protected her with charms to ward off harm, I who was privileged to be her preceptress and guide her emergence into womanhood.

And woman she became—small in stature but well endowed with beauty of face and form. Her hair was lustrous black, her eyes deep gray, her gestures graceful, her voice a caress.

Small wonder then that she was sought as a bride by her cousin, the young heir to the House of Fortal. And when she wed she chose me to serve as her first chamberwoman.

Those were joyous times, and in memory I still hear the echo of her laughter. When the union was blessed with a son, Hylmer, it seemed her happiness was complete. But happiness is hard to come by and harder to hold; it slipped from her grasp all too swiftly with the sudden death of her lord in a hunting accident.

Her grief was great, and I grieved for her. Lady Tephana's beauty was shrouded in the grey garb of widowhood and her position as Mistress of Fortal imperiled by her dead lord's brothers who sought to take power.

It was then that I came to her one dark and dreary day, in the tower chambers which had long since ceased to be warmed by sunlight or her smile.

"Be of good cheer, my lady," I said. "For I bring glad tidings."

"Indeed?" Gray eyes met mine with no luster in their glance. "What might those tidings be that they hold reason to dispel my sorrow?"

"Your time of mourning is over, and your widowhood as well. For even as I speak, a suitor is on his way."

The gray eyes widened. "A suitor? But I do not wish to marry again."

"It is not a question of wish," I said, "but rather one of need. Others plot your downfall here, for you have unfriends within this Keep."

"It is of no great consequence, now that my lord is gone. Whatever comes, the future holds no fears for me."

I shook my head. "And Hylmer, your son—does his welfare mean nothing to you as well? Those who scheme to bring you down will also place his life in peril, for only then can they take power."

Lady Tephana nodded quickly. "You are right, of course. It is Hylmer's safety I must consider. And if I marry again he will be under the protection of my new spouse." She rose and faced me, her eyes at last alert. "But tell me—who is it that would seek my hand in marriage?"

"Ulric, Lord of Ulm." As I spoke I glanced out of the tower window, peering down at a band of horsemen moving toward the castle on the road below, their banners bright against the sun. "And if I mistake not, he comes to claim you even now."

I was not mistaken; it was indeed Ulric who approached the Keep. Nor had I misread his purpose, for it was I, with the aid of certain spells which need not be described, who stirred his thoughts to summon him. Bluntly put, I had ensorceled Lord Ulric with a vision of Lady Tephana and her beauty, hoping to induce his coming.

Of this I spoke not, thinking it wiser that my Lady believe his presence here was prompted only by his own desire. And it pleased me greatly that their meeting bore fruit; he appeared much taken with her charms and lost no time in urging his suit. As for Lady Tephana, she seemed not unmindful of his brave appearance and ardent entreaty. Knowing the safety of her son was at stake, she dispensed with the coquetry of courtship and readily consented to become Ulric's bride.

The ceremony was celebrated quietly, amidst general rejoicing, and sooner than I'd dared believe possible my lady journeyed south to her new lord's land. Hylmer was left behind for a time in the care of trusted chamberwomen, until she felt assured of the stability of her new estate as Lord Ulric's wife.

But I rode with her, and it was I who stayed at her side after our arrival at Ulm. And it was I who soon sensed the coming of a cloud which cast its shadow over the marriage. For while Ulric looked upon her lovingly in the presence of others, I noted that in their private moments his smiles gave way to frowns.

This troubled me, and at last I could keep silent no longer. Seeking out Lady Tephana in her chambers I made bold to question her.

"Forgive my forwardness," I said. "But I speak only out of devotion to your well-being. What is it between you and Lord Ulric which mars this marriage?"

Lady Tephana shrugged. "There is nothing between us." She smiled thinly. "Perhaps it is that which disturbs him."

I stared at her, realizing the full import of her words.

"Do you mean that after a month of wedlock there has been no consummation of the union?"

She nodded quickly and would have turned away, but I deterred her. "How can that be?" I said. "Lord Ulric is indeed somewhat older and less handsome than your late husband, but still he is of noble birth and a fine figure of a man. Is there some secret deformity in his person, some hidden flaw which inspires your repugnance? Surely it is not his indifference that prompts your rejection; even I, who know little of the ways of love, can see how greatly he yearns to follow wedding with bedding."

"Truly said." Lady Tephana faced me now, and I read anger in her eyes. "Ulric does indeed burn with desire to possess me, but his longing has little to do with love, or even lust. To him I am not a person but merely a receptacle to be filled with seed. He does not truly look upon me as wife or woman; he married only to beget an heir."

I nodded. "But this is natural. All men wish for offspring, and a lord needs sons to carry on the line."

"It is more than need which impels him," Lady Tephana said. "Since coming here I have learned much. Soon after Ulric's birth his father's doings brought down a curse upon the House of Ulm, and no further children were born alive thereafter. Mindful of this, Ulric himself married when quite young, hoping to rid the curse and secure an heir. His wife was sickly, but he had little concern for her. He promptly got her with child and when the poor lady died in the birthing he mourned not at this; it was only the loss of the infant which sorrowed him.

"His second wife, the Lady Elva, was wedded in unseemly haste thereafter. It is said she captivated him with the beauty of her fair hair, the slim perfection of her body with its exquisite, pear-shaped breasts. It is also said that he felt true affection for her, but this did not deter him from his purpose. He took her roughly and repeatedly until she too conceived, not once but several times, and always the offspring came before their time so that none survived. Perhaps he loved her truly, but this did not prevent him from dismissing her. He craved a child, and that is why he came to wed me—only because he must father an heir for Ulmsdale.

"As he thinks of naught but his own position, so must I think of mine. And this I swear—I shall not become an instrument of his arrogance, a brood-mare to serve his purpose. Proud he may be, but so am I. Mine is the pride of womanhood, and he shall not humble it."

"Even at the cost of your son's life?" I said softly.

"I will protect Hylmer," she declared.

"With what—a woman's wiles?" I frowned. "How long do you think you can fend Ulric off with talk of headaches or being in your monthly courses? Sooner or later he will insist upon claiming his rights to your person, and if you resist he will surely banish you. Then Hylmer, like yourself, forfeits all protection. You two will wander the Waste to your deaths."

Lady Tephana, she who walked high in her grace, now stood with sagging shoulders, and the white purity of her complexion grayed to ashen pallor.

"But what am I to do?" she cried.

"The answer is simple," I said. "You must conceive."

"Never!" A spark of anger flared from the ashes, reddening her cheeks and flaming from her eyes. "Come what may, Ulric shall not use me thus."

"Consider his position," I counseled. "Ulric acts not out of malice but only to protect Ulm."

"His motives do not matter," Lady Tephana declared. "If I give him a son, the boy becomes his rightful heir, and Hylmer would still have no assurance of safety in the future." Her eyes flashed fire. "I tell you I will not bear Ulric's child."

"I speak only of conception," I murmured. "But the child need not be Ulric's."

Lady Tephana stared at me in puzzlement. "You would have me cuckold him with another man?"

I smiled. "Suppose it was not a man?"

My lady stared, taking my meaning. Then, "You would have me consort with evil?" she whispered.

I shook my head. "Evil is an empty word. The cosmos itself exists only as the interplay of Light and Darkness, which are neither good nor evil—merely opposite aspects of the same power. Power which men seek to control by means we call magic."

"You have knowledge of such magic, then?" Lady Tephana said.

"I do. And I would employ it so that you bear a babe which is not truly of Ulric's blood."

"But what purpose would that serve?"

"Yours," I told her. "If the offspring is not Ulric's it will become your ally, not his. Thus it will grow to protect you and your child. Is that not what you desire?"

Lady Tephana nodded. "More than life itself." She hesitated, grey eyes intent on mine. "But are you certain you can do this?"

"Trust me," I said.

And she did.

So it was that she went to Lord Ulric and cozened him, saying that she would no longer withhold her favors, for now her true desire was as his—to give him a manchild. But when he sought to take her she implored that he wait only a few days longer. First she must make pilgrimage to the shrine of Gunnora, Our Lady of Fruitfulness, and pray to her for the life and good health of Ulric's issue.

Convinced and content, he agreed to her going, wishing her well on the mission.

Before departure I took other steps to guard our safety. When Ulric's former wife, Lady Elva, took refuge in Norsdale Abbey she left behind her own first chamberwoman. This was one Ylas, an ill-favored creature with a harelip, who was skilled in needlework. I was disturbed by her continued presence here and wondered if she had been instructed to stay and spy upon Lady Tephana and her doings. To distract her from such purpose I now sought her out with a smiling face and asked her to weave a scarf for my lady, using fine fabric which I gave her together with drawings of a pattern for her needle to follow. Thus employed I felt she would be unmindful of our own comings and goings.

And go we did next day, accompanied by two guards, though it was not Gunnora's shrine we sought. The guards knew naught of this, for in their provisions was an ample supply of drink containing a potion I concocted to insure sound sleep and direct their dreams. To them those dreams would seem reality, so that next morning upon awakening they would swear they had spent the night in sentry outside the portals of Gunnora's shrine.

But once their slumber was assured, Lady Tephana and I made our way farther into the bleak and barren land where stood another edifice, erected by darker powers for a darker purpose.

It was there, in the crumbling ruins of what had not been raised by human hands, that we came under the cloak of night. And it was there, in a chamber steeped with shadows, that Lady Tephana removed her cloak at my instruction and laid herself upon a slab of stone, baring her body to reveal the richness of its charms.

The slab was cold and the night chill, but it was with fear of the strange shadows that she shuddered and shivered until my words calmed her into repose. Eyes closed, she slumbered, unaware of what transpired in the midnight hours.

As she lay in loveliness I drew forth a short wand fashioned from the spine of an unborn infant and bathed in its blood to confer the power of charmed command.

Power too took added strength from the sound of the

words I muttered in a tongue forgotten by men but well remembered by those who dwell in the Darkness.

The force surged forth to stir the shadows, imbuing them with a life of their own. Swirling into shifting shapes, the shadows took fearsome form as they drew closer to the slab, gathering to gaze on the bared body of my lady. Hands that were more like claws or talons swooped forth, seeking to touch, to grasp, to possess. But with wand and words I kept them back whilst I sought the semblance of one summoned by name—the Darklord Galkur.

And as my lady slept he came, emerging from the striving shapes to tower over the slab with more than a shadow's substance. There was such hunger in his glowing gaze; such emanations of dark desire as to set me atremble so that the wand almost slipped from between my fingers. Hastily I tightened my grip, chanting aloud the ancient ritual which alone could hold the adept's powers of Darklord Galkur in thrall.

Even so, he crept closer to my sleeping lady, closer than any of his shadowy company, tensing above her body as though to hurl himself upon it.

"You want her?" I whispered. "Then listen. Listen, Lord Galkur, and heed me well."

Now, murmuring in the midnight, I proposed my pact —my lady's flesh in return for Galkur's favor. And when I at last concluded, the huge head nodded in eager assent.

"Then it is agreed," I said. The shape made as if to advance upon its prey but with my wand I waved it back. "Leave us now so that I can prepare the way. She shall be yours at moontide of tomorrow's eve."

Shadows lack voices but I fancied my words echoed by Galkur's deeper tones. And then his shape slithered back to merge and mingle with the other phantasmal forms as they swirled away into the darkness, vanishing to leave me alone with Lady Tephana asleep on the stone stained by other sacrifices. Now she too would be sacrificed to seal this pact with Darkness, but mercifully she knew not of the bargain I had struck.

As for me, I slept not, but waited the coming of dawn in silence. When Lady Tephana awoke and sought to question me I told her merely that my efforts had met with success and all would be well. Seeking the guards before the portals of Gunnora's shrine, I bid them bestir themselves. As I had foreseen they were none the wiser for our absence during the night, and now together we made our way back to the Keep.

There, as Lady Tephana rested in her tower chamber, I sped to the kitchen below, for in accordance with my plan I needs must prepare a potion. With me I brought certain herbs and simples gathered from the weed-strung Waste. And while cook and serving-maids stood apart, curious as to my intent yet afraid to question me, I filled a brew pot on the hearth and began the rituals required.

To folk who know not magic it seems strange that potency resides in the leaves and petals of common growths. The secret, of course, lies not in the plants themselves but in their proper mingling. It is much the case as with words. Used singly they lack strength. But when grouped together in certain sentences they can cajole, command, condemn, curse, inspire love or loathing, happiness or hatred. And plants possess similar powers when combined for intended usage.

To compound the efficacy of my concoction I hummed an age-old tune, for musical notes—again when properly assembled—convey a still other power of their own.

All this is the essence of magic's meaning—the informed use of the commonplace to create a linkage with Forces that surround us—and bend those Forces to our bidding.

In the midst of my task I spied the woman Ylas creeping about the kitchen and stealthily observing my every movement. From the look of her she did not relish the odors arising from the bubbling pot before me. And there was an aura about her, as if she were not alone but accompanied by an intangible presence. An image came unbidden to me; that of an eagle-headed gryphon, which is the guardian symbol of the House of Ulm. But what this had to do with the actual and visible Ylas I could not divine; dismissing the vagrant fancy I watched the woman leave after making pretense of eating bread and cheese.

Puzzled, I sent my thoughts after her, informed with a purpose she must fulfil. My sending proved successful, for when I finished my workings and took a portion of my potion to Lady Tephana's tower, Ylas appeared bearing the scarf I had bid her weave. This she presented to the lady, who placed it about her shoulders and praised her work.

But there was about this a matter for unease. Before Ylas arrived I had poured my potion into a golden goblet, and now she recognized its scent. Peering down, she passed her fingers over the goblet's rim, then drew back quickly, and in the twilight of the tower window I saw her misshapen mouth go agape in fear as she turned to depart from the chamber.

"What possesses her?" Lady Tephana exclaimed.

"No matter," I replied. "At best she can but suspect rather than know. As for possession, that in itself is a matter we must now consider. For the night is nigh."

Then, and only then, did I inform the lady of what lay ahead and of the part she was to play in it.

Briefly put, the plan was this. With the coming of darkness Lady Tephana would seek out Lord Ulric and invite him to sup in her tower chambers. Here, with a sumptuous meal prepared, she must greet him with warm and wifely words of welcome while arrayed in a rich robe woven but thinly to cover her charms yet not conceal them. Together they would dine by the light of scented candles, the fragrance of which would mingle with the perfume my lady had applied to her person. And as they enjoyed their repast she would employ the methods of a magic common to womankind—shy gestures, sidelong glances, stifled sighs; such sorceries as need not words to give them meaning. The wine Lord Ulric took with his meal must aid in kindling desire, but nothing could inflame his senses like my lady's unspoken promise of passion to come.

Inevitably he would seek to draw her to the bed, but before the moment of sweet surrender she must invite him to drink first from the golden goblet.

Once the potion passed his lips our aim was accomplished. For even as he drew the garment from her shapely shoulders a strange sleep would steal over him—but a sleep in which he fancied himself still awake. Thus, though he held heaven in his arms and sought the portals of paradise, he would do so only in dream.

Then, as the potion took full effect, Ulric's mortal body would be usurped by the essence of one not completely mortal, as Darklord Galkur took both his place and his pleasure.

Lady Tephana listened and her great gray eyes were haunted with misgiving. "But this is a dreadful thing we do," she whispered.

"A needful thing," I told her. "If there is issue from this union, both it and your son Hylmer will enjoy the protection of Darklord Galkur."

My lady shuddered. "It is said this Galkur is a creature neither animal nor human. How can I freely give myself to such a monster?"

"There is a way," I told her. "When Lord Ulric drinks from the goblet you must signify your desire to drink in turn—not from the goblet, but from his lips, while his mouth still holds the liquid of the potion. This will please him, I know, for there can be no more precious a prelude to the act of love.

"You need but take a sip of the brew to bring the blessing of sleep. Within moments your senses will slumber, though you will appear to be awake. You shall not be aware of Galkur's coming and caresses, nor will he discern that you thus deny him your participation in his pleasuring."

Lady Tephana pondered upon my proposal for a long moment before breaking silence. "There is no other way?"

"None. This is the only course."

She sighed, then nodded. "So be it, then."

Night descended and Lord Ulric ascended to the tower. All was in readiness as arranged, and all went in accordance with my plan.

To assure myself of this I found a station in the room adjoining the bedchamber. Kneeling there in the darkness I put my eye to the keyhole of the chamber door. It was not curiosity which prompted me, but after all my calculation and worrisome workings—and above all, for the sake of my lady—I must be certain of the results obtained.

So it was that I witnessed the meeting of Lord Ulric and his bride, their meal together, her amorous enticement, and its effect upon him. I saw too his draining of the golden goblet and how Lady Tephana drank a portion drawn by a kiss with opened mouth—a kiss that ended only as the lovers sank down upon the bed together.

Together—yet not for long. As the two entwined there seemed a great stirring in the bedchamber, and the candlelight wavered, flames fluttering in a whirl of wind. Then shadows came, though I did not sense their source, filling the room with a swirl of seething sable which spiraled down upon the bed and merged into a single shape.

The shape descended upon Lord Ulric, seeming to absorb his body, so that now Lady Tephana lay beneath a shadow. This shadow was unlike any other, for it had eyes—great eyes, holding a lambent light as they feasted upon my lady's bared beauty, eyes that gloated as fingers of darkness fondled and fastened themselves upon her person. But as the black bulk descended I saw, or seemed to see, a curious change in its contours. For a moment it melted, and in its place appeared the profiled semblance of a great beaked and horned birdlike head borne by a body with widespread wings. But it was Galkur's loins below which thrust forward, and from them darted that which had the hideous likeness of a writhing serpent. At the sight of its writhing and the realization of its intent I cried out in terror, then swooned away before the door.

How long I lay in merciful unawareness I cannot say, but when at last I roused and steeled myself to again peer through the keyhole I saw that Galkur's shadow had vanished, together with all other fearful forms. Now only Lord Ulric and Lady Tephana lay side by side in slumber, their bodies bathed in the warming glow of calm candlelight.

Of what transpired on that fateful evening I spoke not, nor did my lady venture to discuss. But it was apparent that Lord Ulric was unaware of anything amiss and now he looked fondly on his bride—the more so as he perceived the growing evidence of her condition. For it was increasingly obvious she was with child and this pleased him greatly. So fulsome was his favor that Lady Tephana made bold to bring Hylmer to the Keep. Ulric welcomed him warmly and I know he took his place with favor, though I saw him but seldom in the months to come.

As for me, I remained haunted with a vexing uncertainty as to what I had actually witnessed before my fainting spell. Each time I encountered the needlewoman Ylas I wondered if by some mischance she too had wrought a magic of her own.

It was a matter of grave concern, and when Lady Tephana entered the final weeks of her carrying I determined upon a course that would ensnare Ylas, however unwittingly, as a party to the outcome of my plans.

Providing my lady with what was needful, I enlisted her

to summon Ylas to the bedchamber where she lay awaiting the approaching hour of birthing. Here, in accordance with my instruction, she gave Ylas two bolts of cloth—one red, the other white—together with a parchment I prepared bearing a design to be woven into a birth-cloth for the newborn infant.

The design held symbols not usually employed, but I hoped Ylas would feel sufficiently flattered by being entrusted with her task and follow orders to weave the pattern as instructed.

But when I sought her out to take possession of her finished handiwork I perceived instantly that she had betrayed my wishes, for the birthing-cloth bore other symbols—the twin traceries of Gunnora's amulet of protection and the gryphon guardian of the House of Ulm.

Of my displeasure I gave no sign, merely gathering the cloth and wrapping it in the folds of another. Thus shielded, the symbols would possess no power, and Ylas's tampering was thwarted.

Still I could not be assured she might not resort to other means of interfering if left to her own devices; it might be that she was capable of weaving spells as well as cloth.

So three days later, as Lady Tephana's time came upon her, I bade Ylas join us on our journeying. For Lady Tephana had gone to Ulric and asked that she give birth in the shrine of Gunnora. Here, with the favor of the great patroness of womankind, she would bear him a living heir at last to break the curse which beset the House of Ulm. Despite her secret betrayal she was quite sincere in her hope to bear a living child, and felt the need of Gunnora's birth-blessing.

With Lord Ulric's consent we started forth, my lady in a horse litter led by manservants, whilst I bestrode another mare. Ylas and two castle maids followed on foot.

Sullen signs of an approaching storm suffused the sky, and when at last we came unto the hillside we made no attempt to follow the path upward, for the climb was too steep for the horses to mount safely. We turned to go around the hill and reach the shrine from its opposite side, making our way along a road which had been laid by the Old Ones through their land.

Then the storm descended, and in its full fury we could go no farther but needs must seek shelter within the half-leveled structure which long ago the Old Ones had raised as a stopping-place. Placing Lady Tephana's litter in the inner chamber with the women, the men and steeds were left to make do in the outer one as best they could.

Now, as howling wind and hissing rain tore night to tatters, my lady trembled to find herself in this place of darkness instead of Gunnora's shrine. But there was no help for it, and as lightning flashed and thunder boomed she writhed in the pangs of birthing, babbling regret of the pact she had made with other powers. I too felt unease, but it was too late to alter what had been done, and there was naught to do but await the coming of the child.

Thunder heralded its birth, and when the maids drew forth the babe it squirmed and squealed loudly, for it was indeed alive.

As I ministered to my lady, Ylas took the infant and placed it upon the birthing-cloth. Then lightning flickered forth from cracks in the ruined walls and in its glare I turned and beheld the child. Beheld its manly human form which terminated in hooves instead of feet—beheld also the human face whenceforth peered two glowing yellow eyes.

And as I stared stricken, a sound as of the beating of great wings rose above the tumult of the storm, as did the echo of a mighty voice raised triumphant over all.

"Son sealed to me!"

The echo faded but my fright remained. For it was then I knew that we had failed. Despite Galkur's brand upon its body and despite the cry of what I sensed to be the

Gryphon Lord, this was truly Lord Ulric's son.

I moved to place the child beside Lady Tephana, but Ylas shrieked that this was a demon's get, and when my lady saw what she had birthed she screamed and averted her gaze in horror.

Nor would she ever look upon it or hold it in her arms, even when we returned to Ulmsdale and Lord Ulric accepted his heir without question or reproach. He gave the infant into the care of a trusted forester who took him to raise in a place far distant from the Keep.

And I, who had risked and sacrificed so much for my mistress to safeguard her future, found myself without favor in her eyes. Banished from her presence, I now know naught but desolation and despair.

Sometimes I ponder upon that of which I spoke—the nature of a cosmos in which good and evil are illusions, merely the interplay between Light and Darkness which we seek to control by magic so that we ourselves may gain power.

And this I ask myself: what if our power is also an illusion? What if the forces of Light and Darkness are themselves but pawns in some vaster game which we cannot ever comprehend, or hope to master?

The answer to these questions I do not know.

I know only that I am afraid . . .

\* \* \*

## Afterword

*I was introduced to Andre Norton and her business associate Ingrid Zierhut at a convention. The ladies then retired to their room, where Ms. Norton promptly fell asleep and Ms.*

*Zierhut read the ads in the program booklet—thus giving you some idea of the kind of impression I made on them. Still, something did result from our meeting, because when Ms. Norton awoke she announced, "I just had an idea," and Ms. Zierhut responded, "So do I." Whereupon both said, in unison, "Why not ask Mr. Bloch to write a story for* Tales of the Witch World?"

*It was a crazy idea, so of course I agreed. As we all know, somebody—either Shakespeare or Isaac Asimov—wrote, "There are two sides to every story," and "Imitation is the sincerest form of flattery." Actually these quotations come from Diogenes Laertius and Charles Caleb Colton respectively, and both are misquotations. Laertius' term was "question" instead of "story" and Colton didn't qualify his wording with "form of." Nevertheless, I was guided by the incorrect quotes—writing the other side of André Norton's story from the opposite viewpoint of another character, but deliberately imitating the Norton style which, like the lady herself, I greatly admire. "Making a mistake is not always an error," as somebody once said. I think it was me. Having read my story, it's up to you to decide if what I did was right or wrong. At any rate, consider "Heir Apparent" as a tribute to the talented tale-teller who inspired it.*

—ROBERT BLOCH

# FENNECA

## by

## Wilanne Schneider Belden

She was an odd little bit of a child, so tiny the survivors gathered in the burned-out village had no idea of her age, although she seemed far wiser and far more capable than the two-year-old her size indicated. They never knew her parentage, but with so many other children dead, so few people of any age still alive, her very existence made her precious. No one had time or energy left from the desperate attempt to stay alive to inquire into the matter. She never spoke, although she understood—or seemed to understand—whatever was said to her. She attached herself to one after another of the surviving women, wandering away in a day or two to sleep cuddled against another motherly body. At last, she disappeared. They hoped she was all right, but no one could search.

A path, rapidly reverting to woodland, led away from the village. The child walked slowly along it with the caution of the weak. Had the villagers known, they would have benefited. She found and ate several wild, growing things. Fungus. A squirrel's forgotten store. Some roots. She was full-fed for the first time since coming again among people. Food, she must have. People who starved she could do without.

Several days later, she saw the merest thread of smoke. Smoke meant fire, and warmth, and getting dry. It also usually meant people. She was cold and wet and lonely.

She followed the sign and scent of woodfire to a hidden farmstead. Not well-enough hidden. Here, too, she saw the devastation left by the Hounds of Alizon, who killed for enjoyment—and for power and land (if not inhabitants) over which to claim dominion. But having ruined, they had ridden on.

One room of the house looked lived-in, and the beckoning smoke rose from the chimney. The child went in.

Alone in the house, more than half starved, Janya lay on her cot unthinking, long past weeping and despair. When the tiny being entered, Janya believed it hallucination. But the double handful of shelled nuts the child placed by the woman's hand were real. One half nutmeat at a time, slowly, chewing and chewing, swallowing only a little at time, Janya ate. The tiny ragamuffin, clothed in someone's outworn smock, a strip of something around her waist to hold it close and shorten it, watched her solemnly. She went to the fireplace, put the last bits of wood on the dying fire, and went to the door. A signal with "speaking" hands told Janya she would return. Almost an hour passed. When she came back, she dragged after her a branch far too heavy and long for her seeming fragility to manage. Panting and half crying with exhaustion, she wrestled it all into the room. She looked at Janya for help.

Still unbelieving, Janya found the strength to tip over the (now) three-legged table. A part of the branch might break off. It did, and the child put it into the fire.

Her third return—well after dark, shivering so hard she could hardly drag herself through the door—was with the most miraculous gift of all: a fat coney, its neck broken. She dropped the body by Janya's cot and sought the fire, now burning brightly, if small, on the hearth. She sank down, and Janya thought she cried.

The child remained with Janya, who, despite the still-present danger, chose to live in the half ruins of the house she and her husband had built years ago—when there was hope. She might have gone to the village, where perhaps people still existed, but she had no desire to do so. Here lay her life, in graves she had dug out of the near-frozen earth with energy she could have used far better to stay alive longer. She had no wish to live, but live she did.

Perhaps she now knew why.

In their entire first exchanges, the child had not spoken a word, nor, Janya found, did she ever. She was not, however, a true mute, for she sang wordlessly, tunes Janya did not recognize; perhaps she made them up. And she made word-noises, repeating and repeating the same "phrases," never satisfied. She would change a single sound, then two, then three, always searching, it seemed, for exactly what she wanted. Because she understood when Janya spoke to her, the woman did not believe the sounds to be a language, just something the child did to pass the time.

Janya named her Fenneca, calling her Fenny most of the time, and the child responded well. Her surprising smile (flashing through the mask of dirt and despair marking her as one of the few the laughing butchers had missed) was such a delight that, for the first time in months, Janya smiled in response.

Like everyone else, the little girl was bone-thin, ill-clothed in something found—in her case, far too large—and always dirty. Possibly, her hair might be reddish blond (so, Janya thought, it grew in at the roots), but with no way to wash it, one could not be sure. She did have disconcerting eyes, almost green, and the pupils were not exactly circular, although they were close enough to it that Janya did not notice for many weeks. Her dirt-grimed hands were long-fingered and well shaped, and her feet (wrapped in layer after layer of rags) were also long and slim.

Spring was late, preceded by a long month of cold without snow, covered by gray skies, and filled with wolf-teeth winds. Three more of those who had gathered in the village died of starvation, and one more appeared from somewhere, little less skeletal than they who met him. Seed grain was long since eaten, and even the feral, long-toothed rats found themselves hunted as determinedly as they themselves sought food.

True spring came within a week of Fenny's arrival, and the child slid out of the one room into the pale sunshine as if released from a dark cave. She was gone most of the day every day, and came home with her mouth green, her hands full of strange things she insisted were food. Janya doubted, but, as Fenny did not die, the woman chewed and swallowed her portion with grim determination. And lived.

One morning, Fenny returned with her ragged "skirt" so filled with lumpy somethings that she could hardly stagger. She dropped her burden at Janya's feet. They had had no food the day before. Janya, foodless for several days that the child might eat, was hardly able to move, hardly able to think. She reached out a trembling hand. Whatever-it-was could be eaten. Fenny held the hand away. She went to the hearth and held up a pot. She mimed water, cooking, then ran out to the stream to fill the pot.

Janya dragged herself to the table and watched the little hands as they scrubbed the roots, cut out each indentation (leaving a fat cone of the root attached), chopped the rest, and put it into the pan. Fenny picked up a fork, mimed poking, waiting, poking again. Janya nodded. "Yes, when they are soft."

Fenny nodded extravagantly, smiled, and scraped each of the pieces she had set aside into her skirt. She took them outside. Janya could not follow. She could only wait and occasionally poke. The roots took some fifteen minutes to become soft. The odor was minimal, certainly not mouth-watering, but Janya salivated with the mere thought of food. Carefully, carefully, her weakness making the job dangerous, she spooned the diced bits onto a plate. In the moments she waited, anxious, for the roots to become cool enough to try, she wondered. Would she die? If so, she really did not mind, but there was Fenny, and living for Fenny seemed worthwhile, a thought that surprised her.

They ate the roots, wishing for a scraping of salt. Not too much food at once, for Janya. It was sin to waste, and more than a few mouthfuls would come up again from a stomach so shrunken. The taste was bland but pleasant. Later, she ate another mouthful or two from her portion. After a third helping, near twilight, Janya felt strong enough to go outside to find out what so involved Fenneca.

In the old garden, a space some three feet long by six inches wide lay clear of weed and rock and detritus. What an effort for so small a child! Fenny noted Janya's coming, ran to take her hand, and led her to the place. She showed how she had dug and pulled and dug more, until the earth was ready to be planted. For seed, Fenny used the eye-buds she had prepared.

Almost daily, Fenny returned with the results of her foraging. One day she presented Janya with a sort of bouquet. Her mouth was green again, so the woman nibbled at a broad leaf. The taste was a little bitter, but her body craved it. She ate the entire bunch. Fenny found two other roots, also to be boiled, and saved the top half inch, with the leaves, to be planted in her expanding garden. One day, well after dark (Janya was nearly out of her mind with worry), the child returned with a freshly dead ground-fowl and a smeared, teary face. She was not hurt, she mimed, just sorry for what she had had to do.

They feasted that night, and Janya made the meat go far.

Having food, and hope, Janya prepared the soil, making ready for when the next food-crops from the wilds would appear.

Fenny brought little plants, each taken carefully with soil around the roots. Janya expected them to die, but they struggled valiantly, drooped and spread, then began to flourish. They ate wild salads until they nearly burst. Their sores healed, and Janya's gums tightened around her teeth. Fenny's increased rows of the root crop burgeoned. Below the ground, future meals lay growing.

Another fowl, then a rabbit! Tears, always, in Fenny's eyes, but she brought the meat. The next time, the fowl was a hen, and alive. Janya restrained herself from wringing its neck by clutching one hand with the other. Yes, let it live. They could have eggs. Perhaps Fenny might bring more hens. If they did not eat the first eggs, the hens might raise broods. By saving the strongest cockerel, they could start a flock. She did cut off the wing-tips (Fenny cried) so the bird could not fly. In a month, they had five hens, and the first two were brooding.

Stunned rabbits, which Janya penned, made another source of meat.

Still, there were days when they went without, but they could now afford to do so. No longer were they in danger of starving, and to eat their crops and breeders would mean death when winter set in.

As she seemed so well able to do it, Janya let Fenny handle the matter of food. She set to work rebuilding another part of the house, cannibalizing the rest of it for unburned, unbroken pieces of board, whittling pegs to hold them together, and digging again through the rubble for anything usable. She went farther afield, searching other lonely houses. Under a hearth-stone in one she found such treasure as she could hardly believe. A whole leather bag of grain-seed! A new axe-head! Weapons. A small knife she could give to Fenny. She bore them home in triumph. They planted the seed the next day, hoping, hoping that it would grow, that the summer would prove long enough for it to come into seed and ripen.

Every other day Janya went into the edges of the woods for branches to build a huge woodpile. More and more, it seemed that they would live.

None of the other survivors came to their out-of-the-way

homestead. It was several miles from the remains of the village in which they huddled, and few had more energy than enough to keep alive. All did not have that. Janya prayed, almost ceaselessly, that none would come. She and Fenny were so rich in the necessities of life that anyone who came would kill to take them. With terrible shock she discovered what Fenny brought home one night.

She held the hand of a child so distorted with lack of food that he could hardly be recognized as human: eyes gigantic in a huge, hairless head, body covered with the sores of starvation sickness, a belly distended to the size of a giant melon, and filled (Fenny gestured) with dirt to still the hunger pangs.

He could not live, but he did. Janya fed him broth and roots until he had a little strength, then purged him again and again to rid his body of the only thing he had found to fill it. Then more food, a tiny mouthful at a time, and, at last, he began to notice that he lived.

Having brought him, Fenny paid him little attention, as if the bringing was her only responsibility. Janya wondered, but she accepted the new burden. Fenny brought more food. Early berries. Old honey (she had stings, but she just cried and went on). Nothing she brought failed to nourish. The boy filled out, his belly flattened. He even began to grow hair, and his head no longer appeared too large for the rest of him.

Once he had begun to look and act human, Janya reveled in conversation. He spoke seldom while he was so weak and ill, but made up for it almost at once. They talked and talked. His accent indicated his birth to be in one of the Great Houses, but something had happened to his memory. He remembered only his name—Labram—and having had parents, though he did not seem to feel their loss greatly.

Labram's recovery triggered a new need in Janya. She saved every bit of fat, and one windy day, using lye from wood-ashes, Janya made soap. She spent the next week washing things. The first three, of course, were the people.

She had rather expected Labram to wash up well, and he did. With his hair cut off short—it was, of course, impossible to do anything else, so filthy and matted was it—his skin scrubbed with lye soap and sand, his nails trimmed as neatly as they could manage with Fenny's little knife, and clean clothes, Janya had proof of his birth. He had a striking resemblance to a man she had seen only once, but remembered. He and his men had tried to repel the invaders. Dead now, no doubt, but his son lived. It gave her another reason to live. Labram must not be buried away here. Somewhere were people who could educate him, train him, give him a new life, perhaps a new purpose. In a year or two, when they were ready, she would have to find those people.

The change in Fenny astounded Janya. With adequate food, she had grown nearly six inches, and her age now seemed to be about eight, little less than that of Labram, who thought he was ten. Clean (and shorn) she was beautiful in a way that sent strange shudders up Janya's back. All this time, she should have known. A child of no other heritage could have done what—and as—Fenny had done. An old rhyme, two-thirds forgotten, tried to emerge from her welter of earliest memories. Something about . . . "Witch got, Witch borne." She could not resurrect the rest.

She hoped she showed none of her uneasiness. Fenny was hers now, and whatever her people had or were, this beautiful little one had proved beyond doubt that only good could come from such. Janya loved both the children, she finally admitted to herself, as much (if differently) as she had loved her own two. Nothing evil that she could prevent would happen to Fenny, regardless of who/what had got and borne her.

Cleanliness delighted Fenny. When the soap ran out, she came home with armloads of soap-roots, some of which she planted along the edges of the nearby stream where they got their water. With cleanliness came a different life-style. They were a family, and Janya, once an immaculate farmwife, returned to her normal ways. The children reacted to the change as if they had expected it. They washed up before entering the house.

By fall, Labram was outdoors most of the days, with Fenny, who accepted his presences as, Janya was sure, she would never have accepted any adult's. When they came back, he told of learning and teaching. Learning to creep so quietly that no woodland creature knew he was there. Hiding from the few men with strength enough to hunt, and so well that they passed within a foot and never knew. Searching for growing thing to take to Fenny, who knew if they were food. He taught Fenny to hand-catch fish and to spear frogs. The children brought back wild onion and garlic, half a dozen fruits, late berries, many different plant-parts, and, latest of all, backload after backload of nuts.

They dug the root crops, delighted to discover how much larger were these they had cared for than were the wild-grown originals. Backload after backload of ripe grasses were spread on the roof, dried, then stored away for winter food for the fowl and rabbits. All summer long, they saved the seed of the best plants. Next year, they would not have a hungry day. Even this winter, with the fowl and the rabbits, the smoked fish, they should make it through.

The work was endless, and enervating, and frightening to Janya. Alone, she worked desperately to make yet another part of the half-burned house into a place wherein they could pen their animals. She knew of living with animals underfoot, their stench and voidings a constant presence. She would not allow her family to live that way! The children, who worked as endlessly and were driven as hard, seemed not to be children at all. Their whole lives were involved with saving their lives. Had it not been so, they would all have died.

Autumn brought shorter days, but this was the only change from the summer weather. Janya accepted the long, late summer as a gift from the goddess. Their grain ripened. They cut and threshed it, putting by the best and saving every straw. They made new mattresses for themselves and stored the rest to bed the beasts.

Winter arrived overnight, as hard as sudden. When the snows came, and the wolves, and the last but one of those in the village died, the three of them lived snug. In days, no one could pass through the snow-filled, furious cold. The farmstead disappeared beneath a thick, white blanket. They kept openings for air only with difficulty, and melted potful after potful of snow for water. In its own way, the snow was a blessing. Janya, always fearful of someone coming and riving her, again, of what made life worth living, relaxed.

The wolves were another matter. Desperate, they discerned life they could feed upon beneath the snow, and, nightly, they made efforts to dig through to sustenance.

Janya feared. Labram prepared. Fenny ignored.

When the first of the wolves threw himself against the door, Janya shuddered. She had reinforced it, and its hinges, and she could only pray that her work had been adequate. In horror, she watched Labram take the weapons she had found, that day that seemed so long ago, position himself, and nod to Fenny. The woman could not even cry out.

Fenny threw the door open! Labram discharged his weapon. Leaping, the wolf fell dead.

Janya's stasis broke, and she, too, threw herself against the door to prevent entry to the next wolf.

Wolf was not an eatable flesh, but the thick pelt, tanned, would make a warm blanket they sorely needed. In the cold of the morning's weak sunlight, the children dragged the body out and skinned it. By the firelight in the evening, they scraped and scraped and scraped, cleaning every vestige of flesh from the skin. Nightly, another wolf died, although not all were killed as quickly as the first. Daily, another corpse was ready for the remaining wolves. The pile of wolfpelts, frozen stiff as so many slabs of stone, grew higher. Janya scrubbed and scrubbed the wooden floor, trying to eliminate not only the blood, but the odor, and, worse, the sight of Labram's unchildlike skill with a weapon she could hardly put name to.

At last, the pack was no longer a nightly presence. Janya still scrubbed.

When the weather break came, the temperature rose, and the snow developed a heavy crust. They feared for the roof. Desperate, they swathed themselves in every garment, rag, and blanket they owned, stuffing handful after handful of straw between every layer. They cleared the roof, throwing the last basketsful of snow higher than their heads on every side. For the first time, Janya realized that they might not make it through the winter. Food and water they had in plenty, the blanketing snow actually kept them warmer than they would have been without it, and the tremendous woodpile did not disappear into smoke too rapidly. But the snow itself, heavy, turning to ice wherever the warmth inside allowed it to melt during the day, to freeze solid during the terrible cold of the nights, might defeat them.

Fenneca's verbalizations, which had never bothered Janya in the least, became constant. The sounds made an undertone to their lives, never absent, never realized. No longer did these not-speeches seem purposeless—and they had never been random—but the child progressed through impatience to concern, to worry, to what seemed the first evidence of fear she had ever shown. Janya could offer no comfort and became increasingly disturbed. One night, long after Fenneca should have been asleep, the sound continued. Gritting her teeth, Janya endured. "Witch!

Witch! Witch!" pounded through her head. If only the child would be silent! What was she trying to do? Why?

As if in answer, the old rhyme flooded full into her mind. When it poured out of her mouth, however, she knew she spoke the original words, those that frightened, envious people had changed into the parody she had learned. Even in her terror, Janya understood why (if not how) she "knew" the true words of the Call. Need required them of her.

"Witch borne from Witch get,/Witch she is, the pattern set." She spoke more, much more, but she knew she would never remember the words.

Fenneca sat up. Her verbalizations suddenly changed. They flowed, a fully realized, rhythmic, rhymed chant, into the darkness, into the still, windless, starlit night outside and, it seemed to the listening woman, on to the ends of the earth. The triumph behind, beneath the Call sirened so clear that Janya shuddered.

The child lay back, her need, at last, fulfilled. She remained, utterly still, breathing but unconscious, for three days.

The silence following Fenneca's constant trials at "finding" the words of Call she needed should have been a relief to Janya. Instead, she would have called them back, could she. What would follow?

She was unsurprised when, with the last of the light, the man beat against their door. Janya let him in.

He spoke—in what Janya now realized was a language, a language she could never hope to understand—to the still body of the child.

She sat up smiling. That smile still penetrated Janya's innermost being. Now it was directed at the gaunt skeleton of a man who summoned her.

"Father!" she said, and held out her arms. He collapsed into them.

Fenneca began to hum, then to sing.

Janya, desperate, looked at Labram. His face held an expression the woman could not read, his whole being one she did not know. He went to his pallet and lay upon it. He turned to the wall.

Janya, too, sought her bed. Like Labram, she turned toward the wall, shut her eyes against the knowledge that, in the air, there hung a turquoise mist. She pulled her rabbit-skin pillow over her head. She lay awake long, long, hearing the ragged breathing of the man who, unconscious, sprawled across Fenny's bed. Fenny's voice, penetrating through all with which Janya could barrier her ears, was singing again, singing those little melodies Janya had thought only the wandering tunes of a creative, musical child.

She knew the man heard them, wherever his spirit had flown, and that they would bring him back from the place where spirits go when they should die. Her own spirit warred. She could not wish him dead. Not one more life should be given to those who had so treated this land. She could only wish him absent, never to have found his child. *Her* child! Would he take Fenny? Of course he would, and she could do nothing to stop him. Fenny was his.

No! Fenny was *hers*. She would find a way.

And with this, to her own surprise, she was satisfied. She slept.

In the wind-screaming, snow-blowing, sun-deserted morning, Janya woke before the others. She rose, performed her morning activities as if this were any other day, holding to the simple things—the warmth of the water in which she washed, the pleasure of the animals she fed and whose quarters she cleaned (Labram's job, but he, too, remained so alertly asleep that she knew he dreamed dreams the man sent). She refused to allow that thought to do more than pass through her mind.

With what did she have to fight?

She smiled. Going to the hearth, Janya pulled the crane

holding her always-filled pot of hearty broth. She removed the cover.

The man made an inarticulate sound. Janya did not turn; she smiled.

At his awakening, the children roused, too.

Janya ignored him. "Up, slug-a-beds," she called. "Wash and dress. Breakfast is nearly ready."

She crumbled rough bread into four wooden bowls, added a measure of broth, and set them on the table.

When the children came to the table, the man still sat, utterly quiet, utterly spent, upon Fenny's pallet.

"Come, stranger," Janya said. "Break your fast with us. Sit here." She pointed to a stool.

The man could not rise. Fenny and Labram helped him to do so, to shuffle across the room to the table, to collapse upon the stool.

They seated themselves, one on either side, close, that should he topple, they might prevent it. Janya took her own seat. She passed the blessing which always, always, no matter what they placed upon the table, no matter how little, she gave to the goddess who had provided. The children attacked their food with their usual enthusiasm and good manners. Nothing else did Janya allow at her table.

The man stared at his bowl as he might have at Deliverance. Janya remembered how it was to end starvation. She watched him carefully, that he should not gulp. He nodded to her, sipped, waited, sipped again. Slowly, slowly, he drank the broth. Half a mouthful at a time, he spooned up the semisolid in the bottom of the cup.

Fenneca jumped to her feet. She went to her own store of dried herbs. Selecting several, she crumbled them into a pan, poured hot water over them, then poured off the brew into their one whole cup. She blew on it to cool it, then bore it to the man. He sniffed, nodded in recognition, and drank.

When he had eaten, Labram led him to their "convenience," then back to Fenny's pallet. He fell, too deeply unconscious for dream, before he could utter a sound.

Janya nodded to herself. She dared not smile when they could see. She and the children began their morning as if he did not exist.

So the next two days continued. Nights, Fenneca sat by the man's side, her hand in his, and sang the night-shadows from his mind. She slept on Janya's cot during the daytime, lightly, alert, it seemed, to the man's passage into dream. When he slept, she returned to her vigil.

Janya fed the man (whom she refused to think of as her Fenny's father) several times during each day. He received food from her hands, thanking her with his eyes, his gestures, but did not speak. Janya kept her face impassive, her manner pleasant—but that of one who needed no further contact. Labram behaved as if he did not exist. Janya did not allow herself to wonder why.

On the fourth day the man was more alert; he slept less, ate more. Janya continued to treat him as she would any other starving stranger who offered no menace.

But on the following day, he showed clearly that he had business he must transact. With Fenny. They spoke long, if quietly, and did certain things that Janya refused to watch. Labram, still, observing but never a part of what they did, might have been the silent, suffering child Fenny had brought home.

Late in the afternoon, Fenny asked Labram to help her to bring in the wolfpelts. Janya ignored them. The man performed an action resulting in the skins becoming soft, supple, and fashioned into four sets of travel-clothing. The children immediately pulled off their ragged garments and dressed.

The man pointed to a third set of garments and addressed Janya for the first time. "Join us or die," he said, "for so you will if you remain until they come again. We would that you make the first choice, but it is your decision."

His words destroyed all of Janya's barriers to loss and bear. She stared, desperate and terrified, across the space between them, then glanced around, willing her gaze to fall upon anything else, anything.

Labram seemed so wolflike in his silver-gray garments that Janya could hardly recognize him. She cried out. "Why? Why you, too? You're not Witch!"

"I am the guardian, the champion. Why else did she save me? Why did you?"

Janya could not answer.

"I have to accompany her, to walk with her wherever she walks, to guard her sleep, to do what must be done so that she may come to . . ." He paused, then went on. "I do not know where we shall come, but without me, she cannot make it. And she must. For all of us yet alive. For the land, for the right. I did not choose this, nor did she choose me. Our destinies were written in blood and tears long before we were conceived. We must, or we shall die, and all the land with us." Ten, perhaps eleven he might be in body, but his mind, his spirit, were ageless and committed.

"Why should I go with you? What reason is there for me to live?"

Fenneca turned. "Because we love you, and we would not that you should die."

The man nodded. "Without you, the land would have lost one of its last remaining hopes. We would that you go with us to teach what we cannot: mother-love and succor and humanity. Will you deny her what she will need as much as that we can teach? Will you deny him?"

Slowly, half of herself protesting terror, Janya walked over to the garments. Standing aside from her reality, she seemed to watch herself step into a different world, a world where only she was truly human. She bent down and stroked the warm, light, protective clothing. She observed it, then the boy for whom she had planned . . . Labram, too, was full-human. What she had meant to find for him had, instead, sought them out, although she would never have chosen—never known to choose—the course destined.

The truth of the man's statement filled her. She took a deep breath, preparing to speak, though she did not know what she might say. The odor of broiling rabbit, the scent of fresh bread, the spicy aroma of the dried fruits she had concocted into a delicious complement to their meal! Those filled her nostrils—and her mind. Yes. She had the answers to his questions.

She smiled up at him and rose.

"Oh, yes. I will go. But not until we are properly prepared. The Hounds do not travel in winter. They wait for late spring, after the earth is dry, the days long. So long, we are safe here."

The man looked as if he would speak, but Janya overrode whatever he might have upon his lips. "You may believe your Power will enable you to reach wherever it is we go. I know better. We go when all are strong and rested. Do you believe that five days of food after months of starvation will restore you? If so, you are a fool, and I do not believe any of your race are condemned as such. Evil, occasionally, when the need to know more, to step beyond the bounds, yes. Stupid, no. We wait until the weather is friendly. We pack provisions, clothing, supplies, weapons. Whatever is necessary. Or we will not make it. Witch or not, you live in a body, and that body needs care and sustenance, as do ours. Oh, yes, I am needed. And my need tells me of yours."

She turned to the fireplace. Wrapping her hands in rags, she seized the spit, held it over a ready trencher, and pushed off the succulent rabbit. Without further comment, she portioned and served their meal. "Dinner is ready," she stated. "Come."

To the man, she said, "Fenneca has provided food. I have prepared it. When you have eaten, you shall rest. When your strength begins to return, you shall exercise by taking your part in our daily work. Then you shall teach us all to use the sword you wore, the bow . . ." she pointed ". . . you had slung across your back. Even the knife at your side. Perhaps we may even find pack animals—I do not doubt your skill at locating whatever we may need that is not already at hand."

The man stared at her. He crossed the room slowly. Janya watched him, a knowing expression on her face. What he had done with his Power (Janya accepted that he had it, despite her lifelong belief that only women were Witches) had exhausted him again, made him awkward. He slumped onto the stool.

His voice, formerly so strong, was a mere whisper. "You have—full-humans have—always believed us more than we are. I fear that we have believed you less. Is this the time we come together in understanding? Why?"

Fenny laid her arms around his neck, her head against his. "Love," she said quietly in their language—but Janya understood. "And need. Because we love and need each other."

The man nodded against her head. "So be it. So may it be. If we make such a beginning, in love, nothing can stand against us in the end. We may only begin the change, but it will continue."

Labram, garbed in the skins of wolves he had slain to protect them, stepped toward the two at the table. Close, but not too near. "I come for love," he whispered, "not because I am Called."

Fenneca turned to him.

"Then we shall succeed," she said.

After the cleaning up was done, Janya sought her bed. She lay upon it and covered herself. "Come, Fenny. Your father is himself again, and fights his own night-battles."

That might not be true, but Fenny's turquoise eyes had sunken into deep pits. The Power she expended whenever the man dreamed had thinned her, and no amount of food restored the flesh or the energy. The child must sleep, and if he must lie sleepless, so must it be. She did not turn to observe his expression. "We shall share a bed, that he may use yours."

The strange, beautiful child, her red-gold hair now shoulder length, free, and flaring as she turned, nodded slowly. She ran over to the bed, shed her pelts, and danced upon them to keep her toes from the icy floor.

Janya held up the cover. Fenny slipped under and curled herself against the motherly body. She sighed, and in that instant she was asleep.

Unafraid, recognizing why she lived—and why she loved—and welcoming both, Janya sighed, too. She held the little body in her arms, smiling.

The man swayed to his feet, supported himself with strong, hardened hands against the scrubbed-white tabletop. He looked first at the hands, then at Janya across the room. He smiled, too, and the expression filled Janya with the same delight she had felt when the child she had named Fenneca first smiled at her.

The man smiled at Labram. "Sleep, Champion. You, too, are necessary."

The boy smiled, but a different, a lost and left-out smile. "I know," he said. "I know it all."

Janya cringed beneath his weight of loneliness, of aloneness. Human, he could never hope for his love, as mature as his other knowledge, to be returned. Inside her soul, she wept for him.

The boy-man crossed to his pallet, removed his wolfskins, and crawled under the thin blanket.

The man pulled the skins over him. "Perhaps not all. Here, now, we make a new beginning, in hope. Sleep warm tonight, Protector," he said.

More hope, more comfort than she could provide Labram stirred in Janya's heart. Perhaps his future held more than the satisfaction of a job done to the limit of his strength of heart and body. She would hope, too, for him.

Last of all, the man lay upon Fenny's pallet. He seemed to need no covering.

Fenny opened her eyes. "Goodnight," she whispered.

"A good night and good tomorrows to us all," someone said.

Janya never knew whether it was her voice that spoke.

* * *

## Afterword

*For me, an invitation from Andre Norton to contribute to* Witch World *acted like a Spell of Enabling. I've lived there for years, off and on. I am intimately involved with its people and places, with many lives—both of her devising and of my own—lived under its laws. How else? Women my age who came to science fiction early had no other woman author to turn to. Our good fortune in finding her our guide (and, later on, our mentor or our most-positive critic, and our friend) is too great to be unintentional. It all started with André, and because she did it—and does it—well, the door is ajar. To have her open it wide "turned on my head."*

*All my writing begins with characters. Why a woman and a child? Children matter to me. I taught in elementary school for nearly thirty years. I write principally for the juvenile and young people's market. "My children" are the different ones, the kids with too many brains, too much (or too many) talents, and too little understanding of why they don't fit in. The "What ifs . . ." of "Fenneca" began with*

"What if *this child found herself alone after a major disaster? Whom would she contact? How would she be helped—or hindered?"* In Witch World, the disaster could be the passage of the Hounds of Alizon. It could then occur in any of a score of places. Good. The place is only representative; what matters is the consequences of the Hounds "missing" a child and an adult. Other questions that shaped the story were: "As Fenneca is one of the 'different' ones, in what way is she different? Aha! *What importance has this in the development of the story? It is the story!"* Because this one of André's worlds is a witch world into which humans come, I wrote about how, and why, and under what circumstances a witch child and a human woman might discover they loved and needed one another.

—WILANNE SCHNEIDER BELDEN

# BLOODSPELL

## by

## A. C. Crispin

Huge-girthed trees surrounded the forest glade where the young man knelt, laving his face in the chill crystal of a tiny brook. Leaves rustled in the gentle breeze, seemingly whispering in some arcane tongue he heard but could not understand. Allowing the water to still, he bent down, lapping at it, neat as any cat. Even after his thrist was gone he continued gazing at the shining surface, watching his own features form in the ripples, frowning.

There was nothing readily apparent about his countenance to elicit such displeasure: black hair growing into a peak on his forehead topped an oval face, pointed of chin, the jaw strong and determined. Eyebrows angled upward above level eyes the color of the new spring leaves surrounding him.

With an angry hiss, the youth's hand moved, slapping down on his image, shattering it. Absently he rubbed his wet fingers against his furred breeches, then looked up as his ears discerned a sound. His nostrils widened as he tested the breeze, ignoring the rich odors of the flowering trees, the sun-baked earth, the stream—concentrating instead on the musky, heady scent coming from the other side of the screen provided by an ancient weeping willow.

Soundlessly, he stood, narrowing his eyes, and made out the figure of a doe, heavy with young, nibbling at the leaves of the thickets beyond. Her black nose crinkled as she chewed hungrily, her ears flicking back and forth as she listened for any predator's approach.

Instinctively the young man bared his teeth, feeling the first stirring of the Change begin—the heightened rush of blood in his veins, the melting, dizzying *shifting* within him, bringing a sharp pleasure-pain—

*No!* he thought, forcing control over his body, fighting the Were part of him that wanted to Change, so he could hunt four-footed. *The deer is young, and we have plenty of meat now. Let her live to bear her fawn.* He struggled for a moment, then stood once more wholly human—at least to the outward eye.

"Herrel!"

The shouted summons sent the deer crashing away. The youth whirled to see another man, slightly taller and heavier of body, push impatiently through the brush, not bothering to seek out the narrow path. "Daydreaming again, Wronghanded? By Karthen's Swordarm, aren't you ever where you're supposed to be? Hyron has called Pack council—he sent me to find you. Treyval, Overlord of the Silvermantle Clan, has come to bargain for our services."

Herrel's mouth thinned. How like Hyron, Herrel's sire and the leader of the Wereriders, to dispatch Halse to summon him. His father could hardly have missed the fact that Halse the Strongarmed had even less use for his half-blood son than he did. Without a word of acknowledgment, Herrel started back toward those gaunt Gray Towers he still could not count as "home"—even after some ten years within their sorcery-rimed walls.

Despite his greater bulk, Halse moved with the deceptive speed of a charging bear, catching him up easily. "What were you doing, Wronghanded? Trying to bolster your ounce of Power with meditation? Philosophy can hardly be counted as part of our sorcery." His jeering words cut deep, but years of practice in hiding his hurts had made the younger man well shielded—at least outwardly—against his Werekin's jibes. He ignored Halse.

The Strongarmed grunted, sounding almost like his Were alter-ego, the bear. "But when one is desperate, any den in a storm, I suppose . . . anything is better than having a yearling cub at his side in battle, especially one who can scarcely control his Changing. Better you should have never left the Redmantle hold . . . and your slut of a mother."

Herrel's lips tightened fractionally, but he did not rise to the other's bait. Why should he defend a mother he barely remembered, one to whom he had been an embarrassment? The Lady Eldris of Car Do Prawn had been summoned by Hyron's love-spell to his bed-furs, but no true liking had ensued from that brief liaison. When their body-passion died, she had left, and Hyron had not naysaid her going—perhaps because her father had paid sword ransom for her return.

When she had been brought to child-bed, her brother Kardis had granted the infant Herrel full rights as his heir, in keeping with tradition. Hold Daughter, the Lady Eldris had a right to choose the father of the heir she was expected to produce for Car Do Prawn, and none could question her choosing. And the baby seemed fully human . . .

So it was that for the first seven years of his existence, Herrel had led the typical life of a young clan lord—rarely seeing his mother, and then only at a distance. One young man-at-arms, Pergvin, became the closest thing to a friend the young Redmantle lord could claim, teaching him to ride (though that was no easy thing, for no horse, no matter how placid, was ever at ease when the boy was within sight or scent), and instructing him in the rudiments of swordplay.

Then one day when Maleron, Margrave of the Heights, came visiting, Herrel's life changed forever. As the boy crossed the courtyard in the company of Lord Kardis and the rest of the nobles, the formal guesting-cup borne before them by the Lady Eldris, the Margrave's gray war-stallion scented him. Screaming and frothing, the horse reared, snapping its reins, then plunged to attack the child standing helpless in its path. Shrieking, Herrel had cowered away—

—and an instant later the enraged stallion swerved aside, blood streaming from a clawed nose, while a snow cat cub crouched on the stones, squalling and hissing, shaking itself free of the boy's best clothes.

Herrel closed his eyes for an instant, remembering the Lady Eldris's expression as she had faced her brother, her words coming with slow deliberation as she disowned her son. Then she had ceremoniously ripped his red cloak—a smaller version of the one draped over the Lord's seat in the Great Hall—in two, casting it from her.

The next day, the boy, accompanied only by Pergvin and a bag of his clothing, rode out of Car Do Prawn. The Lady Eldris did not appear at the leave-taking.

At first, when Herrel had come to the Gray Towers, Hyron had seemed glad of his presence, though the Pack leader was never one to openly demonstrate liking or approval. But as the years went by, and it became increasingly apparent that Herrel's Were heritage was, after all, truly that of a half-blood, then his father's silences grew cold, his glances stony.

Many times Herrel had thought of taking his Were-bred stallion, Rowan, and riding out of the gates to seek a new life. But what kind of a life could he make for himself, alone, shunned by those of full human blood? Better even the grudging company of his Packmates than complete loneliness . . .

*My courage is as flawed as my Power*, he thought bitterly. *I am a coward.*

His self-contempt was halted by the sight of the silver-blazoned guest banner flapping from the central, biggest Tower. Herrel risked a question of Halse: "Has Treyval said aught of his reason for coming here?" The man's need must be great; few humans would willingly come within a half day's ride of the Wereriders' sorcery-steeped Towers.

"No," Halse said curtly. "But it's to my mind that the Pack has grown soft . . . we need action."

Herrel knew that most of the other Wereriders would agree with Halse's judgment. Ever since the Adept who had created them had vanished through one of the legendary Gates leading to another world, the Pack had ridden in the forefront of any conflict. Bred and born for war, they fought with a beast's savagery—even when they battled in their human forms.

When the two Riders reached the council hall, they found the rest of the Pack assembled, nearly twoscore of them. The Wereriders sat in high-backed seats arranged on either side of a mammoth fireplace, placed so that no Rider's seat was above that of his fellows. The massive hall itself was stone-walled, hung with tapestries depicting hunting scenes (though if one studied those hangings closely, one realized that it was inevitably the *beasts* who were hunting the men). Baskets that gave forth a greenish glow hung on chains, providing a wan illumination.

On the opposite side of the room from the cavernous fireplace was a star, five-pointed with curling runes in its center. Its deeply graven lines were a dull brownish-red, as though those grooves had been traced in long-dried blood.

In the center of the hall, facing the Riders, were two seated figures. One, from his guesting tabard and dagger-of-ceremony, was plainly Treyval, but the other figure went shrouded in a gray cloak and hood, so that it was impossible to make out any features.

Herrel and Halse hurried past the Silvermantle Lord and his unknown companion to take their seats. "The Pack is assembled," Hyron said formally. "You may state your proposition, Lord Treyval."

The taller of the two seated figures rose, holding the argent cloak of his Clan over his arm. Treyval was dark-bearded, well into middle years, with heavy shoulders and too much girth; but the Overlord still bore himself like a fighting man.

He gave the assembled Pack the abbreviated bow used by a noble facing those equal in rank. "My lords, I come here on a matter of gravest urgency to my Clan. Penmyre of Goldmantle has annexed the village of Farmarch, which lies on the western border of my lands. He has done so freely, with the consent of the village council and the folk of Farmarch, and Goldmantle men-at-arms now patrol there to prevent my forces from taking back what is rightfully mine." The Clan Lord's voice was calm enough, but Herrel did not miss the steady tightening of his fingers upon the silver mantle he held.

"And what do you wish of us?" Hyron asked.

"That you retake the village, defeat Goldmantle's forces, and teach those Farmarch traitors that Treyval is not one to overlook insult. For this I will pay in gold, or you may have your pick of our harvest supplies for your next winter's keeping."

"Do you wish the Farmarch council captured and brought to you?"

"That is not necessary, as long as they pay with their lives. Let a few villagers live so they may spread the tale and prevent such insurrection from happening again."

"I see," Hyron said. "Very well then, we must confer. Withdraw to the guesting chambers and we will inform you of our decision."

The Silvermantle Lord bowed, then headed for the entrance, accompanied by that cloaked other. Something about the way that shrouded body moved made Herrel's eyes widen. *A woman? Why would Treyval bring a woman here? Is she his leman? Or his daughter?*

As the two passed the end of the row where Herrel sat, the woman turned her head slightly, and her eyes met the young Rider's. A physical shock raced through him at the force of that dark gaze. He could see nothing of her face, but, somehow, he knew she possessed beauty beyond any that he had seen before. He watched her walk out the door, discerning within the gray folds of cloak a graceful form that was unmistakably female—and the awareness of her sex was as a new-laid fire within him.

The Riders had little to do with women. Occasionally one would leave the Were holding, driven by the demands of his flesh to lurk outside a village or keep, casting a love-spell that would summon some willing partner to share his bed-furs. Such liaisons were short-lived and, until Hyron's encounter with the Lady Eldris, fruitless.

Even Herrel had left once on such an errand, but here, as in so many other things, his Power proved flawed. His love-spell had faltered, lacking in strength and conviction. This failure, though he did not realize it, was chiefly due to his innate distaste for the idea of so using another for his own gratification.

Instead he had Changed, roaming the hills in his snow cat form, letting the animal portion of him have the greater sway, and there he had found a female and mated.

"Are you going to grow roots? Become half tree as well as half Were—and *all* simpleton?" A hard shove accompanied the harsh query, and, startled from his reverie, Herrel turned to find the other Riders staring at him, nudging each other, grinning at Halse's wit. "Wake up, Wrong-handed. Didn't you hear Hyron's summons? We're to discuss Treyval's offer while we sup."

Herrel hastened toward the dining hall. There, amid the good smells of roasting meat and fresh-baked bread, he chewed and swallowed mechanically, absently heeding the discussion that rose and fell around him. He could not forget the woman's dark eyes, and wondered, with a shiver, if she were a sorceress who had cast a spell over him.

"What are your thoughts on the matter, Herrel?" Hyron demanded, after all the other Riders had commented upon the Silvermantle Lord's proposal. "By Pack right, each must have a chance to speak before we vote."

Herrel swallowed hastily, his thoughts racing. Many of the Riders had supported the idea of taking service with Treyval against Farmarch, but not all. He hesitated, half tempted to agree just to avoid the ridicule he would undoubtedly receive from Halse (who was pushing for Pack acceptance of Treyval's proposition), but a sudden sharp memory of the little market town outside the Redmantle Overlord's keep decided him. He had lived among people like those villagers for too many years. *If Halse names me "soft" again, then so be it.*

"It seems to me," he said, not raising his voice, "that the Pack has too much honor to undertake a commission that would only result in our disgrace. We are fighters, are we not? Armed warriors are our proper antagonists, not helpless old people and children—nor yet farmers and tradespeople who have never held a weapon, never marched to battle. If we accept Treyval's offer, it will become a blot upon our reputations that could never be erased. All of Arvon will say—and rightfully so—that the Wereriders are no longer soldiers but have sunk to the level of common cutthroats."

As he finished, Herrel heard approving murmurs from several of the Riders. "The lad speaks well," Harl, who wore an eagle helm when he went into battle as a man, and an eagle body when he fought as a beast, said, rising to address the others. "His words echo my thoughts, better than I could have expressed them. I know how *I* shall vote."

Herrel's eyes widened as the murmurs of support grew into near-shouts, so loud that Hyron must needs pound his tankard on the board for silence. "Let us show hands on the question," he announced. "Halse, to you the count of 'ayes.' Herrel, the 'nays.' First, the ayes.''

Hands went up, but not nearly as many as Herrel had expected. Then Hyron called for the nay vote, and the young Rider was busy counting.

"That settles it, then," Hyron said. "Thirty-one opposed, seven in favor. I will tell Treyval of our refusal in the morn."

Despite the softness of his bed-furs, sleep eluded Herrel that night. He lay staring into the darkness, familiar questions scuttling across his mind, questions that had no answers.

*Why am I here? How is it that I came to be? The Pack was created to be the perfect weapon—a fighting force to defend the Adept who once held this stronghold. He brought Hyron and the others into being by his sorcerous melding of loyal armsmen with wild creatures of this land . . . that is why we are tied to Arvon, attuned to it . . . but, why* me? *The only spawn of a race never meant to breed true, I am naught but a flawed weapon, as much as any broken sword or warped bow . . . full possessing neither Power nor courage . . .*

The thought of the woman's dark eyes touched his mind again, and he turned over, thumping savagely at the feather-stuffed bolster. *She is here, in this building. The guesting quarters are not far away . . . does she lie awake, too?* His mouth twisted. *Of course not, Wronghanded, she sleeps, and knows nothing of your wakefulness. She sleeps—*

"No," whispered a voice from the doorway of his chamber. "I am not asleep."

Herrel sat upright with a jerk that made him dizzy. "Lady?" he whispered, reaching out a hand to the Wereglobe hanging on the wall by his bunk. Just in time, he remembered his nakedness, and, fumbling, drew on his breeches. *Then* he activated the light.

She stepped into the room and drew the door closed behind her, soundlessly. She was wearing naught but a silken nightrobe, and her hair, palest platinum in the Werelight, tumbled unbound down her back. "Lady?" he whispered again, hardly able to believe she was here. He surreptitiously moved one bare foot off the fur rug, and the icy touch of the stone floor reassured him that he was, indeed, awake.

"I would apologize for waking you," her voice was sweet and clear, with an undertone of breathless laughter, "except that I know that you were not asleep. I am Gwenfar, Treyval's niece."

"I am Herrel," he said. "What can I do for you, Lady Gwenfar? Is aught wrong?"

"Nothing, save that I am cold," she said with a sudden shiver. He saw the tiny points of her breasts beneath the thin silk. "And I hoped here might be a place where I would find warmth, and welcome."

Stunned, Herrel sat unmoving as she approached him, placing her small hands on his bare shoulders. *She can't mean what she seems to mean*! he thought wildly. *She*— but his thoughts broke and scattered like chaff before an autumn wind as she leaned down to place her mouth full on his. Her hair fell around them like a curtain, shutting off the world.

Hesitantly, still unable to believe she was here, Herrel responded to her kiss, reaching up to draw her down on the bed beside him. His head spun with the silken feel of her body, the scent of her hair.

Finally he pulled away a little, his breath coming in ragged gasps. She smiled, running her hands across his chest. "Sweet," she said. "You are very sweet, Herrel. And so young."

*Young*? he thought dazedly, daring to lay hand on her hair, gather it up into a fistful of fragrance, and bring it to his lips, *I am young? But she is young, as young as I . . . a maiden, surely?*

But her caresses were too skilled to be virginal, he realized, with a sudden, cold honesty. He leaned forward, looking intently into her eyes, and knew suddenly that this woman, despite the air of innocence and youth her face and slender body gave her, was considerably older than he.

*And so?* he thought, reaching to pull her close again, kiss her eager mouth, *what if it is true? She is therefore truly a woman, and has a right to take her pleasures where she wishes . . .*

But even as he bent her back until they were both lying on the bed, he felt disquiet growing within him.

She moved beneath him, one leg hooking over his, her arms strong across his back, nails digging in. She was kissing his shoulder now, and he felt her teeth nip his flesh, at first gently, then hard enough to sweeten his pleasure with pain. Her thigh was bare beneath his hand, and urgency mounted within him, but at the same moment, his unease grew. Growing, even though he tried to stifle it. It was as though his body were building up a charge of energy, of strength—of *youth.*

*And that energy, that youth, will be transferred from me to Gwenfar, if I take her,* he realized suddenly, fear washing over him.

"No!" he gasped, trying to disentangle himself from limbs that seemed now like silken ropes. "*No!*"

With a wrench he pulled away, stumbled back across the cold floor, his breath coming in great, panicky gulps.

"Herrel?" She reached after him, her expression so guileless that he wondered if he were mad to think such things about her. "What is it? Is it that you have never lain with a woman? I will guide you. All will be well."

"No," he said, his voice still shaky, but gaining conviction with every word. "I will not do this. You would take something from me, something beyond my innocence. Is that how you stay so young, Lady?" His words hung in the air, as though they had been uttered under truthspell.

"I do not understand you," she said indignantly. "Come back here, and I will show you such delights—"

"*Dark* delights, perhaps?" Herrel spat, rage beginning to replace the desire and fear he had felt. "Just as you deal in Dark sorcery, from the Left-Hand Path?"

"What right have you to insult me?" She was angry now, too, her voice like honey poured over honed steel. "If you do not want me, say so, and I will leave. But point no ward-fingers at me! I am no Dark One!"

"You should become a mime in a traveling show, Lady," he snarled, "you play your part to such perfection. You are a sorceress at the very least—for aught I know you are one of the Adepts! Your Power is of the Dark, there is no mistaking it. Get you gone from my sight, and away from the Gray Towers!"

"What is it, little boy?" She made no effort now to disguise her fury—it stung him like a lash. "Are you simply a coward? Or do you confine your lusts to your Packmates?"

Enraged, Herrel did the only thing he could think of that would silence her—he Changed.

Were, his snow cat eyes could *see* the Darkness coiling around her like a smoky halo. He squalled, one paw going out, deliberately extending his claws, baring fangs that could rip flesh, crush bone.

Gwenfar gasped, scrambling off the bed as the snow cat began padding toward her. With a final silken flicker of her night robe, she was gone, out the door, her bare feet running on the time-worn stones.

A moment later, Herrel stood once more a man, her words echoing in his ears. *Coward . . . coward . . . coward . . .*

* * *

After much thought, Herrel did not report his encounter with the sorceress to Hyron. After all, nothing had really happened, he reminded himself. And he knew any confession he made to Hyron would likely reach Halse's ears —and he well knew the mockery that would bring down upon him. Halse would be quick to guess that Herrel had probably been "chosen" by Gwenfar because he, of all the Riders, had never known a woman—that his love spell had failed, as so many other things did for him. "Coward" would be the least of the jibes.

Seething, he prowled the corridors for the remainder of the night in his Were form, but there were no stirrings from the guest chambers.

The next morning, Lord Treyval and his niece rode out of the Gray Towers. The assembled Weres stood gathered as an honor-guard at their leave-taking, as Hyron assisted the Lady Gwenfar to mount. She wore her hood thrown back in the early spring breeze, and strands of her pale, silvery hair wisped around her face. She looked so young, so pure—Herrel found himself pressing the bruised circle of toothmarks marking his shoulder to reassure himself that he had not dreamed the events of the night before.

He could hear his fellow Riders murmuring among themselves, catching a word or two that left no doubt in his mind as to the subject of their conversation. Halse chuckled lewdly, only to be silenced abruptly by Hyron's glare.

*Would that she had picked the bear last night*, Herrel found himself thinking coldly. *Mayhap she would have done me a service, ridding me of Halse.* But then the woman's eyes, black and deep as an underground river, caught and held his. *No*, Herrel amended, *her embrace is something that I could wish on no one, no matter how much an unfriend he has been.* He forced his own gaze to remain steady, but couldn't repress the chill tracing down his spine like a long-dead finger.

Finally, just when Herrel thought he must break that

stare or run mad, the sorceress's mount sidled nervously across the courtyard, severing their eye-lock.

The young Rider watched her back as she rode forth from the Gray Towers, thinking that today he must seek out his private stream and bathe—even its snow-melted chill would be preferable to the memory of her hands on his flesh.

That night, tired as he was from his previous night's sentry-go before the guest chambers, Herrel stayed awake in his chamber, working with a handful of herbs he had purloined from the kitchen. He took pinches of angelica, basil, dill, rosemary, tarragon, and trefoil, crushing them together until they made a pungent powder.

When they were well mixed, he shook them into a small square of white silk, then added a tiny sliver of the blessed blue metal called *quan-iron*. Folding the cloth edges up, he tied them together with red thread, then braided and knotted the thread together until the herbal amulet hung from a red cord long enough to loop over his neck and hang beneath the collar of his jerkin.

Then he took the amulet, holding it in his hand, and breathed upon it. "Trefoil, angelica, rosemary, dill, hinder Dark sorcery—heed my will," he chanted, feeling half foolish. Herbal magic had little to do with the sorcery of the Weres—he was relying instead on human lore he dimly remembered from his childhood. Three times he repeated his clumsily rhymed charm, then concealed the amulet next to his skin.

He slept the dreamless sleep of exhausted youth.

Three days later, a carrier-hawk flapped to a perch on the battlements of the north Tower, a message cylinder strapped to its leg. Hyron broke the seal and scanned the parchment quickly, then looked up at the assembled riders. "Penmyre of Goldmantle asks us to accept employment as border guards for his lands."

The assembled Pack considered the offer, deciding to accept it. Within two days they rode for Goldmantle lands. Their route took them near Farmarch, and Herrel, as he sat astride Rowan, could not help remembering Lady Gwenfar, her silken body. He shifted uneasily in his saddle, wondering just what would have happened to him had he become her lover.

He shook his head, shivering despite the warm afternoon sun. Around the troupe of Riders, the plowed fields surrounding Farmarch smelled rich and earthy with their newly turned furrows. Ahead of the Pack rose the squat, two- and three-story buildings of the town. Herrel could see brightly colored skirts and jerkins against the cobbled streets and buildings, and realized it must be market day.

He smiled, thinking of Car Do Prawn, of the Sowing Festival he had attended once with Pergvin, of—

Herrel gasped, hand going to his throat, feeling a sudden heat from the amulet that lay there. It was almost as though he could *see* something reaching down toward him and the Pack . . . something Dark, malevolent. He summoned breath to cry out, but there was no time—no time!

The other Wereriders had no such warning of danger. One moment they were astride their mounts, weapons in sheaths, the next the entire Pack swayed in their saddles, and, one by one, began to fall.

Herrel barely felt the shock of hitting the hard-packed earth of the road, so intense was the pain sweeping his body. He shrieked, but the sound that emerged was more akin to the battle snarl of a snow cat. He writhed on the ground, convulsing, Darkness sweeping over him in waves of agony, barely hearing the snarls, screeches, neighs, and growls erupting from the throats of his Packmates.

Then the pain was gone, with a suddenness that left him too limp to do aught but lie on the road for long moments. But something within his body would not let him do that . . . instead he was up and padding (padding? Why was he four-footed? He had willed no Change . . . ) toward Farmarch.

Herrel's mind struggled to regain control of his Were shape, but the snow cat mentality held sway—he was trapped, helpless.

And, worse, he was conscious of a new, mounting savagery filling him, drowning the feeble spark that was —had been—Herrel. Bloodlust filled the snow cat mind, a cruel passion for killing that was far from the clean, innocent nature of the creature. The Darkness now filling the snow cat's mind was malignant, unclean.

Herrel, with a fading spark of self-awareness, had only a moment to notice that the Pack jostled around him as they entered Farmarch. A boar, two bears, three wolves (red, gray, and black), a wild stallion (that moments ago had been Hyron), a monstrous eagle, a mountain elk, another, spotted cat, a desert lion—each of the thirty-seven Riders had assumed his Were alter-ego. All the animals were far larger than their wild kindred, their eyes gleaming red as they strode purposefully along the cobbled village streets.

The young Rider glimpsed the terrified faces of the villagers as the Pack advanced on them. He made a last, huge effort to wrest control away from that Dark mind that was now fully controlling his snow cat body . . . but its Power was too strong.

The spark that had been Herrel gasped, then went out.

As if he were an observer outside his own body, Herrel watched the snow cat advance on an old woman who screeched at him, trying to fend him off with a garden rake. With one sweep of his massive paw, the tool went flying. The cat moved forward, then crouched, muscled hindquarters twitching in anticipation of the leap . . .

But there was something wrong . . .

The snow cat pawed distractedly at its throat with a forepaw, its rough pink tongue hanging out of its open mouth as it panted shallowly. The silver-gray flanks heaved as the cat redoubled its effort to breathe, prey forgotten.

With a dizzying rush, Herrel was back in the snow cat body, just in time to share the waves of red-tinged blackness that were sweeping over its eyes. *Air! There's no air! I can't breathe!* He gasped spasmodically, realizing that something around his neck was strangling him, was still tightening—

*Air! Can't . . . breathe . . .*

With a final, convulsive gasp, the blackness became complete, sending Herrel sliding down into it.

He awoke, he never knew how much later, still in his Were form, but fully himself again. The amulet around his throat was no longer chokingly tight, but instead gave off waves of comforting strength and warmth. He lay quiet for a moment, eyes closed, hearing the shrieks of the townspeople and the battle cries of the Weres filling Farmarch. The hot smells of blood and death filled his nostrils.

Bracing himself, Herrel opened his eyes. The old woman lay sprawled beside him, her body ripped from neck to belly. His fur was clotted with splashed blood. Jumbled entrails, sticky-dark, steamed in the breeze. The huge gray wolf who was his Packmate, Hewlor, raised a stained muzzle from the corpse to glare at him from crimson, bestial eyes.

Herrel crawled backward on his belly, trying to make Hewlor see that the snow cat represented no rival for his meat. The wolf snarled, gobbets of flesh hanging from his jaws, but did not leap.

When he had put several lengths between them, the young Rider dared to bound away. He reached the inn, and leaped up onto the driver's seat of a farm wagon standing in front of it, a dead ox collapsed in its yoke. The extra height allowed him to see most of the street.

The carnage that met his eyes made the snow cat whimper sickly; if Herrel had been in his human form he knew he would have vomited. Torn, bloody bodies of

Penmyre's men-at-arms and villagers sprawled at intervals along the street, some still twitching in death-agony. Herrel saw the lion dragging a wailing infant from the limp arms of its dead mother. Even as he watched, it, too, was killed.

*I'm too late*, he thought wretchedly, feeling as though his only escape from the scene before him lay in letting himself sink into forgetfulness, into madness. *It's my fault . . . Gwenfar did this, I know it, I can almost smell her brand of Darkness . . . if I had told Hyron about her, this might not have happened . . .*

Consumed by guilt, he nearly bounded away, tempted to let the snow cat nature take over, become naught but an animal for the rest of his days, but then he saw a small knot of survivors huddled across the town square. A few of them had had time to grab weapons.

The outermost circle of five humans, men and women both, were armed with swords or bows. One woman brandished a pitchfork. Crowded into the center of the group milled a knot of old people and children, many with babies in their arms. The villagers were backing slowly toward the biggest of the Farmarch buildings, stone, with massive double doors, doors that were shut.

Advancing on them were Halse, the red bear; Hyron, the stallion, his forefeet spattered with crimson nearly to the knee; and Hessel, the boar, his tusks dripping with blood not his own. Harl, the eagle, circled above them, shrieking his battle cry. The black wolf, Helder, lay sprawled on the cobbles, throat pierced by an arrow.

*If those doors are locked, they'll all be pulled down*, Herrel thought. *I have to open them!* His snow cat muscles bunched, then strained to the utmost as he flung himself upward, onto the roof of the inn. His front claws scrabbled frantically at the slate shingles, then he was able to pull himself up and over the rain gutter.

Snow cats are also known as mountain cats, with good reason. Herrel bounded from roof to roof as quickly as he would have traveled the rocky heights of the Arvon border.

When he reached the building that was the survivors' destination, he leaped down where the roof was lowest, the shock of the drop nearly knocking his breath out. He could not help the townspeople in his Were form, that was obvious. He'd only earn himself an arrow to match the one that had killed Helder. Herrel Changed.

Human, he leaped for the doors, finding to his relief that they were not locked. He flung them open, then took one quick glance inside to assure himself that none of the Pack had flanked the villagers and were waiting, but the place was empty. High, narrow windows lined the walls. "In here!" he shouted, turning back to the villagers, using the common tongue of Arvon. "*Hurry!*"

The townspeople glanced back to see him gesturing, then, snatching up the smaller children, the unarmed ones raced toward him, leaving their outer circle to spread out, guarding their retreat. They piled into each other, pushing and shoving to get through. Once they were all in, Herrel slammed and barred the doors.

When he turned back to face them, the villagers were staring at him in amazement—naked, bloody, matted with dirt from the road, his hands bare of any blade. "Who are you?" one old man asked, stepping forward.

"Never mind that now," Herrel said. "Close the shutters behind me, fast! They'll be in the windows! Somebody stand by the door to let the others in!"

Turning, he raced over to the nearest window and Changed. Behind him he could hear shrieks of horror. Were again, it was but a moment's work to jump and scrabble his way out the high, narrow window. He landed in an alley, Changed again, then ran around the side of the building, toward the beleaguered rear guard.

Two more of the Pack had joined Hyron and the others; the gray wolf, Hewlor, and the gigantic elk stag, Hathor. His antlers gleamed scarlet, as though some madman had wrapped them with festival ribbons. The archer, Herrel saw, had been at work again—Hanon, the black bear, now lay sprawled beside the wolf.

But the defenders had taken a loss, too. One of them, a sword-wielding woman, had been pulled down and dragged some distance away. The Pack, except for the stallion and the stag, was distracted for the moment while they ripped at the body.

"Get inside, all of you!" Herrel snapped, grabbing at the battered sword held clumsily in the hands of a plowman. "You, give me that knife!" Such was the authority in his tone that the two men he addressed obeyed. "Now go!" They scuttled away, leaving two of their number to stand with the young Rider.

"You two, go also," he ordered. "Barricade the doors behind you."

"We can't leave you!" The wiry woman on his right protested, holding her pitchfork at the ready. "As soon as they're finished"—she gulped, then steadied her voice —"with Annalise, they'll attack again."

"I can hold them off," Herrel said, testing the swing of the old sword. "Is anyone in Farmarch of Wise stock? Any Summoners here?"

"Granther Admon," she replied. "If the ones we were guarding are safe."

"They're safe," Herrel told her. "Tell Admon to call up such a Summoning as he's never done in his life. Only one of the Voices could overmatch the ensorcelment the Pack is under."

"How do you know?" the bowman on his left challenged. "How could you know what spell is at work here?"

"Because I was under it, too," Herrel said, conscious of a grim humor at their reaction when they really *looked* at him. "I'm one of them. So get you back, and leave me to face them. You'll not be abandoning one of your own kind."

He caught the undisguised glance of hatred the archer turned on him, then the man went, dragging the pitchfork-woman with him, over her protests.

Herrel grasped the old sword firmly, his thoughts racing. Behind him he could hear the *thunk* as the villagers slid the oaken bar into place across the door. The sounds of dragging chairs and tables followed. What should he do now?

*If I could just break the ensorcelment for a moment, some of them might recover their minds, as I did,* he thought. For the first time he remembered the amulet that had saved him. Jerking frantically at its cord, he managed to drag it over his head. It was warm in his hand.

But could its protection extend to the other members of the Pack? How could its Power be strengthened?

Herrel thought hard, while part of his mind noticed that the boar, the bear, and the wolf had finished their grim repast and were turning back toward him. Hyron snorted, pawing the ground with a sharp hoof, his eyes gleaming maniacally, no recognition in their depths.

*Strengthen the spell,* Herrel thought frantically. *No Power comes without price.* That was one of the foremost redes of sorcery for both the Right- and the Left-Hand Path. *No Power without price . . . but I have nothing. Only these weapons, and the amulet—*

—and himself. His body, his blood. Blood was a means of strengthening a spell.

*Not my hands, I need them to hold my weapons . . . not my legs, I have to be able to move fast . . . what then? . . . I have it . . .*

Bracing himself, Herrel drew the blade of the dagger across his belly. The taut flesh parted almost without pain, then blood welled into the opening and began dripping. He looked back to find the Pack advancing on him. The urge to Change, to bound away, free, was nearly overwhelming.

Instead, he pressed the amulet against his wound, letting

warmth trickle over his fingers, steeling himself, concentrating all of his Will, every vestige of his Power. *But I am the Wronghanded, the coward, the failure*—some treacherous part of him protested. *Against the whole Pack I can never—*

"Stop!" he shouted, more to himself than to the Wereriders. His voice boomed so loud it startled him in the silence. *Concentrate! You can do this, you must believe to make it so!*

"Brothers we are!" he called, seeing every muzzle pointing in his direction. "Brothers in blood, bloodkin! Look upon me, and fight the Darkness that is making of you worse than beasts! By the Light, by the Cold Steel, by the Rowan, by the Candles of the Weres! Stand as *men* once more!"

He flung his arm aloft, the crimson-dyed amulet dangling from his fingers. "I conjure you, by the blood we share, by the blood I have shed, stand as *men* once more!"

A green mist swirled between them, doubly bright in the westering rays of sunset. When it cleared, the Pack stood two-legged. Each of them swayed, looking dazedly around. Herrel heard mutters of disbelief, then groans of unwilling comprehension as they took in the carnage. Harl collapsed onto hands and knees and was thoroughly sick.

Herrel himself was feeling light-headed from the strain of holding his Will focused at the amulet. *Can I stop now? Is the spell gone?* He blinked, sweat stinging his eyes, thinking that soon he would have to halt, or he would collapse right here onto the cobbles—

*You may cease your efforts, young Rider,* echoed a voice inside his head. *We have removed the ensorcelment.*

Startled, Herrel swung around to see two men step out of the now-open doorway behind him. Though they wore different jerkins and breeches, their faces seemed to have been cast in one mold. One wore his hair cropped short, and it was a strange mixture of black, gray, and brown

—like unto the pelt of some exotic animal. The other's hair was black and sleek, clipped into a short tail at the nape of his neck.

"Who—" Herrel began, then realized the identity of the strangers. He had never imagined that the Voices, those greatest of Adepts, might wear such an ordinary guise. "My lords." He bent knee stiffly, staggering a little as he got up. The earth seemed none too steady.

"Careful, young Herrel," the brindled one on his left said, putting out a hand to catch his arm. "Now is not the time for ceremony. I am Neevor, and this is my brother-in-spirit, Ibycus. Admon Summoned us. It seems Farmarch owes you a debt."

Herrel shook his head. "Not so, my lord. I am to blame for this, for keeping silent when I should have spoken. If I had, the trick to lure us to Farmarch might have been uncovered, and this . . . slaughter . . . prevented." His voice broke a little on the last words. The enormity of what had been done this day washed over him, and for a moment he could not speak at all.

"We know," Ibycus said, coming over to put his hand beneath Herrel's other arm. "We sought the Lady Gwenfar first, but she is gone from Arvon. There has been a troubling in the fabric of this world, and it seems likely she has departed through some Gate. We shall seek Treyval and summon him to an accounting."

"But this was mostly Gwenfar's doing," Herrel whispered bitterly. "She deserves death for what she did. If she were still here, I would hunt her down—"

"But she is not here," Neevor reminded him. "Come, we must see to your wound." Gently, he and his brother laced their fingers together, then laid them over the slash. Herrel felt a sudden warmth and strength filling him, and when they drew their hands away, there was naught but a thin, seemingly long-healed scar.

Later, clad in a pair of hastily borrowed breeches, a

cloak pulled round his bare shoulders, Herrel, with the other Riders, gathered in the Town Hall to hear the judgment of the Voices.

The townspeople were not there, though the Riders could hear them outside, in the darkness, hunting by torch and lantern light for their dead. The soft, keening wails of the women made Herrel want to stop his ears with his fingers, but he forced himself to listen. At least he did not have the memories the others did. Even Halse sat still, his shoulders slumped, staring down at his hands.

"Wereriders," Neevor said. "Since your creation, you have been a thorn in the flesh of Arvon. Your willingness to fight under different banners for hire has enabled those who would not otherwise risk themselves in honest combat to war upon their neighbors. We live in a Shadowed land, and the Dark has many faces. Now that you have been touched by it, you may well fall under its Power more easily next time. This we cannot allow."

When his brother paused, Ibycus continued, as though they were both halves of the same being. "The penalty for what you have done today, by rights, is death. But, knowing that you did not consciously slaughter, but were merely a tool in the hands of another, we extend you mercy . . . partly for the sake of the young Rider, Herrel, without whom there would have been even more killing."

Halse roused from his stupor enough to cast Herrel a glance of undisguised hatred.

"We therefore enjoin you," said Neevor, "to leave Arvon. Now. Tonight. We exile you, that you may learn, during the time of separation, that those who are willing tools for death have no place here."

Hyron raised his head. "How long, my lords? We are blood-tied to Arvon . . . exile for us may be even crueler than clean death."

"For answer, you must follow us," Ibycus said. Silently, the Wereriders filed after the Adepts, out into the night.

"Look up," Neevor instructed them.

Herrel stared, seeing the familiar star-patterns of the Plow, the Hunter, the Lady . . . the Bull. Suddenly they shifted, moved before his eyes, making him sway dizzily. Then they steadied, realigning themselves, into different shapes. Herrel blinked, but even with his eyes closed, those sparkling pinpoints seemed etched in his mind . . . he knew he would never forget them.

When he opened his eyes again, the stars were back in their proper positions.

"You may return to Arvon," Neevor said solemnly, "when the stars take on the patterns we have just shown you."

*So long! How can we live for that long away from here?* Herrel wondered, hearing the dismayed mutterings around him. "My lords," Hyron said. "May we not even return to the Gray Towers to gather supplies . . . our belongings?"

"You have heard our judgment," Ibycus told him.

"But you know that all that has happened here tonight is the witch's fault. *She* should be the one to suffer. We offered her guest-greeting, and she betrayed us. To live, for all those years, away . . . with *this* on our consciences," the Wereleader half protested. "I—we—cannot bear it . . ."

"We grant you one boon," Neevor said. "Your memories of the events of this day, and of Arvon, shall be dulled when you ride out of this land, to help you endure your punishment. Now get you to your mounts, and ride. We shall guide you."

Herrel turned away from the Voices with the others, only to have Ibycus touch his arm. "Wait, Herrel."

"Yes, my lords?"

"Since your hands, alone of your fellows, are unstained with innocent blood, you may remain in Arvon, if such is your choice."

Herrel stood for a long moment, thinking of this land that he loved, of his secret glade by the brook, of the mountains he had roamed four-footed . . . of Arvon, his home—the only real home he could claim.

Finally he sighed, shaking his head. "The fault for today is still partly mine," he said. "That I did not take part in the killing does not change that. And, though they often remind me that I am naught but half-blood, still they are the only kin I have. I will ride with them, my lords."

"You have courage, young Rider," Neevor said. "It is your decision."

"Courage?" Herrel echoed bitterly, following after the knot of Riders, once more alone. "Me?"

"You," Neevor said firmly, falling into step on his right. "You weigh yourself too lightly, Herrel. You are more than you know. Someday, you will learn the truth of what I say . . . just as you will learn to value yourself."

"Perhaps," Herrel said hesitantly, "I was not a coward today, but . . ." He shrugged. "It has gained me nothing in the sight of the Pack. I am still alone. I will always be alone."

"Always is a long time," Ibycus said, sounding faintly amused. "Especially when one is young. Are you then a Voice, to foretell the future?"

"No, my lords," Herrel said, discomfited. "I did not mean to contradict you. But have you seen my future? Do you know if I—"

"Have done, Herrel," Neevor said. "You know we cannot reveal what we may have seen. Simply speaking aloud the course of a life-path may cause it to change, and such direct meddling is forbidden, even to us."

Herrel nodded, accepting it, feeling his momentary eagerness drain away, the old loneliness rise to replace it.

Ibycus cleared his throat. "I will tell you, though, Herrel, that I foresee for you a time when there will be one you can turn to, trust, one who will company with you, even unto a place lying beyond the bounds of death." He paused for a moment. "But it will not be soon."

They reached the horses, and Herrel busied himself dressing, then, after checking the girth, swung onto Rowan's back. Hyron gave the signal, and the Pack turned to follow Neevor, who had mounted himself bareback upon a shaggy mountain pony that had appeared at his whistle. Ibycus, astride on another such beast, brought up the rear.

Herrel touched Rowan with his heel, and the stallion moved out willingly, rested after his long wait. "Ibycus," Herrel said suddenly, urgently, his voice pitched low in the darkness. "I would ask one boon of you, if I may."

"Ask," the Voice said.

"When you draw the veil over our memories, can you . . . leave the one of your foretelling? It would help me during the times when . . ." He hesitated. "It would help," he repeated.

"Very well," Ibycus said.

The long column of silent horsemen rode steadily onward, heading east, toward the mountains and whatever future lay beyond their rugged peaks.

\* \* \*

## Afterword

*"Bloodspell" was a story I wrote to satisfy my own curiosity. Andre first introduced the Wereriders in* Year of the Unicorn, *which told the story of how Herrel and his fellow Riders were finally allowed to return to Arvon . . . after spending thousands of years exiled to the Waste near High Hallack.*

*Nearly two decades after first reading* Year, *I had the honor of meeting Andre when she graciously asked me to* collaborate with her in the Witch World (we co-wrote one book, Gryphon's Eyrie [Tor], and are currently working on another, Songsmith [also Tor]). During a break in one of our recent plotting sessions, I confessed to Andre that, next to Kerovan (our hero in Gryphon's Eyrie), Herrel had always been my favorite Witch World hero. Then I asked her why the Wereriders had been exiled in the first place. "I don't know," she replied. "I just knew that they had been, when I began writing the story."

"They must have done something pretty terrible, to merit such a severe punishment," I said. "Yes, I suppose so," Andre replied, then she added, with a twinkle, "If you really want to know, why don't you write the story of what happened for the new anthology? Then we'd both know!"

My mind was off and running. When Andre had first mentioned my doing a story for this volume, I was delighted at the chance to return to my favorite fantasy universe, and determined to write a humorous piece—but from its inception, "Bloodspell" was obviously not going to be in that vein (sorry 'bout that).

Massacres of innocents have occurred throughout history; My Lai was highly publicized, but hardly unique. My theme, as the storyline developed, became one of responsibility in the aftermath of tragedy.

Gwenfar still has to receive her just due. Andre and I have discussed writing a sequel to The Jargoon Pard someday. Maybe . . . just maybe . . .

—A. C. CRISPIN

# THE WHITE ROAD
## by
## Charles de Lint

The early winter sky was a dirty gray the day Nordendale's men returned from the war. They had marched and ridden out, banners unfurled, helms gleaming in the sun, but returned as stragglers, grimy with the dirt of the road and battle, their uneven column stretched for a quarter of a mile. They returned victorious, having helped drive the Hounds of Alizon from High Hallack, but their haunted eyes, the wounds they bore, the very stoop of their shoulders, witnessed that even in victory, they had lost.

Their lord and his heir were dead. The Dales they returned to had felt the sting of the invaders' attack; the harvest was poor and fields lay untilled. Not one family had emerged unscathed from the final battle at Ruther's Pass.

Saren left her work in the inn when the call came to join the other watchers, her hair tied back in a long braid, wearing men's clothing that hung a size too big on her bony figure. Having turned sixteen this past autumn, she had known nothing but times of trouble in the Dales. The war had dragged on for a score of years, coming to a head only this past year when Wereriders from the Waste, the men of High Hallack, combined with fleets of the Sulcar, to finally put an end to the Alizon menace.

As she watched Gully, with his arm in a sling, avoiding

her gaze, the haywright Capper was carried on a stretcher for he had lost both legs. Big Ran Jenner passed, reduced to a frame as skinny as her own. Theodric's son Nichol came walking alone, carrying his father's axe.

There were no cheers raised to greet them. Only eyes as haunted as those of the returning men, eyes searching the ragged ranks, turning away when a loved one was not to be seen.

Saren turned away herself. A sick feeling rose in her, but it was revulsion at herself. The face she missed was that of her betrothed, Erard, and her first thought had been, by the Hunter's Cup, I'm free! Only gladness quickly soured into guilt. It did not matter that their marriage had been arranged to serve their fathers, nor that—the Moon knew why—Erard himself seemed pleased with the bargain. A man had died in defense of his land and that was no cause for joy. Was she so small-minded that she set another's life against her own happiness?

"Your pardon . . . ?"

Saren started at a touch on her elbow. A stranger regarded her with an apologetic look. But a few years older than herself, he was worn and thin, his clothing threadbare, leaning on a crutch. One leg was shorter and thinner than the other. Another victim of the war.

He pointed to the battered sign hanging above the door. "Is this still an inn?"

"The Herdsman's Halt," Saren replied. "Finest in the Dale. The only one in the Dale, actually."

A brief smile touched the stranger's lips. "Can I get a meal—and a room for the night?"

Saren nodded. "You've picked a poor time of year for traveling," she said, stepping aside to allow him entrance.

The smell of food mingled with that of sour ale and old body odor in a dark room where a broad hearth formed most of a wall. A trestle table with benches, an ale barrel by a smaller table stacked with plates and tankards, and a pair of wooden settles near the hearth were the only furnishings.

"I thought it a good time." Awkwardly he shook out his cloak and laid it across the back of one of the settles, then dropped down. "What with the invaders finally defeated."

"I meant the weather."

He shrugged. "I had nothing before I marched to war and less now. Winter, summer—it makes no difference when you have no home."

"But you can at least camp out-of-doors in the summer."

"One can camp out-of-doors in the winter as well—it's just harder." He stretched out his crippled leg, moving it with his hands into comfortable position. Looking up, he caught her half-shamed glance. "I got this three years ago," he said. "There's not much work for a soldier who can no longer march."

"You were a lord's man?"

"No. I sold my sword as a guardsman in Jorby for a while. Later I rode with Elsdon. Then I got this." He touched his leg. "A wise woman took me in and let me stay on while I mended—fetching and carrying and the like. The work, little though it was, kept my leg from stiffening worse. It was she that told me. . . ." He paused and that half-smile touched his lips again. "Your pardon. I talk too much sometimes. But mine has been a lonely road. I fell in with your men, and they weren't much for talking."

What did the wise woman tell you? Saren wondered, intrigued. But aloud she only observed: "We never had much—and have less now."

The stranger showed a coin in the palm of his hand. "I can pay."

"I didn't doubt that."

She regarded him contemplatively, wondering at the things he'd seen and done. If she'd been born a man, instead of being locked into a Dalesgirl's narrow life—if she'd been free to wander and see the world . . .

The stranger mistook her look. "Did you lose someone?"

"My betrothed."

"I'm sorry."

As she was not, she thought again. Erard's father had a farm and liked his drink. Her own father had seen the profit to be gained in an alliance with a family able to provide cheap provisions for the inn and needed a future for a gawky daughter. A simple bargain had been struck, with her like a coin.

All over now. Her father had died last year, defending the lord's cattle against a far-ranging band of the invaders. Her betrothed fell at Ruther's Pass. All bargains were finished and there was no one but her mother left to make new ones. But Saren didn't intend to be a coin anymore. If a crippled man could travel the Dales in winter, then so could she. She could . . . She blinked, realizing that the stranger was still watching her.

"We've fresh stew," she said quickly, "and home-brewed ale. Will that do?"

He nodded. "I'll take them here by the hearth if I may. My bones need warming."

Saren brought him a plate of the stew and drew an ale from the barrel, then left him to eat while she returned to her chores.

The next morning she watched him go, trudging off under another dirty gray sky. He went up dale, toward the mountains where only herdsmen tended their sheep, instead of south toward the sea where life was somewhat easier. Where had his wise woman bid him to go? she wondered, fingering her braid.

Perhaps he meant to turn off to Grimmerdale. There was a place of mystery there—one of the Old Ones' ruins, standing stones called the Circle of the Toads. But he had not seemed the kind to trust such a chancy site and it was not a place that a wise woman would bid a Dalesman to seek. Then where? If he went far enough he'd come to the Waste and there was nothing there for anyone.

Saren put his destination out of her mind and concentrated on her own troubles. She could go—there was nothing stopping her. Only go where? Be what? If she was a man . . . She touched her braid again and thought, who was to say she couldn't look like one? She didn't have a woman's shape and with her hair cut short . . . A pleased cat's smile touched her lips. Oh, she liked it.

She rounded the back of the inn and set about her morning chores, humming a tune under her breath. Her mother gave her a frown. Saren paid her no mind. To her mother, she was only free labor. This last day Saren meant to go about her chores, but come tomorrow, her mother could look for new help and would find that it did not come cheap.

It was snowing when Saren slipped out of the inn that night. She closed the door cautiously behind her and turned her face to the sky, letting the snowflakes melt on her skin. She could not have asked for a better night. Even if there was pursuit—though it was unlikely that anyone would search for a runaway inn-brat—this snowfall would cover all tracks.

Shouldering her bag, she set off, taking the same path that the crippled stranger had followed earlier. The bag was stuffed with provisions and a change of clothes, a blanket tied on top and a water sack hung below. A heavy load, but she was a strong girl, used to hard work.

Her journey up the Dale passed in the utter silence of a snowfall. The snow tapered off toward the earlier part of the morning, but it looked as though it would stay, for the temperature had dropped. Wind was busy sweeping drifts into hollows and up against the sides of outcrops and trees. Saren's calves ached. She had not thought she would get footsore so soon—after all she was used to being on her feet all day—but she'd been up early and worked hard all day and evening, then left without getting any sleep.

She marched resolutely until the trail dipped into a small valley thick with pines. Slipping and sliding down the incline, she soon padded noiselessly under their snow-hung boughs, across a carpet of pine needles. When she reached the far side of the little forest, where the trees thinned out as they began their march up the slopes once more, she let her bag fall and leaned against a tree.

Before she remembered her short supply she wolfed down two dried apples. There were a few coins in the purse at her belt—taken from a pot in her mother's room, fair payment for years of work, she had decided—however in the wilderness, places to buy provisions would be far and few between. She would have to set snares and live by her skill, see how much she remembered from all the tales of travelers and trappers and the like that she'd listened to over the years.

Seran wasn't worried. Filled with her newfound freedom, all guilt forgotten, she had no room for worry. Everything was too new. She was warmly dressed—from the fat herdsman's hat on her head, complete with ear flaps that tied under her chin, to her thick cloak and the boots of sheepskin with the wooly side turned in. She had provisions and a few coins. And, by the Hunter's Cup, she had her freedom! Only one thing remained to completely sever the past.

She drew her sharp knife and, removing her cap, began to saw away long locks of hair. Sharp though the blade was, it still pulled at times, but, eventually, her hair lay in a tangled pile on her lap. What remained on her head was barely an inch or two at its longest. She shivered as the cold touched her scalp and quickly replaced her hat. Digging a hole in the frozen dirt with her knife, she buried the hair, covering it with pine needles. Now her freedom was complete. Unrolling her blanket, and well bundled against the cold, Saren fell into a deep, well-earned sleep.

She met the road that led to Grimmerdale around mid-morning, pausing there to munch a stick of dried meat. Had yesterday's stranger taken that route? Considering his crippled leg, she did not think he could make very good time and had half expected to come upon him today. Well, if he'd gone to Grimmerdale, he was welcome to it. Saren meant to see something of the world beyond Nordendale's closest neighbor. She passed the road by to continue north.

Just before night settled, she came upon a herdsman's croft set snugly into the side of a hill. The stone walls and turf roof almost appeared to be a part of the land itself. If it had not been for the telltale smoke from its chimney and two men chopping wood outside, she might well have passed it by. She called out in a friendly fashion, taking care to keep her voice somewhat gruff, and was cheered at their welcome.

Father and son, she decided. Wiry, dark-haired men, bearded like goats, in big sheepskin coats. The older man named himself as Forwood, his son as Abear.

"My name's Sardul," Saren told them. "I'm from Jorby originally, but what with the war . . ." She gave a weary shrug.

"That's two of you then," Forwood said, "and in as many days! Is the whole coast moving to the mountains?"

"Two of us?"

Forwood nodded. "There was another lad here yesterday —older than you—with a crooked leg. His name was Carnen—do you know him?"

"Yes . . . yes, I met him—in Ulmsdale, I think it was. I didn't know he'd come this way."

"Looking for a white road," Forwood said.

His son laughed. "And a good time he picked! All roads are white, this time of year."

Saren laughed with them, but she wondered. How had the stranger—Carnen, she corrected herself—managed to come so far, so fast?

"You'll be wanting to stay the night?" Forwood asked.

Saren shook off her thoughts and nodded. "I've coin," she began, but the herdsman shook his head.

"Give us a hand with this wood," he said. "That'll be payment enough."

Saren set her bag down by the croft's door and accepted an axe. The herdsmen returned to their work and Saren bent to the task with them, though her mind was more on what Forwood had told her about the crippled stranger than on the work at hand. *Looking for a white road.* Carnen himself had begun to tell her something about what a wise woman had told him. This white road? It did not make any sense.

She met Forwood's wife Signe and their toddling daughter Torrie, both as dark and slender as their menfolk. After a meal of mutton stew, they sat around the croft's wide hearth, drinking mulled home-brewed honey ale and talking. Saren passed on what news she could, gleaned from customers of the inn, but found that Carnen had already told the most of it. When Forwood began on stories, she settled back, pleased to have someone else do the talking, and listened with delight, and some small dread, as he told of That Which Runs the Ridges, and then a tale of snow faeries that made them all laugh.

"Are you looking for a white road, too?" Signe asked as they went to their beds later.

Saren looked up from unrolling her blankets by the fire and shook her head. "I don't even know what that is."

"Some remnant of the Old Ones, I think," Abear said. "That's what I learned from Carnen. They used a pale stone for their roadworks—did you never see them down by the coast?"

"Not that I remember. We were told to avoid such places."

Forwood nodded. "It's well you did. They're chancy at the best of times." He scratched at his beard and gave Saren a considering look. "Are you looking for a place to winter, Sardul?"

"Well . . ."

"We don't have room here, but Bindon has a bigger place—about three days' march north. He might take you on. Tell him I sent you, lad. Maybe it will help."

"I . . . thank you."

The herdsman said a gruff goodnight as the family went to their beds, leaving Saren the hearth. She stretched out on her blankets, but found sleep elusive, for she kept wondering about Carnen's swift traveling and this white road he seeking. When she finally slept it was to dream fitfully of wise women and ancient ruins, of a crippled man and something that called out to her from a circle of stones to which a white road led.

It snowed again overnight and the day dawned cold with threatening gray skies. Saren took a north trail through the white slopes, blinking at the brightness of the snow. Winter had come to stay.

She passed a number of herdsfolk's crofts during the morning. A word or two with the friendly folk told her she was on the right trail. Carnen had passed ahead of her, still traveling quickly for all that he had a crippled leg. What Saren tried to decide now, as she continued to tramp northward, was why she was following him.

*Looking for a white road.*

*Some remnant of the Old Ones . . .*

What promise had Carnen's wise woman given him? What did he look to find at the end of his white road? She thought of the dreams that had troubled her sleep last night. Something had called to her from a stone henge. It had promised her . . . what? A whisper of summer air in the middle of winter. A hint of wonder. Some marvel stood behind the stones, if she could only find the right road.

Back in the Herdsman's Halt, Saren had heard many old tales. Danger lay in wait for those who meddled with the Old Ones' places of mystery, more so than any gain. Bargains were kept in those sites, but not always in a manner that the seeker had expected.

I'm not a seeker, Saren thought. I'm just . . . curious.

*At the end of a white road,* the memory of last night's dreams whispered to her. *In a circle of stones . . .*

She began to feel as though she'd been ensorceled. By Carnen, perhaps, or by whatever lay at the end of the white road. What she *should* do was turn around and make for the coast. Instead she trudged on through the snow until night fell, and she couldn't have said why she was continuing. Saren only knew that it was something she had to do.

She slept in a hollow that night, curled in her cloak and blanket, face hidden from the cold. Though it snowed lightly around midnight, she was caught fast in her dreams unaware.

Again she dreamed of the road, her footsteps ringing on its surface. That white ribbon of stone sounded hollow underfoot as it ran on through a shifting dreamscape. Saren glided along as might a ghost, or one of the great silver cats that haunted the mountains. Until, suddenly, the henge loomed before her. The sense of a green promise, summer scents and birdsong, came from between the stones, but all she could see inside was a thick gray mist.

A wooden crutch lay on the pale stone at her feet. She thought of Forwood and his tales. That Which Runs the Ridges. Monsters. All the unknown. Underneath this promise of warmth, she sensed something menacing. Only there couldn't be any horror in there! A wise woman had told Carnen to seek it out. A wise woman would not knowingly send someone into danger.

*Yes,* the voice of her fear whispered inside her. *But that wise woman sent him, not you.*

It was cold. Her teeth chattered. And there was the promise of warmth beyond that swirl of mist. She took one step, a second. The mist clung to her face like cobwebs. A third step on and it began to clear. The cold disappeared. She saw a woodland glade, held fast in summer. Her mouth formed a delighted "O," until, rising from the fresh green sward underfoot, pushing aside the sod with bone finger curled like claws, came dead men.

Fear held her motionless until the first fleshless hand rasped across her boots. She cowered away, her skin crawling with revulsion. Something snapped underfoot with the sharp crack of shattered bone. The clawing hands of the dead clutched, and she flailed at them only to—

—wake up screaming.

The echo of her scream rang in the still mountain air as she sat up, hugging herself. The cold had settled deep in her bones and she shivered as much from it as from the terror she'd woken from.

"Dream," she muttered through chattering teeth. "J-j-just a dream."

Building a fire she huddled over it, waiting for snow to melt in her pot so that she could make tea. Not until the scalding liquid spread its warmth through her was she able to relax. Sweet Gunnora, the dream had been vivid. She was not used to nightmares. This had seemed a warning. She knew as well, without knowing how she knew, that the place she had dreamed of was real and that she would find it. What she did not understand was why.

It was close to dawn now, so rather than trying to sleep longer, she rolled up her blanket, doused the fire with handfuls of snow, and was on her way when the sun came creeping up above the horizon. She learned that Carnen was still ahead of her from a family of herdsfolk she met later in the morning, but Carnen himself and his white road continued to elude her until she stopped at yet another croft late in the day.

"Bindon's holding is a day and a half's journey from here," the father of the household told her. "But there's nothing in between. Just . . ." He hesitated.

"Just what?" Saren asked.

The herdsman looked uncomfortable. "A road," he said. "Left over from the time of the Old Ones."

"Where does it lead?" Saren asked.

The man shook his head. "No one knows. No one's been fool enough to follow it."

"All the same," Saren said. "I have to go on."

"There's a storm brewing," the herdsman warned.

"I'll be careful."

"It's not care that's needed to survive a storm in these mountains," he told her. "It's shelter and warmth. Blind luck won't get you through."

Saren thought of Carnen who was still ahead of her and of the dreams that held both threat and promise.

"I'll have to trust to luck," she said. "It's all I've got."

The herdsman shrugged. "Well, luck go with you then —with the both of you. I warned your friend as well, but he wouldn't listen either. With a crippled leg, he won't make Bindon's keep by nightfall—that's for sure."

"Thank you for the tea," Saren said. Before the herdsman could continue with his warnings, she set off, leaving him standing and shaking his head as he watched her go.

She found the road of the Old Ones before midnight. The storm still gathered in the night skies above her, clouding the stars. Wind flung sharp pellets of snow against her skin so that she wore a strip of cloth torn from her blanket as a protecting scarf. Drifts filled hollows, making for deceptive footing. But she found the road. Weary, she sighted down its length, scuffing the toe of one boot against the snow until she'd cleared a slab of the flat rock that formed the road's length.

Easy to find, she thought.

If it was so easy to find, what made it special? Anyone could seek it out, even a crippled man in the first storms of winter. But that didn't gainsay the threat that might lie at its end, for how many *would* follow it? Only the brave or fools sought out the places of the Old Ones. Or those with hidden knowledge. Carnen might have such, gleaned from his wise woman. What did she herself have? A dream —half promise, half warning. Sighing, Saren set off.

The way was easy to follow, even when the storm blustered about her. Thick flakes drove in swirling gusts all around, but something about the road kept Saren from straying. The cold wasn't as easy to deal with. Her limbs went numb, as much from the bitter chill as weariness. She shuffled forward bemused, half asleep. When the snow let up, the cold crept through the layers of her clothes. She unwrapped her blanket with stiff fingers and wore it as a second cloak.

It was hard to see with the cloud cover hiding the stars and all around the wind-driven snow. When the wind finally died down, the girl stopped. The mountains were gone. Instead, she was on a vast plain, an empty white expanse stretching out as far as the eye could see. She scuffed at the snow, clearing a spot. The road was still underfoot. The sky had cleared. Stars speckled the night sky, but the constellations they formed didn't seem familiar.

Carnen's white road. It had taken her . . . elsewhere.

She shivered with the cold and the strangeness, then sighed, shuffling on. The past was gone. Nordendale, her mother, the inn. The crofts of the herdsfolk and the mountains. What lay ahead, she didn't know, but it had to be something. Perhaps better, perhaps worse than she'd known, but with the past gone, she had no choice but to go on.

Her mind drifted to the memory of the men of Nordendale returning home from the war and she felt a kinship with them now. Soldiers were coin, spent on a battlefield. Her own life had been a kind of dying as well; a coin, its value lying in what it could be bartered for, not for what it was itself. This kind of thinking made her head ache. And Carnen, she wondered. Was he some wise woman's coin?

She paused again, slowly lifting her head. The wind blasted her face with a sharp sting of snow, and a headache made it hard to concentrate. She blinked, eyelids moving so slowly she was sure they were almost frozen, rimmed with frost. The henge stood in front of her, tall and brooding.

The stones were darker than she'd dreamed them, more foreboding. A summery scent came to her from between the stones where a mist crept to the breath of a different wind than the one that tugged at her clothes. She looked down at her feet and saw Carnen's crutch lying there.

She bent down and picked it up. Was he inside now, a wise woman's coin spent? Another whiff of summer escaped the space between the stones. Apple blossoms, a faint smell of roses, the scent of grass and wildflowers and green growing things. Strawberries and lilacs.

She stepped forward, determined to see. The mists clung to her as she stepped between the stones. She shivered, anticipating the touch of bones.

Once inside she had a momentary glimpse of the summer glade shown to her in her dream. Apple trees were in blossom, yet the trees bore fruit at the same time. Rose bushes bore both bud and flower on their thorny branches. She heard a birdsong, sweet and clear. At her feet, yellow and red and pale blue flowers grew in a circular scatter amongst the grass.

She took another step forward, then everything flickered. A rushing sound filled her head. Scent and sight vanished. She gave a guttoral cry as weariness came over her in a rush. She tried to use Carnen's crutch to keep to her feet, but it slipped from under her when she put her weight on it and she pitched forward into the darkness.

When Saren woke it was to find herself in a long dark hall, a gloomy light entering windows set high in its walls. A hearth stood at its far end, cold ash inside. Two carved chairs on the dais were both empty. Three trestle tables ran the length of the room with rough benches along either side. Moldering tapestries hung from the walls, too time-dimmed to show patterns.

Saren pushed herself up from the stone floor to sit on her haunches. A winter chill still lapped her round and she trembled despite herself. Where was she now? In some ruined keep of the Old Ones? Dreaming? Dead?

The hall's one door creaked open. Saren scrambled to her feet, backing away. She tripped against the dais and fell backward, quickly pulling her legs under her. Crouching there, biting at her lower lip, her gaze centered on the slowly opening door.

It had not been foolishness that brought her here, she thought, watching that door. It had been utter madness. True, Carnen had preceded her, but she didn't doubt that his wise woman had let him know what to expect. There would be formalities to observe, certain approaches that the seeker after the Old Ones must take, secret knowledge —none of which she had. Where Carnen must have had some idea as to what he faced—by the Hunter's Cup, he'd know *why* he was on the road in the first place and what he sought at its end—she was only muddling along. Toying with disaster. And now—

Her worst fears were realized as the door opened wide enough for the hall's inhabitants to enter. Raw fear clawed through her. She knew now where she was. In a hall of the dead.

Corpses, like those of her dream, shuffled in to take seats at the tables. Some were newly dead, their wounds still inflamed. Others were white-fleshed and swollen—corpses that had lain a week or so in their graves. The worst were those whose flesh was so moldered that the white bone showed through tattered skin. Bone white figures with skull faces.

Sweet Gunnora, she moaned. I never meant . . .

"Meant what?" one of the dead demanded. It stepped close to the dais and bent down until its ravaged features were only inches from her own. A maggot hung from the corner of its mouth, wriggling into the flesh. "Never meant to wish me dead?"

"I . . ."

Bile rose in Saren's throat as she recognized the creature for her betrothed Erard. Behind it another figure approached and this one she recognized not so much from its features—for there was little recognizable in that skull-face with the tatters of flesh and scalp still hanging from it—as from the clothing she'd last seen it wear when it was alive. Her father.

"Is this how you repay the years of love I gave you?" the dead thing demanded. "To come here in your flesh and mock me?"

"You . . . you never loved me . . ."

"Small wonder. What father was ever cursed with such a poor excuse of a daughter? One that would steal coins from her own mother."

Fear and sickness warred inside Saren, but she shook her head slowly. "*I* was the coin," she said.

"Hard times," Erard said. "War makes for hard times. We all had our part to play, our coin to spend and be spent in turn."

"No!" Saren cried. "It wasn't for love of Nordendale

that I was to be spent, but for my father's greed and whatever use you meant to make of me."

"Witch blood," Erard said. "A wise woman told me you had witch blood and that if our lines joined, I would prosper. Yet you denied me, Saren. You let the war take me and spend my life in battle with your ill-wishing."

"I never ill-wished you! I never loved you, but I never wished you harm."

"You never sprang from my loins," her father said. "A bard spilled his seed in your mother, but I wed her all the same. I raised you as though you were my own, but what return did you give me?"

"Lives are not to be bartered and sold."

"No?" Erard asked. "Then what are they for?"

More of the creatures were pressing forward now to hear her answer. Saren stared at their ruined visages, fear thrumming in her. Her head spun with what she'd just heard.

*Witch blood.*

*A bard spilled his seed in your mother.*

A bard's witch blood. Was that what the road had recognized inside her and used to draw her into this trap?

"Tell us," one of the dead demanded. A half-fleshed face pushed forward, ravaged fingers held out to her. Fat white grubs fell to the floor as it moved its arm.

"What are lives for?" another asked.

"Coins to spend—what else!" a third cried.

The voices came hard and fast, in jeering demand that made her press her hands against her ears. She wept and her tears froze on her cheeks. The stink of rotting flesh and the proximity of the dead made her empty stomach lurch and boil with acid. Thin fingers plucked at her.

She screamed when the dead flesh and bone touched her face. The corpses began to pull her into their midst and she huddled into herself more. Dead hands grabbed at her arms, jerking them from her ears. She flailed at the creatures. Where she struck them, bones shattered, arms were tugged from shoulder sockets to fall to the floor.

"What is life?" her father demanded.

"We had life," another of the dead told her, "but our coin was spent and we have nothing now."

"If not coin, what is it?" Erard shouted at her.

"A gift!" Saren wailed. "A gift—do you understand? Not coin to be spent. Not something to be bartered for profit. But a gift, freely given!"

The grip of the creatures loosened and she was able to pull free and stumble to her feet. She staggered back a pace or two and stared at them. Mist roiled about their feet. The rotten smell of opened graves was thick in the air.

"Nothing is freely given," one of the corpses said. "There is always a payment needed or else why are we here? Why do we die? What sent us here?"

Saren shook her head, trying to clear it. How could she be here, discussing such concerns with the dead? By the Hunter's Cup, she *had* gone mad. But she thought on what the corpse had asked her and an answer came slowly all the same. Right or wrong, she did not know, but it was all she had.

"Did you never give a bouquet of flowers to a loved one?" she asked.

Here and there, gruesome heads nodded.

"And when the flowers withered—did that make less the moment of giving? A life is like that gift of flowers. While we bloom, we make the best of the promise in it. When we die, it's not a gift taken back, but a natural part of all."

"Words!" her father spat. "In this place—"

"You're in this place because you can't see the gift!" Saren broke in. "Because life is just coin for you and nothing more. That is what you made of the gift's promise, so you must abide by it."

The creatures began to advance on her again, muttering and waving their stick-thin arms at her. She backed away against the wall and could go no farther. There sounded a rushing sound, as though a great wind blew. Dizziness swept over her, corpses and hall spinning in her sight. She lowered herself until she was sitting on her ankles, back against the wall. She tried to stay erect, but she couldn't.

The dead creatures came boiling up over the lip of the dais, but Saren fell over on her side, great clouds of darkness swimming in her sight and taking her away once more. But just before she was gone, before the dark took her or the dead touched her, she saw a woman's face in her mind's eye. It was a broad, serene face, blue-eyed and framed by a spill of corn-yellow hair. There was a hint of a green dress on a rounded shoulder, a breath of summer fields that cut across the grave stench in the hall.

"Oh, well-spoken, daughter," the woman said.

Then the darkness swept up and took Saren away.

When Saren's eyes fluttered open, she found herself warming by a friendly fire blazing merrily away in front of her. The hall was gone and she was inside the henge, stone under her blankets. The tall pillars didn't seem so foreboding in the flickering light. Sitting beside her was the crippled stranger that she'd followed from the Herdsman's Halt, always a day or so out of step with him.

Seeing him, she felt a sudden calm. She sat up, held out her hands to the fire, and studied her companion. He was sitting in a way that made her think that perhaps the crutch she'd found hadn't been dropped so much as thrown away because it wasn't needed any longer.

"Hello, Carnen," she said.

"And you're the girl from the inn," he replied. "I didn't recognize you when I first found you here. What brought you?"

"Your white road."

"But I said nothing of it to you."

Saren shrugged. "You told the herdsfolk and they told

me." She pointed at his leg. "You seem to be in better shape than when I first met you."

"It was a charm of Andnor's," he explained. "The wise woman I told you of. Each step I took on my search helped to ease it—the charm being completed if I reached the end."

"So that's why you made such good time—your leg kept getting better."

He nodded. "And you—was it your witch blood that brought you?"

Saren lifted a hand to touch her cheek, then let it drop to her lap. She told him of her experience, following the road. "But I don't feel as though I have witch blood."

"I saw it in you when I first met you—a small trace, but there nevertheless. Without it, you wouldn't have survived the white road."

The henge they were in, Saren realized, was not the one the road had led her to. This one stood in the mountains, high on a ridge. The night skies were clear above them, dotted with familiar stars. The slopes were white with snow, but the henge itself was clear.

"Was it all a dream?" she asked. "The plain, the other henge, the . . ." She shivered. "The hall of the dead?"

Carnen shook his head. "The stoneworks of the Old Ones are connected. It is possible to step from one to the other in the blink of an eye. The road tests us, you see. That's what Andnor told me. I . . . I went to my own hall of the dead, though it was different from yours."

"And the woman in green—the one that called me daughter?"

"I never saw her," Carnen said. "I saw a man—a man with stag antlers springing from his brow. He never spoke at all." He poured tea from a pot by the fire and handed it to her. "What will you do now, Saren?"

"If life's a gift," she said, "then I want to use its promise wisely. I want to . . ." She looked at him across the top of her mug. "To follow a green road, I think. One into summer. I want to give of myself to others, freely, with no bartering and no coin. I'd like to tell stories, maybe, or learn to play an instrument. Become a healer. I don't know. I just want to do something useful."

Carnen lifted his mug. "I think I'd like to travel that green road with you—if you wouldn't mind the company."

"Together, instead of me trailing a day or so behind you?"

Carnen smiled.

"To the green road, then," Saren said, clinking her mug against his. "Good fortune to us both!"

"Good fortune," Carnen repeated and they drank to the toast.

In a green wood, in a place Saren might have called "elsewhere," a corn-haired woman sat back from a pool that held an image on its surface, an image of a henge and two well-worn travelers toasting each other. She looked at her companion, a tall, broad-shouldered man with stag's antlers sprouting from his brow.

"There's one for each of us now," she said.

The antlered man nodded. "And there will be more. The Dark has had its time, holding the land in the thrall of war. I think its coin is spent."

"For a while at least."

"And our coin?"

The woman in green put a finger against his mouth and shook her head. "We have no coin—only gifts," she said. "And a gift can only prosper."

"Is that a promise?" the antlered man asked.

"A hope," she replied. "Nothing more." Looking at the two figures still reflected in the pool, the longstones rearing above them, the light of their fire flickering against the gray stone, she sighed. "I pray it will be enough," she added.

\* \* \*

# Afterword

"The White Road" is set in the dales of High Hallack, soon after the end of the Kolder War, but it isn't a direct sequel to any existing Witch World novel or story. Instead, I was trying to capture the flavor of Andre's "coming of age" stories as a tribute to all the years of pleasure I've had from her writing.

I discovered her work at that perfect time—my early teens—and retain a fond memory of her books to this day, particularly those that fit into the Witch World series. Being asked by Andre to contribute a story of my own to that mythos and getting to work with her in the editing stages of the story has easily been one of the high points of my professional writing career. I just hope that in "The White Road" I've managed to capture some measure of the wonder that I found in her writing as a small repayment for all that she's given me.

—CHARLES DE LINT

# CAT AND THE OTHER
## by
## Marylois Dunn

Cat, who through a series of skirmishes, had won the right to sleep on the castle window ledge in the only spot of sunshine in the great room, woke and opened his eyes widely. He was different. He was Cat and something else.

Laughter rang in the room and Cat sat up blinking, curious to see if it was directed at him. He did not like to be the butt of laughter. The humans were looking in his direction and laughing but they did not seem to be laughing at him.

He licked his left paw tentatively, wondering if he should jump down and check out the readiness of the evening meal. He felt . . . different . . . strange. Frightened. Frightened? No. That was a mistake. He was truly confused. Cat had never in his life been afraid. Startled, on occasion. Upset, once or twice. Angry, often. But frightened? Never!

Yet, what was this cold, churning lump that had settled itself where his digested lunch should lie in easy comfort? It was fear. He opened his small mouth and panted a few breaths, like a great hound, to cool the sodden lump of his innards. Fear. Of what had he to be afraid?

It was not himself. He knew it. There was something Other within him. Something small and terror-stricken had hidden itself within his inviolate person. How dare it? How dare it!

115

Cat's eyes flashed yellow fire. His dark slitted pupils spread to cover the golden iris and his claws sprang from their velvet cushions.

NO, NO, the terror-stricken voice shouted in his head. SHOW NOTHING. BE CAT. DO NOT LET ANYONE NOTICE A DIFFERENCE IN YOU.

*Who are you? What are you? How come you are inside my being?* Cat demanded. Interested in this Other inside himself, he blinked his eyes, drew in his claws and stretched out again in the sun, folding his paws under his chest. Cat faced inward, watching the goings-on in the room through slitted eyes.

LOOK THERE ON THE HEARTH. SEE THE YOUTH WHO LIES THERE SEEMING LIFELESS?

Cat flicked one ear. *Is he dead?*

NOT DEAD, the Other said. THE WITCH WOMAN HAS DRAWN OUT THE SPIRIT. SHE SPEAKS OF IT NOW. DO YOU UNDERSTAND HER?

Cat laid back both ears and shifted his hindquarters in impatience. *Of course, I understand.* He focused his attention on the Witch Woman, she who had been laughing.

"Don't you see?" she was saying to the lord of the Keep. "The lad's spirit is flown."

"I see not how this benefits us. The lad is the beloved of his father. Would you have us in a war over his death?"

"Would you have his affection for the maid to become a choosing? She is a witch-to-be. Already she feels a bond to the lad, Kharis. Another month would have found her tainted, her gift gone."

"You suppose this only."

She smiled at him. "Am I ever wrong?"

The lord bent over the seeming lifeless body. "He breathes. Can he waken?"

"Only if his spirit returns to his body before one of the hawks catches it."

"Hawks? I do not understand."

"When I drew forth his spirit, I loosed it and cast it through yonder window. A loosed spirit will enter the first living thing it encounters. It now resides in the fat feathered body of one of those pigeons on the stable roof."

The lord walked to the window and looked out on the pigeons.

Cat remained perfectly still, seeming to be sleeping in the sun. The lord rubbed Cat's ears absently and Cat raised a small purr. Then he turned back to look at the Witch Woman. "Are you sure the spirit reached the pigeons?"

The Witch Woman laughed again, a cold, unpleasant trill. "Into the cat? Not likely. My aim is better than that. Anyway, see how quietly he sleeps in the sun? No. Cat would be running frantically, scared out of his wits by the strangeness within. See how the pigeons stir? They fly. They circle about. One of them is most disturbed and he is upsetting the rest. I assure you, Kharis's spirit will soon fall prey to a hawk and we will be free of him without having to resort to murder. Until then, we must lovingly tend the lad, who has had some kind of a seizure, while we send for the father. There must be no hint of spirit casting. Not now. Not ever."

The lord looked again through the window, and as he watched, the entire flock of pigeons lifted suddenly into the air with a loud whistle of wings. The birds were distressed, beating first one way and then, on some signal imperceptible to human eyes, turning as one to fly swiftly in the opposite direction. Their maneuvering did them no good. A wide-winged, dark shadow swooped from the sky, the wind whistle of his wings audible above the sounds of frantic pigeon wings. A hawk clutched one of them in his sharp talons and soared to the top of a nearby conifer, jesses trailing.

It tore at the pigeon's breast and the lord could see, in the sunlight, the bright blood of its dying. He looked to the still figure beside the fireplace.

"He lives," the Witch Woman said. "That was not the one."

Cat sat up and stretched, first the right hind leg all the way out to the widespread toes; then the left. He arched his back and stretched forward as far as the front claws could reach, scratching the fabric of the needlepointed pillow he slept on as he did.

"Stop that, Cat." The woman made a threatening gesture toward him. "You know better than to tear the pillows."

Cat was insulted to have his stretch interrupted rudely. He leaped down and made his way slowly toward the kitchen, tail haughtily erect. *Who does she think she is?* he grumbled. *I won the pillow fairly in battle. It's mine to rip if I want to.*

DO YOU DARE DEFY HER? the Other asked. LOOK WHAT HAPPENED TO ME. AREN'T YOU AFRAID OF WHAT SHE WILL DO IF SHE FINDS OUT WHERE I AM?

*Who will tell her?* Cat said. *A feline who keeps his wits about him has little to fear here or anywhere else.*

YOU DON'T SEEM UPSET THAT I SHARE YOUR BODY.

*Are you going to cause me a lot of grief? Are you going to be afraid all the time or try to make me do something foolish against my will?*

WELL, ACTUALLY, I WAS AFRAID AT FIRST, BUT YOU SEEM TO BE WELL IN CONTROL OF THE SITUATION. IF YOU DON'T MIND MY PRESENCE, I'LL ABIDE UNTIL WE CAN DEVISE SOME WAY TO GET ME BACK INTO MY OWN BODY. I WON'T BE ANY TROUBLE TO YOU. I PROMISE.

*Very well. I am rather enjoying having someone I can communicate with directly. It is a great burden to live your life in pantomime amongst such dullards.*

IS IT JUST THIS HOUSEHOLD THAT IS FULL OF

DULLARDS, OR IS IT THE SAME EVERYWHERE?

*I haven't been everywhere. From what I hear from other cats and from those stupid slavering hounds, it is the same everywhere. Humans have lost the capacity to communicate with superior beings.*

I'VE HEARD THE FALCONERS KNOW WHAT THEIR BIRDS ARE THINKING.

*Nonsense. Birds don't think. They act and react. Definitely a subspecies. And, what is this about "we" getting you back into your own body? I am not a volunteer in this project. I make you welcome because it seems the sensible course, but I have not joined up for any machinations against the Witch Woman. She rules here. I know which way the fur is stroked.*

The Other was silent.

Cat stopped at the kitchen door looking around for his favorite cook. When he saw her, he fixed his gaze on her and said, *Have you a preference in food? I can get almost anything I want from that one.*

DOES NOT MATTER TO ME, the Other said. IT SEEMS MY SPIRIT DOES NOT HUNGER.

*I see she is plucking geese. Perhaps I can wangle a liver.* Cat padded over to the cook he favored, avoiding the other kitchen help as he did. He slipped under her wide skirts and announced himself by first rubbing his head against the calf of her leg, then pressing the full length of his body between her ankles. He finished his performance by stroking the back of her knees with his stiffened tail.

"O-oh, Cat." Cook stomped her feet and whooshed him from under her skirts. "Don't start something you can't finish." She laughed as she reached down to give him a rub.

Cat responded with a loud rasping purr, pushing his back up into her stroking hand.

"You are a love," she crooned. "The dairymen have come with fresh milk. Would you like a bowl?"

Cat responded by standing against her knee and rubbing

his face against her thigh.

"You shall have cream." She chuckled and poured him a saucerful which she placed under a table safe from the passing feet of the other cooks and kitchen help.

*You see why I like this one?* Cat asked.

DO YOU GET ALL YOUR FOOD THIS WAY, BEGGING?

Cat stopped lapping and groomed his whiskers. *I do not think of it as begging. I pay in affection for what she gives.*

He returned to his saucer of cream unaware of the bustle of feet around the table and the clatter of voices and cooking utensils as they prepared the evening feast. Cook dropped half of a goose liver under the table when no one was watching and Cat pounced on it, chewed, savored, and swallowed it quickly. He waited around for a while to see if any more good things were forthcoming but Cook was too busy to tend to his stomach's desires.

While he waited, Cat washed himself carefully. He gave extra attention to the hair between his back toes which had become clogged with something sticky and distasteful. He pulled, tugged, licked at the toes until the Other said, ENOUGH. ENOUGH. YOU WILL SCRAPE ALL THE SKIN FROM YOUR TOES IF YOU CONTINUE. IF YOU MUST WASH, MOVE ON. WASH SOMETHING ELSE.

*I thought you were not going to interfere,* Cat grumbled, but he shifted and, putting one forepaw on the tip of his long tail, held it in place for a full wash from root to tip.

HOW OFTEN DO YOU WASH? THIS IS TWICE SINCE I HAVE JOINED YOU.

*As often as needed,* Cat said. *I wash when I feel the need of it, when I am bored, when some foul hand touches my fur. I wash when I wish to appear disinterested in their doings. Washing is a wonderful way to misdirect their attention. If your kind did more washing, you would have less time to get into trouble.*

The Other chuckled. YOU MAY BE RIGHT.

Then the Other gave such a start that Cat, already unbalanced while trying to wash his lower backbone, almost fell over. *What is it?*

LISTEN. IT IS SHE. THE MAID. LISTEN!

*The one who got you into trouble?*

HUSH. LISTEN!

"Oh, Hurbis. Please can't you fix a tray that I may take to my chambers? I can't bear to go down to the great hall to eat while I listen to them crow over what they have done to Kharis."

"What have they done to the lad?"

"I don't know. Cast a spell on him, or given him some kind of sleeping potion. They won't tell me. I know he lies in his chamber senseless and still. It is as if he were dead, yet he breathes. He is still warm. But I don't know for how long."

"Perhaps it is a spell that will last only until you are safely initiated into the Way."

"I would gladly give over the calling if it would save Kharis's life. I would not have him die over me."

"You care for him?"

"I don't know. I like him. He is a warm and friendly lad and I like to talk with him. He is the only one in this hall who treats me like a person instead of a witch-to-be. Except you, of course."

"Tosh, Child. I have seen others of your kind come here before. They are all treated the same. If you do not learn to separate yourself from folk, you will not ever be Witch Woman. It is in the separation that the magic comes."

"But that is such a lonely way to live."

"True. And now is the time to decide if you want it or not. If you want husband and family, leave this place at once. Join yourself to a young man. Kharis will do. It matters not who. But you must do that which makes you unfit to be a witch before you take the vows. Once you cross the line between what is and what is-to-be, there is no turning back. Happiness for each person is a different thing. You are no child. You must decide and quickly where your happiness lies. If you do not want to be a witch, make your choice quickly."

"I need time to think."

"I think you do not have time."

I THINK THE COOK IS RIGHT. THERE IS NO TIME, CAT. WHAT CAN WE DO?

*There goes that "we" again. I don't know what to do. Because I am a male feline in the house of a Witch Woman does not make me her confidant.* Cat switched his tail angrily from side to side. *She does her spell making under the eyes of a female cat who keeps herself quite removed from the rest of us mere felines.*

COULD YOU ASK HER? PERHAPS SHE WOULD KNOW SOMETHING THAT COULD BE DONE TO GET ME BACK IN MY BODY. THEN I COULD TALK TO THE MAIDEN. I LOVE HER VERY MUCH, CAT. I COULD MAKE HER HAPPY AS A MORTAL WOMAN. THIS WITCH BUSINESS DOES NOT SEEM LIKE A NORMAL LIFE TO ME.

*"Normal" is like "median." It depends upon where you are standing when you make the measure.*

PLEASE!

*Oh, all right. I will go up to the tower and see if her preciousness will talk to me. But, you be still. Don't distract me. No matter what happens.*

I PROMISE, the Other said and subsided to a silent presence which Cat carried inside himself as he made his way silently up the circling staircase to the top of the donjon tower.

It was, as Cat had said, a long way to the top of the tower. On the way they met and avoided the feet of many humans on their varying tasks around the keep. Some were servants, some guards. Some were guests of the castle lord and some were tradesmen come to sell their wares to whomever was interested in their trade. The hounds they met avoided Cat, slinking by him on the outer edge of the stairway. Cats they met were greeted by whisker touching, silent communication of everyday things: *I saw a great rat, just the size you like to catch, down in the cellars this morning.* Some were met with hisses, side-carried tail, and arched back. The Other marveled at how Cat commanded each and every creature he met with an economy of gestures. He was truly a prince of cats whether or not he admitted it.

At the tower's crest, an apartment of three rooms covered the entire upper floor; the largest was a room of books and tables, bottles and leather bags full of herbs and potions. It was obviously the Witch Woman's chamber for preparing the spells she cast. A smaller room was her bedchamber and it was in there they found the cat they sought.

She was not beautiful: White. Lean. Blue-eyed. There was a strangeness about her that made Cat uneasy in his innermost self though he would admit it to no one, not even himself.

*What brings you to my chamber?* Her thought was as clear to the Other as it was to Cat.

*I have not seen you for a long time. No one seems to know much about you. I wondered how you are?*

She was amused. *How is the little gray tabby I watched you pursuing down at the stables last week? Should you not have more concern for her well-being than for mine? I will bear you no kits.*

*That is not by my choice.* Cat said. *The offer is always open.*

*La!* she said. *It is as good an offer as I have had lately, Cat. I will keep it in mind. Now. What is the real reason you have come up all those stairs?*

*So practical as well as beautiful,* Cat murmured. *I do*

*have a question. There is a maid I have taken a liking to
who is witch-to-be. Do you know her?*

The white cat's eyes narrowed to slits and she licked one
paw to smooth back her whiskers. *I know her.*

*Did you know she does not want to be a witch? She is in
love with the lad, Kharis.*

She stood up and the fur on her back rose. She hissed.
*Has she said such in your hearing? I knew the little tart was
not fit for the honor. Tell me the words she spoke. I want to
know the very words.*

Cat backed off and went from a sitting position to a
prone one to placate her. *Honestly, the maiden has spoken
no such words in my presence. Perhaps she has not even
thought them consciously. But I watch. I see. I understand
these humans, sometimes better than they understand
themselves. I know this is so but I cannot give you words she
has not spoken.*

*I wish you could. If I had her very words, I could transfer
them to my mistress and she would be sent packing. No one
becomes Witch unless they have a true heart for the calling.*

Cat licked at his forepaws nervously. *I have heard there is
a way to forestall her training.*

She hissed again. *There are many ways.*

*An easy way.*

The white cat composed herself and sat primly, front
paws together, tail wrapped around them. *Yes. You would
think that was the easy way. But I know the mistress has
cast his spirit into a pigeon. He lies now senseless. Unless he
comes to his senses and talks the maiden into his lair, it is
not a likely way.*

Cat bit delicately at an itchy spot on his forearm as he
appeared to be thinking. *Isn't there some way to bring back
his spirit to his body? It seems to me, without that, there is
no chance at all to turn the maid from witch-to-be.*

The white cat was silent for some time, her thoughts

hidden. At last she said, *Of course, I know the spell. But you would have to catch the very pigeon which holds his spirit and bring it, alive, to the chamber where the lad lies.*

*That would be a lot of trouble,* Cat said. *But I think I know the very bird. I was watching when she cast the spirit and I saw this one particular pigeon begin to act most unpigeonlike. I suppose I could catch him if you think it worth the trouble.*

*Of course, it is worth the trouble. Would you have one unworthy become a Witch Woman? She is a stupid girl. If you can catch the bird, I will come to the chamber where the lad is tonight. I will reunite him with his body. At last I have a task worthy of my calling. Can you do that, Cat? Can you catch the pigeon who carries the lad's spirit?*

Cat stretched to his full height on the tips of all four paws. *I think I can promise you positively to have the lad's spirit there waiting for you tonight.*

She came down from the bed and gave Cat's ear a thank-you lick and they left her purring happily to herself as they made their way down the long spiral stair to the stableyard outside.

YOU DID IT, CAT. IF SHE CAN REALLY CHANGE THE SPELL, I WILL TRY TO DO MY PART TO MAKE THE MAID GO WITH ME FROM THIS PLACE.

*It remains to be seen if the cat can do as she promises or not. Some cats brag above their powers.*

PEOPLE TOO. BUT I HAVE A FEELING SHE WAS NOT BRAGGING. I BELIEVE SHE CAN DO AS SHE SAYS.

*Oh. I do not doubt for a moment. She is old and wise and she has been with the Witch Woman since they were both kits. I am sure she has the knowledge of the human if only she has the physical ability to use it.*

PHYSICAL ABILITY?

*Yes. Some spells require the use of a jewel the Witch*

*Woman wears around her neck. Others do not. I was asleep
when she cast your spirit from your body. I don't know
which she used.*

THE CAT MUST KNOW AND SHE MUST KNOW
SHE CAN DO IT.

Cat hummed to himself. He knew that some cats were
inclined to believe themselves wiser than they were. He
only hoped this were not the case here. If it was, he was
going to a lot of trouble for nothing. He took them out the
dog gate, an opening in the wall which allowed the hounds
and the other animals of the keep to come and go as they
pleased. It greatly aided the servants in keeping the floors
clean. The stupid dogs knew enough to go outside for their
physical cleansings, even if they did not have enough pride
to cover their leavings. Outside, Cat made his way to the
stable roof and stretched out on the sunny side of the
pigeon cote. After dark, when the birds were settled down,
he could choose a small one to carry in. White cat would
not perform the ritual if he did not bring the bird. Or,
worse, she might suspect where the Other really hid and
run straight to her mistress with the information. She was
just that type.

He slept and the Other did not bother him with conversation. Perhaps he, too, rested if a spirit needed to rest. Cat
held down the thought that he would be glad to be alone
again and attending to his own business. This carrying
around a human spirit was most upsetting. He washed his
paws when he woke and gave his face and ears a thorough
cleaning. The pigeons were quiet in their cote, making the
cooing sounds of pigeons and shuffling as they pushed each
other for better position on the roosts.

They sat on the roof until the sounds of the evening feast
ceased in the great hall and the last lamps were carried
upstairs to the bedrooms. Only the evening torches were
lit, flickering in the windows.

*Let us go,* Cat said at last. *It is time.*

I HAVE BEEN LONG READY. I WANTED TO LET YOU REST AS MUCH AS YOU COULD. THIS WILL BE DIFFICULT FOR YOU, I KNOW.

*Not so difficult. I have caught many a pigeon in my day.*

AND CARRIED IT STRUGGLING AND COOING INTO THE GREAT HALL?

*Not the great hall, thank the Powers. We go to the lad's bedchamber for which we should be grateful.*

I AM. I AM. IS THERE ANYTHING I CAN DO TO HELP YOU?

*Be still and be quiet. Don't distract me. Hunting is not the easiest profession.*

AS YOU SAY. I WILL BE QUIET. GOOD LUCK, CAT.

*Luck has nothing to do with it,* Cat grumbled to himself as he crawled forward on his belly around to the open door of the pigeon cote. His coming did not disturb the birds, who were already sleeping. He lay quietly assessing his prey and deciding which one would be the easiest to catch. When he decided, his leap from the ground was so quick and silent that only the birds nearest the victim were disturbed and they did not murmur for long. Instead, they shuffled around glad of the room on the perch and went back to sleep.

Cat lay on the bottom of the cote, the startled pigeon grasped in jaw and claw. Because it was dark, the bird struggled very little and, gradually, Cat shifted his grip until he had the bird by the back of the neck. Pulling its skin tight had the effect of partly choking it so its few struggles ceased after a short time. It lay as one unconscious in Cat's grip. He stood then, shuddering when he thought of the cleaning he would have to do to his coat when this was done, threw his head back so the weight of the pigeon was on his shoulders and made his way carefully down from the roof, to the fence, to the woodpile, across the stableyard and into the dog gate.

The castle was quiet. Most of the people were gone to

bed and what servants crept about were attending to their own business paying no attention to the animals within the walls. The hounds smelled the pigeon when Cat brought it in and one of them came over to see why the bird was in the castle. Cat, whose teeth were otherwise occupied, glared a baleful yellow-eyed glare at the dog and stood on toes which showed their weapons. The hound went back to the fireplace and lay down to chew on his tasteless bone with nothing more than a sniff. He was smart enough to know Cat could defend himself and his pigeon if he wanted to.

Cat made his way up the stairs slowly. The bird was awkward and somewhat heavy to carry. Dead, it would have been no problem. He would have dragged it up the stairs without ceremony but he could not kill this one until the white cat cast her spell. And, he had to keep his grip on the bird while she did it so he could be in the way when spells were cast. He did not think it would matter from whom the spell were cast as long as she said the words correctly. The Other would leave its present hiding place and reenter its body. That was, after all, what they were after.

He found the bedchamber of the lad and found the door closed. That was no help at all. He stood up against the door, but his weight was not enough to push the heavy portal.

*Rat's Eyes,* he growled. *They never close a door in this place. Why this door? Why now?*

PROBABLY DON'T WANT PEOPLE LOOKING IN. The Other spoke for the first time in some hours. WHERE IS THE MAID'S ROOM? PERHAPS YOU COULD GO AND LEAD HER HERE.

*With a live pigeon in my teeth? She would think me mad and at the least, take it away from me. We need this bird to make the white cat cast her spell.*

SCRATCH ON THE DOOR. PERHAPS SOMEONE IS INSIDE.

Cat grumbled but he rearranged the pigeon again and stood as tall as he could to make scratching noises against the door. Someone stirred inside the room and the door opened slowly. Cat dropped close to the floor in the shadows and as the door opened, slid inside quickly and without waiting to see who it was, dashed under the bed. From the safety of its woven covers, he peeped out.

The Other gave a start. IT IS SHE! IN HERE! WITH MY BODY! WHAT IS SHE DOING IN HERE?

*I cannot imagine,* Cat said.

*I can.* Another voice spoke from the deep shadows under the bed. Cat turned to look. It was the white cat lying comfortably on a pillow she had pulled under the bed. *I have been here for hours. I was beginning to think you weren't coming.*

Cat swung the pigeon around in front of him where it fluttered briefly when he changed his grip on its neck. *I was occupied with this stupid bird,* Cat said.

*Oh? I thought you would charm him into flying into the room on his own. It is for his own benefit.*

*I have not your talent for charms. I said I would bring him and I have. Now, can you do your spell so I can either let him go or eat him?*

*All you toms are interested in is your bellies.*

*Not quite all,* Cat said with a leer.

*I wish the stupid girl would go. She has been sniveling over the lad's body since everyone else went to bed. If my mistress knew it, she would be furious.*

*Can't you send her a thought?* Cat asked. *Do you communicate with her at all?*

The white cat licked her paw and smoothed her whiskers. *Not really. I know what she is thinking, but I don't think she knows what I think. Or even if I think. She is a wise woman but in that, no wiser than any other human.*

*Too bad.* Cat started to say something else but a noise in the corridor interrupted. The door swung inward on its unoiled hinges and leather-clad feet moved angrily toward the bed.

"And what, exactly, are you doing in this chamber, miss?" It was the Witch Woman's voice.

"I came to see how Kharis fares. I see he still lives but there is no change. Is he going to die?"

"Probably so. Do you care? Are you lovers? Or do you just wish it so? Are you so eager to give up your gift? You ungrateful wench. This is a choice you have to make right now. This instant. I can give you more power than you have ever dreamed possible. He can give you nothing of value. Sex. Children."

LOVE, the Other said. Cat cringed.

"I know the gift is of great value. I thought I wanted it, but when I see how it is used. I am not so sure. I like the lad. He is kind."

"Do you love him?"

"I do not know what love is," the maid cried.

"If he lives and you have the opportunity to find out, will you choose him?"

The maid was sobbing. "I do not know. I do not know."

"Go to your room. I will have your answer in the morning."

The girl's small feet ran from the room and in a few moments the Witch Woman's leather-clad feet followed. She closed the door firmly behind her.

The white cat hissed angrily. *You see. I told you she is not worthy to have the calling. I knew it all along.*

*Well, you may be right. Let's get on with this spell-making and see what happens. If the lad's spirit returns to his body, he may make the decision for her and she will be out of your fur.*

*True.* She stood and pushed past the woven coverlets into the room. Her paws disappeared from sight as she leaped onto the bed.

Cat took a better grip on the bird and dragged it from under the bed. He looked at the leap he must make and took an even firmer hold, then made the leap with seemingly little effort. Only the Other knew what it cost him to make the leap. *Where do you want the bird?*

*Can you put it on the lad's chest and hold it still?*

Cat lifted the bird onto the boy's chest and stepped up after it. He stretched out and held the bird in his paws keeping his grip on its neck.

*That's good. Just like that.* She began to go through some kind of sing-song words which were meaningless to both Cat and the Other. Cat watched as she closed her blue eyes and began to sway back and forth, mewling, growling, purring aloud, all time keeping up a stream of magic words in her thoughts.

Cat began to feel strange. Dizzy. He almost lost his grip on the bird and when he felt a sharp stabbing pain in his head, he did let go his mouth grip to shake his head. Then, quite suddenly the feeling was gone. The Other was gone. Cat was alone inside himself. Beneath him, the youth began to stir.

Kharis opened his eyes and, feeling a weight on his chest, held up his head. "Hello," he said. "How come I here to my chamber and what are you doing on my chest? Have you brought me a bird, Cat?"

Cat let the pigeon go and stepped off of Kharis's chest with great dignity. *Too bad. You don't remember a thing, do you?*

*What are you talking about, Cat? Would you have him retain his pigeon thoughts?* The white cat asked.

The lad curled his legs around the cats and picked up the bird. He carried it to the window and put it on the ledge.

"In the morning you can fly back to your mates." He turned back to the cats. "You are good to keep me company." He stroked both of them. "But I have a feeling that I would do well to leave this place tonight, before the sun rises. The Witch Woman has no love for me."

*You have that right,* the white cat said. *Come, Cat. This person does not have any idea what we have done for him.* She leaped down from the bed and trotted to the door asking in pantomime to be let out.

Kharis picked up Cat and held him close for a moment before putting him down. "I feel a closeness to you, Cat. There is something . . . Faugh! I can't remember. But I thank you anyway for whatever it is." He nuzzled the cat for a moment before putting it down. "You smell like a pigeon cote."

Cat looked at him. *Think nothing of it. My pleasure.* He turned to follow the white cat when a gesture of Kharis's stopped him. The lad licked the tips of his fingers and smoothed first one eyebrow and then the other. Then he licked his fingers again and slicked down his hair before he followed the cats into the hall to go seeking the maid he loved.

Cat purred aloud following the white cat down the hall. *Why are you so happy, Cat? It is I who am pleased. Perhaps he will take the little snip with him when he goes.*

*Oh, I don't know. When we can do a little good here and there, it makes me happy. And perhaps the lad has learned more than he knows. Most humans would be the better for having a bit of cat in them.*

*You are really a very wise fellow. Come on up to my quarters, there will be a bowl of cream waiting for me. Many things are better shared.*

Cat moved up to her shoulder where he could walk beside her, and then in a bold mood, he touched her face quickly with his rough tongue. *So true,* he said. *So true.*

* * *

## Afterword

*I have been a denizen of the Witch World for many years but I, like all other readers, have had to enter by casting my spirit into the characters created by the Master, Andre Norton. When I learned* Tales of The Witch World *was open to other writers I was excited and eager to be allowed to enter through the castle gates for a change.*

*Cat Himself, an orange and cream tom who drops by my door each morning at breakfast time to cadge a handout, suggested this story to me when his personality abruptly changed. For over a week, he was someone else entirely: sour, cynical, angry, and more than a little confused. One day he arrived with an upright tail and a twinkle in his eyes and announced that Cat Himself was here again. I was certainly glad to see that whatever had possessed him was gone.*

*When I read him "Cat and the Other"—over a bowl of eggs scrambled with bacon and cream—he licked his whiskers, smiled, and seemed to say,* That's just about the way it is, Sis.

—MARYLOIS DUNN

# OATH-BOUND
## by
## Pauline Griffin

The Water Swallow still heaved so in the aftermath of the great storm that Tronel had to put out his hand to steady himself as he bent to pass through the door of the captain's cabin.

The Sulcar were a tall people, fortunately, requiring high ceilings, and once inside, he was able to straighten again despite the wings on his helm and hold himself erect in the correct manner for a shield man before the one to whom he had bound his sword.

Helmgard half sat, half lay upon his bunk, scowling at his freshly splinted leg.

He glanced up in the next instant.

"Sit, Bird Warrior. I would ask of you, not command, and I dislike straining my neck to see those with whom I speak." The Falconer complied.

"What would you have of me, Captain?" Helmgard said nothing for a moment, as if he must gather his thoughts or brace himself for a hard duty.

"The Water Swallow sailed these southern waters before, making landfall on the large, hitherto unknown island which is our current destination.

"My eldest son did not return with the others we set to exploring it. They reported he had become separated from them and they had found him again only as he vanished into a strange circle of stone trees which they were unable to penetrate themselves.

"I did."

He stared straight forward, not seeing for a moment the man whom he addressed.

"It was a gate, of course, or the precinct of a gate. Those inside informed me that Bretor had passed through and that the nature of the passage precluded his return. As weregild, I was granted command over one of them for a period of seven years, the Lady Qu'el who has served me since as my bondswoman. That period is now at an end, and I must return her to the gate."

He slapped his injured leg with a big hand.

"This prevents me from accompanying her myself, and I swore that no other of my own people would ever set foot beyond the beaches of that accursed island again, yet I cannot send her alone. The journey will take the better part of two days, and although it was safe enough in the past, I understand from her that this may no longer be the case."

"So you would have me escort her?" His face was unreadable beneath the masking helm, his voice cold. Helmgard nodded.

"I ask you to serve so in my stead. Your people's feeling against womankind is well known, and I do not demand what I know would be distasteful to you at the very least. If you do refuse, then I must be forsworn to my folk since I cannot fail in my duty to her."

Slow yellow fires burned in his screened eyes, but Tronel answered as the other knew full well he must. The spar which had put the Sulcarman on that bunk would have struck him instead had Helmgard not cast him out of its way.

"It falls within the bounds of my oath. Falconers serve thus when we ride escort to some lord's retinue . . . When?"

"The storm worked with us in this," he replied. "We

should sight land with the dawn and be ready to set ye ashore by noon."

The morning was still very young when Tronel came on deck. The ill-famed island lay on the horizon, filling most of it. Distance and the still-heavy shadows aided the heavy covering of vegetation characteristic of most southern lands in softening it, so that from here it looked almost as if it were covered with feathers or fur.

No matter. Helmgard's directions would bring them to the gate, and Storm Lord was aloft and should already be soaring over the island, scanning it with his sharp eyes. Once the falcon returned, he should have more than enough knowledge for his purpose. Mercenaries were not accustomed to the luxury of fighting on ground of which they had intimate knowledge.

His lips tightened a fraction. This was to be escort duty only, insurance against trouble but not an anticipation of it. In truth, he had no will at all to face down any witchery issuing out of a gate . . .

He stiffened and instinctively stepped back into the deep shadow cast by the bridge superstructure. Another was approaching this normally secluded part of the deck, and he was not minded for company, not even that of his own comrades.

To his surprise, the intruder was his unwelcome charge.

Tronel's first thought was to withdraw at once, but he forced himself to remain where he was and study her. Falconers hated women and feared them for the terrible danger they represented to his kind, but over the long years since their migration north, contempt had risen up as well, and that was in itself a threat. It had so blinded them that neither he nor any of his companions had even suspected the eldritch history of this female despite her patent strangeness. That weakness must be altered, now and in the future.

Qu'el was human, or seemingly human, right enough, but her delicately wrought features had a cast to them that told they were not likely to have originated here, save, possibly, in Escore . . .

Her complexion was pale, fairer even than that of the Old Race, and her hair was of a rich honey color. The eyes were large, nearly too large in the small face, heavily lashed and piercingly black, the most obviously alien feature about her.

He frowned slightly. What purpose had this creature of the gate served apart from satisfying the need for vengeance for the captain's loss? She did not work the ship alongside the Sulcarmen and women. Helmgard might have used her for his pleasure, of course, but he imagined that she had more likely performed some other, more significant, function.

Qu'el stopped some five feet from him and stood by the rail, asking no support from it, while she fixed her eyes on the distant island.

Her coming here now was no cause for amazement at least. If that were indeed her homeland, or an entrance to it, she would naturally be eager for a sight of it after an absence of seven years.

Whatever her feelings might be, her expression at first remained absolutely impassive, then suddenly, her head snapped skyward, and such joy and exultation and splendor filled her that his lips parted a little in wonder.

She gave a low, infinitely glad cry of welcome and lifted her arms as if to embrace one much loved.

A black speck showed there, still high against the sun, but descending so rapidly that it soon took discernible form.

His heart seemed to stop. The white vee on the breast was visible now. Storm Lord, and he was coming, not to his battle-brother, but to this-female.

Tronel watched, frozen with dread and the feeling of

betrayal, as the falcon came to rest on Qu'el's arm, his sharp talons closing so gently that they scarcely rumpled the material of her sleeve. She drew him to her until he caressed her pale cheek with his head.

The man waited to see no more.

"Release him, Witch!"

She stepped back with a startled cry, but before he could reach her, the bird was between them, calling in the language they shared that she had done him no ill.

The woman fled. He did not try to follow. The Water Swallow was not so large that he would not be able to locate her quickly if he needed to do so. For the moment, all his concern rested with Storm Lord.

Man and bird knew one another well. They had been paired since the then-newly-fledged falcon had chosen to ride his arm and no other's, and it was not long before Tronel was able to assure himself that no bond or block or change seemed to be set on him. His feathered brother had but responded to the heart-cry and gladness of the woman.

The Falconer's interest in viewing the island was temporarily spent, however, and he hastened below to the cramped bow section allotted to the mercenaries.

Noon came soon, too soon for Tronel. The Water Swallow was anchored in the center of a small bay, as close as she dared come to the shore, and he was in his place in the prow of the boat that would shortly ferry him and his charge to land.

He glanced somberly at the pink-white sand glistening under the bright sun and the vivid green wall of vegetation behind it. It would not be long before they disappeared into those trees, perhaps permanently.

He quelled that thought. He did not fear the island, not any more seriously than was prudent for a warrior approaching unfamiliar territory. What he dreaded was the one even now settling herself opposite him in the stern.

This was not a man's plaything, not merely a body formed for the production of fighters, but an entity come out of a place of Power and proven possessed of the ability to draw to her a being he had believed responsive to himself alone. What other gifts were hers to wield, he wondered, and how would she choose to use them now that her period of bondage was ended? If she would exact vengeance for that servitude, there might be very little a sword or knife or muscle could do against her.

Qu'el, for her part, sat absolutely still, giving no backward glance at the ship and and seeming to look right through him.

Tronel saw one slender hand dip over the side and thought she frowned slightly.

He ran his own fingers through the water. At first, he was puzzled, then he drew a quick breath. The sea was cold! This was more like the water on Estcarp's coast than a shallow, sun-warmed bay so far south.

The breeze was cool, too, enough so, he realized suddenly, that he was comfortable in his mail. Before this, he had found the noon and afternoon temperatures nearly as debilitating as a wound.

He fixed his attention on Qu'el. Her features were frozen into their mask again, her body quiet, but the eyes were alive, darting from sea to sky to the fast-nearing land.

So. No immediate danger, but she sensed enough of its shadow or enough strangeness to be very much on the alert. It behooved him to hold his own guard as well.

They made land without mishap. Tronel sprang lightly to the sand and stood back while the nearer of the Sulcar men handed the woman out.

Her head lowered once to acknowledge the service, then she walked swiftly toward the trees, moving so quickly that he found he had to press himself to overtake her.

Qu'el came to a halt just beyond the first of the screening

trunks. She stood with eyes closed, her head tilted slightly back.

She drew in a great lungful of air and slowly released it again.

"Free . . ." Her eyes opened and fixed on him, the question in them so clear that he responded as if she had spoken it.

"I am but your escort, lady. What lay between you and the Sulcar is none of my concern or interest."

She nodded even as she had to the oarsman but then looked somberly upon him once more.

"I am sorry for having spoken to your falcon," she told him softly. "I knew that to be a breach, but he in his flight was the fairest and finest sight I had seen in an eternal seven years, and the call went out from me before I even realized I had sent it forth."

"He seems to have suffered no hurt," the man responded gruffly.

"None. Storm Lord came to me through his own generosity." Tronel made her no answer. He would gladly have terminated all conversation with her, but her earlier unease troubled him. If she had any knowledge or suspicion which might bear upon his mission, he would feel the better for sharing it.

"Something disturbed you out there, the cold of the water, I think."

She smiled. "You are a miner of thoughts, Falconer! I had believed I concealed my reaction well." In the next moment, she was grave again.

"It troubles me because it is unnatural to this place." The great eyes raised, and he felt them lock with his despite the screening of his helm.

"I fear that no part of all this world is as safe as it was when I came into it. Wars have been fought and are being fought. Balances have been altered. Gates, old and new, have been wrenched open." A shudder passed through her of which she seemed unaware.

"I say to you, Bird Warrior, that if the peoples of your realm knew what powers, knew the lords of the Inner Dark, lurking just beyond, groping for any entrance by which they might come against Light and life, ye would no more battle human against human, equal against equal, but would rather embrace one another as brothers-and-sisters-in-arms against the horror that might at any moment come upon ye."

"You believe this chilling is of the Dark? That Dark?" he asked sharply. She shook her head.

"I do not know, but it is wrong for here, and anything in violation of nature must be watched carefully until it has firmly been proven beneficial or harmless."

"You know so well what is right for this world, this island? You are not native to either."

She nodded. "I do. The gate we seek has been set here a long time."

"We must move as warriors in a hostile land, then, with silence and care and with our senses open to receive sign of any foe before he can leap out upon us."

Although the afternoon passed swiftly and peacefully, Tronel's face was tense and strained by the time the first shadows began to fall, and when he chose a campsite, it was with both concealment and ease of defense in mind.

After some deliberation, he allowed a small, well-hidden fire, one that might be kicked out in a moment should the need arise.

He chewed some of the dried meat from his pack without really tasting it. Everything was so silent around them that his very breath seemed to trumpet like the blast of a war horn. That was the working of his imagination, but he knew full well that they had good cause for concern.

"Where are the animals?" he whispered to his companion.

"Hiding," Qu'el answered. "A great terror is on them."

"Of what?"

"I know not, but, Falconer, I would end your service now and have you return to the ship did I not fear that it would do you no good."

"You believe some Dark power is here?"

"This has the feel of the Dark." He saw one hand lift to press against her eyes.

"My realm has bred many of the like, and no gate is so mightily guarded that its defenses are not occasionally breached." She straightened as if girding herself for a struggle.

"Here, such a break would be temporary, but much havoc could be wrought before it was won again and the invaders destroyed or driven out once more. It is mine to prevent that, but to do so, to act effectively against any but the most menial of the Shadow's slaves, I must reach the gate and actually enter into it. Only then will my strength be returned to me."

"We shall reach it," he assured her, feeling in his heart that they had no other choice if the half of what she seemed to fear was true.

Unless she herself was of the Dark.

Tronel put that thought from him. The Sulcar did not deal with the like, and even should Helmgard and his clan be deceived as to a Dark One's nature, Storm Lord would have known, as would the other falcons, before his company ever set foot aboard the Water Swallow. Their vision was clearer than any human's in such matters.

"Did you not serve Helmgard with Power?" he ventured.

He could see her rueful smile in the flickering light.

"I served him as I cannot serve us. I brought him luck."

"What?"

"There are many times when choice or chance affect a man's or a people's life. My function was to always bring him and his to the most favorable course, and I succeeded so well that his wealth and clan have increased despite the turmoil which has reduced so many others, to the point that he has been able to help reoutfit and man other Sulcar vessels, lessening the need to hire hands outside their own blood."

He stared at her for several long seconds.

"You cannot help us so now?" he managed to ask at last.

"That is absolutely forbidden. The Power simply would not rise for me." Her head lowered as the burden settled on her again.

"Perhaps it is not as I fear."

"Perhaps not."

"You do not believe that," she responded dully.

"Nay. . . . How came you to be stripped of your strength, lady?" Qu'el stared into the fire.

"I mishandled the gate. It was through me that Helmgard's son came to be lost." Her head lowered.

"He chanced upon us as we were attempting to contain a breakthrough. The nature of our foes was obvious enough, as was the fact that we were hard-pressed, and he brought his sword to bare in our cause, helping to turn the issue in our favor.

"People from your world can cross into ours if it be their will to do so and their purpose is sufficiently strong, and when he was told that the threat to his realm was a continuing one, he demanded his right to take part in the defense.

"Both my own sword-comrade and my sister had gone down in the fighting, and my thoughts were more with my losses than with him. I failed to see that, though he could function very well in most respects, he was as a child in his ability to grasp deep or complex concepts, that he could neither truly appreciate the gravity or permanence of his decision nor comprehend at all the stark horror of the foes he was dooming himself to battle. In my accursed preoccupation with my own pain, I condemned that-child to a war he was no more fit to fight than a babe laughing in its mother's arms." She took hold of herself.

"When his sire came, we admitted our guilt. We could not restore his son to him, but so that some good might come to him and his from the disaster, I was commanded to accompany him after the most of my Power was taken from me and ordered to serve him as I have described. It is much to Helmgard's credit that he never used me other than courteously, although he was given free play as to how he might deal with me."

"When you return to your own?" the man asked after a moment.

"I shall be given charge of no more gates, but all I had will again be mine along with whatever increase to it my efforts here will have gained for me. Power is strengthened by the exercising of it, even in such a manner as I did among the Sulcar."

He frowned.

"You were harshly judged."

She shrugged. "It was just. An officer must bear the burden of his mistakes." There was no answer Tronel could make to that, and his inability to do so both made him aware of his discomfort and spurred a need to withdraw out of this discussion.

"We had best rest now. I shall take the first guard." His companion accepted that without any show of surprise and immediately curled herself into a ball, drawing as close as she could to the fire.

The Falconer watched her for a moment. Normal night cooling had joined with the unnatural chill so that it was now quite cold. Her clothing was light, designed for the warmth normal to the island, not for the temperature presently punishing them. Almost without thinking, he loosened his cloak and dropped it over her. Qu'el looked up, and Tronel turned hurriedly away.

"It would be a hindrance to me," he lied as he hastened from the circle of light.

He relaxed a little once he had drawn apart from the camp and set himself for his watch.

His fingers absently stroked Storm Lord. The feathered one was the more effective sentry, and, as on many a similar occasion before, he gave fervent thanks for his presence and for his fierce courage.

He shivered as the claws of a particularly sharp wind gust penetrated the thick canopy to tear at him.

This was probably needless, he thought sourly, just complication and difficulty forced on them by a female's ridiculous hysteria.

Reason gave the lie to that. The Lady Qu'el did not strike him as one who gave herself over to panic, and if she did so weaken now, her fear was born of such solid base that he still durst not discount it.

Dawn found the small party already on the move. The chill was stronger than ever, the silence even more oppressive than it had been the previous day. It ate at them all, so much so that Storm Lord limited his scouting to short forward spurts followed by quick retreat to the illusory safety of his companions' company. Although the man would have preferred to have more advance knowledge of their route, he did not have the heart to demand greater effort from the falcon. His own fear was too strong.

They continued on thus for three hours, and Tronel was beginning to hope that they would reach the gate without suffering worse than this trial to their nerve when Storm Lord returned from one of his scouting flights with real purpose on him. He had discovered something he neither understood nor liked.

The two humans followed after him until they came to a halt before a newly made path, a swath of destruction ten feet across that followed a course roughly parallel to their own. All within it was blackened and slain.

The Falconer's eyes narrowed as he bent to examine some of the blasted vegetation. He had initially imagined it had been charred but now saw that it was cold-killed.

He looked to his companion.

"Do you know what might have done this, lady?"

"Aye," she replied grimly, "hunters in the service of a particularly vile and powerful lord. We had best make haste. They track by sensing body heat, and they were heading in the general direction of our camp. They are sure to strike our trail at some point, and when they do, they will be back after us. They move very swiftly when seeking to give death." She straightened.

"Let me have your knife, Bird Warrior. My Power may be chained as yet, but there are no bonds on my body."

He gave the weapon to her and stepped onto the black road. The invaders appeared to have come from the gate or at least from that direction. They would save time if they kept to the path their foes had made.

Half an hour passed and ten minutes longer, then he became aware of sounds behind them.

Tronel's arm caught Qu'el, forced her off the blighted trail. He followed fast after her, keeping his body between her and whatever was approaching.

He saw them, two creatures, biped in form and slightly taller than a big man but without any great breadth of shoulder or muscular development. Their uncovered skin, or what passed for skin, was a stark white. The heads were long and lacking in what humans called features. A slit existed about where eyes might be, and another, shorter one was positioned an inch beneath it, but that was all. Their arms ended in gaping circular holes where hands or other appendages might be expected to begin.

Those last were weapons. Even as he watched, the nearest hunter pointed toward a clump of tall ferns. A cloud issued from the arm, and the plants shriveled.

They were aware of the humans—that much was certain

from the way they moved—and the Falconer braced himself to meet their assault.

He raised his eyes to peer into the dead blackness lying beyond the slits in the helmetlike heads.

Helmet? He wondered if what he saw before him was actually the creature or merely some artificial covering akin to his own mail. Qu'el confirmed that wild surmise in the next instant.

"Break their cases. The light will soon finish them." After that, there was no more time for speech.

Both sprang aside and apart as the Dark hunters sprayed with their icy mist the place where they had lain. Tronel saw the women cast her dagger, saw it penetrate the foremost being's cheek, but his own opponent gave him no opportunity to observe the result.

A greater distance lay between him and his target. Qu'el's blow had shown that the thing's armor could be pierced, but the surprise of their counterattack was over, and the hunter's reactions were quick. It loosed its deadly weapon even as he dove for it.

The man leaped to avoid it, did escape it himself, but he could not lower his sword in time. It met the stream, only its point, but such a surge of cold ran up its length that his arm dropped, useless, by his side.

His left hand caught the weapon as it fell. He swung with it and struck home only to see the now-brittle metal shatter into gleaming splinters.

The creature's arm raised again. Tronel tried to bring up what remained of his sword but knew his blow must come too late.

"The face! Tear the mask!" His eyes raised to it, but he had no hope of reaching it . . .

A black missile tore through the air above him. Incredibly fast, fierce, almost an embodiment of battle fury in this moment of his master's peril, the falcon threw himself at the Dark hunter. His powerful talons, his beak, seized the narrow strip separating the two slits, wrenched at it until it tore out and stood at a right angle to the face.

For one moment, there was an outpouring of murky shadow and piercing cold, then that vanished, and the emptied shell toppled. It struck the man, knocking him, but there was little real weight to it, and his own armor prevented him from taking injury from the blow.

Tronel came to his feet in the next instant, still gripping the remnant of his sword, but he saw the other invader was down as well and Qu'el was standing beside it. Storm Lord's concerned call told him the falcon, too, had come through the encounter unscathed.

Working his fingers to ease the throbbing of returning circulation, he sheathed his weapon and joined the woman.

"We still go for the gate?" he asked.

"Aye, though what we shall find there . . ." Her shoulders squared.

"We shall never know until we make the test. A few more minutes will give us the answer."

They crept forward, every sense alert, so that it seemed an eternity before they found themselves facing the place Helmgard had described.

It was indeed strange and to Tronel fearsome because of that strangeness. Twenty great stones had been set in a circle, or had grown thus, for their form was that of trees, and bright, living leaves sprouted from the branches. In their center stood a plain arch fashioned of the same gray rock.

At first he relaxed, for all seemed well, but then he detected a faint shadow, a sooty mist flecked with red, hovering around the arch.

"Too late," Qu'el whispered, despair plain on her. "Our guards must be slain."

"The Dark lord?"

"Nay, a servant awaiting his coming, but it is not one which can be fought without Power."

He watched the shadow-thing. It seemed to grow ever more substantial as his eyes became accustomed to fixing on it.

"Is it like to those hunters?"

"Nay. It is quite mindless but a perfect choice of guardian here. It will sweep down on us if we try to approach the gate."

"We cannot fight through it?"

She shook her head. "There is no hope of that, not with the weapons we possess."

"What will happen?"

"Its master and probably others will come, to the great grief of this world."

The Falconer was silent awhile.

"You say it will sweep down upon an intruder, lady. If I were to move against it first and draw it to me, would it be possible for you to slip in and gain the gate?" She studied him closely, then the guardian at the arch.

"Perhaps, if you could hold it for even a few seconds. The chance is slight, and there would be very little hope of your survival." He merely shrugged.

"Warriors have made that choice before now." He drew his broken weapon.

"The edge is still sound. We shall soon see if it will bite upon mist." Tronel hesitated.

"If you win through, send Storm Lord back to my people aboard the Water Swallow. There is no point in sacrificing him as well, and he will answer to you."

Her head bowed. "So let it be."

The Falconer made his charge. He crossed the ground separating him from the stone trees quickly, passed between the nearest of them.

A great red-shot darkness loomed up before him. What had seemed mist at a distance proved something more cohesive at closer range, a thin ooze that was, in a terrible, mindless sense, somehow alive, obscenely alive.

It flowed toward him. He braced himself to meet it, not daring to hesitate or even to think lest his fear break him and he flee. If once that happened, hope was indeed dead.

It was on him then, pouring over him like the tide over a boulder in its path—or quicksand swallowing the last trace of its victim—a blind hunger and cold and a death that was deeper than any dying.

The horror seemed to seep into his very being, body, mind, and soul, draining the light and life out of him. He could not struggle, could do nothing at all as the warmth was leached out of him but fix his mind on the memory of a bright sun and a falcon soaring high against it. He remembered the joy lighting a woman's face at the sight of that falcon . . .

It was nearly over. He imagined he saw a new light, a vibrant green that tore into the black and red, but he was too spent for even delirium to hold him, and he retreated into full night.


Tronel became aware of heat, of a gentle touch that sent warmth pouring into his body. His eyes opened to find Qu'el bent over him.

He started to draw back, but memory returned, and he compelled himself to lay still.

Her eyes closed a moment, as if in relief, and her hand lifted in a gesture of greeting.

"It is good to have you back in this realm, Bird Warrior. For a time there, I feared not even the Green Fire would be sufficient to warm you again. He frowned at that. Green Fire? In that first moment of awareness, he had thought her surrounded by emerald flame, as if it emanated from her . . . His vision was clear now, and she was but a woman.

"It is victory, then?"

"Victory. That Dark One will not come again, nor will

many of the retinue he planned to bring with him." Her expression shadowed for a moment.

"They were a bad lot, worse even than I had feared." The man's strength was returning rapidly. He sat up after one failed effort and tried to take stock of himself. Qu'el read his desire easily enough.

"Both you and Storm Lord are sound. You still have your dagger, though your sword can but serve as a reminder of this day." She held it up, or, rather, the hilt of it. Only a small sliver of the blade now remained.

"You managed to get in a few strokes, no mean feat, and they did tell. As for the rest, your mail is nigh unto useless, I fear, but your helm somehow escaped damage save for a bent wing, which can readily be set to rights."

She handed it to him. He took it from her, but rose to his feet and stood looking at it without attempting to set it on his head.

"You will rejoin your people now?" he asked.

"Aye." He took a deep breath. "I would make this war mine."

"Do you know what you say? There is no withdrawing or release from such service." His eyes met hers.

"I am no mind-damaged boy, lady. Having seen this enemy and fought it, I cannot again go back to slaughtering my own kind, those who should be brothers-in-arms with me as you yourself named them." The lady was silent for many long seconds.

"You have shown yourself to be all we could wish in an ally, yet there are difficulties, maybe insurmountable ones, for you.

"You overcame your distrust of me and your lesser feelings to work with me in this need, and you overcame your indifference for compassion's sake, which is, perhaps, an even greater measure of you, but just now, you had to will yourself not to recoil when you wakened to find me beside you.

"The war we wage is harsh. Our enemies are awesomely powerful, and we have learned it is necessary, essential, to pair our warriors, male with female, so that each is balanced by the gifts of the other and both are strengthened thereby. The penalties of failing to effect that partnership are inescapable, and, Bird Warrior, they are heavy. Could you bind yourself to serve with a woman even as you now do with Storm Lord?" It was his turn to fall silent.

"If I must," he said in the end.

"The decision of a moment is not enough. Are you willing to battle with yourself, with your own past? It will come to that, month after weary month."

"If I must," Tronel replied again.

He hesitated then, knowing himself well enough to realize that in such a war, rout might come more frequently than advance.

"If my partner realizes that I am battling." Qu'el regarded him more closely, seemingly with greater respect.

"Very well, Falconer," she said, speaking slowly, thoughtfully. "Wait one year. Think well and use the time well. Spend some of it at Lormt, that repository of ancient knowledge, if you can, following whatever trails catch your fancy. If at the end of that period, you are still firm in your resolve, then we shall welcome you gladly, you and your feathered brother both."

She smiled, silencing the question he had been about to raise.

"Do not fear for the gate. There are others besides this one. The way will be opened for you . . . You are content?"

He nodded, concealing the keenness of his disappointment.

"I must make myself content."

"Well answered . . . Good journey, Comrade, until we join forces again." The Lady Qu'el stepped back, toward the arch. He watched her, knowing she went to face enemies like to those they had challenged this day.

His hand raised in the salute of his race.

"May you soar high on fortune's wings, Lady."

With that, because he found he did not wish to see her go, he turned and, calling Storm Lord to him, left the area of the gate to begin his journey back to the coast.

\* \* \*

## Afterword

*I have been captivated by Andre Norton's Witch World ever since discovering it. The Falconers, however, fascinate me above all its other inhabitants, a race hating and fearing both women and sorcery with excellent reason.*

*Given this interest, I leaped at the chance to work with such a man—one honorable in himself and possessing the integrity and courage to put his prejudice and fear aside for duty's sake and then to acknowledge the need to battle them under the double challenge of universal peril and the evidence that presented itself against them. It was a story I thoroughly enjoyed doing, and I would very much like to develop the character further.*

—PAULINE GRIFFIN

# OF ANCIENT SWORDS AND EVIL MIST

## by

## James R. Heidbrink

Ships, three-masted vessels of war, swiftly slicing through the waves as they head out on yet another adventure, their mighty sails dove white and billowing in the breeze. Ah, the open sea; the piercing cry of a gull, the biting taste of the salt air and another chance for a Sulcarman to loosen his blade and flex the talent of a good sword arm.

Pain, searing hot, like an all-consuming fire that shoots throughout the body and bursts into the brain with a multitude of colors.

Ah, women; those beautiful, well-endowed wenches that inhabit the various waterfront inns and bars in all those ports of call. What talents they possess, to make a lonely seaman completely forget about all that ails him, providing he has the money of course. Those soft rounded shoulders, their full bosoms, the smell of perfume and . . . Pain again, this time even sharper than before, strong enough to end all dreams, replacing them instead with the harshness of reality.

Jobec opened his eyes very slowly, his lids at first refusing to yield, as though they had somehow been glued together. Gone were the peaceful visions of mighty ships and even mightier women, to be replaced with a close-up view of sand. Sand and something that must have truly crawled out of a nightmare. A creature that was all claws, legs, eyes, and evil intentions.

With a startled cry, Jobec pushed his massive frame up into a sitting position, his head spinning violently with the sudden effort on his part. From his new viewpoint, the blue-shelled crab didn't appear nearly as ferocious as it had at eye level. Actually, the little beach crawler was quite content to remain where it was, happily chewing on something it held in its claws. With a revulsion that caused him to retch, Jobec realized exactly what it was that the hungry crab was so busily eating.

If anything, his head was now somewhat clearer after dumping the salt-water contents of his stomach on the sand. Rising a little unsteadily to his feet, Jobec watched with amusement as three more of the shelled predators scurried back out of his way. "Ho my lads, breakfast time, is it?" he said with a laugh, his voice booming out against the quiet serenity of the beach. "Or is it lunch? Either way, you'll be getting no more of ol' Jobec Stardith to munch on, mind you."

Lunch, his stomach rumbled at the mere thought of it. How long had it been since he had eaten last? But even more pressing than that was his overpowering thirst, already his throat felt as if it were rapidly closing upon itself.

Brushing as much sand as he could from his clothing and body, he shaded his eyes to scan the vast horizon of blue, searching for any sign of the ship he had been on, or the ones that sailed with it. But, unfortunately, no such sight met his eyes. Had they all perished in the storm? Ah, what a storm it had been, the likes of which would rival many a good bard song.

They had been returning from a raiding mission in the northernmost section of the country of Alizon. Five warships, riding low in the water, their bellies loaded with plundered loot. Jobec was the captain of the Red Dawn and under him was a rough and tumble crew of Sulcarmen, along with a few Falconers who had hired on as marines. It was a loyal and fierce crew, one that would make any captain of the sea proud.

Ordinarily, the families of the Sulcarmen would have ridden on board, turning each of the ships into a floating village. But this time the men had decided it best to leave their loved ones behind, since they would be raiding too far to the north for it to be safe.

A good thing that they had too, for the devils of Alizon had almost crept up on them by surprise. It was only through superior naval and fighting skills that they had managed to crush the enemy assault, turning it instead into a victory for the Sulcar ships. That victory hadn't come easily, though, the decks had run red with blood and many a good man went down under enemy steel during the vicious infighting that occurred.

It was on the return trip home, however, when their battle luck had seemed to fail them. This time it was their own ally, the sea, that had attacked them with a storm, the likes of which Jobec hadn't seen in his thirty-six years at sea.

First they had done the natural thing and tried to outrun it, but failed as the weight of the captured goods they were carrying slowed them down. Then they were left with only one possible option, to tie everything down and ride the squall out.

Hitting them full force, the wind had screamed and howled like a wounded werewolf caught in a woodman's trap. With the wind came the waves, the size of which threatened to capsize the ship at any moment.

It was during one of these waves that a piece of the rigging had snapped free of the aft mast. Swinging down, it had caught Jobec between the shoulder blades, tearing him from where he clung to the stern of the ship. He was carried over and away from the hull of the ship, his cry for help being drowned out by the howling of the storm. That he had managed to survive a watery death was amazing, but had any of the others? Again he searched the horizon, but no sign of a ship or any debris could be seen, nothing but water.

Water, once more he felt his throat tighten at the thought. Something had to be done to answer that awful thirst, but where?

Facing inland, he searched for something to set his bearings on. This tiny section of the coast was unfamiliar to him, but then again, rarely did they set sail this far north into Alizon territory, except on raiding missions. That he was now in hostile territory Jobec had little doubt, which only added to his already growing list of problems.

The beach itself was surrounded on three sides by rocky white cliffs that rose straight up to a height of about fifty feet, forming a natural cove. But to his left he noticed what appeared to be a small path or perhaps a game trail that ran at an angle, leading up through the cliffs. "Very well . . ." Jobec said aloud, ". . . that way it is.

"Sorry I can't stay to join you, my little friends, but I must be going now," he said to the small group of crabs that were still sitting there intently watching him. "Remind me when I return, to tell you the story about the two redheaded sisters of Kars. Ah, now that is an adventure story!"

With a hearty laugh, he started off in the direction of the trail, pausing just long enough before leaving the beach to spit over his shoulder for luck. For luck he would truly have need of, seeing how he lacked food and water or any weapon with which to defend himself, if the need arose.

The climb up the cliff was harder than he had anticipated, and by the time Jobec had made it to the top he was sweating and panting for air. Trails and paths weren't for him. Ah, what he wouldn't give for the feel of a rolling ship once again beneath his feet.

Before him now stretched a vast open field of grassland that ended at the base of some rolling foothills, barely visible in the distance. Oddly enough, the path he had been following didn't lead in that direction, instead it veered sharply to the left, heading through a rather dense section of woods that bordered on the field. Now Jobec didn't think too highly of venturing along on that shadowy trail that cut through the forest, but neither did he of being caught unarmed and out in the open by the Hounds of Alizon—those vicious white dogs that were trained to hunt men. So the woods it was, maybe there he would find some water and a few edible plants to fill a rapidly shrinking belly.

One thing that struck him as a little odd, as he made his way down that twisting path, was the complete silence that seemed to hang in the air. Not once had he heard so much as a single cry of a bird or the rustling movements of a woodland creature. Even the buzzing and biting flies that so often annoyed one while in the woods seemed to be absent today. As he continued, the silence grew even more disturbing and he often caught himself glancing back over his shoulder as though he expected to see someone or something dogging his trail.

The path itself had grown somewhat wider. Upon closer investigation Jobec discovered that he trod upon gray blocks of stone that lay hidden under the fallen vegetation of the forest. So the path was made by someone of intelligence rather than animals, even though all signs pointed to the fact that it was no longer used regularly by whomever made it.

It was quite late in the afternoon before Jobec chanced upon water, but it was not so much the small stream that caught his attention, as what lay directly on the other side of it.

At one time it might have served as an assembly hall of

some kind, so great was its size. The structure appeared to be made from the same gray blocks that formed the path. A roof, barely visible under the vines that grew upon it, still sheltered the back section of the building, while the front part had long since crumbled into decay, exposing the massive pillars that had at one time supported it. Running along the side of the building, just beneath the overhang of the roof, were carven images of men, animals, and creatures Jobec couldn't identify, their features eroded by time and the elements. For what purpose and by whom this structure had been built, he couldn't be certain. But that it was very ancient there was little doubt.

The silence that had accompanied Jobec throughout the day seemed to hang heaviest in and about this building. It was as though it gave off a feeling of sadness, sorrow, or perhaps dread.

Jobec's thirst had been quenched by the cold running waters of the stream, but his hunger still remained, growing stronger with every passing moment. But it was something that he would have to live with a little while longer, as already the sun was sinking low in the western sky, casting strange shadows everywhere. It would be best to seek shelter for the night, as it was common knowledge that the darkness belonged to the predators who hunted the woods. Ah, but what he wouldn't give for so much as a single piece of tasteless journey bread. His stomach rumbled at the thought.

Crossing the stream, he headed up the last of the path, which ended at the front of the building. With a little extra caution, he climbed the three steps that were there, walking past the first row of the massive pillars. Jobec paused briefly to try to read the runes that were carved on the pillars, but their meaning and origin were unknown to him. The feeling of dread he felt was so strong now that it was almost a physical blow. Moving carefully amidst the rubble, he proceeded toward the still erect section in the back, his eyes gradually adjusting to the gloom.

It was there, much to his horror, that he discovered what might have been part of the reason for the feeling that he picked out of the air.

Before him sat eight massive tables, each apparently carved from a single block of grayish-blue stone. They were arranged end to end, four tables to a row. Scattered on, beside, and beneath the tables were numerous skeletons of fighting men, still wearing the now rusting armor and chain mail they had died in. At one time comrades-in-arms had toasted cups in this hall, as was evident by the numerous goblets and drinking vessels scattered about. But a battle had interrupted that celebration and many had been killed.

"Earth take that which is of earth. Water accept that of water. And that which is now freed, let it be free to follow the high path," Jobec said aloud, following the burial oath that is custom to many a fighting man. He doubted seriously that the words had ever been said before over those that lay here.

Moving among the dead, Jobec began to realize that there was something very wrong with his original theory about what had happened in this place. Although all those in the building had been armed fighting men, nowhere could he see any evidence that a fight had taken place. Not one skull had been cleaved or any weapon drawn. It was as though the enemy had been able to descend upon these poor souls completely by surprise.

What kind of enemy had it been, to come so upon this dwelling and take all those inside totally unaware? At least fifty armed men had perished here. If only the dead could speak, then maybe he might know an answer to the riddle that lay before him.

Jobec failed to recognize any of the crests on the rusting shields and helmets as any he had ever seen or heard legend of. So ancient must this race have been.

It was during his investigation that he chanced upon a sword partially hidden upon one of the tables, covered over with eons and eons of dust. The weapon was smaller and much lighter than those carried by the Sulcarmen, the blade being forged from an unknown bluish metal, with a handle that appeared to be somehow made from a solid piece of precious red stone, polished smooth. Although the scabbard had long since crumbled with rot, nowhere were there any nicks, pits, or other signs of age upon the sword itself. Catching the dim light in the room, the handle and blade seemed to glisten with fire. This indeed was a fine weapon for a Sulcar captain!

Grasping the handle tightly, Jobec bowed to the skeleton that lay next to it, raising the sword in salute. "I thank you, noble sir, for such a fine weapon. You may rest assured that it shall only be used bravely and with honor." Having now obtained water and that with which to arm himself, that left only food. But that was a problem that he would have to live with until the morning.

In the back of the building Jobec discovered a wooden ladder, still sturdy, that led up to a small, open attic. Possibly at one time it had been used as a storeroom for supplies, but for now it would serve nicely as a place to rest. He hadn't exactly relished the thought of sleeping on the first floor with the dead. Sitting back against a far wall, he watched as the shadows in the room below lengthened and grew dark.

It was more of a mental warning than any actual sound that awoke Jobec from a sound sleep. Remaining perfectly still, he listened intently as his eyes grew accustomed to the darkness about him. Sweat ran down his bearded face as his heart began to beat faster. With what? Fear, yes that was it, the very air around him carried a feeling of it.

Straining his eyes to cut through the darkness, he could see nothing wrong, or could he? It wasn't anything definite, but didn't the shadows appear to be moving and growing somewhat darker? No, not shadows—shadow! It had just moved into the front of the room on the first floor, spreading out gradually as it did. This was not the shadow of a man, animal of prey, or for that matter, any living creature he knew of. As a fog it appeared, but one that blocked out the background as it moved slowly among the dead.

Fear, again a warning, so strong now that it was like a scream. Jobec clutched the hilt of the sword even tighter, his knuckles turning white. To face a man in battle was one thing, but this.

"You cannot defeat it, brave warrior." Words, spoken words that he heard, but not with his ears, with his mind. Startled, he looked about, but there was no one to be seen. Then, before him an area of the attic began to lighten noticeably. Within the light a form was beginning to appear, to take on shape. Whatever was appearing there in that glow meant him no harm, he was certain of that, although he was unsure exactly how he knew that. "You have nothing to fear from me, fighting man." Once again the words danced in his head.

Before him now stood a woman, small of frame, long hair the color of a spider's web tumbled down about her shoulders. She was clothed in a glistening tunic of silver and blue, closely fitting her body, leaving bare her arms and legs. About a delicate neck hung a string of blue jewels that matched those in the bracelets she wore. She was thin of face with a pointed chin and slanting eyes that appeared to shine in the darkness much as would those of a cat.

"Who are you?" Jobec asked slowly, forming the words in his mind.

"I am not one of your world, Jobec Stardith" the reply came.

"You know my name?" he asked, surprised.

"This and other things can I pick from your thoughts."

"Then the advantage is all yours, my dear lady, unless you would be so kind as to tell me your name."

"In my time I was called Salith."

"Your time?"

"One that has long since past."

"I don't understand . . ." Jobec protested, shaking his blond head slowly, ". . . I can see you—you are here now."

"Only an image, I assure you."

"But, if this is indeed true, why then do you come?"

"To deliver a warning to someone who is good of heart."

"A warning?" he asked, his eyebrows raising.

"Can you not feel it, oh man of the sea? Your very presence in this forbidden place has upset the balance of age-old powers. It has awakened things which have long since slept, things that should not have been awakened."

Jobec turned, looking out across the room below. That growing mist was coming closer now, darker, blocking out the view of the room behind it.

"Hurry!" Her voice was sharp in his mind. "There is not much time left, you must flee now, while you can."

"Flee?" Jobec thought, amused. "My dear lady, you underestimate me. I have never been one to retreat from a battle, not as long as I am still able to swing a sword or draw a breath."

"A battle yes . . ." she said, ". . . but it is not merely armed men that you face here tonight. Rather it is something that is very ancient and very evil, something that was accidentally released by those who dabbled in magical powers they knew not how to control. Think you that you can stop something that all those who lay below could not? Look, warrior!" she cried, pointing to the darkness below.

Jobec did, and what he saw there made his skin crawl. Before him, he still saw a room where the shadows deepened, but superimposed over that he also saw an image of a room as it once had been. A room well lit with flickering torches and alive with the bodies and voices of hearty fighting men. Then something out of the very blackness of evil itself had entered that room, to descend upon those brave men and suck away the life force in each of them. This shapeless mass of foulness had fed on the very souls of that wretched company, cursing them to an everlasting eternity of suffering and unrest. Jobec's vision blurred and once again he found himself looking at a darkened room, long since devoid of any life.

"Dear lady . . ." he thought, his fear racing to overcome him, ". . . is this then the very thing that comes tonight?"

"Not tonight, now, this minute, and for you!"

"Why for me?"

"Because your life is what draws it, much as the scent of blood does a hunting beast."

"And there is no way to fight this thing?"

"None that you know of, Jobec Stardith. Your only chance is to escape while you still can."

"But surely it will give chase."

"It cannot. This building is a place of power—of evil power in which the thing is trapped. It cannot go outside these walls," she said.

The shadow had now reached the base of the ladder and was slowly making its way up toward them. Jobec could feel the hairs on the back of his neck begin to rise in terror.

"Come . . ." she cried, ". . . there is no more time!"

He was on his feet instantly, springing across the small room after the fleeing figure of the girl. Already the shadow had reached the top of the ladder and was pouring into the attic. At the other end of the room Salith knelt by what appeared to be nothing more than a bare wall.

"There was once a window here, though it has been covered over with rocks. Use your strength to open it, warrior!"

One glance over his shoulder at that growing mass of blackness reaching out for them was all it took for Jobec to summon the strength of several men. With a mighty swing, he sent the sword crashing against the spot she had pointed to. Sparks flew as steel and stone met, but still the barrier remained. "Sul!" he shouted, yelling the battle cry of the Sulcarmen, as the blade once more arced through the air to crash against the wall, scattering rocks out into the night. The opening now lay clear, but there was no time to waste, they must act quickly. Already he could feel that evil mist closing its grip about them. A sickly sweet smell of death and decay filled the air.

"Climb down and hurry!" Salith cried, pointing to a thick vine that hung just to the outside of the opening.

"You first," Jobec argued.

"This is not the time nor the place for gallantry, man of the sea. You face things here you do not understand," she said.

"Maybe so, but what I do understand is that I will not flee and leave an unarmed woman, illusion or otherwise, behind to face whatever manner of thing that it is we face. Now go!" he ordered.

"Brave, foolish man," she said with a smile, before she disappeared through the opening.

Thrusting the red-hilted sword into a strap of his tunic, Jobec squeezed his massive shoulders through the small opening, leaving behind a layer of skin in the process. He was most of the way out when something grabbed hold of his legs, slowly dragging him back inside. Instantly the fear rose in him as he screamed aloud, kicking and struggling with all his might to tear himself free from the viselike grasp. There was a strain, then a pop as he found himself falling end over end, through the air.

He lay slightly dazed at the base of the building, but luckily the ground was soft and he was not seriously hurt in the fall. It was then that he heard a loud scream from above that turned the blood in his veins to ice water and sent him running as fast as he could away from the building, not even realizing at the time that he was barefoot. Whatever manner of evil had been in that building, it obviously wasn't satisfied with just the moldy leather boots of a Sulcarman.

Pulling up short at a tree, his heart about to explode, he thought of the girl, Salith. Where was she; for that matter, where was he? Surely he had run so hard without any direction that he was now completely lost.

"Fear not my brave warrior, for Salith is still with you." The words cut into his thoughts.

"But where?" he thought.

"Here, just follow the light."

Up ahead, he saw a strange bluish glow that bobbed and weaved among the trees, appearing much as the light of a candle when blown by a soft summer breeze. Jobec raced to catch up with it, ignoring the pain of going barefoot over stubble and thorns. On through the night he chased after that glow, but no matter how fast he went or how hard he tried, he could not close the distance between himself and the elusive light.

Through brush and thickets and around trees he continued to run, until at last, totally exhausted, he could go no more. Sitting down with his back braced against a tree, he closed his eyes for a moment to rest.

Voices, real voices and those of men, coming closer. Jobec awoke instantly, his hand reaching out for the hilt of the sword that lay beside him. It was broad daylight now, the brightness of the sun hurting his eyes. Although certain that when he had closed his eyes to rest his back had been firmly planted against the trunk of a tree, he now found that he was once again lying on the warm sand of a beach. Not only was he now in the open, he was fully exposed to whomever was coming up behind him.

Ah, but Jobec Stardith would not be one to go down without a fight, and surely his would not be the only blood that would flow freely today. Jumping quickly to his feet, he spun around, prepared to match cold steel with those who were upon him.

"Ho, Jobec, you old sea dog. It is good to see that you still live and are as anxious for a fight as ever."

Surprise overwhelmed him. Instead of facing a scouting party of armed Alizon soldiers as he expected, he now fronted six Sulcar blood brothers and cup comrades from his own ship. Nor could he mistake the graceful lines of the war vessel that sat anchored in the distance as being anything other than the Red Dawn.

"Ho, Captain, you look as though you've seen a ghost. Does the sight of a fellow Sulcarman disturb you so?" the tall muscular man leading the party of six asked.

"Disturb? No, Haylor, that it doesn't. But puzzle it does. I thought surely that the ship and all those on board had been lost," Jobec replied.

"Nay, it will take more than just a little wind and rain to defeat the crew of the Red Dawn. If only I could say as much of her captain."

His remark had been said in humor and good spirit, with no ill feelings meant, as well Jobec knew, for he and Haylor had been blood brothers since the time they were both old enough to use a sword. Many an adventure the two men had shared and many a good time. But, even as the men hugged each other in an embrace of companionship, Jobec's mind whirled as he tried desperately to put together all the pieces of the previous night. This was definitely not the same beach where he had washed ashore after the storm, but how did he get here? More so, how in the world did they find him here?

"What troubles you, brother?" Haylor asked, concerned, reading the expression on the other man's face.

"I was just wondering about how I happened to get to this particular beach, and how you happened to find me here."

"As for how you got here, I wouldn't know . . ." Haylor

answered, ". . . but the finding of you took some doing. We were about to call off the search and give you up for dead, when we happened to spot your signal fire."

"Fire? But I didn't light any fire."

"Maybe not, but somebody did," Haylor said, pointing.

He was right; there on the beach, a little over forty feet away, were signs of where a fire had burned, though it was not much more than a smoldering pit of ashes now. The sand around the fire was still wet, and in it Jobec could see numerous bare footprints. They were small and slim, like those made by a child, or perhaps a woman of small frame. Lying just beyond the fire was a scarf made of a shimmery silver and blue material. Jobec stooped down to carefully pick it up.

"It appears that our captain has had an adventure of his own since the other night," Haylor said with a grin, his gaze going from the scarf to the red-handled sword in Jobec's tunic and finally resting on the captain's bootless, cut, and bruised feet.

"That I have had, brother Haylor."

"Maybe then, there shall be a tale that will be told."

"Aye, and it is such a tale as you have never heard before," Jobec replied.

"Better then than the tale of yours about the two redheaded sisters from Kars?"

"Much better, my friend," Jobec said with a laugh.

"This tale I must hear."

"And that you shall, provided that I will only have to tell it to you over a hearty meal and a good bottle of wine."

"Ho, Jobec, you have just made yourself a deal."

As both men walked back down the beach to join the others who already awaited them in the skiff, Jobec paused to face back toward the woods. "Salith," he whispered aloud, forming the words clearly in his mind. But no answer came. Could it be then that she was indeed nothing more than an illusion, as she had claimed. Maybe so, but surely illusions didn't leave footprints in the sand, and wasn't the piece of material that he now held in his hand real enough?

Jobec carefully tucked the scarf inside his tunic as he turned and walked toward the water. Yes, it would be good to regain once again the ship and the life he loved at sea, but he knew that he would one day soon return to this deserted little section of the coastline, to once more walk that shadowy trail that led through the woods. For there were still certain questions that had been left unanswered and a thank-you that had been left unsaid.

\* \* \*

## Afterword

*Through the gifted writing of Andre Norton, I've spent so much time in Witch World that I often feel a little guilty about not having to pay taxes or file for official residency there.*

*It was during one of my more recent trips that Jobec the Sulcarman, captain of the Red Dawn, told me the tale that you have just read. At first I doubted the authenticity of the story, thinking that it had come from all the mugs of ale we drank that night. But when Jobec showed me the red-hilted sword and the scarf of shimmering silver and blue material, I no longer had any doubts to the truth of it. The last I heard, he had set sail with the intention of returning to that mysterious stretch of woods, with its winding path and dark secrets. I truly hope that he finds what he is looking for—somehow I think he will.*

—JAMES R. HEIDBRINK

# NINE WORDS IN WINTER

## by

## Caralyn Inks

"By the Marshmist's seventh daughter," Mag'ra yelled. "They even stole my false teeth!" She couldn't remember the last time she was so angry. Danner the Potter made those teeth for her in payment for bringing both his wife and child through a difficult birthing alive. Sure, she never wore them except when she visited the villagers or company called. Even a woman her age had her pride. She'd have worn them more often, but she loathed the taste of the glue-paste that kept the things fixed to her gums. Nothing, she believed, was so repulsive as bare gums in a woman's mouth. It made one look a crone.

For eighty-one years she'd lived in these hills as Lore Mistress and healer for the small villages strung throughout the long narrow valley called Min's Hold. Even the brigands who lived in the high places, the Sharoon Hills, came to her for healing and the old knowledge. No one had ever disturbed her privacy, until now.

Mag'ra bent over and picked up a pottery shard. Once it had held an elixir that would ease pain. It was lost. All her healing stores were ground into powder or had soaked into the dirt floor. Such wanton destruction of that which would give succor to all who needed aide was beyond her understanding.

She tossed the shard aside. The fools had stripped the

meat house of the food which would have seen her through to spring. "I'll not eat meat at another's table without my teeth! And I am not so old that I have to suck gruel." She shivered and pulled her cape tight about her.

This winter was the worst she'd ever experienced. Usually the high tors rimming Min's Hold shielded them. Not this season. The cold winds were unrelenting.

Every winter the villagers and the brigands worked together in fairly peaceful coexistence. For the most part, these outlaws had lost their homes and families in the long war with the Hounds of Alizon and the resultant internal strife in High Hallack. If truth be told, all, including herself, had cause to be grateful for their presence. Desperate for a place of their own, they fought to keep the valley free from the Hounds.

But now, the wind of human voices had borne to her the rumors of a shift of power among the brigands. Radnor, the new lord, was said to be one who used the Dark forces to gain a foothold in the valley.

She'd enjoyed working with the old lord, Alesanfar. To keep Min's Hold secure, they each used their own strengths. Alesanfar used his gift of leadership and his men, and she by drawing on the Power of an Old One, Min, to whom she'd given herself a long time ago. But Alesanfar would have no power over forces of the Dark, if this Radnor proved to be. Even without proof Mag'ra knew this to be true. An uneasy feeling rode her, like a bad taste one could not remove from the mouth.

Someone outside shouted her name. She stepped around the shattered remains of her furniture and herb bottles and went to the door. Danner the Potter was running up the hill leading to her home.

"Dame Mag'ra!" He panted, bracing himself on her door. "Are you all right?"

"Yes. I was over to Old Stern's and missed the ruckus.

His prized sow went into labor before her time last night. You know how he loves that beast."

Danner nodded. "The bandits—they raided the town —took all our food." He grabbed her arm. "You've got to do something!"

"I intend to," she said, holding her lips in such a way that she hoped he did not see her teeth were missing. "Do you know where the raiders came from or who they were?"

"I recognized one of Alesanfar's men."

"Alesanfar? That doesn't ring true. Unless . . ." She was silent a moment, then asked, "Was anyone hurt?"

"No. Surprisingly."

"Not so surprising. If the villagers were all dead the brigands would have to travel a long distance to find the supplies they need." She examined Danner. He was hiding something. "Out with it! What are you not telling me?"

"I am sorry, Dame Mag'ra, among the women taken was Zaya."

"My craft-daughter?" At his nod fury began to build anew in her. This was not Alesanfar's doing, not the destruction of her home nor her supplies or the taking of her craft-daughter. He respected their friendship and the Power he knew was hers to command. Never would he insult her like this. No longer did she doubt the rumors of a new lord. Alesanfar had been displaced by one of the Dark. Radnor. And in his power was her craft-daughter.

Zaya was fourteen years old. Granted her talent was small, but the girl was the only one she found with any trace of the Gift at all. She must pass on her knowledge. No fool, Mag'ra knew time was running out. She tamped down her anger and stored it. Emotion was a form of energy, energy that she could put to better use than expending it on empty air.

"I will get Zaya." And, she added to herself, my teeth! "About the supplies, I may not be so lucky. You organize the people and see what stores remain. The raiders did not have time to get them all. I'll return when I can."

Mag'ra brushed her gelding until he glistened; even his gray hairs took on a dull shine. One did not go to battle dirty. The past two seasons she'd had to cut Horse's oats to slim down his middle. Her legs refused to spread as far as they used to.

She glanced down at the earth. Though the snow-laden clouds hid the sun there was enough light to cast shadows. Their length revealed it was close to nooning. If she made good time, dusk would see her at Sharoon Keep, the abandoned hold the brigands had made their own.

It was a good thing Old Stern's sow was in labor last night, even if she had forgotten her teeth in her efforts to calm him. The brigands probably didn't even know the hermit existed or more than likely she wouldn't have the clothes on her back, or Horse to ride this day. She did not doubt that the Old One, Min of the Nine Words, had her hand in that!

The villagers were scared silly. She didn't blame them, but she was to old to be silly. Death no longer frightened her. It only created a sense of loss. To prevent that loss she needed Zaya or, hopefully, someone like Zaya with a stronger Gift. The people needed her lore knowledge and healing skills to survive, but more important, she must pass on to another the Gift of Min and the Power of the Old One's Nine Words. Today she'd use that Power, she knew that by its restless surging inside her. Min would not tolerate the Dark trying root itself in Her soil! As the Old One's Handmaiden she'd go forth to battle to prevent that!

Min's Nine Words directed her life. Her throat and tongue were not formed to utter the Old One's language and of necessity she had had to render them into human speech. Over the years of serving Min she'd come to realize the Power of words, all words. They shaped all life which spoke, for good or ill. It grieved her to see people destroy themselves by the words they used all unknowing what they did or the forces freed by their utterances. Few were those she found willing to learn this truth.

Mag'ra slapped Horse's neck. "I want my craft-daughter and my teeth back." With a grunt she mounted Horse and directed him toward the heights. Pulling her ankle-length, fur-lined cape around her, she arranged it so the folds, as much as possible, covered Horse. The cold hurt his bones, too.

Mag'ra watched for signs. The Old One would show her what Words were needed. Two of the Words she knew already. Sleep and renewal. The land itself told her. It was covered with snow, the cold sleep. Underneath winter's bounty earth-life slept silently, bearing in its slow beating heart, renewal.

The Old One cared more for life which went winged or on all fours than for those who walked upright. Even so, those who walked Min's ways were protected. Min also loved the earth and the life which rooted itself in soil.

Beneath an evergreen tree, in the late afternoon, the third Word revealed itself—Death. A winter fox, fur-breast spotted with blood, devoured the crow it had killed.

The snow creaked beneath Horse's feet, as with care he set down each hoof. Mag'ra leaned forward to ease his way up the increasingly steep incline. It wouldn't be long before the Keep's posted guards spotted her and gave challenge.

She listened and watched for Min's sign, warning her of the guards. If she was alert enough she'd see it. To her chagrin she'd missed them in the past. Ahead, on a snow-covered bush perched a field mouse, feeding on a small, apple-green berry. Its bright eyes met hers for a moment, then it spun, kicking up a miniature flurry of snow as it darted for cover. Mag'ra smiled. She cherished the Old One's flashes of Humor. Humor. Her fourth Word and Min's warning of the guards.

She drew back on Horse's reins and called out, "Ho, there! Guardians. I am Lore Mistress Mag'ra. Aid from the Lord of Sharoon Keep I come to claim."

Before and behind her two men stepped from their hiding places. They were dressed in white fur and gray leather. The man behind held a bow, arrow nocked and aimed at her. The young man to the fore carried a long staff. She recognized him. Not so long ago he'd come to her for healing.

"How are your ears, Guardsman Lentor?"

"They are well, Healer," he said. "What would you have of us?"

"To be taken to your lord."

"It is no fit place for you, mistress. Ask of me your need. Maybe I can help."

Mag'ra sought his eyes and held them with her own gaze. He was sincere and for that she gave answer. "I seem to have lost two things which are mine. One is my craft-daughter, the other is not your concern. It is said the men of Sharoon Keep know all the hiding places in the high hills and the valley of Min's Hold. I would ask of your lord assistance in finding and returning that which is mine."

"I . . . I can not. I . . . mean." He stuttered. Lentor glanced at the man behind her and his look was answered.

The older man walked up and took hold of Horse's bridle. "Lentor, she knows who has her property." He looked up at her. "What do you think you can do, Old Woman? Lord Radnor will crush your brittle bones, then throw your remains to carrion feeders!"

"Not necessarily," Mag'ra answered.

"Bah! You," he spat at the snow, "are a fool."

"Bass!" Lentor exclaimed. "Do not speak to Lore Mistress Mag'ra like that. She deserves your respect. She's saved many of our lives."

"Then let her save her own!"

Mag'ra waited until Bass looked at her. She held his gaze as she had Lentor's. His speech betrayed a good education; his face, fatigue and the bitterness that comes from deep grief. A man who'd lost all he held dear. Pity stirred within her. She hesitated, then shrugged. What she planned to do would not permanently hurt him. No one named Min's daughter fool. Mag'ra pointed a finger at him and spoke.

"Silence."

Bass backed away from her, his lips forming vowels of nothingness. He stumbled. Fell. His hands clutched his throat.

"Bass!" shouted Lentor. He knelt beside his friend, supporting his shoulders. "Mistress, what have you done?"

"For a time, sealed a fool's tongue. Now will you take me to Sharoon Keep?"

"On pain of death, we cannot leave our post."

Mag'ra thought for a moment. "You remain behind and watch and ward. Bass can lead me. Though his voice doesn't work, his legs do. You have mounts?" At his nod, she said, "Get one. We'll wait here for you."

"Bass, get up." She reined Horse over to him. Mag'ra chuckled at the look on his face. "You don't much like an old woman giving you orders. Well, I don't intend to continue if you decide to be reasonable." Holding out her hand she said, "Grab hold." Bass hesitated, then clasped her hand and stood. She pulled free and leaned down, touching his throat with her fingers.

"Speak." Mag'ra straightened in the saddle, rearranging her cape. "Haven't you anything to say?"

"I . . . I—"

"Be at peace. I did that to you to demonstrate old I may be—and at times foolish—still I am not without Power.

"You knew I was aware of who took my property and so you might, also, have guessed that I full well know my way to Sharoon Keep?"

Bass brushed the snow off his pants and said, "I have seen you there before when Lord Alesanfar ruled." He turned toward Lentor who led a gray-spotted black mare to him. He mounted.

"Come up beside me." Mag'ra kept careful watch on the sky and land around them. She needed five more Words. Nine Words in winter must be spoken for the Power she intended to invoke to come full circle. If not completed it would turn wild, possibly even seeking the Dark in its need to be complete. "The old lord, Alesanfar, was a good man. How are his children taking his death?"

"He's not . . ."

Mag'ra reined in Horse. "You mean he lives?"

"No. Yes."

"How can you say a man is dead and alive?" Bass had not halted his mount's progress. She urged Horse to once again match paces with him. When he did not answer, she asked, "His son and daughter?" Several moments went by and still he did not reply. She reached out and touched him. "I mean them no harm, only good!"

"Many children were killed when Radnor took the Keep. Alesanfar's son was one of these. Felde, his seven-year-old daughter, lives though she is hidden among the servants. Radnor believes she is also dead."

"Good." Leaving the question of Alesanfar for a moment she asked, "Have you seen Radnor practice sorcery?"

Bass shook his head. "I have not, but . . ."

"Go on. Do not hesitate to speak. I have heard rumors."

"I have led men in my time, mistress, and followed many more. Radnor's displines are harsh. What he wants, he takes. That is not so different from other men. Even his dark pleasure in the power he holds over us is like many men I've served under. But, never have I seen a man strip and destroy another's will."

"How does he do this?" She watched Bass's face grow still, then whiten.

"His eyes. Radnor's eyes." He shuddered and looked fearfully at her.

"I took not your mind, but your voice for a time," she reminded him.

"True." Bass sighed, turned, and looked full at her. "You intend to fight Radnor?" At her nod he said, "Alesanfar is tied to the cross beams in the Great Hall. Radnor is starving him to death. Most of the men have no idea how he continues to exist."

"But you do."

"One night, just before cock crow, I saw his daughter crawling across the beams bringing him food and water, which she fed him."

Mag'ra shut her eyes and sighed. Another Word. Courage. "Tell me. How is it that Radnor hasn't taken your will from you? I sense no touch of the Dark on you, except the blackness of grief."

"I obey every order that's given me."

"If Radnor tells you to kill me?"

"I will do it."

Mag'ra nodded in satisfaction. "To save your true lord and Felde, you will do anything?"

"I would."

Loyalty. The seventh Word was now hers. Ahead Mag'ra saw the open gates of Sharoon Keep.

"What have you there, Bass?" One of the men called out as they entered the inner ward of the Keep. "A spy?"

"No. A visitor for Radnor," answered Bass, dismounting and then helping her down from Horse. "Come with me."

They passed between two guards standing at attention just inside the Great Hall. Mag'ra was surprised to see how immaculate it was. More so than during Alesanfar's time. The rushes covering the stone floor were clean, the tables were stacked neatly against one wall. Fires burned in relatively ash-free hearths at the far ends of the oblong room. The only sound in the room came from the rustling of the rushes they walked on.

She preferred the noisy activity and the homey clutter of before.

The discordant notes in the Hall came from the emaciated, naked body, arms outstretched and lashed to an oak girder, hanging in the middle of the cross beam above them, and from the man sitting in the lord's chair on the dias.

Radnor was clean-shaven and dressed in a yellow, fur-trimmed robe. The light from the twin fires reflected off his dark hair and set the white streaks in it aglow.

Mag'ra focused her gaze on Radnor's nose, not ready to test her powers against his. She'd caught just a glimpse of his eyes when she stepped into the room. Yet even that was enough. For a moment she had almost faltered. His eyes were as yellow as his robes—completely yellow. Where white-rimmed irises and dark pupils should be was an abnormal, nearly complete blankness. Across the expanse of his saffron orbs swirled moving ribbons of red. Mag'ra shuddered at the thought of what the Sorcerer gazed upon, for she did not doubt that he could indeed see. A stench, that she associated only with the Dark, came from him, permeating the room.

She moved away from Bass and stood directly beneath Alesanfar, silently speaking the eighth Word Min revealed to her. Sacrifice.

When Radnor began to speak, the sound of his voice not only echoed throughout the room but his words set up a pounding wave of Power inside her that sought out her own. Mag'ra let his seeking Words meet one of Min's: Silence. And his Words were swallowed up.

"Radnor. I am Lore Mistress Mag'ra, and I come seeking aid from you and yours."

"Aid?" he asked.

"Yes. Early this morning our village was raided by brigands. Two of the things taken belong to me. I want them back."

"Are you saying that I have these things?" Radnor asked. the sardonic tones of his voice a sharp contrast to hers.

"Not at all. But the men of Sharoon Keep know the hills and valley as no others. I hoped you might ask them to watch for my belongings."

Radnor leaned forward in his chair. "What are these things? My men went on a foraging run this morning, maybe they have already discovered what you seek?"

"My craft-daughter Zaya. A girl of fourteen. She has brown hair and eyes."

"You only mention one item," Radnor said. "What is the other?"

"A gift."

"And what might that be? I insist on knowing."

By the tone of his voice Mag'ra knew he meant it, but she was not about to reveal it was her false teeth she sought. Even before one belonging to the Dark, a woman had her pride and more important, the lack of his knowledge might help defeat him.

"You may insist," she answered, "but I do not intend to tell you."

"Enough of this verbal fencing! You know my men raided your village. What I take I keep." He leaned forward. "Look at me!"

"No."

"Seize her!" he shouted.

Bass reached for her.

Before she could be restrained Mag'ra raised her hands and formed them into a small, cauldronlike hollow, cupping them around her lips and nose. The Old One's daughter whispered into them. As if she were presenting a most precious gift Mag'ra opened her hands, keeping the edges of the palms close together and her wrists touching her chin. She breathed upon the Power she held and dispersed Min's Word into the room. All heard the Word. Sleep. All responded to Min's command and slumped to the floor except for herself and Radnor.

"So," Radnor said, drawing out the small word. He stood. "You are more than a Lore Mistress. I was hoping to flush out one such as you."

She must be cautious. Each word they now spoke would carry deeper meaning.

Mag'ra thought of the snow fox she'd seen on the way here. The red blood of its prey on the fox's white breast had betrayed its presence. If she was to succeed by no gesture or word must she reveal the source of her Power. Each small bit of knowledge Radnor gained he could use against her. But that went for her, too. Mag'ra smiled, and spoke not.

"Old woman." Radnor laughed mockingly. "You have defeated yourself by betraying that which you sought. Two things you said. Your craft-daughter Zaya and something else. A thing?" He snorted. "I doubt that as you called it a gift. The chance you took in coming here to retrieve it indicates the gift is of great value. This I would indeed see for only Power wrapped in flesh and blood could be worth such a risk."

The Sorcerer lifted his hands and began to chant. His words slurred one into the other, until they sounded like the off-key drone of many hornets. The words, bound tight to one another, began to spiral outward as would the spinning waters of a whirlpool. A suck, drag, pull of force.

Mag'ra heard the doors to the Great Hall open, but she did not turn from Radnor. Footsteps sounded on the stone floors, barely stirring the rushes, and passed her, halting to one side of the steps leading to the dais. It was Zaya. Her clothing was disheveled and bruises marked her face; otherwise she appeared unhurt.

Beneath the sound of the sorcerer's chant came a small noise—a clattering and then a scraping on the stone floor behind her. Mag'ra listened intently. It was moving closer.

She was distracted by the sound of another set of footsteps moving through the doorway, though this person fought the summoning. These feet stumbled and dragged and at one point fell over one of the sleeping guards. Who could it be? Mag'ra silenced her instinctive urge to call the child's name as she came into view and halted just behind Zaya. It was Felde, Alesanfar's daughter. Piled up on child's feet, clear to the ankles, were rushes—mute evidence of her fight against Radnor's will.

The moment Radnor stopped chanting Mag'ra felt something bump against her foot. With a quick glance she looked down. She nearly laughed. It was her false teeth! The "thing" had responded. Radnor was deceived. Two young girls stood in answer to his summoning, not the true gift. Somehow she must find a way to use this hidden knowledge as a weapon against him.

"I have what you came for. Foolish woman, why a kitchen drudge?" When Mag'ra refused to answer he bent his thoughts upon the girl. "Lord Alesanfar's daughter. Thank you, Mistress Mag'ra. You have placed in my hands tools which I will wield. Two virgins. And one holding within her great untapped Power of her own. A gift indeed, of great price!" he exclaimed.

For a moment his words confused her. Zaya? She has but little of the Gift. What can the man be speaking of? Then she, too, looked at Felde with the Power. The girl, though immobilized by Radnor's summoning, still fought. Her eyes burned with rage. It was she who held a full Gifting! One such as Felde Mag'ra had sought for many years. The extremity of Felde's situation had forced an early birth of her Gift; usually the onset of womanhood brought that about.

The Dark will not have her. I claim Felde for the Light!

Mag'ra breathed in and tapped the reservoir of anger-induced energy she'd stored for this moment. She moved toward Radnor, sliding her teeth along with her foot.

"Halt!" Radnor commanded.

Mag'ra kept moving.

"I was drawn to this valley," the Dark's Sorcerer spoke, "because of the Power I sensed here. Though I sought, I did not find. You are its receptacle. And now it and you are mine! Be seated and bound to my will." He moved his hands in a sweeping motion.

Mag'ra staggered as his Power sought to draw her feet from beneath her. She regained her balance, and again slid her false teeth another few inches.

Radnor frowned. He raised clenched fists to shoulder height and looked fixedly at her. As if he were fighting against an unseen resistance Radnor began to move his fists together.

In response to the Sorcerer's action an invisible force pushed against either side of her head. Her ears felt as if they were being slowly pulverized by a vise. Mag'ra spoke the Word Courage in her mind. A fresh surge of Min's Power blossomed in answer. Mag'ra channeled that down her leg and into the teeth.

The Power focused on the teeth, she began to chant the Nine Words Min had given to her for this task. The teeth moved! She continued to chant. Renewal. Death. Humor. Silence. Loyalty. Sacrifice. Courage.

She faltered. The teeth slowed. Stopped. There was a gap in the circle of Min's Power. One Word was missing! Mag'ra fought off fear, not allowing herself to foster it, claiming Hope in its stead. In the opening moves with Radnor she'd forgotten that somewhere she'd missed the sign pertaining to the Old One's ninth Word. Without it, all would fail.

Min's Power and the Dark's met inside her and she rocked with the unleashed forces.

Through pain-filled eyes Mag'ra saw Radnor's fists move a fraction closer. She screamed. The pressure building within her head threatened to burst through her skull; frantically she diverted it to her nose. Blood spurted from it in response. A piece of her ear fell onto her shoulder and stopped its downward slide on her breast. Her eyes closed and she fell to her knees. To keep the Dark from taking root in Min's Hold she'd gladly Sacrifice both her ears. As with any strong emotion Mag'ra knew pain generated energy, too. She gathered the pain-induced force Radnor was battering her with and channeled it toward her teeth.

Mag'ra opened her eyes. The teeth had reached Radnor and they hung from the fur edging his cloak. The small silver rings hinging them sparkled in the firelight as they made their way upward. She must keep his attention solely on her.

"Young man, why are you having such a hard time defeating an old woman? Or didn't you realize just how withered I am. Of course you couldn't know," Mag'ra said in mocking tones of pity. "You are blind, aren't you?" She watched Radnor's yellow eyes through lowered lashes; she wasn't ready for a direct locking of will, yet. Across his orbs the red threads twisted in agitation.

Radnor grunted. His face contorted as he twisted his fists back and forth.

Mag'ra gasped. She had no breath to scream. More flesh and blood spattered from her ears. She fought to keep open the outlet that she was using to direct the pain's intense power toward the teeth.

Out of the corner of her eyes she saw Felde move jerkily toward Radnor. The child was watching the teeth! With Radnor expending energy on their battle, less of his will went to binding the girls.

Mag'ra dared not look at her false teeth nor the child, or she'd betray them both. Her physical strength was nearly gone. Summoning her will she lifted her hands, cupping them. A full circle of Power she did not have; even so she must act!

"Min. Min," she mouthed desperately. "Hear this Word and let it be used as your Handmaiden wills it!" Across the hollows of her hands she spoke, making full eye contact with Radnor for the first time, locking his gaze to hers. She breathed upon the Word, willing the Power up through her body, out of her eyes and across the invisible bridge that connected Radnor's eyes with hers. Using the pain he'd dealt her as a springboard she screamed.

"Death!"

He staggered, his hand dug at his eyes! Now it was her turn to hear Radnor scream. The Power he had used against her abruptly ceased.

Felde! The child had climbed up on the chair behind Radnor. Mag'ra watched her pluck the false teeth from his back. Radnor turned. Felde threw them!

In the firelight Mag'ra could see those porcelain fangs, the tips of the teeth Power changed! They gleamed in the light like shards of pointed ice. False no longer they became in truth Min's weapon.

The teeth latched onto Radnor's throat, sinking deep into his flesh and ripping it out! Blood stained his yellow robes. The Sorcerer fell to the floor, Min's Word taking full possession of him.

Mag'ra felt like laughing but did not have the strength. Who'd have guessed that a seven-year-old child and a pair of false teeth could defeat one of the Dark? She lay full-length upon the floor and fought to retain consciousness long enough to chant each of Min's Words one more time, to set the Power free to act. "Renewal. Death.

Humor . . ." Pain and fatigue overcame her; she could speak no more. Just for a moment she'd shut her eyes.

Someone kept shaking her. The side of her head pressed to the floor rocked on the rushes. She wanted to scream at the fool who touched her. Instead she opened her eyes. It was Zaya. She forced herself to focus on the girl. Her cheeks were wet from tears and her eyes revealed fear and confusion. As always, Zaya needed direction, something to do to keep her busy. Action shaped her life, inactivity made her feel uncertain. What can I give her to do? Ahh!

"Zaya, find Danner and tell him I need a new pair of teeth." At the look on her face Mag'ra chuckled. Above Zaya she saw Felde walking the beams to her father. Maybe Alesanfar would allow Felde to become her craft-child, too. But for now, that could wait.

Just as welcome sleep claimed her, Min's Ninth Word revealed itself. This was one of Min's touches of humor. An Afterward. Mag'ra laughed dryly. Humor could be painful at times. But she was the Old One's Handmaiden and across the years she'd come to appreciate these wry moments. Mag'ra smiled and as she whispered the last Word, felt the Old One's healing touch upon her ears.

"Triumph!"

\* \* \*

## Afterword

*The title "Nine Words in Winter" came first and the tale emerged from it. It was a story that told itself.*

*Historically the setting is near the time of Ully the Piper. Min's Hold is not too far from Coombfrome.*

*I grew up on the fruit of Andre's imagination and her Witch World tales stimulated mine. In that special place of "what happens next," I yearned to continue her stories. I feel privileged to have had the opportunity of doing just that.*

—CARALYN INKS

# WERE-HUNTER

## by

## Mercedes Lackey

It had been raining all day; cold, and dismal. Glenda trudged through it, sneakers soaked; beneath her cheap plastic raincoat her jeans were soggy to the knees. It was hours past sunset now, and still raining, and the city streets were deserted by all but the most hardy, the most desperate, and the faded few with nothing to lose.

Glenda was numbered among those last. This morning she'd spent her last change getting a bus to the welfare office, only to be told that she hadn't been a resident long enough to qualify for aid. The supercilious clerk had taken in her age and inexperience at a glance. If he had begun processing her, he'd have been late for lunch. He guessed she wouldn't know enough to contradict him, and he'd been right. And years of her aunt's browbeating ("Isn't one 'no' good enough for you?") had drummed into her the lesson that there were no second chances. This afternoon she'd eaten ketchup and crackers—there was nothing left in her larder that even resembled food. There were three days left in the month; three days of shelter, then she'd be kicked out of her shoddy efficiency and into the street.

When her Social Security orphan's benefits had run out when she'd turned eighteen, her aunt had "suggested" she find a job and support herself—elsewhere. The suggestion had come in the form of finding her belongings in boxes on the front porch with a letter to that effect on top of them.

So she'd tried, moving to this place near the university; a marginal neighborhood surrounded by bad blocks on three sides. There were no jobs if you had no experience—but how did you get experience without a job? Her aunt had never let her apply for a job. Her meager savings (meant, at one time, to pay for college tuition) were soon gone.

She rubbed the ring on her left hand, unthinkingly. That ring was all she had of the mother her aunt would never discuss. It was silver, and heavy; made in the shape of a crouching cat with tiny glints of topaz for eyes. Much as she treasured it, she would gladly have sold it—but she couldn't get it off her finger, she'd worn it for so long.

She splashed through the puddles, peering listlessly out from under the hood of her raincoat. Her lank, mouse-brown hair straggled into her eyes as she squinted against the glare of headlights on rain-glazed pavement. Despair had driven her into the street; despair kept her here. She could see no way out of this trap—except maybe by killing herself.

But then a chill of fear trickled down her backbone like a drop of icy rain, driving all thoughts of suicide from her, as behind her she recognized the sounds of footsteps.

She didn't have to turn around to know she was being followed, and by more than one. On a night like tonight, there was no one on the street but the fools—and the hunters.

One thing in her favor—she knew this neighborhood intimately; curiosity had kept her poking into every corner when job leads ran out. That curiosity had paid off in material things—as the old people who lived around here died off or were sent to nursing homes their belongings often ended up piled in the alleys. Glenda had made more than one windfall find in those dusty old cartons.

These scavenging hunts had also given her a mental map of every possible bolt-hole for use in an emergency.

There was only one such attainable at this hour—hiding in the backyard of the "witchhouse" wasn't appealing, but the alternative of facing those who dogged her heels now was less so.

The rain would help; she quickened her pace—not running, as that would only set them off, but moving just a tiny bit faster than they were. She dodged around a corner, taking a few steps at a run, then resuming her fast walk. The rain lashed her face; she stumbled but kept moving.

Around another corner; dart across the street just under the headlights of a car—squealing brakes and a string of obscenities marked that her pursuers were delayed just a few more seconds. She glanced back—there were five of them, wearing dark jackets with gang-symbols painted on them. She ducked around another corner; the mouth of the alley she sought was just ahead.

It wasn't much of an alley. *They* might not know it was there—even if they did, they couldn't know what lay at the end of it. She dodged inside, feeling her way, until one of the two buildings gave way to a seven-foot privacy fence.

She came to the dead end, the high board fence on the left. She listened, straining her ears for sounds behind her, taut with fear. Nothing; they'd passed the alley by, or hadn't reached it.

Quickly, before they could find the entrance, she ran her hand along the boards of the fence, counting them from the dead end. When she touched the sixth one, she gave it a shove sideways, getting a handful of splinters. But the board moved, and she squeezed through the gap into the yard beyond, pulling the board back in place behind her.

Just in time; echoing off the stone and brick of the alley were harsh young male voices. She leaned against the fence and shook from head to toe, clenching her teeth to keep them from chattering, as they searched the alley, found nothing, and finally (after hours, it seemed) went away.

"Well, you've got yourself in a fine mess," she said dully.

"Now what? You don't dare leave, not yet—they might have left someone in the street, watching. So now you get to spend the rest of the night in the backyard of a spookhouse. You'd just better hope the spook isn't home."

She peered through the dark at the shapeless bulk of the tri-story town house, relic of a previous century, hoping not to see any signs of life. The place had an uncanny reputation; even the gangs left it alone. People had vanished here. But the police had been over the house and grounds more than once, and never found anything. No bodies were buried in the backyard—the ground was as hard as cement under the inch-deep layer of soft sand that covered it. There was nothing at all but the sand and the rocks; the crazy woman that lived here told the police it was a "Zen garden." But it didn't look like any Zen garden *she* had ever read about. The sand wasn't groomed into wave-patterns, and the rocks looked more like something out of Stonehenge.

There were four of those rocks—one like a garden bench, three that formed a primitive arch. Glenda felt her way toward them in the dark, trusting to memory to find them. She barked her shin painfully on the "bench" rock, and her legs gave out, so that she sprawled ungracefully over it.

She sat huddled on the top of it in the dark, trying to judge what time it was. Dawn couldn't be too far off. When dawn came, and there were more people in the street, she could probably get safely back to her apartment.

For all the good it would do her.

Her stomach cramped with hunger, and despair clamped down on her again. She shouldn't have run—she was only delaying the inevitable. In two days she'd be out on the street, and this time with nowhere to hide; easy prey.

"So wouldn't you like to escape altogether?"

The soft voice out of the darkness nearly caused Glenda's heart to stop. Then the voice laughed, and oddly enough, the laughter seemed to make her fright wash out of her. There was nothing malicious about it—it was kind-sounding, gentle. Not crazy.

"Oh, I like to make people think I'm crazy; they leave me alone that way." The speaker was a dim shadow.

"Who—"

"I am the keeper of this place; not the first, certainly not the last. So there is nothing in this city—in this world—to hold you here anymore?"

"How—did you know that?" Glenda tried to see the speaker in the dim light reflected off the clouds, but could make out no details, just a human-shaped outline. Her eyes blurred. Reaction to her narrow escape, the cold, hunger; all three were conspiring to make her light-headed.

"The only ones who come to me are those who have no place *here,* yet still have the will to live. If another world opened before you, would you walk into it, not knowing what it held?"

This was surreal. Well, why not go along? "Sure, why not? It couldn't be any worse than here. It might be better."

"Then turn, and look behind you—and choose."

Glenda hesitated, then swung her legs over the bench-stone. The sky was lighter in that direction—dawn was breaking.

Now she *knew* she was hallucinating—for framed within the arch was no shadowy glimpse of board fence and rain-soaked sand, but a patch of reddening sky, and another dawn—

A dawn that broke over rolling hills covered with waving grass, grass stirred by a breeze that carried the scent of flowers, not the exhaust-tainted air of the city.

Glenda stood, unaware that she had done so. She reached forward with one hand, yearningly. The place seemed to call to something buried deep in her heart—and she wanted to answer.

"Here—or there? Choose now, child."

With an inarticulate cry, she stumbled toward the stones—

And found herself standing alone on a grassy hill.

After several hours of walking in wet, soggy tennis shoes, growing more spacey by the minute from hunger, she was beginning to think she'd made a mistake. Somewhere back behind her she'd lost her raincoat; she couldn't remember when she'd taken it off. The situation was frustrating, maddening; there was food all around her, on four feet, on wings—surely, even some of the plants were edible—but it was totally inaccessible to a city-bred girl who'd never gotten food from anywhere but a grocery or restaurant. She might just as well be on the moon.

Just as she thought that, she topped another rise to find herself looking at a strange, weatherbeaten man standing beside a rough pounded-dirt road.

She blinked in dumb amazement. He looked like something out of a King Arthur epic. He was stocky, blond-haired; he wore a shabby brown tunic and patched, shapeless trousers tucked into equally patched boots. He was also holding a strung bow, with an arrow nocked to it, and frowning—a most unfriendly expression.

He gabbled something at her. She blinked again. She knew a little Spanish; she'd taken German and French in high school. This didn't sound like any of those.

He repeated himself, a distinct edge to his voice. To emphasize his words, he jerked the point of the arrow off back the way she had come. It was pretty obvious he was telling her to be on her way.

"No, wait—please—" She stepped toward him, her hands outstretched pleadingly. The only reaction she got was that he raised the arrow to point at her chest, and drew it back.

"Look—I haven't got any weapons! I'm lost, I'm *hungry*—"

He drew the arrow a bit farther.

Suddenly it was all too much. She'd spent all her life being pushed and pushed—this was the last time *anybody* was going to back her into a corner—this time she was going to fight!

"Damn you!" She was so angry she could hardly think. "You stupid clod! *I need help!*" Red flashes interfered with her vision, her ears began to buzz, and her hands crooked into involuntary claws. *"Damn you and everybody that looks like you!"*

He backed up a pace, his blue eyes wide with surprise.

She was filled with fury that grew past controlling—she couldn't see, couldn't think. Suddenly she gasped as pain lanced from the top of her head to her toes, like a bolt of lightning—

—her vision blacked out; she fell to her hands and knees on the grass, her legs unable to hold her; convulsing with surges of pain in her arms and legs. Her feet, her hands felt as if she'd shoved them in a fire—her face felt as if someone were stretching it out of shape. And the ring finger of her left hand—it burned with more agony than both hands and feet put together! She shook her head; it spun around in dizzying circles. Her ears rang. There was a sound of cloth tearing—

Her sight cleared—distorted. She looked up at the man, who had dropped his bow and was backing away from her slowly, his face white with terror. She started to say something to him—

—and it came out a snarl.

With that, the man screeched, turned, and ran.

And she caught sight of her hand. It wasn't a hand anymore. It was a paw. A leopard's paw. Scattered around her were the ragged scraps of cloth that had once been her clothing.

Glenda lay in the sun on top of a rock, warm and drowsy with full-bellied contentment. Idly she washed one paw with her tongue, cleaning the last taint of blood from it. Before she'd had a chance to panic or go crazy back there when she'd realized what had happened to her, a rabbitlike creature had broken cover practically beneath her nose. Semistarvation and confusion had kept her dazed long enough for leopard-instincts to take over. She'd caught and killed the thing and had half eaten it before the reality of what she'd done and become broke through to her. But raw rabbit-thing tasted *fine* to leopard-Glenda; when she realized that, she relaxed and finished it. Now for the first time in weeks she was warm and content, and for the first time in years *she* was something to be afraid of. She gazed about her, taking in the grassy hills and breathing in the warm, hay-scented air with a growing contentment.

Becoming a leopard might not be a bad transformation.

Ears keener than a human's picked up the sound of dogs in the distance. It might be that the man she'd frightened went back home for help. They just *could* be hunting her.

Time to go.

She leaped down from her rock. Her sense of smell, so heightened now that it might have been a new sense altogether, had picked up the cool of running water off this way, and running water was a good way to break a trail; she'd read that.

Reveling in the power of the muscles beneath her sleek coat, she ran lightly over the slopes, moving through the grass that had been such a waist-high tangle to girl-Glenda with no impediment whatsoever. In almost no time at all, it seemed, she was pacing the side of the stream that she had scented.

It was quite wide, twenty feet or so, and seemed fairly deep in the middle. She waded into it up to her stomach, hissing a little at the cold and the feel of the water on her fur, trotting upstream until she found a place where the course had narrowed a little. It was still over her head, but she found she could swim it. The stream wound between the grassy hills, but there was rarely any more cover along them than a few scattered bushes. Something told her that she would be no match for the endurance of the hunting pack if she tried to escape across the grasslands. She stayed in the watercourse until she came to a wide valley. There were trees here; she waded onward until she found one leaning well over the streambed. Gathering herself and eyeing one broad branch, she leaped for it; landing awkwardly, having to scrabble with her claws fully extended to keep her balance.

She sprawled over it for a moment, panting, hearing the dogs nearing.

Time to move again. She climbed the tree up into the higher branches, finding a wide perch at least fifty or sixty feet off the ground. It was high enough that it was unlikely that anyone would spot her dappled hide among the dappled leaf-shadows, and afforded to leopard-eyes a good view of the ground and the stream.

As she'd expected, the humans with the dogs had figured out her scent-breaking ploy, and had split the pack, taking half along each side of the stream. She noted the man who had stopped her, and filed his scent away in her memory for the future. The others with him were dressed much the same as he, and carried knives and bows. They looked angry, confused; their voices held notes of fear. They looked into and under the trees with noticeable apprehension, evidently fearing what might dwell under their shade. Finally they gave up, and pulled the hounds off the fruitless quest; leaving her invisible above them, purring.

Several weeks later Glenda had found a place to lair up; a cave amid a tumble of boulders deep in the forest. She had also discovered why the hunters hadn't wanted to pursue her into the forest itself. There was a—thing—an evil presence, malicious, but invisible, that lurked in a circle of standing stones that glowed at night with a sickly yellow color. Fortunately it seemed unable to go beyond the bounds of the stones themselves. Glenda had been chasing a half-grown deer-beast that had run straight into the middle of the circle. She had nearly been caught there herself, and only the thing's preoccupation with the first prey had saved her. *That* had frightened her for a day.

Other than that peril, easily avoided, the forest seemed safe enough. She'd found the village the man had come from by following the dirt road; she'd spent long hours when she wasn't hunting lurking within range of sight and hearing of the place. Aided by some new sense she wasn't sure that she understood she was beginning to make some sense of their language. She understood at least two-thirds of what was being said now, and could usually guess the rest.

These people seemed to be stuck at some kind of feudal level—had been overrun by invaders the generation before, and were only now recovering from that. The hereditary rulers had mostly been killed in that war, and the population decimated. The man who'd stopped her had been on guard-duty and had mistrusted her appearance out of what they called "the Waste," and her strange clothing. When she'd transformed in front of his eyes, he must have decided she was some kind of witch.

Glenda had soon hunted the more easily caught game out; now when hunger drove her, she supplemented her diet with raids on the villagers' livestock. She was getting better at hunting, but she still was far from being an expert, and letting leopard-instincts take over involved surrendering herself to those instincts. She had the uneasy feeling that every time she did this she lost a little more of her humanity. Life as leopard-Glenda was much easier than as girl-Glenda, but it might be getting to be time to think about trying to regain her former shape—before she was lost to the leopard entirely.

She'd never been one for horror or fantasy stories, so her

only guide was vague recollections of fairy-tales and late-night werewolf movies.

But—maybe the light of the full moon would help.

She waited until full dark before setting off for her goal, a still pond in the far edge of the forest, well away from the stone circle, in a clearing that never seemed to become overgrown. It held a stone, too; a single pillar of some kind of bluish rock. That pillar had never "glowed" at night, at least not while Glenda had been there, but the pond and the clearing seemed to form a little pocket of peace. Whatever evil might lurk the forest, she was somehow sure it was barred from there.

The moon was well up by the time she reached it. White flowers had opened to the light, and a faint, crisp scent came from them. Glenda paced to the pool-side, and looked down into the dark, still water. She could see her leopard form reflected clearly, and over her right shoulder, the full moon.

Well, anger had gotten her into this shape, maybe anger would get her out. She closed her eyes for a moment, then began summoning all the force of that emotion she could —*willing* herself back into the form she'd always worn. Whatever power was playing games with her was *not* going to find her clay to be molded at will!

As nothing happened, her frustration mounted; soon she was at the boiling point. Damn everything! She—would —not—be—played—with—

The same incoherent fury that had seized her when she first changed washed over her a second time—and the same agonizing pain sent blackness in front of her eyes and flung her to lie twitching helplessly beside the pool. Her left forepaw felt like it was afire—

Then it was over, and she found herself sprawling beside the pond, shivering with cold and reaction, and totally naked. Naked, that is, except for the silver cat-ring, whose topaz eyes glowed hotly at her for a long moment before the light left them.

The second time she transformed to leopard was much easier; except for the pain. She decided against staying human—after finding herself in a perilously vulnerable and helpless form, leopard-Glenda seemed a much more viable alternative.

But the ability to switch back and forth proved to be very handy. The villagers had taken note of her raids on their stock; they began mounting a series of systematic hunts for her, even penetrating into the forest so long as it was by daylight. She learned, or remembered from reading, countless tricks to throw the hunters off, and being able to change from human to leopard and back again helped. There *were* places girl-Glenda could climb and hide that leopard-Glenda couldn't, and the switch in scents when she changed confused and frightened the dog-pack. She began feeling an amused sort of contempt for the villagers, often leading individual hunters on wild-goose chases for the fun of it when she became bored.

But on the whole, it was better to be leopard; leopard-Glenda was comfortable and content sleeping on rocks or on the dried leaves of her lair—girl-Glenda shivered and ached and wished for her roach-infested efficiency. Leopard-Glenda was perfectly happy on a diet of raw fish, flesh, and fowl—girl-Glenda wanted to throw up when she thought about it. Leopard-Glenda was content with nothing to do but tease the villagers and sleep in the sun when she wasn't hunting—girl-Glenda fretted, longed for a book, wondered if what she was doing was right . . .

So matters stood until midsummer.

Glenda woke, shivering, with a mouth gone dry with panic.

It wasn't just a nightmare. This dream had been so real she'd expected to wake with an arrow in her ribs. She was still panting with fright even now.

There had been a man—he hadn't looked much like any of the villagers; they were mostly blond or brown-haired, and of the kind of hefty build her aunt used to call "peasant-stock" in a tone of contempt. No, he had resembled her in a way—as if she were a kind of washed-out copy of the template from which his kind had been cut. Where her hair was a dark mousey-brown, his was just as dark, but the color was more intense. They had the same general build; thin, with prominent cheekbones. His eyes—

Her aunt had called her "cat-eyed," for she didn't have eyes of a normal brown, but more of a vague yellow, as washed-out as her hair. But *his* had been truly and intensely gold, with a greenish back-reflection like the eyes of a wild animal at night.

And those eyes had been filled with hunter-awareness; the eyes of a predator. And she had been his quarry!

The dream came back to her with extraordinary vividness; it had begun as she'd reached the edge of the forest, with him hot on her trail. He had no dogs, no aid but his own senses—yet nothing she'd done had confused him for more than a second. She'd even laid a false trail into the stone circle, something she'd never done before, but she was beginning to panic—he'd neatly avoided the trap. The hunt had begun near midmorning; by false dawn he'd brought her to bay and trapped her—

And that was when she'd awakened.

She spent the early hours of the morning pacing beside the pond, feeling almost impelled to go into the village yet afraid to do so. Finally the need to *see* grew too great; she crept to the edge of the village past the guards, and slipped into the maze of whole and half-ruined buildings that comprised it.

There was a larger market-crowd today; the usual market stalls had been augmented by strangers with more luxurious goods, foodstuffs, and even a couple of ragged entertainers. Evidently this was some sort of fair. With so many strangers about, Glenda was able to remain unseen. Her courage came back as she skirted the edge of the market-place, keeping to shadows and sheltering within half-tumbled walls, and the terror of the night seemed to become just one more shadow.

Finally she found an ideal perch—hiding in the shadow just under the eaves of a half-ruined building that had evidently once belonged to the local lordling, and in whose courtyard the market was usually held. From here she could see the entire court and yet remain unseen by humans and unscented by livestock.

She had begun to think her fears were entirely groundless—when she caught sight of a stranger coming out of the door of what passed for an inn here, speaking earnestly with the village headman. Her blood chilled, for the man was tall, dark-haired, and lean, and dressed entirely in dark leathers—like her dream.

He was too far away for her to see his face clearly, and she froze in place, following him intently without moving a muscle. The headman left him with a satisfied air, and the man gazed about him, as if looking for something—

He finally turned in her direction, and Glenda nearly died of fright—for the face was that of the man in her dream, and he was staring directly at her hiding place as though he knew exactly where and what she was!

She broke every rule she'd ever made for herself—broke cover, in full sight of the entire village. In the panicked, screaming mob, the hunter could only curse—for the milling, terror-struck villagers were only interested in fleeing in the opposite direction from where Glenda stood, tail lashing and snarling with fear.

She took advantage of the confusion to leap the wall of the courtyard and sprint for the safety of the forest. Halfway there she changed into human for a short run —there was no one to see her, and it might throw him off the track. Then at forest edge, once on the springy moss that would hold no tracks, she changed back to leopard. She paused in the shade for a moment, to get a quick drink from the stream, and to rest, for the full-out run from the village had tired her badly—only to look up, to see him standing directly across the stream from her. He was shading his eyes with one hand against the sun that beat down on him, and it seemed to her that he was smiling in triumph.

She choked on the water, and fled.

She called upon every trick she'd ever learned, laying false trails by the dozen; fording the stream as it threaded through the forest not once but several times; breaking her trail entirely by taking to the treetops on an area where she could cross several hundred feet without once having to set foot to the ground. She even drove a chance-met herd of deer-creatures across her back-trail, muddling the tracks past following. She didn't remember doing any of this in her dream. At last, panting with weariness, she doubled back to lair-up in the crotch of a huge tree, looking back down the way she had passed, certain that she would see him give up in frustration.

He walked so softly that even *her* keen ears couldn't detect his tread; she was only aware that he was there when she saw him. She froze—she hadn't really expected he'd get *this* far! But surely when he came to the place she'd taken to the branches, he would be baffled, for she'd first climbed as girl-Glenda, and there wasn't anyplace where the claw-marks of the leopard scored the trunks within sight of the ground.

He came to the place where her tracks ended—and closed his eyes, a frown-line between his brows. Late-afternoon sun filtered through the branches and touched his face; Glenda thought then that he had been totally fooled by her trick. He carried a strung bow; black as his clothing and highly polished, and wore a sword, which none of the villagers ever did. As her fear ebbed, she had time to think that he couldn't have been much older than she—and was very, very attractive.

As if that thought had touched something that signaled him, his eyes snapped open—and he looked straight through the branches that concealed her to rivet his own gaze on *her* eyes.

With a mew of terror she leaped out of the tree and ran in mindless panic as fast as she could set paw to ground.

The sun was reddening everything; she cringed and thought of blood. Then she thought of her dream, and the dweller-in-the-circle. If, instead of a false trail, she laid a *true* one—waiting for him at the end of it—

If she rushed him suddenly, she could probably startle him into the power of the thing that lived within the shelter of those stones. Once in the throes of its mental grip, she doubted he'd be able to escape.

It seemed a heaven-sent plan; she ran, leaving a clear trail behind her, to the place of the circle. By the time she reached its vicinity it was full dark—and she knew the power of the dweller was at its height in darkness. Yet, the closer she drew to those glowing stones, the slower her paws moved; and a building reluctance to do this thing weighed heavily on her. Soon she could see the stones shining ahead of her; in her mind she pictured the man's capture—his terror—his inevitable end.

Leopard-Glenda urged—kill!

Girl-Glenda wailed in fear of him, but stubbornly refused to put him in the power of *that*.

The two sides of her struggled, nearly tearing her physically in two as she half-shifted from one to the other, her outward form paralleling the struggle within.

At last, with a pathetic cry, the leopard turned in her tracks and ran from the circle. The will of girl-Glenda had won.

Whenever she paused to rest, she could hear him coming long before she'd even caught her breath. The stamina of a leopard is no match for that of a human; they are built for the short chase, not the long, and she was exhausted. He had driven her through the moon-lit clearings of the forest she knew out beyond the territory she had ranged before. This forest must extend deep into the Waste, and this was the direction he had driven her. Now she stumbled as she ran, no longer capable of clever tricks. Her eyes were glazed; her mind numb with terror. Her sides heaved as she panted, and her mouth was dry, her thirst a raging fire inside her.

It seemed as if her foe knew this section of the wilderness as well or better than she knew her own territory. She could not rid herself of the feeling that she was being driven to some goal only he knew.

Suddenly, as rock-cliff loomed before her, she realized that her worst fears were correct. He had herded her into a dead-end ravine, and there was no escape for the leopard.

The rock before her was sheer; to either side it slanted inward. The stone itself was brittle shale; almost unclimable—yet she began shifting into her human form to make that attempt. Then a sound from behind her told her that it was too late.

She whirled at bay, half human, half leopard, flanks heaving as she sucked in pain-filled gasps of air. He blocked the way out; dark and grim on the path, drawn bow in hand. She thought she saw his eyes shine with fierce joy even in the darkness of the ravine. She had no doubts that he could see her as easily as she saw him. There was nowhere to hide on either side of her.

Again leopard-instinct urged—kill!

Her claws extended, and she growled deep in her throat, half in fear, half in warning. He paced one step closer,

She could—she could fight him. She could dodge the arrow—at this range he could never get off the second. If she closed with him, she could kill him! His blood—

Kill!

*No!* Never, never had she harmed another human being,

not even the man who had denied her succor. No!

*Kill!*

She fought the leopard within, knowing that if it won, there would never be a girl-Glenda again; only the predator, the beast. And that would be the death of her—a death as real as that which any arrow could bring her.

And he watched from the shadows; terrible and menacing, yet—he did not move, not so much as a single muscle. If he had, perhaps the leopard would have won; fear triumphing over will. But he was still, so it was the human side of her that conquered.

And she waited, eyes fixed on his, for death.

:Gentle, lady.:

She started as the voice spoke in her head—then shook it wildly, certain that she had been driven mad at last.

:Be easy—do not fear me.:

Again that voice! She stared at him, wild-eyed—was he some kind of magician, to speak in her very thoughts?

And as if that were not startlement enough, she watched, dumbfounded, as he knelt, slowly—eased the arrow off the string of his bow—and laid both to one side. He held out hands now empty, his face fully in the moonlight—and *smiled.*

And rose—and—

At first she thought it was the moonlight that made him seem to writhe and blur. Then she thought that certainly her senses were deceiving her as her mind had—for his body *was* blurring, shifting, changing before her eyes, like a figure made of clay softening and blurring and becoming another shape altogether—

Until, where the hunter had been, stood a black leopard.

Glenda stared into the flames of the campfire, sipping at the warm wine, wrapped in a fur cloak, weary and drowsy. The wine, the cloak, and the campfire were all Harwin's.

For that was the name of the hunter—Harwin. He had coaxed her into her following him; then, once his camp had been reached, into human form again. He had given her no time to be shamed by her nakedness, for he had shrouded her in the cloak almost before the transformation was complete. Then he had built this warming fire from the banked coals of the old, and fed her, then pressed the wine on her. And all with slow, reassuring movements, as if he was quite well aware how readily she could be startled into transforming back and fleeing into the forest. And all without speaking much besides telling her his name; his silence not unfriendly, but as if he were waiting with patient courtesy for her to speak first.

She cleared her throat, and tentatively spoke her first words in this alien tongue, her own voice strange in her ears.

"Who—are you? *What* are you?"

He cocked his head to one side, his eyes narrowing in concentration, as he listened to her halting words.

"You speak the speech of the Dales as one who knows it only indifferently, lady," he replied, his words measured, slow, and pronounced with care, as if he guessed she needed slow speech to understand. "Yet you do not have the accent of Arvon—and I do not think you are one of the Old Ones. If I tell you who and what I am, will you do me like courtesy?"

"I—my name is Glenda. I couldn't do—this—at home. Wherever home is. I—I'm not sure what I am, or where."

"Then your home is not of this world?"

"There was"— it all seemed so vague, like a dream now— "a city. I—lived there, but not well. I was hunted—I found a place—a woman. I thought she was crazy, but—she said she knew an escape, and I saw this place—and I had to come—"

"A Gate, I think, and a Gate-Keeper." He nodded, as if to himself. "That explains much. So you found yourself here?"

"In the Waste. I walked—I met a man—I was tired, starving, and he tried to drive me away. I got mad."

"The rest I know," he said. "For Elvath himself told me of how you went Were before his eyes. Poor lady—how bewildered you must have been, with no one to tell you what was happening to you! And then?"

Haltingly, with much encouragement, she told him of her life in the forest; her learning to control her changes —and her side of the night's hunt.

"And the woman won over the beast," he finished. "And well for you that it did." His gold eyes were very somber, and he spoke with emphasis heavy in his words. "Had you turned on me, I doubt that you would ever have been able to become human again."

She shuddered. "What am I?" she asked at last, her eyes fixed pleadingly on his. "And where am I? And why has all this been happening to me?"

"I cannot answer the last for you, save only that I think you are here because your spirit never fit truly in that strange world from which you came. As for where—you are in the Dale lands of High Hallack, on the edge of the Waste—which tells you nothing, I know. And what you are—like me, you are plainly of some far-off strain of Were-blood. Well, perhaps not quite like me; among my kind the females are not known for being able to shape-change, and I myself am of half-blood only. My mother is Kildas of the Dales; my father Harl of the Wereriders. And I—I am Harwin," he smiled, ruefully, "of no place in particular."

"Why—why did you hunt me?" she asked. "Why did they want *you* to hunt me?"

"Because they had no notion of my Were-blood," he replied frankly. "They only know of my reputation as a hunter—shall I begin at the beginning? Perhaps it will give you some understanding of this world you have fallen into."

She nodded eagerly.

"Well—you may have learned that in my father's time the Dales were overrun by the Hounds of Alizon?" At her nod, he continued. "They had strange weapons at their disposal, and came very close to destroying all who opposed them. At that time my father and his brother-kin lived in the Waste, exiled for certain actions in the past from the land of Arvon, which lies to the north of the Waste. They—as I, as you—have the power of shape-change, and other powers as well. It came to the defenders of the Dales that one must battle strangeness with strangeness, and power with power; they made a pact with the Wereriders. In exchange for aid, they would send to them at the end of the war in the Year of the Unicorn twelve brides and one. You see, if all went well, the Wereriders' exile was to end then—but if all was not well, they would have remained in exile, and they did not wish their kind to die away. The war ended, the brides came—the exile ended. But one of the bridegrooms was—like me—of half-blood. And one of the brides was a maiden of Power. There was much trouble for them; when the trouble was at an end they left Arvon together. Now we come to my part of the tale. My mother Kildas has gifted my father with three children, of which two are a pleasure to his heart and of like mind with him. But I—"

"You're the misfit? The rebel?" she guessed.

"If by that you mean the one who seems destined always to anger his kin with all he says and does—aye. We cannot agree, my father and I. One day in his anger, he swore that I was another such as Herrel. Well, that was the first that *I* had ever heard of one of Were-blood who was like-minded with me—I plagued my mother and father both until they gave me the tale of Herrel Half-blood and his Witch-bride. And from that moment, I had no peace until I set out to find them. For surely, I thought, I would find true kin-feeling with them."

"And did you find them?"

"Not yet," he admitted. "At my mother's request I came here first, to give word to her kin that she was well, and happy, and greatly honored by her lord. Which is the entire truth. My father—loves her dearly; grants her every wish before she has a chance to voice it. I could wish to find a lady with whom—well, that was one of the reasons that I sought Herrel and his lady."

He was silent for so long, staring broodingly into the flames, that Glenda ventured to prompt him.

"So—you came here?"

"Eh? Oh, aye. And understandably enough, earned no small reputation among my mother-kin for hunting, though they little guessed in what form I did my tracking!" He grinned at her, and she found herself grinning back. "So when there were rumors of another Were here at the edge of the Waste—and a Were that thoughtlessly preyed on the beasts of these people as well as its rightful game—understandably enough, I came to hear of it. I thought at first that it must be Herrel, or a son. Imagine my surprise on coming here to learn that the Were was female! My reputation preceded me—the headman begged me to help—" He spread his hands wide. "The rest, you know."

"What—what will you do with me now?" she asked in a small, fearful voice.

"Do with you?" He seemed surprised. "Nothing—nothing not of your own will, lady. I am not going to harm you—and I am not like my father and brother, to force a one in my hand into anything against her wishes. I—I go forward as I had intended—to find Herrel. You, now that you know what your actions should *not* be, may remain here—"

"And?"

"And I shall tell them I have killed the monster. You shall be safe enough—only remember that you must *never* let the leopard control you, or you are lost. Truly, you should have someone to guide and teach you, though—"

"I—know that, now," she replied, very much aware of how attractive he was, gold eyes fixed on the fire, a lock of dark hair falling over his forehead. But no man had ever found her to be company to be sought-after. There was no reason to think that he might be hinting—

No reason, that is, until he looked full into her eyes, and she saw the wistful loneliness there, and a touch of pleading.

"I would be glad to teach you, lady," he said softly. "Forgive me if I am over-forward, and clumsy in my speech. But—I think you and I could companion well together on this quest of mine—and—I—" he dropped his eyes to the flames again, and blushed hotly "—I think you very fair."

"Me?" she squeaked, more startled than she had been since he transformed before her.

"Can you doubt it?" he replied softly, looking up eagerly. He held out one hand to her. "Would you—come with me?"

She touched his fingers with the hesitation of one who fears to break something. "You mean you really want me with you?"

"Since I touched your mind—lady, more than you could dream! We are mind-kin, I think."

She smiled suddenly, feeling almost light-headed with the revelations of the past few hours—then giggled, as an irrelevant thought came to her. "Harwin—what happens to your clothes?"

"My *what?*" He stared at her for a moment as if she had broken into a foreign tongue—then looked at her, and back at himself—and blushed, then grinned.

"Well? I mean, *I* left bits of jeans and T-shirt all over the Waste when *I* changed—"

"What happens to your ring, lady?"

"It—" Her forehead furrowed in thought. "I don't know, really. It's gone when I change, it's back when I change back." She regarded the tiny beast thoughtfully, and it seemed as if one of its topaz eyes closed in a slow wink.

"Were-magic, lady. And magic I think I shall let you avail yourself of, seeing as I can hardly let you go skyclad if you are to accompany me—" He rummaged briefly in his pack and came up with a shirt and breeches, both far too large for her, but that was soon remedied with a belt and much rolling of sleeves and cuffs. She dressed quickly under the shelter of his cloak.

"They'll really change with me?" She looked down at herself doubtfully.

"Why not try them?" He stood, and held out his hand—then blurred in that disconcerting way. The black leopard looked across the fire at her with eyes that glowed with warmth and approval.

:The night still has time to run, Glenda-my-lady. Will you not run with it, and me?:

The eyes of the cat-ring glowed with equal warmth, and Glenda found herself filled with a feeling of joy and freedom—and of *belonging*—that she tossed back her head and laughed aloud as she had never in her life done before. She stretched her own arms to the stars, and called on the power within her for the first time with joy instead of anger—

And there was no pain—only peace—as she transformed into a slim, lithe she-leopard, whose eyes met that of the he with a happiness that was heart-filling.

:Oh *yes*, Harwin-my-lord! Let us run the night to dawn!:

\* \* \*

## Afterword

*This used to be a song; one now called "Golden Eyes,"
although the original name was the same as the story's.*

*Then came the invitation from Andre to come play in her world. . . . Well, this was literally a dream come true, for ever since I had first set eyes on Witch World as a lonely misfit adolescent, I had longed to go there. Failing that, I longed to be able to write something set there, something Andre might see—and, dare I hope?—like.*

*It occurred to me immediately that since there was far more going on in the original song that I had written, this would be a perfect plot—especially since of all the peoples and creatures of Witch World, I felt most drawn to the Wereriders. But there was a problem: the females of that group do not share the shapechanging powers of the males. But then again—Estcarp males do not share Witch powers . . . and there was my answer. As with Simon Tregarth, my heroine would have to come from outside—our world. I checked with Andre, who told me that although the Gates were set to drop travelers in one particular spot (so Simon's Gate was out) she was certain there were several connecting here and there. And for my hero—who better than an offspring of one of the other thirteen brides from Year of the Unicorn. I chose Harl and Kildas because they were the most sympathetic of the couples to Herrel and Gillan, and perhaps the most likely to have birthed another Were-misfit. So there you have it, misfit from our world, misfit from theirs, finding that together they aren't such misfits after all. And a fantasy-dream held for twenty years come true. Thanks, Andre.*

—MERCEDES LACKEY

# NEITHER REST NOR REFUGE
## by
## Ardath Mayhar

I lay beside one of the small streams that feed into the wide, lazy rivers of Kars. The damp of the black soil was seeping into my clothing, and more than one crawling creature was finding refuge in my boots or my loose shirt, but I didn't move. Concealed by a thick screen of greenery, I watched a line of Duke Yvian's mercenaries as they rode along the road toward Gartholm.

I had no personal quarrel with the duke, to be sure, but when one is a refugee from one's own people one tends to be wary of everyone. Lying there, hearing the thud of the horses' hooves and the distant mutter of voices, the clink of weapons, I thought of the last day of my life in Estcarp. I had hidden, even there in my homeland.

It had been easy to conceal my unusual talents from the witches. Our stead was a remote one on the edge of the southern mountains. My mother was of the Old Race and knew how to deal with those who came to examine her daughters for the Talent they nurtured so jealously. Not one of them ever thought of testing my mother's son. Such things did not occur . . . males did not harbor that gift, though even we had heard rumors of an outlander who had some sort of power that made the witches squirm with discomfort.

My sisters had not desired to go to the training required

of those with such gifts. Both had managed to find lovers at incredibly early ages and so disqualify themselves. Their husbands now helped my father with the work of the stead, and my mother was pleased with the turn of events. Perhaps she had even advised and abetted my sisters in their method of escape.

My own betrayal came by no one's fault. I had been sent to a neighboring stead, across a wooded steep, after the seeds for which we traded each year. I had taken a shortcut, far above the road that had been cut into the hill, because two of the witches were traveling along it.

As I approached a steep bluff that had been undercut by the winter's rains, I saw the soil begin to shift. A landslide in those hills was always a thing to fear, and I knew that the women riding along the road would be buried alive if I did not act.

My years of secret practice, my covert lessoning at my mother's knee were the only possible sources of help. I braced myself against a treetrunk, well clear of the loosened spot, and strained to stabilize the creeping earth before it could become an avalanche. The boulders that were loosed in their places were diverted to strike big trees farther down the slope, so coming to a stop before they could do any damage.

I should have known that no use of such power could escape the notice of those on the road. The use of gifts, even without the utilization of the jewels they wore, could only bring them seeking the source of the disturbance they sensed.

I knew that whatever their reaction, it could only be terrible for me and for my mother. When I heard them climbing the slope, I fled. Without goodbye to my family, without any supplies other than those I carried for the short journey to our neighbor's stead, I left Estcarp and went up into the mountains.

The Falconers watched me, I knew, as I crossed along

their trails. Perhaps I might even have joined them, but I disliked the mountains. Driven to flight, I found myself strangely delighted with the notion of seeing strange places and meeting people different from those I knew.

The line of men was out of sight. I heaved a sigh of relief and crawled along the side of the stream until I came to a path. It was well-worn . . . probably being the one used by some neighboring village for reaching the water. A scrubbing-stone assured me that that must be the case, and I followed the track cautiously.

Before I had gone very far I stopped in my tracks. There was a village ahead . . . I could smell the distinctive odor that gathers where human beings group themselves. But there was another stench. Fire. Burnt meat. Death, which I had now learned to recognize a long way off.

Those men of Yvian's had come from this direction, though along the road instead of by the path. What had they done there?

I crept into the shrubbery edging the path, through a belt of trees, across a field whose crop of grain was tall enough to conceal me. As I drew nearer, the foreboding in my heart became stronger. As did the smell. Burnt bodies would smell so, I thought.

There were six houses grouped about a green knoll where a few sheep still huddled, looking about in a bewildered manner. Two of the houses were burning fiercely, and from the other four there came no sign of life.

I lay again behind a screen of greenery, trying to think why Yvian should be attacking his own people. It was not a thing that anyone with a brain would do, so far as I could see.

There were sprawled shapes lying about the area between the houses and the knoll. Not one moved as one of the houses collapsed with a roar, its thatch roof sinking into its fiery interior.

I crawled from my concealment and stood, looking

about. Then I went to bend over one of the bodies, that of an elderly woman. She had been brutally mistreated before having her throat cut. And she was of my own kind, though her black hair was strongly laced with gray, and her ivory skin was stained with age and blood.

My heart thudding painfully, I went from body to body. All were of the Old Race. All had been not only murdered but foully used before death. They had been left, too, for the birds and scavenger beasts to maul. That I could prevent.

I dragged them, one by one, to the door of the other burning house and laid them decently straight along its line. Then I brought armloads of the stacked wood left from the winter store and piled it over them. When that roof collapsed, it would fire the pyre and take their pitiful bodies with it.

As I worked, I found that I was crying. Until now, even though my danger had been real, it had seemed remote. Here I had found that to be of my kind was sufficient grounds for being condemned to death. That is a bitter lesson, and I, Jorem, at the age of nineteen, learned it with pain and passion.

Gulping back a sob, I set the last load of wood over the last pitiful body. A child. When I straightened my back I stood for a moment in the blazing heat so near the burning building, and I cursed long and bitterly, using terms that I had heard but never used before.

I thought for a moment that I had gone mad. Another voice was echoing my curses. It came from a pile of cattle fodder stacked along a stone wall. Even as I stood away from the burning house and started toward it, the hay began to stir. From beneath the pile came a slight figure that began sneezing and shaking itself free of straw and dust.

I hesitated to help, though many times I had assisted my sisters in such difficulties. She had probably been terrified.

Now she could not know that I was to be trusted, so I stood back and let her tidy herself as well as she could.

Even as I waited, others of the houses began to show signs of smoke . . . the fire must have been cast into less hospitable spots there, I thought. The girl stopped her efforts and turned to watch the next roof burst into flames.

"My father's house!" she moaned. "Mother?" She turned frantic eyes toward me.

I had to shake my head. "I saw no one living as I put them to rest. There were six women, four men, five children. If your mother is there, I will try to find her, but it will be a perilous business."

She shook her head, in turn. "There were only six women here. Four men. Six children . . . I am the only one left, and I am no longer to be considered a child. But what will become of me? Everyone . . . everything . . . all is gone!"

Something in the air seemed to be trying to warn me . . . I could not know of what. I reached for her hand.

"This is no place to stay and ask questions. Someone is coming. We must hide ourselves, unless we want to join your people. And there will be nobody left to burn our bodies. Come!"

I led her quickly into the field from which I had crawled, and we dropped to hands and knees and made our way to the wood-plot beyond. There we crouched behind a fallen log, risking peeps from our shadowy retreat.

Six horsemen rode into the blazing village. Their mounts shied and snorted at the smoke and the smell of death, but their riders pulled them up and sat staring about. One, seemingly the leader by his fine mail shirt and ornate helm, gestured about.

"He has seen that someone survived . . . the bodies in the fire . . . he wants to know who. The duke evidently wants all of us dead." The girl's voice was quiet, but its edge was steely.

I didn't wait to ask her why or how. I slid backward toward the stream, and we went into the water and slipped downstream beneath the cover of the ferny banks until we were far below the path that had led to that dead village.

When we came out, we were sodden, chilled, and the sun was down. "We must have a fire," I said. "We will catch our deaths, if we stay wet all night."

She put out a warning hand, barely visible in the tenuous twilight. "We of the Old Race were thrice horned! Everyone will hunt us. We cannot risk it."

"Horned? Why?" I was stunned, though I should have suspected that something of the kind had happened.

"They read a proclamation. There was something about a raid out of Estcarp. Nonsense, and all of us knew it, but it changed nothing. The mercenaries attacked at once. I had just time to dive into the hay and burrow deep. I . . . didn't watch."

I reached to take her hand. "What is your name?" I asked, simply to change the direction of her thoughts.

"Thelia. Daughter of . . ." She choked quiet.

"I, too, have lost my people. Not through death, but it seems to be just as final as that might be." I looked down at her in the dim light. "And what will be final is our deaths, if we don't have fire. Come with me."

I went into a thick wood, filled with deadfall and tangles of vine. It was evident that no one had come here, even to gather fuel, in generations. The thick crown of treetops above would surely hide our smoke.

There was no problem in finding enough dried stuff to make fire. Quick work with flint and steel set a spark, which grew into a tiny blaze. I left Thelia to nurse it along as I cleared a wide space around the area to keep the flame from spreading. Then I went blundering into the darkness and brought back armloads of branches broken from fallen trees.

"Dry wood makes little smoke. The light cannot be

seen . . . this wood is too thick to let any light through. We can dry ourselves. Then, if we feel the need, we can move away from this spot before daylight."

She stared up at me, her triangular face ivory-pale, smudged with smoke and tears and dust. Even our journey in the stream hadn't succeeded in cleaning away the traces of her experience. But her gaze was now steady and fearless. Something in her look made me wonder how any rider of Duke Yvian's would fare if he encountered her armed and ready.

I shrugged out of my loose shirt, spread the things out of my small pack to dry beside the blaze. The warmth was grateful against my skin, and I turned about, hearing the cloth of my nether garments begin to steam.

Thelia watched for a moment; then she slipped off her over-tunic and spread it beside my own things. She stood beside me, back to the fire. I could hear her sigh of relief when the clammy cloth began to warm.

I tried not to stare, but the wet material of her undergarment outlined her slender body with great fidelity. She was, as she had said, no child, no matter how lacking she might be in inches. Her pale face was beginning to flush with the warmth. She was no beauty, but there was something about her that tugged at me. She was not unlike one of my sisters . . . yet what I was beginning to feel I had never felt toward a sister. It embarrassed me, and I turned about to warm my other side.

There came a light chuckle from behind me. I began to blush and felt that go down my neck and over my bare chest. Blast! She could see me blushing. The chuckle grew stronger.

I turned around again and sighed. The lines of stress that had made her small face so stark and grim were now eased. She looked at once younger and more mature.

"Jorem, you're a very nice person," she said. "I am glad it was you who came. But where are we going now? We cannot stay in the woods. We cannot go by the roads. Anyone seeing us is justified in killing us on sight. What are we to do?"

I had been thinking along those lines myself. The Old Race was stamped on my own face, as well as hers, for I resembled my mother, not my Sulcar father. I, too, was subject to that horning, caught in the same web of vicious intent that had destroyed Thelia's home.

I sat and patted the ground beside me. She dropped to sit there.

"It is time I told you of myself," I said. "You should be warned, for you may see things that shock you . . . that you believe are impossible. I . . ." I glanced sidewise at her . . . "I have something of the gift the women of our kind possess."

She turned to look squarely into my eyes. "You? A male? How can that be? It is considered impossible!"

I turned my gaze to the fire. "I am not trained . . . only insofar as my mother knew a few matters she could pass on to me. She had no great gift herself, though my sisters did until they . . . disqualified themselves. I seldom can accomplish anything if I set about it intentionally."

I risked another glance at her, and she was still staring. "An emergency seems to—to pull it out of me. Once one of our cattle was swept downstream in the spring flooding. I reached out, in some way I didn't understand at all, and pulled her back to a spot shallow enough for her to find her footing. That was how my people learned that they had spawned a freak."

"Is that why you are here?" she asked. "Because of what you are? I can imagine that the Witches do not approve of such exceptions to their rules."

"I kept a hillside from sliding down on a pair of them. That would not have made any difference in their treatment of me—or of my mother—if they had seen that it was a man who saved them. So I hid, and then I ran. They may suspect, but suspicion is not enough to empower them to make trouble for my folk. I have done a few things since . . . small matters to save my own skin . . . that make me understand something of the gift. Are you shocked?"

A small hand took mine. "No. After today, nothing will ever shock me again. No gift saved my people. No Witch came to do so much as ease their dying. You were there, and you did what you could to help. I cannot go back to my people, and you cannot go to yours. We will be our own people, a family perhaps, for a time. Will you do that?"

I closed my fingers about hers. It was a comfort, after all those weeks of homeless tramping, to feel a human touch and concern for another. We were young. We were probably helpless, if faced with armed men or fully trained power, but until such time we would do what we could. I felt the same thought in her.

In the end, we went down the stream. It would end, I knew at the start, at a river. And rivers led to the sea. My father's blood, while it didn't show in my face or body, ran strong in my spirit. I had never seen a sea, yet I knew what it must be. Pounding waves sometimes accompanied my dreams, and vessels rigged with tall sails somehow lived inside my mind. A Sulcarman, no matter if he be a generation removed from it, could survive in or near the broad waters.

It was not an easy or a safe journey. Only the fact that only those aboard boats or barges were expected to be traveling along a river saved us from discovery. We contrived a raft that looked like floating brush. Buried in the nestlike mess atop it, we drifted slowly past villages, past Gartholm itself, and approached the environs of Kars.

I would have liked to pass by night, but there was no way to steer our makeshift craft to shore. We came by day, at midafternoon, and we burrowed deep into the brush on our raft to avoid detection by anyone on the river or ashore.

Strangely, I could see no guard set at the docks. The city was covered with a thin layer of smoke, as if houses had burned recently. The horning must have begun there, to spread outward like ripples on a pond. Straining to see between branches, we peered at the city as long as it was within sight. It was frustrating not to know what was happening there.

A deep bend below Kars brought us to near-disaster. There was an eddy there that sucked down our raft and, almost, our struggling bodies. We made it to shore breathless and exhausted. This was no well-wooded riverbank but a low, sandy curve backed by open fields and a road that seemed well used. Even as we pulled ourselves onto the sand, hoofbeats came along that road, and a voice roared an order.

I looked up in time to see an armored figure scoop Thelia beneath one arm and head toward a horse, ignoring her struggles. Another was coming toward me, dart-gun at the ready. I saw my own death in the eyes of the man who now stood over me.

He moved slowly, a grin splitting his thin-lipped mouth. Fury ran through me in a hot flood. Hatred for anyone who could kill so casually and causelessly.

Something took me into its hands and began to wring me in its grip. Darkness behind my eyes . . . darkness and anger and red rage . . . I felt my head bursting with pressure. Something went from me in a sear of force, and I lay limp on the sandy edge of the road, facedown, shaking.

After a time there was a touch at my shoulder. Light. Tentative. Almost fearful?

I groaned and turned myself to face upward.

Thelia sat on the ground beside me. Her eyes were wide, and her face was even paler than it had been after her ordeal.

I sat convulsively. Pain shot through me, and I gasped as I looked around us. Four men lay on the road, with their horses collapsed either under or beside them.

"What happened?" I asked.

She shook her head. "I don't know, precisely. But you did it, whatever it was. They just . . . fell. Unconscious. They're not dead. We'd better do something before they come back to consciousness."

The horses were beginning to twitch. Even as I watched, one quivered and tried to rise and stand, failed, then succeeded. That drove me to hurry to the side of the nearest man. I rolled him over, stripped off his mail and helm, then tied him with strips torn from his own leather undercoat. When I looked up, Thelia was serving another the same way. Before any of them recovered their senses, we had them well trussed and rolled into a small ditch in the field.

We tumbled the extra two saddles into the ditch with them and loaded the extra horses, now recovered, to look like pack animals. The trappings taken from one of the men fitted me fairly well, but the smallest of them had worn mail large enough to swallow Thelia. She hadn't the stature to masquerade as a soldier, anyway. So we cut away her long black hair, put a metal cap on her head, and contrived breeches from her short leather skirt. She made a passable boy, perched on the smallest of the horses.

Then, bold as suns, we set out along the road that led, Thelia assured me, to the coast and the sea, ending at the sea-keep called Verlaine. The few patrols we passed did not challenge us. Before two days were gone, we had passed beyond the well-traveled portion of that road and were in rocky country where there were no farms or villages.

All the way, I was half watching for danger and half concerned inside myself with the last manifestation of the gift that had come, so unsought and unexpected, to me. It was a frightening thing. Before this, I had consciously done something to cause the effects I'd achieved. This had come from some layer of me that I had not known was there.

Fired by anger, it had brought up from my own depths a destructive power I had not known I possessed.

Thelia, riding silently behind me, had said nothing. She knew, I think, what turmoil was troubling me. When we camped, at last, beside the cliff on whose other side the waves thundered, she spoke.

We were sitting beside a skimpy fire built of sea-wrack brought up from a small cove. The horses had grazed a bit on the salt grass and returned to the fire, standing about with eyes sparking reflections of the firelight.

Thelia put a chunk of anonymous wood onto the flames, and the fire burned blue and green for a time. When it had turned red again, she turned to face me.

"You are troubled. About that power you possess . . . or that possesses you. Why? It saved us both, you from death, me from death after . . . much worse. What gives you cause for concern?"

I had been asking myself the same question. While I had been reared in a remote place, we had known visitors, tale-tellers, people who knew the ways of Estcarp and other parts of our world. I was not ignorant, for all my inexperience. I knew that power, however come by, no matter how unexpected or unorthodox, is better than no power at all. Yet my qualms were real, for all that.

"I think it may be that I cannot control this thing. I have no training that gives me a rein on it. It takes over, as you have seen, and does things that I only know about afterward. It is frightening. I want to know what I do and to do it purposely. I feel helpless and in the grip of something stronger and more dangerous than I want to become."

It sounded strange, even to me. Weak. Even cowardly. But Thelia seemed to understand.

She nodded, her face bright in the firelight. "I see. I understand. You need training. I may be able to help you."

Something came alert inside me. "You . . . have been so trained?"

She laughed. "No. Not I. But I went with my youngest sister, when she was sent by my mother for such training. She had less than enough talent and came home again, but I know the woman who can teach such skills. I can find her, I believe. Few can . . . she does not advertise herself to the world."

"I did not know that any in Karsten practiced such witcheries as are done in Estcarp," I said.

"Few do. None have ever done it openly. Those able to teach what is needful can be numbered on one hand—or could be. Possibly only Sabyl is left, now. She lives in such a remote spot that even those carrying the word of the horning could not find her and would not know to seek for her."

"You call her name? I thought that was never done."

Thelia sighed. "She is no longer a practicing witch. She married, but for some reason a part of her gift remained with her. Enough for teaching those with the power how to use it. Now, widowed, she lives alone in a cove . . ." she glanced up shyly from beneath her straight black brows . . . "on the coast."

I sat straight, hope blossoming inside me. "You can find her? She can teach me?"

"If she is not too appalled at your sex to make the attempt. If she has not been found by accident and done to death. If I can find her again." Thelia smiled across the blaze.

For the first time since that burst of black anger, I felt a lightening of the spirit. If I could only be trained, be made to feel that I was not some sort of dangerous creature that might explode into destructive violence to the detriment of those about me, I could live with what I was.

I might return home again, an equal to those women who had frightened me into flight . . . For a moment I dreamed. Then I relinquished the dream. Whatever befell, those would not relent toward any man who challenged their sole possession of power. My mother had known that. I knew it.

But with Thelia I did not need others. In the time since our first meeting, she had worked herself into my heart.

If she brought me to Sabyl, and if Sabyl taught me what was needful, the two of us might well find a way to redress some of the wrongs done to her people. Thelia, small as she was, held determination worthy of one twice her size. I had a talent that was useless in my own place but, just perhaps, highly valuable in hers.

I smiled back at her. "If I can learn what she has to teach . . . would you be interested in going back with me? Back into Karsten? To learn what has been done to our people? Even . . ." I set a stick carefully across the flames . . . "to require some payment for the suffering of your family and all those others destroyed by the horning?"

The blaze leaped up in a crackle of green and orange and blue. Her eyes were gleaming in the paleness of her face.

"You would go to war? At my side? Then I will surely find Sabyl. We will go back together into Karsten, and we will work our will upon this foul duke, or, lacking him, upon his mercenaries."

The coals were growing red, and their color shaded her face. She nodded, once, decisively. "Jorem of Estcarp, we will go to war together."

And afterward? I found it didn't matter, so long as we went side by side.

\* \* \*

## Afterword

*Having been led gently into the world of fantasy by Andre Norton at a tender age, it is natural that I should feel that I* live, at least partially, in her Witch World. The musical language, the mind-expanding concepts she used in the series of books dealing with that world seem to have helped my own creative imagination to flower.

The horning, as described in the first book, has always intrigued me . . . what shocking and unexpected devastation was visited upon those unsuspecting members of the Old Race! I also liked the concept that a male *could* possess the powers that the witches claimed solely for female use. The combination of ideas grew into this story, which was a lot of fun to write.

—ARDATH MAYHAR

# TO REBUILD THE EYRIE
## by
## Sasha Miller

Eirran shook her hands until the blood began working back through them. She rubbed her mouth; it felt as if it had been stretched out of shape from the gag the man had stuffed in it. The man had knotted the rope into a hobble, tied her feet, and tethered her to a tree as if she were an animal. Well, at least the blindfold was off. She squinted until the light no longer hurt her eyes. She wanted to get a good look at her captor.

"You!" she said, sounding more surprised than she felt. It was just as she had surmised; after all, she had spent the entire day pressed against his body. He was the young man from last night at the tavern. The good-looking one.

"Silence, woman," he said.

"What? You bind and gag me while I'm sleeping, take me who knows where, finally let me down off that splay-footed, awkward gaited nag of yours and then bid me keep silence? I'll show you what kind of silence I'll keep!" She clenched her fists at her sides and began to scream. The man merely glanced at her and paid no attention to her outcries.

"You can scream until you lose your voice," he said calmly. "Nobody will hear you."

Eirran stopped screaming; she had begun to hiccup.

"Damn you," she muttered. *"Hic!"* They were hard hiccups, deep and painful, but not hurting as much as the discomfort of the day's ride. The man had set her in front of him in the saddle, holding her without regard to how she fared or where she was bruised. The cast-off shift she used as nightgown was nearly torn off her by now. She had heard and felt him ripping pieces away as they rode, and panic threatened to overcome her. The brambles had caught at her flesh, and her legs were scratched and bloody. "They'll come looking for—*hic!*—me, you know."

The man shrugged. Now that she had a chance to look at him in the day's fading light, she could see that he was young, with brown hair and eyes that gave off golden glints when seen at certain angles. Why would such a one be moved to kidnap a tavern-keeper's niece?

"Let them look," the man said. He gave a shrill whistle and a bird came swooping down from the clouds to settle on his wrist. It was black, marked with a deep V on its breast. Jesses hung from its feet. She could swear that the man and the bird spoke to each other, making *eek-ik-eek* noises back and forth. Once more the bird lifted itself into the air. It soared, riding the air currents above the small valley the man had chosen for their evening camp. "My feathered brother will give me ample warning if anyone should be able to decipher the false trails I've left this day."

Eirran shuddered and hiccupped again. A Falconer! It could be no other. But why? How? A dozen questions crowded into her mouth, but the only one that made it past her teeth was perhaps the least important and certainly the least likely to be answered. "What is your name?"

He turned and looked at her, and the golden flecks in his eyes flashed in the late-day sun. "That is no concern of yours, woman. I've let you rest. You have room enough to move around. Get busy now. Make a fire. Prepare a meal."

Her temper flared again. "Make your own fire if you want one, and your own meal, too! I'm not doing anything for you, not until I find out who you are, and what you intend to do with me!"

He shrugged again. "As you wish," he said, and went to tend to his horse. It was a rough-coated beast, not beautiful to look upon, but it didn't seem particularly wearied by the double burden it had carried that day. It had to be one of the fabled Torgian breed. The Falconer took off the saddle pad and the leather bags, rubbed down the horse, and turned it loose to find forage. There was plenty of high grass nearby, and presently Eirran heard the animal munching contentedly. The sound reminded her she had neither eaten nor drunk since the previous night.

"I'm your prisoner," she said, trying to appear more calm, not anger him in turn. "Your—*hic!*—captive. I don't have any obligation to take care of you. Don't you even know that much?"

He stared at her. "You're my woman—a woman," he corrected himself. "If you don't work, you don't eat. But you can have some water." He tossed a half-full skin toward her and she nearly dropped it. Her hands still weren't working properly.

"Thank you," she said. She drank greedily, and her hiccups ceased. She put the stopper back in the neck of the skin and watched while he made camp.

He took something out of the bag, wrapped in a cloth whose weave she recognized. It was the end of the hind-quarter of mutton she had put away in the kitchen the previous night. He gnawed at the bone, tearing off strips of meat with strong white teeth. She turned away, appetite suddenly gone. She heard him opening the bag again, closing it. He got to his feet and came toward her.

The moment she had been dreading arrived. She knew little about Falconers, just the stories men told in her uncle's public house on the road between Kars and Verlaine, and then they were seldom the main part of the tales. Falconers were supposed to be woman-haters, but she could think of no other reason for any man to steal a woman from her bed in the night save one. The one her uncle had recently begun to urge her to. For money. Money that she wouldn't be allowed to keep. She stared at the Falconer across the flickering fire.

"No matter how you covered your trail, they'll still come looking for me," she said. She rubbed her hands. They were only a little less swollen, and her mother's ring cut cruelly into her finger. She was surprised she still had it.

"They won't find us." He stared up at the sky at a dot that grew larger as the falcon came down at last and perched on a nearby limb. "They haven't discovered the trail I left for them yet. By tomorrow night we'll be beyond tracking."

"Where are you taking me?" Anything to distract him, to keep him talking.

He looked at her. She was struck by the expression of dislike that was plain on his face. "No reason to hide it, I suppose. We're going into the mountains. You're the first. When I'm finished, there'll be a new Eyrie, a new women's village."

Cautiously, lest she dry up his words, she probed further. "But—but I thought the Falconer way of life was no more."

He scowled. "So everyone thinks. The Old Ones, the enemies. But I have decided to bring it back."

"With me."

"Yes. I—I watched you, last night at the tavern."

She had done her share of looking at him as well, at the young man sitting in the shadows, his hood drawn up, and only an occasional gleam of fire or lamp showing his attractive features, and took pleasure in the fact that she was being observed. She hadn't had any idea he was a Falconer. "Yes," she said. "I saw you looking."

"I heard your name," he continued as if she hadn't spoken, "and then I knew. Eirran. It sounded so—so—"

She almost jumped, startled. Eirran, Eyrie. The sounds were close. "And for that—" she said incredulously, "for *that* you stole me away? For a *name?*"

"It was a sign. You're a woman and the truth is not in you, but you'll do for a start. And later, when my brothers in flesh come and see, they'll bring women also. We'll keep them in the village, just like in the old days. The Falconers will flourish once more!"

"Never!" she exclaimed.

The spell broke. If he had once been considering forcing himself on her, that thought was gone now. He turned and stared coldly at her, the amber flecks in his eyes catching sparks from the firelight. Then he got up and rummaged in the saddlebags once more, coming back to where she sat. He flung some garments at her; if she hadn't put up her arms they would have hit her across the face. "Put these on," he said curtly.

She examined the clothing—it was man's gear, trews and tunic. It was wrinkled and smelled of the saddlebag, but the clothing was clean enough. Probably some of his spare garments; she recognized none of them as having been stolen from the tavern. She looked up at him and let her lip curl with disgust. "And how do you suggest I get into these—these things?" She indicated the rope hobble on her ankles. The intricate knots were beyond her ability to untie with her swollen hands. She could barely flex her fingers, and there were deep marks scored on her wrists.

For the first time, he appeared flustered, not entirely in command. "I don't want to untie you—"

"You'll have to, if I'm to dress myself in other than these rags." She brushed at her tattered nightgown. A bare thigh gleamed in the firelight. She knew now that he had ripped bits of cloth from the garment during the day's journey to use while he was laying the false trail. "Don't worry, I won't run away." She wriggled her toes. "You didn't think to bring my shoes, and I warrant you've no second pair of boots. Anyway, I'm more afraid of what's out there—" she indicated the darkness outside the circle of their fire "—than I am of *you.*" She put all the scorn and derision she felt at that moment into the word.

Stung, he glared at her. But he untied the rope and coiled it away. "You'll learn better," he muttered.

"Ha!" She tossed her head. "Now, where's my blanket? Or am I to cover myself with branches?"

He threw a blanket at her even more forcefully than he had the clothing. "Here!" he said. "Do as you please! I'm beginning to be sorry I ever brought you with me!"

She took the blanket and headed for the shelter of a bush. Presently she returned, clad in his spare garments. They were too big for her, but anything was better than the ruined shift. He had banked the coals of their fire and was asleep or pretending to be, wrapped in his cloak. She neither knew nor cared. She put the blanket on the opposite side of the little fire pit. Worn out by the day's events, she quickly fell asleep.

Next morning, he started to bury her cast-off shift, but she stopped him in time. "We need the cloth," she said, "since you didn't allow me the luxury of throwing a few things into a sack to bring with me."

She tore away part of the shift and wrapped pieces of the thin fabric around her feet. "I don't suppose you've got any thongs or thin cords, do you," she said as she worked. "Only ropes."

But he surprised her by producing a set of leather ribbons, red-dyed. She recognized them as more elaborate versions of those the bird bore. He whistled the falcon to him, and changed the jesses with a surprisingly gentle touch. "Newhold can wear his good one," he said, and handed her the old set.

Her mother used to touch her like that. Her mother— Quickly, she tied the cloth wraps in place and stood up.

"We could have breakfast from those berries over there," she said, indicating a bush just outside the circle of their camp.

He frowned. "What makes you think they're not poisonous?"

"Other birds, smaller ones. They've been at the berries and they won't bother harmful ones," she said patiently. "They're not there now, of course, lest your falcon make his own breakfast from one of them."

"Eat, if you wish," he said, and shrugged. She realized he was refusing to admit a morning hunger, out of pride, or disdain. Yet he had rested the night before, and eaten too.

She made a pocket of the hem of her tunic, filling it with more berries than she could eat, and brought them back to where he was burying the last traces of the fire pit.

"Here," she said. Almost as if he had no interest in the food, he reached out a hand and sampled one.

"Good enough," he said indifferently. "Tart." But he ate his full share before they were all gone.

That day's journey was somewhat easier on Eirran. She still rode in front of him and he kept one arm firmly around her waist, but she was neither bound nor gagged. And she could keep the forked horn on which the bird usually rode from digging into her flesh with every step. The bird shunned it now.

Because she could see where they were going, she could move with the rough-coated Torgian rather than be jounced about like a sack of grain. She glanced at the sun's position. North. They were headed north and east, in the direction the ruined Eyrie of the Falconers was rumored to lie. Mountain peaks were already growing around them, high and broken as they had been when the Old Ones in Estcarp had shattered the land in the Great War.

She looked back at her companion, curious as to what sort of man he was under his Falconer's guise. He bore a dart-gun at his waist and had a half-filled bandolier slung over his shoulder. He carried no sword, only a long hunting-dagger strapped to his thigh. There was a bundle behind him, covered with oiled cloth. She guessed by the size of it that it held bird helm and mail shirt. The falcon scorned to ride near her. It appeared to consider itself deprived of its perch, alternately soaring overhead and riding on the man's shoulder. She couldn't tell whether it was war-trained or not.

Around mid-morning, she began to grow bored with the countryside and the fruitless speculation about her captor. "If we're to rebuild the Eyrie, don't you think it might be nice to get acquainted?"

"Why?"

"Oh, I don't know. It would pass the time. And I'm no Falconer woman—not yet, anyway. I like to know things."

Her apparent acceptance of her fate seemed to soften him a trifle. He shifted his arm around her waist, settling her more comfortably against him. "What sort of things would you know?"

"Oh, how you came to be at my uncle's tavern last night, what you used to do before you decided to rebuild the Eyrie." She paused, cautious. "How to please you best. You know."

Hesitantly, he began to speak. At first they talked of inconsequential things. But she began to pick up hints about his background. She had always known that a man talked most eagerly about himself, and this Falconer was, after all, a man.

He was young, not much past twenty, a year or two older than herself. He had until lately served as a marine guard in one of the few Sulcar ships that still plied the waters to the west. But even more than with other Falconers who followed the same path, he cared not for the sea. He became ill from the motion of a ship even when it lay at anchor. And so he had left that service, determined to seek another as a mercenary, a blank shield. He had come to the tavern, seen Eirran and heard her name, and this new plan sprang into his mind full-formed, like a waking dream.

Eirran thought about this a while. She could understand dreams; she had had many of her own. The most persistent had her in a cottage with two gardens outside, one for food, a smaller for flowers. Within, all was immaculate and tidy; she sat at the table concocting some herbal mixture while a kettle sang on the hob, a cat purred on the hearth, a baby lay gurgling happily in the cradle.

Well, old Juvva was teaching—had been teaching her herblore. Cats and kettles were easily come by, but to get a baby and do it the right way she would have to marry one of the dullwits who came to the tavern. As Eirran grew and her shape became more attractive to men, they began slipping her an occasional coin in appreciation of a smile, a bit of extra service, or the infrequent glimpse down her bodice when she bent over to put the flagons on the table. She saved these coins the tavern's patrons handed her with a single-minded fierceness. Someday, she would have enough to purchase her own cottage. Like Juvva, she would brew potions and remedies, earning her way, and there live alone, beholden to no man, a tribe she had learned to dislike.

She knew her uncle suspected she had this store of coin, though she kept it well hidden behind a loose board in the loft. At night it was under her pillow when she slept. She dimly remembered the sound of the pouch falling to the floor when the Falconer had taken her. She wondered if her uncle had stopped after finding it and not bothered to search for her.

Their camp that night was easier than it had been the day before. She watched him with interest. His motions were economical, graceful. He dug a small fire pit, ringing it with stones, and kindled a flame. He fed it with small twigs until it was well caught, then added larger bits of wood. She noted that the fire made little smoke.

When the bed of coals suited him, he put a small kettle into the pit and poured some water into it. He opened the parcel of provisions, setting aside the mutton-bone for another time, and took out a lump of smoked meat instead. He prepared to slice it into the water.

"No, no," she said, coming close. "That's not the way. That meat has to be fried first. Slice it into a pan, and save the grease to flavor some trail-biscuit." She squatted on her heels beside him.

"Here, you do it," the man said. He got out a shallow pan and lined it with slices of meat. He didn't trust her with the knife, but he did trim a forked stick for her so she could spear the bits of meat and turn them. As they browned, she began dropping them into the pot.

"I don't suppose you thought to steal some vegetables," she said.

"Yes, I did." He opened another parcel and produced some carrots and a few leeks.

"Chop them," she ordered, "and then go look around and see if you can find anything else for the pot. Wild turnips, garlic, edible roots. I've seen a lot growing around here as we rode. And give me that packet of flour and something to stir with."

"I don't know which plants to look for," he said. "I'm a warrior, not a farmer."

Without a word, she turned over the watching of the rest of the frying meat to him while she gathered what she needed. He prepared the roots she'd found and dropped them into the stew while she stirred up the trail-biscuit and set it to cooking on a hot stone. Good smells filled the campsite.

"Men," she said, shaking her head. "You don't know how to do anything."

"I've made out well enough until now."

"I don't see how," she said, and ladled out half the stew for him. He had only a single metal dish and one spoon. He kept the dish but gave the spoon to her, using the forked stick for himself. He speared the chunks, blowing on them before putting them into his mouth while she ate out of the pot. They put the pan of grease-flavored trail-biscuit between them and used it to soak up the broth. Together they cleaned the pots and utensils with sand. Newhold the falcon and the Torgian had long since fed, each in its own manner, and now slept nearby.

He and Eirran stared at each other across the fire.

"You're a good enough trail companion," he said, "even if you are just a woman."

"And you can probably learn, even if you are just a man." She stared into the flames. "I've no more liking for your ilk than you have of mine, Falconer. But I'll say one thing for you. I haven't had to slap your hands away from me every moment."

The memory of how his arms had brushed across her breasts during the day as he held her while they rode hung in the air between them. But that, she thought, had been accidental, the consequence of the manner in which they traveled.

"Sleep, woman," he said. "Tomorrow we begin to climb in earnest."

She settled down under the blanket, but sleep didn't come as easily as it had the night before. She found herself wondering about Falconers, and how they had come to have such disdain of women. Her own dislike of the man-tribe was easily understood; she had dodged too many grasping hands and pinching fingers in her time. But what had caused such a rift between Falconer men and women?

Perhaps, she thought, back in the before-time, when the Old Ones ruled in Estcarp and wars were fought by men and not by Power-wielding witches breaking mountains and tossing the land about, there had been a chief of the Falconers whose wife had been a bad woman. Perhaps she

smiled at other men, younger men, stronger, and lied to
her husband. And later, when he discovered this, as
husbands are bound to do with their wives, or wives with
their husbands, perhaps he moved her to a house in a
faraway fold of the mountains, where her lovers couldn't
visit her without being missed in the warren of caves and
cliffs that comprised the mountain fortress that was the
Eyrie.

And perhaps, Eirran thought, warming to the story she
was spinning for herself, others of the Falconers decided to
do the same with their wives, lest they be tempted to follow
the same paths the chief's wife had taken. Both sides were
proud, unyielding, turning their natural yearnings for each
other into disdain and indifference, men for women and
women for men. And with the passing of the years, both
sides had come to regard the arrangement as the only
proper one to have.

But the indifference was merely feigned, Eirran realized.
She had long ago learned that that which a man most
loudly professes to despise was that which he longed for
the greatest. If there had been true indifference between
the men and women of the Falconers, their entire tribe
would have died out long since.

Somehow, that thought troubled her more than anything
else that had happened to her the last two days. Her
dreams were uneasy that night.


The next day dawned gray and full of clouds, and
Newhold was reluctant to fly in the heavy air. But the
Falconer urged the bird aloft anyway.

"Rumors have it that strange beasts live in these mountains, since the Great War," he said. "We must be alert."

When the rain began he spread his cloak over the horse's
rump and drew Eirran close against him, sheltering all as
best he could against the cold drizzle. The Torgian trudged
on, finding it slow going over the mud and stone. And then

Newhold came swooping down from the sky, screaming a warning. The bird was nearly too late; the dark, misshapen beast was on them almost before the Falconer could draw his dart gun. Eirran found herself in the mud as he threw her to one side. She screamed in pain as her shoulder struck a rock.

He cursed and fired, and Eirran's scream was drowned in the roar of outrage from the beast as the darts struck home. Newhold screeched and stooped, utterly fearless in the defense of the Falconer. The horse fought also, rearing and striking out with its hooves, and where they hit, the sound was dark and solid. She heard more snarls and screams, a sound of underbrush being trampled as something crashed through it, and then the Falconer was kneeling beside her where she lay.

"Is—is it dead?" she asked fearfully.

"I don't think so," he said. "But we drove it off, Newhold and Rangin and me. How do you fare?"

"I don't know," she said. With his help, she tried to sit up and she groaned in pain and clutched her shoulder.

"We'll take shelter," the Falconer said. "We've come close to the Karsten gap, the place we once called the Keyhole. Even though the Keyhole is no more and the mountains are shivered and rent, there must still be a cave someplace nearby."

"Maybe it's taken already by that—that monstrosity," she said, and shuddered.

"I'll make certain it's a place with a narrow entrance, where the beast cannot go," he said. "If I help you, can you ride?"

"Yes, I think so."

He put her on Rangin's back, putting his hand on the halter and leading the way slowly through the worsening rain. To her relief, they found a shelter almost at once, a narrow cleft in the broken mountain. She dismounted, but the horse had to be unsaddled before it could squeeze

through the opening. She found comfort in this fact.
Newhold was already perched on an outcropping of stone
just overhead.

"I've got a lamp somewhere," the Falconer said, "and a
flask of oil. We can have a light, even if we can't hope for a
fire. But Rangin gives off a lot of heat."

He struck steel to flint, and presently they were able to
see the interior of the cave.

The room they were in wasn't a large one, nor was the
floor even. It had once been sand-covered, but the upheaval of the Great War had pushed underlying stones through
the sand and all but hid it from view. Eirran sat down on
one of the larger stones while the Falconer shoved others to
one side, hastily making a rough barricade between them
and the entrance to the cave.

"When the rain stops, I'll go search for firewood," he
said. "In the meantime, let's have a look at your shoulder."

She would have loosed the fastening at the throat of the
tunic and pulled the garment down on one side, but he
would have none of that. Brusquely, he pulled it off her,
over her uninjured arm and down the one that was hurt.
She gasped and clutched the garment against her exposed
breasts, but he took no notice. Intent on examining her for
injuries, he moved the arm this way and that, ignoring her
protests. His face cleared.

"Nothing is broken," he said, and she realized he had
been worried and concerned over her. He looked at her
anew, and frowned. "You're a mess!"

She touched her hair, uncombed for two days and now
wet and full of mud. She opened her mouth, a sharp retort
springing to her lips, but then he took her in his arms.

"It was my fault," he said. "You are in my care. It's a
miracle you weren't killed or seriously injured. But you're
alive. We're both still alive." He stroked her face. He was
rain-wet, and his hands muddy; he must be leaving smears
on her cheeks. "You are beautiful, you know. So very

beautiful." He held her against him for a long moment while her heart raced at the unexpected pleasure of this contact, so different from the way they had pressed together while they rode. Then, she thought dimly, it had been from necessity. But now, the thumping of his own heart, reaching her ear where it was pressed against his chest, told her he held her because he wanted to, because he wanted her—as much, she realized, as she wanted him.

They sank down together onto the sandy floor of the little cave.

Later, he cradled her head on his shoulder. "It was your first time, wasn't it?" he said quietly.

"Yes."

"I didn't dare dream—" He closed his lips on the thought. "It was my first time also."

"Ah." She reached a hand up to stroke his face, and winced. She had forgotten her bruised shoulder. "I—I don't know what to call you."

"We don't give our true names lightly. But you, this, this is different. I'm known as Yareth."

"Yareth," she repeated, liking the sound of it. Then she flung herself against him again, heart leaping, but this time in terror.

Something snuffled and howled outside. She heard the sound of claws against stone, felt the ground shake when the beast tore away a piece of the mountain and let it drop. Newhold bated and screeched, eager to attack. Knowing it would be the bird's doom, Yareth sat up at once, uttering a shrill whistle and holding out his arm for a perch. The falcon reluctantly obeyed. Its talons dug in and drew blood from Yareth's unprotected skin before he could transfer the bird to the saddle-fork and secure the leash. Behind them, Rangin stamped angrily. A misshapen limb ending in a four-clawed thing like a hand, groped into the cavern mouth. The hand encountered a stone, one of the ones Yareth had moved there. The beast grasped the stone, pulled it outside. There was a yowl of rage and frustration; then the area above the opening shivered, and a shower of rubble tumbled down from where the beast had smashed the stone against the mountain face.

"And you fought that?" Eirran whispered, appalled.

"It didn't expect opposition, and retreated to think things over," he replied, just as softly. He reached over and pinched out the lamp.

"What do we do now?" she said. The darkness pressed in on her and she was grateful when he moved close.

"We wait. If I'm correct, this is a something that likes not the light. If we have been traveling on a sunny day, we would surely have met it while we slept."

She shuddered. Following his example, she groped for her clothing and put it on again. "Will the mountain hold it off?" she said fearfully.

"I don't know. We'll just have to wait and see. But never fear." A movement told her he had his dart gun in one hand and had drawn the hunting-knife with the other. "If it gets in, it won't find us alive. Any of us."

They huddled together, the four of them, all through the rest of the day and night. The man and woman scarcely dared utter a word, though they found as time passed that they knew each other's minds and thoughts better than if they spoke. She began to hiccup again from fear, and automatically he handed her the water-skin. When he whistled softly to the falcon or stroked the Torgian's rough coat and then touched her breast it meant, I would have you in my arms but dare not. And when she touched his face it meant in return, I desire you as well and we will embrace again if only in death. Sometime during the night he handed her the knife and she pressed his hand. I'll do what needs to be done, her touch said, if it comes to that.

Now and then the beast left the cave mouth for a short time. They could only surmise that it went away to feed, for when it returned its onslaughts against the opening were even fiercer than before. She began to understand that the beast wanted them not so much for food, but because of some hatred it carried in its bones, that only the feel of their flesh under its claws could slake.

Toward morning, they began to strain their eyes, searching for a dawn without clouds, for the sun to return. And little by little, the light came. Eirran thought it was her imagination, but then she could see Yareth's face in the gloom. Outside, the beast uttered a last howl of frustrated rage and shuffled off to find its lair before the sun came up fully.

Yareth got up, shaking the stiffness out of his limbs. "We have to get out of here now, while we can," he said.

"Yes. I'll tend those talon cuts on your arm later."

They gathered their few belongings and ventured out of the cave. Eirran sucked in her breath; the face of the mountain was deeply scored, and slivers of stone lay everywhere, marking the ferocity of the beast's assaults against it. They had to clear a path through the rubble before they dared lead even the sure-footed Torgian through it. Once outside, Yareth saddled Rangin quickly and pulled Eirran up before him. Then he turned the horse's head back in the direction they had come the previous day, and dug his heels into Rangin's belly. The Torgian grew high-rumped with the steepness of the path it found, going down much more quickly than it had come up.

"Aren't we going on, searching for where the Falconers' Eyrie used to be?" she said, startled.

"No. If beasts like that now walk the mountains in the dark, there might be worse ones who go in light," he said. "It's true. The Falconers' way of life, as we knew it, is no more." He shrugged. "Everything ends. Perhaps it's better so."

She turned in his embrace, looking up at him, but he refused to meet her gaze. He stared off into the distance, frowning. Well then, it couldn't be easy for him, giving up his dream. No more than it was for her, giving up her own as she must now. The cottage, the coins that were now almost enough to pay for it— She sighed.

"What is it?" he said. "Are you in pain?"

"No. I was just thinking. I had a dream too, and a little money I was saving to buy a place of my own. It's gone now."

This time he turned her in his arms. For the first time, he smiled, and looking at him, she realized she loved him. "Your money is here, in the bottom of one of the saddlebags!" he said. "I brought it with us, so you could use it and buy things to comfort yourself with, later! I almost had to tear your fingers from the pouch when I tied your hands together, you know."

She began to laugh. She slipped one hand around his neck and pulled his face down to hers while the Torgian carried them to a future full of new dreams neither could have had imagined only a few short hours before. The falcon, Newhold, swooped down and took its accustomed perch on the saddle fork.

\* \* \*

## Afterword

*The curious relationship between Falconers and their women has always intrigued me. Both sides refuse to yield; each side thinks it is correct, the other wrong. When two such proud factions are at odds like this—and particularly when these factions are made up of men, and women —there has to be an attraction even greater than that which normally exists between the sexes. That which is desired must become that which is shunned, or the stability of the entire society is threatened.*

*When the Eyrie was destroyed in the Great War, the Falconer way of life went with it. What if, I thought, there was a young Falconer, too youthful to have actually lived in the Eyrie. He would doubtless have a head full of romantic notions of what it must have been like, never having experienced it first-hand. And what if he met a young woman and decided to try to make his dreams come true? And what if she also had her dreams—which might not coincide with his? And what if this enormous mutual attraction worked between them, despite their differences? What would happen then? Given this premise, "To Build the Eyrie" practically wrote itself. The people came alive for me so much that I want to write another story, about what happened to them later.*

—SASHA MILLER

# MILK FROM A MAIDEN'S BREAST

## by

## Elizabeth Scarborough

Trugemma was the bravest, the most powerful, the most beautiful, and altogether the most wondrous warrior in all Escore. Everyone said so. Her name was in everyone's thoughts, on everyone's lips. For she, with her many brilliant and decisive victories in the field, was Escore's hope against Darkness. She was absolutely marvelous, even in a land where marvels were routine, and absolutely undefeated. That is, until the day the weres cornered her and her small expeditionary band on the edge of the deep Moss Forest and growled and howled with the expectation of turning Trugemma into a lot of brave, powerful, beautiful bloody tatters.

This was *not* how it was supposed to go, and the moss wife Freyti hopped from one frost-furred foot to the other in agitation as she watched from moss cover at the edge of the deep woods.

Trugemma the triumphant would have had no problem with a few measly weres, Freyti knew, had winter not allied itself with darkness. Out there, where the trees stood naked and solitary, snow drifted deep from trunk to trunk, glittering beneath an anemic moon from which it seemed

251

to have sucked all light. Into this sparkling morass the horses of Trugemma and her band sunk, their efforts to turn, to go backward or forward, utterly useless in the drifts. Fretyi had become aware of their predicament while she was still far back in the woods, for she had, as had all her people, the ability to hear at a short distance unspoken thoughts and feelings. She had set Fiibs, her babe, high in the fork of a tree, where she would keep until Freyti was ready to fetch her, and had scurried forth to offer her assistance.

The weres, unfortunately, also picked up unspoken thoughts and feelings and had come ahead of her, yipping taunts at the trapped Trugemma, flecking the snow with the blood of horses and riders, darting into shadow where the force whips could not reach. The riders, buried to their knees, could not maneuver to lash from a more effective angle. Slowly but deliberately, distributing their weight to keep them atop the snow and within striking range, the gray werewolves circled, snarling—twice around went the lead bitch. A third time and all would be lost, Trugemma and her band imprisoned, unable to help themselves with muscle or magic.

The wolves thus far had been unable to hamstring the horses only because the horses' hams had sunk below snowline. With the small band immobilized, the pickings would be easy. Already Trugemma and her men, wearied by months of siege and battle, felt the strength drain from their arms and the cold grip them hip-high as their leggings were torn loose by snapping teeth.

Freyti fretted to think that the small detour she had perhaps subliminally encouraged her heroine to take had resulted in this. She had not realized the snow would stop the warrior maid and her followers. Snow was no problem to moss women, who were mostly sheltered from it, and whose large hairy feet were as good as snowshoes when need be. And avoiding weres was as much second nature to the moss people as avoiding hounds was to rabbits. The weres had about the same attitude toward Freyti's folk, too. She had personally never seen them close up before but she knew them with the knowing of her race and the knowing sent shivers up her that had nothing to do with the cold.

Still, standing around shivering all night would do no one any good. Her jeopardy would be slight. She knew the deep woods and the moss walls and the limbs for fast climbing as well as she knew her own gnarled hands, or the long gray hairs that fell in front of her face. Sprinting forth over the snow she shoved her hair behind her shoulders, her thumbs between her teeth and whistled, sharply.

"Ho, wolfie! Come play with me!" she shouted at the pack, and turned back toward her woods, knowing her heroine would cover her back and make short work of the pursuing pack while Freyti found her saving tree limb. But when she turned for the woods she saw the moss curtain away and part and knew she was lost. Fiibs had found her way down from her perch and toddled toward the edge of the snow. Freyti swung round at once and flew across the snow, toward the thinner trees.

She was only three steps beyond weres and riders when her momentum brought her down, her feet in their speed no longer skimming the surface, but sinking with the added pressure of her bounding. The weres abandoned their first sport and fell upon her, tearing at what they could reach without sinking into the snow themselves. At first it was only her long, concealing hair, and this they tore from her head and strangled in the strands that snarled them in its tangles.

As the fangs found her flesh, Freyti felt Fiibs's cry, puzzled and afraid, but the teeth and claws were tearing her then and she screamed as the lead bitch tore at her exposed belly. A thundering rent the air and the ground throbbed with power, though Freyti did not know if it was the power of Light or the power of death.

The weres exploded around her, but even as she saw Trugemma bending over her, she felt the blood pouring from her and the pain slicing her into halves and knew that her heroine had delivered her somewhat belatedly.

"Courage, poor creature," the warrior-witch told her as she bent near, her wide green eyes and golden hair close enough for Freyti to touch, had she the strength left. "I'll give you a bit of a spell now to ease your passing. And notify your next-of-kin, of course."

"Fiibs—" The name gushed out of Freyti with what was left of her life. "Take Fiibs—"

"I beg your pardon?" Trugemma said, but she saw the spirit pass out of Freyti's eyes then and stood, saying to her executive officer, "These last wishes would be carried out more frequently if only the dying weren't so incomprehensible. What on earth, do you suppose, is a Feeb?"

"Maaaaaa!" cried a small gurgling voice as what seemed to be a foot-high hairball tottered forth with its twiggy arms outstretched to the battered creature bloodying the snow.

"By the Lady!" Trugemma swore, swinging the hairball aside and scooping it up at arm's length for inspection. "What is this?"

Her executive officer coughed. "I think, ma'am, that may be one of the feeb things our late comrade here was referrin' to. Looks like what I've heard tell a moss wife looks like." His eyes scanned the deep forest with its heavily fringed trees. "Country for it, all right."

"Smaller, though. And I've never heard them called feebses before. It might be—"

Fiibs, however, knew what she was and what Trugemma was, and upon hearing herself named stuck out her arms again and grabbed the glamorous general around the neck, clinging hard. "Ma," she said, and would not let go.

With her soldiers bearing the body of Freyti and herself bearing Fiibs, Trugemma led her band and their horses out of the drifts and into the shelter of the deep woods, where they were soon met by a delegation of hanging-haired mosswives who coagulated out of the mossy background without warning.

"How can it be that Freyti is dead?" someone's mind touched Trugemma's with wondering and a shade of resentment. "You have the power to blast the weres. You did so—"

Trugemma started, and the damp hairy thing she held snuffled unattractively. A good officer neither explains nor excuses herself, but a defense sprang unbidden into Trugemma's mind. "We were surprised and I was too busy fighting and too weary to gather the right words. I know it's not supposed to happen but *you* try campaigning for three years solid and see how well your vocabulary works. When she drew them off, the words came to me and of course I acted at once but . . ." The "but" was self-evident. Rather lamely, she said aloud, "She was very brave. A good trooper. Saved all of us and this child besides. I don't suppose any of you are next-of-kin?"

She had not intended to allow herself to be separated from her men, but when she and the moss woman in front of her stepped through the curtain, the others were not beside or behind them. She didn't notice it until she was halfway through another curtain. She was really overly tired and the weight of the child on her exhausted arms occupied most of her concentration. The ground beneath her feet was frosty but soft and spongelike and she had to pick her boots up and set them down again very carefully to keep from falling. She started to protest to her guide about being separated, but the child clung to her so that she knew she couldn't free her arms to back up her insistence. Besides, for a change she was among proven allies. Probably the woman was just showing her to a sleeping place. She yawned and stumbled forward, across the threshold of a remarkable dwelling and almost into the lap of an equally remarkable creature who greeted her with a grunt.

"So. This is Escore's best hope since the Tregarths, is it?" came a grumbling thought from the creature. Trugemma knew her for the leader at once.

"Bush-Grandmother," someone whispered shyly.

The Bush-Grandmother sat among her minions. Any of them could have been mistaken for the child's mother, except the Bush-Grandmother herself, who was twice as wide and whose hair was twice as bushy and whose back was not humbly hunched and whose eyes were not downcast or hidden behind the mesh of hair. Small star-shaped flowers speckled the mossy floor and wound up the tree trunk, and from these emanated a pearly glow that showed clearly the predominant color of these people as well as their home was gray—gray hair, gray skin, furrowed like that of tree trunks or the very elderly, though Trugemma received an almost childlike feeling from many of them.

Not the Bush-Grandmother though. Though she stayed seated and still, her manner was bristling enough to cause Trugemma to wish a clearer path to her sword than her living burden allowed. She turned toward the helpful whisper to offer the babe to a relative, but no one stood where the whisper had been. She knew the others were there, but now they were blending with the mossy walls, or sitting still as tussocks, leaving her to the auspices of their leader.

"Well, girl," the Bush-Grandmother said in the same tone Trugemma's fencing master had once used when she was—just once—less than perfect. "What have you to say for yourself?"

"I say thank you very much for the kind comparison, but I've not the honor of being related to the Tregarths, though I did sit in council with one—I think it was Kyllan—and I say also that I think someone had better relieve me of this child. She's a bit damp and—" No one moved forward though she felt titters and rustlings around the edges. The Bush-Grandmother only stared stonily at her. It was less a last attempt at diplomacy than her knees giving way that caused Trugemma to sink down to the moss then, carefully hanging the bottom ends of Fiibs' hair and with it, she hoped, the bottom end of Fiibs, over the springy, moisture-absorbing ground cover. She found her legs and arms were trembling as she sank down and finally she managed to brace the baby with one arm and undo her sword with the other. She slid it hilt-first toward the glowering Bush-Grandmother, making the first gesture of truce.

"Somehow there has been a misunderstanding," she projected with ploddingly careful emphasis to each word, so that her tired thoughts did not tangle themselves. "I am not your enemy. I ride for Escore—not a blank shield but with my own company, entrusted with the companies of others, in the service of the Light. *I* did not kill your kinswoman. The weres did that. They would have killed my men and me as well or left us trussed for the Sarn Riders had not your kinswoman—"

"Freyti," the Bush-Grandmother said, and her thought broke. "Her name was Freyti. She knew your name. Can you not learn hers?"

"We were not introduced," Trugemma snapped, her patience spent with the Bush-Grandmother's antagonism. Where were the modest, self-effacing little creatures of which the legends told?

"We are not as you expected," the Bush-Grandmother said. "And you are not as we expected, Trugemma called Darksbane. Not as Freyti expected. She idealized you. I could have warned her to take no sides, to think not so highly on any of the race of man. But it made her pleased to think she might serve you. That is why she slipped past the wards that guard us from our enemies. In your service, she need fear no enemies—"

Trugemma jerked her untouched sword back to her and Fiibs began to howl. Two mossy forms clustered close to pat the child to stillness but did not lift her weight from Trugemma's arm. Trugemma glared. "If I wished to waste my time in guilt, Old One, I have far more dire matters to take precedence. I did not come to bear your scorn or your judgment but to bring you your kin's—Freyti's body, and her child. Since we are evidently not welcome here, my men and I will be on our way if you will only be good enough to take this child."

At that Fiibs began howling again and clung to Trugemma in a stranglehold.

"Her mother died in your service, lady," the Bush-Grandmother said. "Fiibs is your child now. Take her and go."

"*My* child!" Trugemma was truly choking now and had to pull the little gnarled claws from her neck to catch her breath.

She stared for a moment with distaste at the drooling puckered mouth in the weathered little face, the tearing big eyes under heavy furred lashes, the tree-twig arms clutching and clinging like the moss itself. "Madame, that is impossible. You obviously have no idea what war is like." That she said aloud. What rushed to her mind were the images of the children who had died waiting too long for her to deliver them from siege—children more human than this one, and children cut down in battle, and children murdered in the aftermath, and the were whelps and kephan foals and thas kits she had wiped out herself. They were evil, of course, but still young. War was no place for the young, battle no respecter of innocence. The image came back to her of the supposedly evil—all magic said so, of course, and it wouldn't lie—face of a kephan colt, startled and wobbly as it tried to climb toward its mother, and of her own sword. "Impossible," she said, but now she buried her face in Fiibs's hair. Fiibs's tears would have to do. Hers had steamed away in the heat of battle long ago.

"Young woman," the Bush-Grandmother said, but for the first time not unkindly. "It will be inconvenient for you, I agree. But you are the chosen foster mother. Freyti chose you herself to nurse her child and foster it—"

"Impossible—" Trugemma echoed her previous statement then raised her head enough to mutter, "She could not have known her babe would have need of another mother—"

"We of the moss always seek humans to nurse and foster our children—the most admirable we can find, and if sometimes that is not very, well, we don't any of us get what we want in this life always, do we?"

Trugemma's curiosity was not great but it was there and enough for the Bush-Grandmother to continue. "You have been thinking that you find us alien-looking, inhuman. What do you think we are? Vegetable? Moss itself? Mothers-in-law and ugly stepsisters to the beautiful woods nymphs men sometimes wish we were? That is not so far wrong, you know. Except that it had little to do with the moss or the woods to begin with. Our ancestress was beautiful as you are beautiful and more."

"That is not so very beautiful," Trugemma thought as she imagined to herself. By now she frequently forgot that the old one could hear her and she did not especially care. Somewhere beyond her own self-pity and self-reproach she realized that she was about to hear yet another tale of the early days of Escore, when the adepts experimented to find the perfect inhabitants for their domain. Each of the mutated races in Escore had their own version of this creation myth, but somehow she had assumed that the moss wives had always been separate—were a true magical race and not a mutation.

"She was the daughter of the leaders of the adepts—not

much more than that has come down to us except that they were reasonably good folk, with a sense of responsibility toward their fellows and their creations. Our ancestress —Flita was her name—was very talented with all growing things, could change them and raise them and make them grow bigger or smaller or in strange shapes. She spent hours making ornamental gardens and growing orchards with fruits offering full-course meals with all of the nutritional requirements of her people. She had a flaw, though —she was very impressionable. Her figure was not the only willowy thing about her. She was easily swayed. She fell in with an evil companion—a fellow adept, not so talented as she, but with large ideas for creating monstrous crawly things that ate nobler life-forms.

"She was too blinded by his handsome face and the reflection of her own loveliness in his eyes to see the potential ugliness of his imagination, and she agreed to marry him. Her parents, who suspected their colleague of being a bad lot and who had hoped for a better influence for their daughter, tried to forbid it. But her lover used his own talent for creeping and crawling and stealth to steal her away. To stall any future opposition to their union and his ambitions, he persuaded Flita to help him grow a vine that would encircle her parents' dwelling and choke it to smithereens. Flita enjoyed engineering the plant to please her lover, but it is very doubtful that she knew that he planned to use it to kill her parents.

"Fortunately for them, they were quite a bit smarter than their would-be son-in-law. They saw the vine coming and destroyed it, foot by foot, following it backward until they found their daughter and her lover. By then Flita's lover had confessed to her his plan and had promised that the two of them would be together and would take unto themselves all of the power and prestige possessed by her supposedly departed forebears. She was already weeping when her parents arrived, and when she saw them she flung

herself at their feet and wept even more bitterly, in relief
and for forgiveness. She also prayed that they would spare
her lover, and told them that she had disobeyed them
because she needed him so.

"Her parents were far less emotional by nature than
Flita. They saw that not only had she disobeyed them and
become an accomplice at their attempted murder, but with
her talent so easily subverted could become a menace to all
Escore. Already they were fighting with colleagues of like
mind to the lover, who wished to branch out from mutat-
ing creatures into better adapting species and try to create
other, darker things, just to see if they could. The daughter
with her talent would be a constant threat to humanity
while she was so easily influenced, and so attractive to
those who would use her.

"Her mother and father talked this over among themselves and then explained it to Flita, saying that they felt
they had no choice but to do something harsh to save the
world from her and her from herself—and also they
needed to do something about that lover. She begged for
his life and pleaded that she would reform him, that they
would change, and her father bade her to stand on her own
two feet then, and gave her twelve hours to change them
into something harmless, and preferably benevolent. He
further charged her that since she was a danger to mankind, the beauty that was the gift of himself and his wife to
her was to be removed, so that people would no longer be
fooled. They felt she was ugly inside, you see, instead of
merely weak, but she was their child.

"Thus charged, the girl had to face up to the fact that her
lover really was not a good person, although she loved him
still and needed to cling to him as much as ever. As soon as
her parents' backs were turned he tried to get her to plot
with him again. She tried to heed her father's words and be
strong, but her lover was so handsome he made everything
seem reasonable, so she clawed her hair over her face so

she could not see him. Still he did not stop, but reached for her, still talking, so she changed him into a still and silent thing—a tree. And then she thought she could see his reproachful face in the pattern of the bark so she covered his branches and limbs with moss as gray as the despair she felt. She was trying to change herself into the same when her parents returned, and stopped the transformation, for when they saw how hard she had tried to obey them and the cost to her, they remembered that they loved her and did not want her to be forever lost to them. Already her skin had become barklike and her limbs—er—limblike, and her hair had gone from gold to the gray of the moss. But her eyes were large and loving and she clung to the tree. Then her parents promised her that the tree could become a creature like herself for one hour every year and be her mate, and that, if in subsequent years she and her progeny could prove to mankind their inner beauty, despite their outward hideousness, and be always healers and of service, they might be redeemed. For that reason, we of the moss always offer service to those humans who seem good and try whenever possible to persuade the humans to nurse and foster our children."

"Excuse me, could you repeat that last bit. I missed it—" Trugemma said, bouncing Fiibs furiously, for the baby had begun whining near the end of the story and now was squawling louder than a were's howl. Thought transference didn't help. Trugemma could no longer hear herself think much less hear the thoughts of the Bush-Grandmother.

But she had heard much of the story, and now when she felt like shaking the screaming Fiibs, she looked down at that puckered little face and those tightly clenched eyes and wondered if the other children she had seen, the inhuman ones, were truly human too, or—or at least *like* her, in how they felt, despite their various bizarre appearances. How *would* this youngling grow if kept by a suitable mother—not herself, of course, not a soldier with killing to do but a warm and loving human mother who would be kind to her. Not these poor pathetic creatures who scuttled about forever ashamed of themselves, serving probably highly unsuitable people because they had, as a race, a stupid tendency to cling to unfeeling trees, which changed into mates so wicked they could be allowed only one hour a year before they must disappear again. But then she remembered Freyti and wondered, trying to think if she knew of any human woman who would have first risked her unarmed self to enemies to save a band of armed soldiers. And she wondered how many, though there was much talk of motherly sacrifice, would have knowingly led the weres upon herself to save a child as ugly and presently as unpleasant as Fiibs. Though she had seen some valiant acts on the part of human mothers for their children, in her experience such courage was not as common among people, even people of the Light, as it was among animals.

Fiibs cried, but somewhat more quietly as Trugemma stopped bouncing her and rocked her thoughtfully. But though the crying was softer, it was insistent, and Trugemma looked rather desperately back to the Bush-Grandmother. "She must be hungry," she said, feeling almost as useless as she had when coming upon the aftermath of the siege.

"Freyti was her mother and Freyti is gone," the Bush-Grandmother said. "We are none of *us* her mother."

"But a wet-nurse surely, or some substitute?"

"There is none. We may each of us nurse only the children of our bodies. Only a human nurse will suffice for second-milk."

"That's very convenient for you in this circumstance," Trugemma observed. "But even if I were inclined to take this little one with me—strictly as a debt of honor, you understand—the facts do not change. I spend long hours in the saddle and sleep under the stars or in the rain. I ride among enemies and cannot pause to clean a child's messes and if I had her to defend, I would always be preoccupied, not able to be as ruthless as—as ruthless as—as I need be at times," and her mind strayed back again and she was filled with such a bleakness and a grimness that she wondered that the child in her arms did not feel how the darkness clouded her heart and cry all the louder. "Besides," she said finally, "I am a maiden and to keep my witch powers, untrained as they are, I must a maiden remain. As a warrior, and as a maiden, I have nothing with which to nourish this child."

The Bush-Grandmother blew an errant strand of hair back over her shoulder and considered. "If that is so, Freyti was farther from the mark than she usually was. Though I did not agree with her in her adulation of you and in her following the thoughts of anyone who passed near enough for word of your deeds, I did not chasten her. Freyti always knew, somehow, what needed to be done. She was the best healer of us all, and not just with herbs and medicine. She knew where a pain was and what thing, however unlikely, would soothe it. She saw in you beauty and brilliance, it is true, but often she spoke of how your talent for war would be as strong for life and peace, if ever this land's ills permitted it. I wonder if she knew when she saw you that that talent was being poisoned by the very qualities that she admired—that because you are kind, you despise yourself when you cannot prevent unkindness. And that because you are responsible, you cannot help but commit unkindnesses yourself to prevent future ones on the part of those less scrupulous than yourself. And that with every act you perform that goes against your peaceful nature, you injure yourself and an infection of darkness sets in."

Now it was Trugemma who clung to Fiibs, cradling her furry warmth and mingling the tears she thought she no

longer had with the babe's. Her thoughts came out broken-
ly: "All that I could do was not enough, will not be enough.
I—everything—anything—makes less. Destroys, withers,
blights, burns. It none of it does any good—there is no
building, only tearing apart."

"My child." The Bush-Grandmother's voice was tender
now, and somehow she had moved to the place beside
Trugemma. "Nourish for a time instead of destroying.
Fiibs will cling to you so you need not fear losing her—we
of the moss are very good at that—but more importantly
she will be a healer, of great use to you and your men.
Protect her as her mother protected you, and you will see."

Trugemma wiped her eyes in Fiibs's hair. If only she
were able to do as the Bush-Grandmother urged. A child of
her own might teach her how to deal with enemy whelps in
a way that would not bring to her own soul the blight she
ascribed to them. But if she let herself care for this legacy
of Freyti's the child would stand a good chance of being
killed, or worse. But then, that might happen anyway, if
Darkness won its way into these woods.

She was not plagued with false modesty. She knew her
own importance to her cause. Her effectiveness would be
hindered by having to care for a baby. On the other hand,
it was hindered perhaps more, and in a more insidious way
that boded real ill, by this slow groping coldness that
worked its way through her bloodstream and into her
heart. It seemed self-indulgent and fool-hardy to wish for
something—someone—of her own—but she suddenly
had such a yearning wistfulness, after years of consigning
life to rot, to help it grow instead.

Fiibs cried again, a snuffling whimper and it seemed to
Trugemma the child grew lighter and frailer as she held
her.

"She is hungry," the Bush-Grandmother repeated.

"Then for pity's sake find someone to feed her—" Trugemma said, trying to disentangle her hair from Fiibs's clinging fists.

"Maaa—" Fiibs said feebly.

The Bush-Grandmother did not need to answer. Trugemma knew no other mother was possible for the little creature. She could not disengage the tiny claws so she held Fiibs and rocked her and felt her grow flimsy, brittle somehow, like moss torn from its roots to crumble to powder, fine and dry. Fiibs was withering even as she held her, without her mother, or a human nurse to sustain her.

Trugemma hardly realized she was weeping again but she wished she had never come to this place. While she was cold, she was numb, and now everything was hot and hard and painful and the wounds reopened, the blood flowing with the tears, the sweat flowing in the dead of winter with a fever of remorse. Her tunic was soaked beneath her armor and she struggled to pull loose from the armor while cradling Fiibs. Twiggy hands tugged to help her and it was free. The front of her tunic was soaked, but not with blood or sweat. Fiibs quieted and snuggled eagerly toward her neckline.

The Bush-Grandmother sighed deeply with relief—this was some moss-magic then, but a wholly cooperative miracle. Trugemma's body and heart had consented to cooperate without consulting her head. The Bush-Grandmother nodded gravely, and Trugemma opened the neck of her tunic. "Well, my dear," she said aloud to Fiibs, who nuzzled her greedily. "I see you are a sensible creature who will do well on campaign after all. Very wise to provide yourself with magical rations and escape the camp cook's gruel."

Fiibs didn't answer, but clung hard, as was her nature, and she continued to do so until she was old enough that others clung to her strength instead. And though she was known throughout Escore as Fiibs Mossdotter, no one was sure what her last name meant, for most only recalled that she was the child of the venerable General Trugemma, one of the early engineers of peace and mutual understanding among all of the creatures in Escore. No one ever mentioned anything unusual about Fiibs's appearance, except for her long silvery hair, which was the envy of many maids. One old soldier, reminiscing about the time when he and his comrades had been bewildered for a night, stumbling aimlessly through a deep forest, before the general and her baby had finally found them and led them out, spat appreciatively and said, "Must have been bein' born in them woods made her hair like that—silver as that moss with the snow shinin' on it. Otherwise, of course, she was the spittin' image of her mother, and that's sayin' somethin'. For my money, no woman ever walked this land who was more beautiful, inside and out, than them two."

*   *   *

## Afterword

*For all its intricately woven background of science and magic, the Witch World is an awfully lot like the real world. It has so much conflict, so much war, so many people who see its problems in terms of black and white, good and evil. I liked the Moss Wives, who seemed like ordinary folks minding their own business to me. I decided to contrast them with your typical sword-wielding Amazonian thewier-than-thou princess type. At the same time I was thinking about this story, I was trying to write a proposal for a book based on my own experiences in Vietnam. More than half of my patients were Vietnamese. So when I started to write about Trugemma the warrior, she just wasn't funny to me anymore. Like many veterans I've known, she is unable to deal with the relatively innocent civilians because she is so contaminated by what she knows to be her own evil actions in the name of good. I couldn't solve a problem like that in a lighthearted manner so the Witch World anthology inspired my only-so-far serious story.*

—ELIZABETH SCARBOROUGH

# NIGHT HOUND'S MOON

## by

## Mary H. Schaub

He knew that something unimaginably horrid was going to happen after the moon set. The moon was only a waning sliver, scarcely bright enough to cast a shadow, but Kennard felt painfully certain that its silver light had to be banished before whatever evil brooded here would manifest itself. He and Jarrel—the potential victims—were clearly in no condition to run away. Kennard, who ordinarily had trouble breathing while lying down, was straining for each breath against the thongs cutting into his cloak and tunic. The outlaws who had initially captured them had not bound them so cruelly tight; but then, to the outlaws, their captive trio had been a salable commodity, not to be carelessly damaged without affecting their price.

Kennard concentrated on his breathing, a mental exercise that necessarily pushed aside most other external sensations. He ignored the chill, gritty stone surface of the platform where they had been placed. He tried to ignore the thongs trussing him up like a piece of meat for roasting—this was harder to do, but gradually he focused solely on the rhythm of his breathing. His heartbeat slowed, reducing the pulsating thumps in his ears as well as the fiery pain of overstressed rib muscles. As always at such times, he recalled Rubeth's irascible voice badgering him during his worst seizures. "Listen, boy! *Think* on what you're doing. Count to yourself. Breathe as deeply as you can. The more excited you get, the worse you are, as you well know." She had been right, of course. Wise women, especially old experienced ones, tended to know about illnesses and how to treat them. Not for the first time, Kennard wished he had learned more from Rubeth. He should have listened with more attention to her endless discourses on plants and herbs, but he had been a small boy, easily distracted from what seemed to him to be dry, useless knowledge. . . .

He squirmed, unsuccessfully trying to stretch cramped muscles. The one herbal remedy he was familiar with and which would be eminently helpful now was lodged uncomfortably underneath his ribs where he couldn't possibly reach it. Rubeth had bartered with a trader for those oddly wedge-shaped leaves. The trader wasn't sure where they had come from, but he had been told that they could ease breathing difficulties. Rubeth had brewed a tiny sample for Kennard to try, and ever since, he had prized the diminishing remnant of the packet, to be chewed only when all else failed.

The rough paving stones abrading his cheek seemed to exude a moldy dampness that caught in Kennard's throat, setting him coughing. He tried to suppress the irritation. Coughing always made his wheezing worse, and if it was very prolonged, would leave his rib muscles aching. Rubeth herself had died of the coughing sickness three winters before. The remote valley in the Dales where she settled was too far from any trade route or travelers' trail to attract another wise woman unless one might wander there by chance. Kennard had been separated from his parents as a small child in one of the frequent violent skirmishes that afflicted the Dales in those days. Rubeth had always assured him that she would never have noticed him lying in the underbrush if he hadn't sneezed loudly when she passed by on one of her plant-gathering trips. She had brought him back to her cluttered hut and considered him a professional challenge. "Not every person would know to make a brew of bronzeroot to halt sneezing," she had often remarked. He missed Rubeth's birdlike quickness, and thought now that her craftiness would be a valuable asset if only he could ask her what he should try to do in this situation. Jarrel's experienced advice would also be sound, he was sure, but the old soldier was turned away from him, and isolated too far to call to unless Kennard raised his voice. Somehow, the boy knew it would be wiser to keep silent. The longer he escaped attention here, the better.

The last few days, Kennard reflected bitterly, had been haunted by ill fortune. This current predicament was only the most immediate crown to the tally of woeful incidents. There had been two times, he thought, when his luck seemed to have turned for the better. His encountering Jarrel was one, but the first had been his finding the great hound by moonlight. He could see it in his mind as clearly as if it were just occurring.

Kennard had been wandering alone in this remote area of the Dales near the border of the ominous Waste. He hadn't truly known what he was looking for; he supposed that he was hoping to chance upon another wise woman like Rubeth who might allow him to accompany her in exchange for his unskilled help. He wasn't as strong as the boys of his general age that he'd seen in the few scattered villages Rubeth had visited. Rubeth had guessed that Kennard was about five years old when she found him, thus making him about twelve now. His breathing sickness rarely forced him to bed, but he had never gained much weight, and couldn't run or exert himself without bringing on the wheezing and viselike tightness in his chest. Although he hadn't realized it at the time, Kennard had learned many things from Rubeth. He had developed a good memory for trails and taking directions, and knew which irritating or poisonous plants to avoid. His hands were deft for fine work like sorting or weaving. He also had an inborn friendliness for animals, often helping Rubeth mend a bird's broken wing or treat a small wild thing's injury.

He supposed it might have been that feeling for an animal in distress those few nights before that had spurred him out of a solid sleep to sit up, blinking in the cold moonlight. Kennard had wrapped himself in his cloak and carried his only weapon, a sturdy wooden staff that he had smoothed and shaped from a tree limb. He wasn't guided to the spot by any noise, but he had clambered down a steep slope as if he had known where he was going. A dim, pale shape had been moving at the foot of the incline, but the movements were cautious and strictly limited, as if there were a tether that pulled each motion up short. Kennard had approached with care, not wanting to find himself attacked by an injured but still lethal mountain cat. But it hadn't been a cat at all—it had been a dog, a huge dog, bigger than any Kennard had ever seen before. Kennard had spoken to it soothingly. "Don't be afraid. I want to help you. Let me see—were you caught in a rock fall?" He had eased closer and the great head had swung partly toward him. He had supposed it must be some breed of hound, but it had looked as large as a hill pony, with a short, thick coat and alert, pointed ears. In the moonlight, it had seemed all pale gray, even its eyes. To Kennard's surprise, it hadn't made a sound, not a whine or a growl as one might expect from a trapped beast. It had been securely trapped. Kennard had been able to see the cause of its distress as soon as he had come within reach of the animal. It had been wearing a collar of silvery metal woven almost like a plaited band, and a protruding tree root had snagged the collar presumably when the dog had slid into the gulley in a subsidence of loose gravel. Kennard had kept talking softly to the dog as he had gingerly inserted his fingers between the collar and the gnarled root. There had been no way to know how long the dog had been held there; it had sensibly chosen to lie quiet rather than thrash about and possibly strangle itself. With some effort, Kennard had finally worried the collar free from the root. The dog had pulled away and shaken itself, but it hadn't bolted. Instead, it had stood still and let Kennard feel over it to make sure no bones had been broken. When the boy had turned at last and reluctantly started to climb back up to the forest track, he had been delighted to hear the dog scrambling after him. Kennard had never before had a companion animal; he couldn't believe that this creature fit to course beside a high noble's horse might deign to stay with him, if only for a brief time. It had seemed uncanny, though, that the creature made no expectably doggy noises. It had given a low grunt when it stretched out to sleep against Kennard's back. Kennard had felt as if he were being guarded by a fabulous beast out of a songsmith's tale.

The next morning, Kennard had discovered that his color sense had been misled in the moonlight. The dog's eyes were light blue, like the clear waters of a mountain lake. Its coat was dusky gray all over, with no sign of white hair on foot or belly. They had traveled all that day in agreeable silence, stopping only for a frugal midday meal from Kennard's supply bag. He had been thinking that perhaps the dog could help him hunt some small game to stretch his scant number of journey cakes when the dog's ears had pricked up.

The dog had turned toward the brush-choked mouth of a narrow valley branching off from the half overgrown trail they had been traveling. Kennard had followed the dog through a mass of clinging brambles, wondering what had so attracted its attention. Then he had also heard the confused sounds of a struggle—muffled blows, sharp cries, and calls by different voices. As they rounded a dense bush, the scene had been all too clear before them. Four or five ruffians were unmercifully assailing two travelers, one of them a white-haired old man, the other a soldier from his dress and long sword. Kennard had clutched his staff, not sure how he could help. The dog had not hesitated. It had plunged into the fray, bowling over two of the outlaws before they realized what was upon them. The embattled soldier had taken advantage of the sudden respite to help the older man to his feet and stumble uphill to a more defensible position. As the dog had seized one outlaw's arm, the chief of the assailants had slammed it across the head with his thick club. Kennard had cried out and run toward the dog, unfortunately attracting similar attention. He had been struck a glancing blow to the head by one of the outlaws, and his next conscious sensation was being jolted across the back of a rough-haired mountain horse.

After dark, the raiding party had stopped and made camp, giving Kennard his first opportunity to speak to his fellow captives. The outlaws had simply tossed all three close together out of the way while they had built a fire and set about sorting through their victim's belongings. Tumbled close as they were, the captives had been given no chance of freeing one another. One of the outlaws had squatted near enough to prevent any efforts to escape. The first words had come from the older man, but they had made no sense to Kennard. The man he had thought was a soldier had tried to soothe his companion. "Lie easy, Brehm," he had said in a low voice.

Brehm had continued to babble something about metal, then he had abruptly fallen quiet.

The soldier had rolled his shoulders as far as he could in Kennard's direction. For an instant, a flare of light from the campfire had illuminated the soldier's face, with the weathered features of an experienced fighter. From Kennard's years with Rubeth, he also suspected that it was the face of a blind man. The soldier's next words confirmed Kennard's guess, for the two of them were lying in clear sight of one another.

"Stranger? Are you there? Can you hear me?"

"Yes," Kennard had said. "I'm awake."

"I thank you for coming to our aid. I am Jarrel, and this poor muddled fellow is Brehm, a prospector in these cursed border lands."

"My name is Kennard. I don't suppose you know what happened to the dog?"

Jarrel had shaken his head. "I heard no dog. Since the blow that cracked my helm at Morlan, I have been nearly blind. I can tell day from night, but that is all. You sound young, like a lad."

"I am, sir. I believe that I am twelve, or so said the wise woman who reared me. I am worried about the great dog that tried to rescue you. One of the outlaws struck his head with a club. I fell soon after, before I could reach him."

"A brave dog, then, to dare such odds," Jarrel had said. "We shall hope that he recovered from the blow. If he is a large beast, then likely he was but stunned."

"Do you think so?" Kennard's hopes had soared. He couldn't bear to think of the elegant creature lying dead in the trampled weeds. He had described how he had found the dog, and then Jarrel had explained that he had chanced upon Brehm at an inn farther down in the Dales. Brehm had wanted a swordsman to accompany him on a prospecting trip to the edges of the Waste seeking the rare remnants of metal sometimes buried in ancient ruins. Given Brehm's eccentric reputation, no sensible swordsman had been interested.

"When I said I'd go with him," Jarrel had recalled ruefully, "there was much merriment in the crowd. But we had some fortune in our searching, before Brehm became confused. I was trying to fix his attention on the trail when we were set upon by these thieves."

Jarrel had been interrupted at that point by raucous cries from the outlaws, who had just discovered Brehm's hoard of metal.

"Look here, Grund," one ruffian had said, flourishing the semimelted lumps as he transferred them to his own bag. "They be pleased at Darst to see these . . . but not that," he had added, shunning a small mass of silvery metal. He had hastily thrown a dirty rag over it to avoid touching it and had tossed it down a nearby ravine.

"Why throw away good metal?" a younger outlaw had asked.

Grund, the apparent chief of the band, had cuffed him. "Lackwit! Them at Darst want naught to do with moon stuff." In the firelight, his scar-seamed face had taken on an avaricious leer. "That be why our pay is in gold for all we bring as be useful to them."

Having ransacked the saddlebags on Brehm's horses, the outlaws had turned to their captives, prying into every purse and pocket. To Kennard's immeasurable relief, the man who pawed him missed the thin cloth packet containing his precious dried leaves. It had been during this search that Grund had announced it was senseless to trouble traveling any farther with the delirious Brehm. With one practiced swipe of his knife, he had cut the prospector's throat. "The Purple Robes will pay us no gold for a witless man. You, Foss—strip off his clothes. No need leaving them to waste."

Kennard had cried out at the murder, earning himself another dazing blow to the head. He had later recalled little of the rest of that night. The outlaws had broken camp fairly early in the morning, eager to reach the Purple Robes and their reward for delivering their captives.

At twilight the next day, they had arrived at an eerie space cluttered by randomly set standing stones. Very little vegetation seemed to dare intrude on the flat soil at the bases of the stones. Kennard had felt a chill unease caused by more than just the presence of so much cold rock. Grund had dismounted and had struck a blackened metal bell suspended in a niche in one roughly squared stone. With startling suddenness, a form swathed in purple had glided out from between two larger stones. Kennard hadn't liked the color of the robes—they were a sullen purple-red, like an old, unhealed wound.

In contrast to his usual bluster to his men, Grund's manner to the robed personage had been affected and obsequious. His eyes had kept shifting restlessly, as if he wanted to conclude his business as speedily as possible. Kennard had been too far away to hear what Grund said, but the robed man had a high, whining voice that carried. "Only two?" he had complained. He had peered toward Kennard and Jarrel. "One blind and one a mere lad. We are not pleased." Grund had muttered some apology, and the other had grudgingly counted out several broad coins made of a dark red gold like none Kennard had ever seen before. Grund had seized the coins and harried his men into feverish activity. Kennard and Jarrel had been jerked from the horses and trussed more securely, then hauled by two grunting outlaws to a bare stone platform where the robed man fussed about their placement. The outlaws hadn't even taken time to lead Brehm's stolen horses by their reins, but had driven them along running loose in their midst. They had in fact withdrawn so hastily that Kennard had deduced they didn't want to observe what was going to happen next. That conclusion had not been at all reassuring.

More men shrouded in purple-red had emerged from among the standing stones edging the platform. They had woven in and out in a silent, intricate pattern for a time, then one had chanted some sounds that pierced Kennard's ears and set his already throbbing head aching anew. As quickly as they had materialized, the robed men were gone, leaving Kennard and Jarrel alone in the wan moonlight.

The boy was just succeeding in lowering his breathing rate back near normal when Jarrel ventured to speak. "Lad? Can you hear me? I dare not speak your name in such a place. It might give them power over you."

Kennard grasped the sense behind the other's reticence. "I'm here, sir, safe as may be."

Jarrel sighed. "I would that you had not come upon Brehm and me. This is indeed poor reward for your trying to aid travelers in distress."

"Never mind, sir," said Kennard, anxious to encourage

his fellow prisoner. "It was the dog who led me to you."

"Whatever happens to us," Jarrel said loudly enough for any hidden listeners to hear, "hold fast to those beliefs you cherish. Remember what your wise woman must have said to you about things of the Light, for I feel in my bones that this place has naught to do with the Light. The firmer we can fix our thoughts on those Powers that aid men, the more can we thwart what purposes are lurking here."

Kennard was engaged in trying to follow Jarrel's advice while still regulating his breathing when the scant illumination from the moon faded away. Pale starlight enabled him to make out the standing stones' bulky uprights as well as Jarrel's shadowy form lying dark against the gray paving. He realized that there was another darker shape beyond Jarrel, a slowly swelling pool of blackness that seemed to be spilling up from one corner of the platform. Using a trick that Rubeth had taught him, Kennard glanced to one side of what he was trying to see, achieving a better impression of it in the dimness. It was definitely getting larger, and as it grew, tendrils of dark vapor were peeling off from the initial mass.

Kennard called to warn Jarrel. "There's a misty stuff coming toward you, like a black fog. Oh, do try to roll away from it if you can! Roll toward me—I'm over this way."

Jarrel tried to twist himself and roll, but he was too tightly bound to do much more than rock back and forth. The vapor spilled around him, blotting him from Kennard's sight.

Kennard was also straining to move, and of course his convulsive activity was robbing him of air. He squeezed his eyes shut and desperately counted to himself as Rubeth had drummed into him. Abruptly, he felt a cold, damp touch on his cheek. He would have cried out if he'd had the breath. A sharp tug at his shoulder rolled him over enough so that he could see a silvery shape looming over him. Unbelievably, it was the dog.

"I thought you were dead," Kennard gasped.

The dog didn't pause for conversation. It worried briefly at the thongs binding Kennard, then seized the boy's cloak firmly in its teeth and started dragging Kennard toward a gap between the nearest standing stones. A wave of black vapor pulsed about them. The dog rumbled low in its throat, the first sound that Kennard had ever heard it make.

Kennard tried hard not to breathe, but had to. For an instant, he felt a sickening dizziness, a pressure inside his head, as if an oppressive force were clamoring to be admitted. The vapor's fetid odor immediately set Kennard sneezing, and as always happened, repeated sneezing set him wheezing. He couldn't spare any thought for repelling a mental assault; his sole priority was to breathe. He groped for his memory of Rubeth's brisk voice. "Shut out everything else, boy. All that matters is your breathing." He wasn't aware of the scrapes and bumps his body was enduring as he bounced across the uneven paving stones.

The air was suddenly cold but clean. Kennard opened his eyes. He had been pulled completely away from the platform, into a narrow ravine. The dog was its old silent self again, chewing quietly at the thongs until they were shredded. Kennard lay prone while feeling returned to his numbed limbs. As soon as he could use his hands, he pulled out his remnant of Rubeth's leaves and chewed a dried fragment. The pungent sourness made him wince, but his aching rib muscles immediately relaxed as his breathing slowed and deepened. To his surprise, the dog poked its nose inquiringly toward the packet. Catching the distinctive scent, it snorted and drew back.

Kennard tucked his packet back next to his chest and stretched his arm across the dog's back to help himself to his feet. "We must return and try to help Jarrel," he whispered, as if the dog could understand the words. Moving as quietly as possible, Kennard crept up the rubble-strewn ravine, keeping a sharp watch for any of the robed attendants. Soon he was easing around the rough flank of one of the standing stones. To his relief, no one else was in sight except Jarrel's prone body, twitching slightly in a pool of receding vapor. Kennard hastily pulled a fold of his cloak across his nose and mouth and ran to crouch beside Jarrel. "I'm back," he whispered urgently. "The dog has come back, too—it must have tracked us. You must get up now so we can escape from here."

The dog had immediately set about gnawing at the soldier's bonds. Suddenly, Kennard's own pressing fear was realized. A robed attendant slipped out onto the platform to check on the condition of the helpless victims. Seeing Kennard free instead of stupefied or worse, he gave a shout and darted away to spread the alarm.

Jarrel, who seemed dazed, fumbled at his throat, murmuring, "Metal . . . medal." Kennard frantically hauled at his shoulders, trying to prop him up. With the dog's great bulk to lean against, Jarrel was swaying on his feet when a flare of red torchlight preceded their enemies' return.

There were five robed figures, but the aura of Power and the Dark that reeked from one tall, gaunt man proclaimed him the master; the others were mere underlings. Those with torches thrust them in sockets bored in the standing stones. Two attendants advanced toward Kennard, but the dog bared a daunting set of fangs at them and they faltered and stood still. In spite of the ruddy torchlight, the dog's collar gleamed pure silver, as did the smooth hair of its coat. When one attendant dared take another step forward, the dog bristled and threatened to charge at him.

"Moon monster!" screamed the attendant, whirling to retreat.

"Fool." The gaunt master gestured with a blunt black wand, and the hysterical attendant dropped, quivering, to the stone floor. Turning toward Kennard and Jarrel, the master gestured again. Kennard felt as if all the energy was being drained from his body, and was trembling, about to fall, when Jarrel finally extracted a metal amulet suspended on a fine chain around his neck.

In a firm voice, Jarrel asserted, "By the Flame, by the Sword wielded in a just cause, by all that stands with the Light, we claim protection."

Strength surged back into Kennard. The master stepped back a pace, as if surprised. These were feeble victims supposed to be stripped of all will to resist. It was rather like finding a supposedly helpless mouse clamping sharp teeth in the predator's paw. The master frowned at such insolence. He moved his wand, leaving black-red strokes hanging in the air. As he began to chant a fell summons, he was abruptly interrupted.

To everyone's amazement—especially Kennard's—the dog threw up its head and howled. A great, roaring echo filled the open space, vibrating against the standing stones. The attendants fell to the pavement, screaming and clutching their ears. The master looked pained, but stood his ground, and pointed his wand at Jarrel.

Without knowing why, but suddenly certain of what he was doing, Kennard seized Jarrel's hand holding the amulet and turned the medal toward the master. Unbidden, words came to Kennard, and he shouted, "Beware the Moon's Hound!"

The amulet blazed silver, as did the dog's collar, dazzling the eyes. Kennard had to shade his from the brilliance. A searing beam from the amulet riveted the master, who shrieked, and, as Kennard gazed in astonishment, shrank and withered within his purple robes until all that remained on the paving was a heap of garments. One attendant scrambled to his feet and fled; the other three lay blasted like their master.

Jarrel stood frozen, clutching at his amulet, which had reverted to its ordinary appearance. "I found this many years ago," he said in a wondering voice. "It was half buried in sand at the base of an ancient guard post in the northern mountains. It must be a thing of Power, as is the collar on that dog. I could see the light from the collar just now, and then the beam from my amulet, brighter than midday. Tell me what has fared, for I am surely at a loss."

Kennard described what he had seen, as best he could, his own voice shaken by his witnessing such forces wielded too near mortal flesh.

"My wits still seem half-curdled by that fog you tell me of," said Jarrel. "I thought that someone was trying to shout at me within my head—a most unpleasant sensation. By fortune, I recalled my amulet, and thinking on it steadied me until you and the good dog returned to rescue me. The dog is still with us?"

Kennard glanced around, suddenly aware that the dog had slipped away, but even as he peered about for a flash of silvered fur, the dog returned, shepherding a riderless pack horse which Jarrel said he recognized at once by touch to be one of Brehm's animals. "Let us leave this place," Jarrel added. "Although its servants are dead or fleeing, I do not like the smell of it."

Because he was somewhat unsteady, Jarrel at last agreed to ride on the horse while Kennard and the dog paced alongside. By the time the sun rose, they were entering a quiet valley that felt far removed from the blighted lair of the Purple Robes. Kennard divided a slightly stale journey cake salvaged from one of Brehm's saddlebags. When they had eaten and drunk from a nearby stream, Jarrel stretched his hands out toward the dog, who sat up as if it knew it was the focus of attention.

"I thank you for your valiant help," Jarrel said to the dog, as gravely as he would have addressed a person. "We likely could not have stood against those servants of the Dark had it not been for you and my amulet." He pulled the metal pendant out into the sunlight. The dog cocked its head to one side, watching the glittering amulet. "Would you come with me as companion?" Jarrel asked the dog. "I feel a drawing toward you like none I've felt since my sword brother died. I know not your name, but if it please you, I shall call you 'Silver.'"

The dog gave a vast, contented sigh, and snuggled up to Jarrel, nearly knocking him down.

"He must think you are his lost master," suggested Kennard.

"No, he would not mistake me so, but perhaps I may stand in the place of one he has lost, if only for a time."

The dog licked Jarrel's hand, then marched in a businesslike way to Kennard, tugging at his sleeve. The boy had to follow the persistent animal through a stand of ferns to the edge of the stream, where the dog freed Kennard and sat down, looking very pleased with itself. Kennard glanced all around, seeking some reason for the activity, and suddenly recognized a clump of shiny, wedge-shaped leaves. "My medicine!" he exclaimed. The dog wagged its tail, and loped back to Jarrel's side as if satisfied that it had rendered one good service in return for another.

Kennard gathered an ample supply of fresh leaves and packed them carefully between layers of cloth as he'd seen Rubeth do. Jarrel had rubbed down the horse, readying it for the trail.

"Brehm told me there was an inhabited Dale to the west," Jarrel said. "If we continue on, we might find it. I must admit I feel at a disadvantage without my sword at my belt. As soon as I can, I should like to trade for a new blade. Brehm said he must watch for a distinctive peak with a great rock near its summit shaped like a snow cat's head."

"But . . . but," said Kennard, excited, "I can see such a rock from here, above those trees to the west."

"Lead on, then," said Jarrel. "No doubt we shall surprise some landholder when we arrive on his doorstep, for we are a strangely assorted trio." To Kennard's surprise, Jarrel suddenly laughed. "Do you realize, lad, that while we have been otherwise occupied, the year has turned. We are no longer in the Year of the Raven; we are now in the Year of the Night Hound." He ran his hand lightly over Silver's graceful head. "And we have our very own hound companion fit to defend us against any perils of the night. It must be a sign of a change for the better in our fortunes."

Kennard gave a contented sigh of his own. He had finally found someone to travel with and belong to again. The road ahead shone brightly in the sun.

\*    \*    \*

## Afterword

*I have been keeping one mental foot in the Witch World ever since I read the first book in the series. When I was asked to contribute a story set there, it was both a joy and a special challenge. At the time my father was having serious surgery, so between waiting outside Intensive Care and worrying at home, I slipped off to the Witch World to try to construct a story.*

*For some reason, the idea of a great dog presented itself, along with a young man reared by a wise woman far up in the Dales. Medical matters being on my mind, I also thought my young man might be familiar with the asthma I knew as a child . . . and why not have him encounter some particularly nasty outlaws with links to even worse forces? The story shaped itself from there. I found my title the instant I saw the Year of the Night Hound in the Witch World calendar. I am thankful to say that my father's surgery was successful. I hope that my story may divert readers as pleasantly as it did me during a trying time.*

—MARY H. SCHAUB

# ISLE OF ILLUSION
## by
## Carol Severance

Metae chanted in time as, hand over hand, she hauled in her fishline. The small boat rocked with her steady pulls. This was her seventh catch of the day, and from the weight of it she suspected she had another fine-sized taape on her hook. She grinned as she envisioned her Uncle Taggart's sour expression when told of her success. He did not approve of her fishing the icy, winter seas along with the men. Just as he did not approve of much that she did.

"It is unfitting," he had snapped that very morning, "that a young woman, the heir to Komlin Keep, should dress like a commoner and place herself at risk on the open sea. When your Aunt Kelana drowned years ago, she caused chaos in the realm."

It wasn't Kelana who had caused the chaos, Metae thought. Aloud, she said, "I'm perfectly safe, Uncle. I've fished since I was a child. My father insisted I learn. *He* was not unwilling to go among the commoners."

Taggart's expression had grown hard then, and he turned away as he always did when she spoke of her father. Twenty years before, after their elder sister had disappeared into the sea, the twin brothers had fought over leadership of the isolated hold. Metae's father had won. But now he, too, was gone, and her uncle reigned as regent until Metae was old enough to take the leadership herself. Taggart was a harsh and bitter man and Metae was not the only one eager for the next few months to pass.

Metae grinned. For all his complaints, Taggart had not stopped her from joining the fishing fleet, and now, sitting alone in the cold wind and spray, working hard with her hands, she knew she had the right of it. How better to prepare for leadership than to live in the way of her people?

The wind shifted suddenly, causing the boat to jerk from its rhythm. Quickly, Metae tossed the fishline to where she could hold it with her foot, and reached for the oars. She must turn into the wind. Her move came too late! An erratic wave lifted the tiny vessel high and Metae was forced to grab the gunwale with both hands to keep from being thrown overboard.

"Gunnora, protect me!" she cried as the wind whistled in her ears and the fury of the waves rose. Her foot slipped and the unprotected fishline tangled around her ankles as it started sliding back into the sea. Only her full weight kept it from pulling her overboard. The slate gray sky dissolved into inky green and Metae detected the foul smell of evil in the air. This was no ordinary storm. The stench, along with the surging sea, set her stomach to churning along with the waves.

Her heavy woolen jacket and leather breeches and boots were little protection against the unearthly cold. She flinched as ice, formed of the salt spray, struck at her like flying needles. More ice slicked the edges of the boat.

*Am I to die here?* she wondered. *Am I to drown in these frigid waters like my aunt before me?* She envisioned her body washing ashore with ice clogging her lungs; or, like her aunt's before her, disappearing forever into the cold Komlin sea.

Then Metae remembered that she was not alone on the sea. Others of the Komlin fishing fleet had been scattered across the waters as they followed the taape schools. It was not likely any of them had more warning than she of the coming storm. All must have been caught unaware. The men would be fighting now for their very lives. Her own peril seemed less important in her concern for her people.

*Uncle Taggart will be well pleased with this day's catch,* she thought bitterly. Not only would her own death place the Keep firmly in his hands at last, but the most loyal of her followers would be removed from his concern as well.

A huge wave swept across the gunwale, tearing Metae from her hold and smashing her down onto the tangles of fishline. Another great wave washed over the boat and swept her and all else that was loose into the sea.

Metae tried to kick off her heavy boots and to disentangle herself from the line, but she was tossed so violently in the waves that she was unable to do either. She was pulled beneath the waves, swallowing icy brine. Then she was thrown again to the surface, caught in a rough, powerful current.

Exhaustion and the cold could not be denied long in the icy water, and though she struggled against it, Metae soon admitted that she was lost. She welcomed unconsciousness, for it hid the evil green clouds that blanketed the sky.

*I'm hot!*

Metae's first conscious thought convinced her that she had indeed drowned in the storm. Never had such moist and luscious heat as now touched her skin existed in the harsh lands bordering the northern sea. Never could it have. She lay unmoving, satisfied that in death she was at least, and at last, warm.

"You'll fry like a lanagoot's egg if you stay in the sun much longer."

The unexpected voice made Metae jump. A ripple of pain shimmered through her bruised and strained muscles.

"Mother of Min," she moaned ruefully, "I'm alive." She forced her eyes open. Then instantly squeezed them shut again to keep out the glare.

"Oooh! What is this place? I am blinded!" She tried to move again. "Oooow!"

"Tsssk! You even sound like a lanagoot."

Metae coughed and forced back tears. She was terrified to look up and see who the owner of this strange voice was. The storm had been no natural one and who knew what monstrous things might have been brought to life by its passing.

"Get up, youngster—if youngster you be," the voice said. "I'll help you into the shade." Metae felt hands tugging at her sore shoulders and she forced herself up onto her knees as much to avoid the pain as to follow the voice's order. She waited for the dizziness to stop, then opened her eyes and tried to stand.

She promptly landed back in the sand with a painful thump. Her ankles were tied together! Frantically, Metae jerked away from the old woman who leaned over her, thinking it must have been she who had bound her legs.

"Humph," said her wizened companion. "You come trussed ready for the spit. I thought that was just seaweed." At Metae's look of terror, the woman added, "Don't worry, I'm not planning to eat you. I'm no witch for all that I live in this evil place."

Metae looked again at her feet. It was only the fishline that held her, still tangled around her legs. She slumped back on the sand in relief and watched as the old woman pulled a sharp stone from her belt. With a few deft strokes, she cut Metae free. Metae was pleased to see that the woman cut the line carefully, conserving the longest pieces intact. Good fishline was a precious commodity.

"Who are you?" she asked as the woman tugged the remaining line in from the edge of the sea. It was twisted among large tangles of seaweed.

"By the Nine Words of Min!" the old woman cried, ignoring her question. "A taape! And it's still fresh enough to eat. I never thought I'd live to taste another cold water fish. Oh, this is a happy day indeed. Come on, girl, let's get this back to the fire before it starts to spoil." She clambered to her feet and scuttled off along the beach. "I could eat this raw and be satisfied," Metae heard her mutter as she moved away.

Metae struggled painfully to her knees and stared after her. Looking around, she saw that she was no longer anywhere near Komlin Keep. She was nowhere near the Eastern Continent unless her teachings had been all been wrong or there had been some magical change in the climate.

Her homeland, located as it was to the far north of Quayth, was cold and gray through most of the year, especially so in winter. And while Komlin had little contact with the outside world, Metae's father had shared with her all the news brought by occasional Sulcar trading vessels and even rarer visitors from across the high mountains. She had never heard of a place like this.

It was hot and humid. Sweat ran down Metae's back and under her arms even after she shrugged off her jacket. Her damp breeches stuck fast to her legs, the salt-encrusted leather scratching against her skin. She sniffed for the presence of evil, but the wind carried only the sweet tang of the sea and the rich, heavy fragrance of lush vegetation.

The water was emerald green with streaks of blue more beautiful than any Metae had ever imagined, while landward stretched a line of verdant foliage. Moisture glistened in golden sunlight.

Where was the rocky shore of Komlin, the barren islets that fringed the harbor? Where, indeed, was anything beyond this bit of sunlit land? Metae could see nothing across the sea except the clear azure sky. She shivered in spite of the heat.

Stumbling after the old woman, she called, "Who are you? What place is this?"

The old woman looked back, studying her with squinted

eyes. "You should wash the salt off before it chafes," she said. Then her expression softened. "Come, we'll talk while you soak and the fish bakes."

She led Metae to a nearby pool of clear water and showed her leaves to crush into sudsy wads for washing. As Metae began rinsing away the sea brine, the woman gutted the taape and wrapped it in wide green leaves. She slid the package into the coals of the well-used fire pit.

"I am Kelana," she said after a time. "Ah, I see you know my name. You must be Komlin bred."

Metae nodded, mouth agape. She closed it abruptly at the acrid taste of the suds. "I know your name well, Aunt," she said after spitting away the suds. "My father was your brother Garrin, Holder of Komlin Keep."

"Garrin?" the old woman replied. Her face lit with sudden pleasure and Metae saw that she must once have been a beautiful woman, just as the stories told. "Garrin became Holder?" Then Kelana's expression changed. "You said 'was.'"

Metae dropped her gaze. "Father died five months ago. Uncle Taggart stands as regent until I am installed one month hence."

"Ahhhhh," sighed Kelana. She sank back onto the mossy bank and rubbed her forehead with her hand. "So, Taggart has won Komlin at last."

"No!" cried Metae. "That evil man will not rule Komlin. Not while I yet live!"

Kelana gave a bitter laugh. "So said I twenty years ago. But the very day I was to accept the crown, Taggart worked his treachery on me. I had gone to Grayson Heights alone that morning to mourn our father. As I walked atop the cliffs, a sudden gust of wind pushed me over the edge and I fell, not onto the rocks, but into a great sea storm that had not been existent moments before. A current dragged me through the frigid water like a helpless tangle of seaweed and later threw me up onto one of the barren outer isles."

"But how did you get here?" Metae asked, lifting her

hands to indicate the lush vegetation. "This is no barren Komlin land."

"Do not trust all that you see, child," Kelana said. "This is the very island I first set foot on."

Metae frowned, wondering not for the first time if the old woman could be trusted to speak the truth. She seemed sincere enough, and she did resemble her father in voice and look.

"I was near frozen by the time I was thrown onto the rocks," Kelana went on. "With the last of my strength, I called on Gunnora to aid me and to whatever unknown gods might rest in this place. In so calling, I must have disturbed the evil force that Taggart had employed to entrap me here.

"The sky suddenly blackened and the air grew even colder. Then, as if in answer, a blue flash streaked the sky and the cold receded somewhat. A mighty wind arose and I thought I would be blown back into the sea, but just as quickly, trees and heavy foliage sprouted and sheltered me from the icy blasts. Rain poured; it only made the vegetation grow, and grow. It was as if the forces of evil and good fought some battle of their own here, with my life as the winner's prize.

"The more harsh and dangerous the evil thrusts became, the more gentle and lush became the hospitality of the good, until at last the entire isle had changed to the way you see it now. I have but to reach out my hand for ripe fruits, toss a line into the coral sea for fish to feed my hunger." She glanced toward the fire pit where the fish was cooking, poked at the glowing coals. "Though none is so good as a Komlin-caught taape.

"The battle went on for days before the darkness finally retreated and the air turned eternally warm and moist," she said. "That was when I learned that my chance for escape was gone forever. As the power of good altered the land to make it livable for me, the strength of the evil poured into a wall of invisibility around the island. It could not kill me, so it trapped me here instead. Had I lit a signal fire soon enough, it might have been seen from the mainland."

Kelana sighed. "But I did not. And so for twenty years I have lived but a few miles from home with no one the wiser."

She handed Metae a length of coarsely woven cloth.

"Does Taggart know that you . . . we live?" Metae asked as she wrapped the cloth around her. It seemed strange to leave her shoulders and arms bare to the sun, but the sensation was not at all unpleasant.

"I think not," Kelana said. "He dared not kill either of us directly. We are too close kin. The blacklash would have been too great for his limited powers. I think he expected each of us to die of exposure here where our bodies would never be found. He had no way of knowing the island had changed. No, I believe he thinks us both dead by now."

Metae sniffed appreciatively as Kelana pulled the fish from the coals. She drew forth roasted tubers as well, brown and crackling with escaping steam. Gingerly, she handed one of the tubers to Metae.

"Taggart claims that in your grief, you jumped from Grayson Heights, that you sought your own death," Metae said as she took a careful bite; it tasted like roasted nutmeats although the texture was not at all the same. She burned her tongue taking a second bite.

"Jumped, did I?" Kelana muttered. She divided the fish into equal portions and carefully licked the juice from her fingers. "Do you believe that?"

Metae snorted. "Taggart also claims that a woman cannot fish with the skill of a man." She saluted her aunt with a fistful of steaming taape. "I rarely believe anything my uncle says."

The days passed quickly on the island. Too quickly for Metae. She was desperate to escape before Taggart could take full control of Komlin. When she was not staring at the sea, devising impossible plans to defeat the invisible wall, she talked with Kelana about all that had taken place since her disappearance. She described what she knew of the struggle for leadership between Garrin and Taggart —how Garrin had relied on the will and support of the people while Taggart employed strange and sometimes magical tactics acquired from the Sulcars and on secret forays into the mountains. The use of magic was not commonplace in Komlin, though all knew that at one time the entire district had been inhabited by Old Ones; the people resented Taggart's efforts to sway them with magic that was not rightfully his. They stood by Metae's father. In return he brought them many years of peace and prosperity.

"I had hoped to continue that peace when the lands lay under my hand," Metae said, growing discouraged. "Taggart wishes to expand Komlin's borders, and thus his own power, by force and treachery."

In return, Kelana told Metae about the island. They walked the reef together, fishing and searching for edible seafood as well as for colorful shells. These last Metae buried to kill and clean the animal from inside, then displayed on a shelf in Kelana's front-roofed hut. During the warm evenings, Kelana taught her how to coax the tiny hermit crabs from their secondhand shells by blowing on them and singing softly until the creatures crawled far enough out to be snatched in her fingers.

"Hermit crabs make the best bait," Kalana said. "But don't let your nice shells lay about, because these little thieves will come and steal the prettiest of them away. They exchange shells whenever they find an empty, roomier one available."

"Is there no way to leave this island?" Metae asked her aunt. "No way to break the spell that keeps us hidden?"

"Only by finding and destroying the evil force that holds the spell in place," Kelana said. "What little power I had, I lost during that first fight between good and evil. I don't suppose you . . . ?"

Metae shook her head. "Taggart seems to be the only one of our kin able to call at will on magical forces."

"Which only proves that he's sold his soul to some foul thing," Kelana replied. "Our family's never been known to hold the power. The source of evil must be embodied in some living thing near here," she went on. "But it is impossible to search every plant and living creature on this island. My protector, whoever it might have been, did the job too well. I have searched every day for twenty years to no avail. No, child, there is no escape."

Metae was not willing to give up hope, however. She moved about the island each day, watching and listening always for some clue. The times she enjoyed most were when she was in the sea. She walked in the shallows, treading the treacherous coral in sandals which Kelana wove from dried vines, and swam in deeper water, often trailing a line for the ever-eager fish. Her wraps of pounded bark tended to dissolve in the seawater, but as they were alone on the island, she found it of little consequence.

One day, while swimming after a large blue fish, Metae found herself near a particularly ragged coral outgrowth. She shivered. The place was dangerous, many of its coral polyps poisonous enough to leave her ill for days if she should foolishly allow her bare skin to brush against them. Though she was fascinated by the fish, she turned away to seek others more safely accessible.

When she related the incident later, her aunt gave her a sharp look. Had she seen anything there but the fish and the coral? Kelana asked. An eel perhaps, hiding in one of the holes? Or some other dark creature of the sea?

"I looked no further than the coral," Metae replied. "The place made me feel unsafe, as if some evil dwelled—"

She stared at her aunt for a moment, not believing what

she had just said. Then she jumped to her feet and raced back toward the sea. Kelana followed. Splashing through the shallows, Metae hurried back to the place where the blue fish had disappeared.

She swam around the coral head, carefully avoiding the red sections which she knew to be most poisonous. Again she felt herself shivering as though the water were colder here. When she glanced back at Kalana, she saw that the older woman had stopped some distance away and was standing on a coral shelf. She was hugging herself as if the air and water were freezing.

"I can come no nearer," Kelana gasped when she caught Metae's eye. "It is too cold, the repulsion too great. The evil is near here. You must find it."

Metae nodded. "Good fortune," she heard her aunt call as she dove again to inspect the coral formation. She circled it. The area was not large. She came up for air.

"Go back," she called to her aunt, for she could see that Kelana was being assailed by whatever evil force lay here. She knew that the old woman did not have the strength to repel the attack for long.

But Kelana would not leave. "Its attention is focused on me now," she cried. "Find it before it realizes you are here."

Metae dove again.

There! She saw it! A pulsating green-black mass deep inside a pocket of red coral. There was no way to reach it without contacting the poison. She popped up for another breath.

Kelana's eyes were squeezed shut. She swayed in the water with the same rhythm as the creature below. "Gunnora protect us both," Metae muttered as she pulled a sharpened stone from her belt and dove again. Without hesitating, she reached into the hole.

The coral burned like fire against her skin, but she forced her arm farther through the jagged opening. Fighting every instinct, she thrust her cutting stone into the slimy, quivering mass. To her horror, the stone struck something solid. It slipped from her hand. Suddenly the creature split down the center and retreated from where she had first touched it. It slid apart slowly, retreating like a layer of slime beneath the golden globe around which it had been wrapped.

Metae almost gasped as she recognized the golden shape. It was a shell! The most beautiful she had ever seen. *Of course,* she thought, *the shell embodies the good in this place. It and the evil creature inside are trapped together here in the sea.*

Her lungs felt as if they would burst, but Metae pushed her arm yet farther into the hole. She knew that if she rose now to get air, she would never be able to brave that fiery opening again. She only prayed for courage—and that the creature would have no poisonous stinger as did some shelled animals. She lifted the shell in trembling fingers.

Exciting the red coral passage was worse than entering had been. Waves of agony swept along her arm and a horror of cold grew ever nearer her fingertips. The creature was sliding back outside the shell, trying to reach her. She felt it at the same time trying to curl around the inside of her mind. She stopped it by brushing the bottom of the shell against the coral to force the creature back inside. When she was free at last, Metae could barely gather the strength to push herself back to the surface.

As soon as she had air in her lungs, Metae fumbled open the woven bag at her waist. She dropped in the shell and cinched the bag tight. Fighting both pain and fatigue, she made her way back to Kelana. Together they stumbled back across the reef, each trying to aid the other, each barely able to stand alone.

Ashore, Metea moved into the shade well above the high water line and immediately began scratching in the sand. She dug a hole three hands deep and opened the bag above it to drop in the shell. The emerging creature slid rapidly back into the shell as it brushed against the dry sand. Metae used sticks to brace the shell so that it stood on one end with the largest of its openings down. Then she and Kelana covered it with sand.

Metae was ill for many days after burying the shell. The coral poison raged through her body, while the fury of the trapped and rotting evil raged through her mind. There were times in her delirium when she thought that it was her own body trapped inside the shell, slowly dying and rotting away, draining like foul black oil into the sand. It was only due to Kelana, who was barely able to function on her own behalf, that Metae survived.

When she woke at last, weak but lucid, Metae was startled to feel a chill in the air. "Have we lost, Aunt?" she cried out. "Did the creature escape?"

Kelana hurried to her side. "Thank the gods you have returned," she said. "No, the creature did not escape. Its death is causing the illusion to break down. The island is reverting to its natural state." She helped Metae lift her head. "Look, the wall around us is dissolving, you can see the shadow of the mainland there across the sea. In a few days more, we will be fully back in the real world and we can light a signal fire to alert those at the Keep."

Metae stared at the misty gray horizon for a moment, then looked down at her arm. The pain was not so great now, but ragged scars streaked across her once-fair skin. When she cried out at the sight, Kelana comforted her. "It is only the outside of your arm that looks bad," she said. "If you do not injure it again soon, you will regain the arm's full use." Metae wept as she drank the broth Kelana urged on her, then sank into a deep and troubled sleep. When she next awoke, Kelana greeted her with more warm broth and encouraging words. "The coral reef has disappeared," she said. "The sand is almost gone, the beach turned back to stones as it was before. The foliage has returned to scrub plants and salt-resistant brush."

"The signal fire?" Metae asked in a little more than a whisper. It was all she could manage. She rubbed her arm but did not look down at it.

"I've begun gathering driftwood," her aunt said. "But the job goes slow. When you are well, you can help." Metae looked more carefully at her aunt then. She was shocked to see how the woman had changed. Kelana appeared years older than she had before her struggle on the reef. Now she looked frail and fragile, her body too thin under the ragged woolen dress that she wore to keep off the growing cold. It was the dress she had been wearing when she washed up on the island.

"You must rest, aunt," Metae said, struggling to rise. "I can prepare the fire."

"You can't even sit up, girl," Kelana snapped. "Drink this, and let the gods finish this thing at their own speed. I'll survive."

It was many more days before Metae felt her full strength returning. She spent the time staring at the distant Komlin shoreline, watching it grow ever more visible across the sea. As soon as she could, she began making short trips along the beach to scavenge for driftwood. Dry fuel had never been abundant on the island of illusion, and what little remained of that earlier stuff dissolved in Metae's hands as she carried it to the fire site. She was forced to go ever farther away to find wood from the real world.

"We will have only one chance," Kelana said as they struggled with a jagged, salt-encrusted log. "This signal must be seen or we will die here in the cold. There will be neither wood nor time to build a second signal." She shivered in the icy wind.

Metae struggled harder, gritting her teeth against the pain in her damaged arm as she pulled at the log. When Kelana noticed, she made her niece stop working for a time, insisting that the fire could wait, Metae's arm must be saved.

When they were sure the evil creature had been completely scoured from the golden shell, by the ravages of disintegration and the predation of ants and other underground insects, the two women dug up the shell. Its color was brilliant, even in the paler, winter sun of Komlin. When Metae sniffed at it carefully, she could smell no hint of its earlier foul occupant. She rinsed it in the sea, then set it on a driftwood shelf inside their makeshift shelter.

Some days later, she noticed that the shell had been moved. Thinking her aunt had shifted it for her own reasons, she paid little attention. The weather was somewhat warmer that morning and she wished to search the far side of the isle for any remaining fuel.

The following day, the shell had been moved again. This time, Metae found it on the sand near the doorway. She picked it up and when she turned it over, gave a giggle of surprise. A tiny hermit crab had taken up residence in the great golden shell. It was unusual for a crab to choose a shell of this shape and size, but Metae applauded the creature's courage in choosing so fine a home.

She did not want to lose the shell, however, so she tried to tease the crab out. She spent the entire morning singing and blowing softly into the opening, but the crab stayed firmly coiled, locked inside the shell. Finally, Metae gave up in disgust and tossed the shell into a high-sided basket. It was too late to get to the other side of the island and back before dark, so she spent the afternoon helping her aunt rearrange the wood they already had.

"Perhaps we should light the fire with what we have," Kelana said that evening. "I distrust this warmer weather. If it heralds a storm, we may lose our only change to signal for help."

"Be patient a day longer, aunt," Metae replied. "There are several more large pieces of wood on the far side of the isle. I will gather them tomorrow and we will light the signal the morning after."

The next day, the shell was gone again. Metae searched the shelter, then the entire clearing, calling on her aunt for help. It was past noon before they found the tiny crab slowly dragging its adopted home across the rocks and toward the sea. The two women laughed and brought the shell back. Kelana wove a stout basket of twigs, and after placing the shell inside, secured the basket's opening with a lid of twisted grasses. They placed other, more appropriate shells just outside the cage to tempt the crab into shifting domiciles in the night. The signal fire, they agreed, could wait one more day.

It was quite warm the following morning, and Metae was startled to see new growth along the edges of the rocky shoreline. She shrugged out of her heavy jacket, then cursed when she saw that the crab had escaped with the shell again. It had torn a hole through the tough grass lid. As she searched, she noticed that patches of sand had reappeared and that the water was exceptionally blue.

"Oh gods!" she whispered when she looked toward the mainland. Only the vaguest of outlines showed against the horizon. The island was reverting to illusion.

"The crab!" she cried. "Taggart's evil must have drained from the sea creature into the only living thing that could reclaim the shell. A hermit crab! Gunnora forgive me for being so stupid."

It was too late to light the fire. The illusion was back in place. Their signal would never been seen.

Metae called for Kelana and together they searched again for the golden shell. They kept close watch on the entrance to the sea, for that was where the crab been headed the day before. Late in the afternoon, when Metae had all but given up hope, Kelana spotted a flash of gold at the edge of the water. She raced to the spot then screamed and threw herself back.

"I cannot touch it!" she cried as she lay in the sand.

Metae fought a wall of revulsion and fear to reach the shell; it was like walking through congealing pitch. Unable to reach the shell with her hands, she lifted a stick and swung it, knocking the shell back from the water's edge. She swung her stick again and again, forcing the evil crab to retreat inside the shell as it tumbled up across the rocks and sand. With each strike, fire raced through the damaged muscles of her arm.

Metae maneuvered the shell until it lay atop a flat area of stone. Then she lifted a large rock in her pain-benumbed hands.

"No!" cried Kelana from behind her. "Do not crush the shell! The powers of good are embodied in it and all will be lost if it is destroyed. We would be left unprotected and the evil free to take us for its own!"

Metae stared at her aunt in horror, then back at the shell. Already, the crab was pulling its burden back toward the sea. Metae picked up the stick and whacked the shell again, keeping it trapped in the cleared space around the fire pit.

"What can we do?" she asked, shuddering under the onslaught of real and illusory pain.

"There is nothing we can do," Kelana said. "We cannot kill the evil by burying the crab, for unlike the sea creature, it can simply crawl away, taking the shell with it. It will never come out on its own and we cannot crush the shell." She sank down beside Metae, wiping away tears. "We can only set it free and hope that enough of the real world still exists here on the island to allow our signal fire to be seen in the morning." It was clear from her voice that she held no real hope for rescue.

"No!" Metae replied. "That would leave Taggart free to use this foul thing again and again. We must kill it. This time for good." She whacked the shell back into the center of the clearing, then tossed the stick to her aunt and ran toward the small fire pit.

"What are you doing?" Kelana cried as Metae returned with a burning brand. "You can't light the fire now! The smoke will never be seen in the night and the fire will be burned to coals by morning!"

"Better that we should live out our lives on this unnatural island than that we should set this creature free," Metae said as she thrust the brand into the base of the driftwood pile. The dry wood caught quickly and burned as the moisture-laden wood of illusion never had. Flames crackled high and lit the evening sky.

No amount of prodding with sticks and smooth stones could get the shell into the fire or keep it there. Metae shuddered as she realized that she would have to touch it again. Shielding her face with her left arm, and ignoring her aunt's cry of warning, Metae reached out with her right hand to snatch up the shell. Instantly, she felt the mantle of darkness curling again around her mind. Forcing it away, she thrust her arm into the flames.

It was the tunnel of red coral all over again. She screamed, wavered, would have withdrawn her arm but for her terror of the black smear riding at the edge of her vision. She caught an image of herself, one-armed, useless, unable to pull a fishline into a rocking boat. She could not continue. Abruptly, cool hands touched her face, protecting it from the heat. A thin, frail shape pressed between her body and the fire. *Ah, Kelana,* Metae thought, *once again you bring me back from the darkness.* She held the shell steady in the flames.

Finally, when it seemed that nothing existed in all the world except the searing pain in her arm, Metae felt the crab let go. In her mind she felt it loosen and uncoil from the inner chambers of the shell and drop at last into the burning coals. Slowly, she opened her eyes and withdrew her hand. The empty shell remained clenched in her charred and bloody fist.

Metae and Kelana watched as the crab burned. They

were both numb now to the heat and the crab's piteous attempts to reach them. It shriveled slowly and turned to black ash, then iridescent slime. The fire had been built on solid rock so the oily residue could not escape back into the earth. It bubbled and hissed, and finally puffed into black, foul-smelling smoke.

The smoke thickened, rising in billowing clouds all out of proportion to the size of the animal that had served as their source. It swirled and expanded and formed into a great green-black column rising high into the sky. Across the light of the first evening stars, Metae could see it spreading like a thick blanket across the sky. They watched it until they could see no more.

Daylight came without warning to Metae and her aunt. They awoke huddled together in a cold wind, stiff from passing the night on unyielding stone. The fire had burnt to embers and the only trace of smoke was a thin smudge of dirty green high in the slate-gray sky. It disappeared even as Metae turned her gaze upon it.

"Hoy! Metae, is that you? Hoy, there!"

The voice brought Metae fully awake and she twisted to look back at the beach. There were men there, and boats. A whole fleet of boats, bobbing side by side in the rough winter seas. She tried to wave, but was too exhausted to lift her hand from the ground.

"Auntie," she whispered, "look. It's the fishing fleet. They have found us."

Kelana blinked her eyes and sat up slowly. She tried to pull her ancient winter cape around her shoulders but it shredded into a scattering of scorched rags. She patted at the burnt ends of her hair.

Metae smiled at her vanity and a few moments later took great pride in introducing their rescuers to the rightful Komlin heir. The older men recognized Kelana immediately for they had known her well before her disappearance. They came forward quickly to offer her aid.

"Humph," Kelana grumbled goodheartedly. "It's about time you got here." She refused their offers of loyalty, insisting their allegiance should remain with her niece.

"I'm too old for politics," she said. "I've been away too long. All I want now is a warm room with a cold wind blowing outside and an endless supply of taape." The men laughed and gave her their solumn promises.

"What news of Taggart?" Metae asked, sorry to be bringing a look of concern back to her aunt's face, but knowing the responsibility for the realm was now hers and Taggart must be dealt with.

The men shifted their feet and glanced sideways at one another.

"Regent Taggart is dead, mistress," one of them said at last. He glanced again at his companions. "It happened just last night. As the crown was being placed upon his head, Taggart suddenly screamed and pulled away. He lifted his hands and we saw that his fingers were burning. We tried to douse the flames, truly we tried to help the man, but the fire crept unquenchable along his limbs leaving nothing but black ash. The ash fluttered bit by bit to the stone floor of the hall. His feet burned at the same time, and his legs." The man stopped to take a deep breath.

"After the fire had consumed him entirely, the ash slowly changed to liquid. It was as foul smelling and full of evil as the man himself had been." He hesitated, knowing he had spoken out of turn, but Metae motioned for him to continue. "That foul oil remained for a time on the stone floor, then finally puffed into a cloud of smoke. We followed it outside and saw that it drifted this way. At dawn, this island appeared where no island had been before. We realized then that more than Taggart's evil magic was afoot and came to investigate."

"Evil always seeks its own in the end," Kelana said. "Taggart's failed scheme carried a high price." She glanced down at Metae's ravaged arm. She still held the shell clenched in her fist. Abruptly, a look of joy lit Kelana's gaunt features.

Following her aunt's stare, Metae saw that the skin nearest the shell had taken on a pink tone; it was shining and healthy with new growth. She looked up at her aunt in triumph. She understood now, that with the shell's help, her arm would grow back whole. The scars from the coral and those from the fire would remain with her forever, but the muscles and strength would return. She would be able to use the arm again to put taape on Kelana's table. Metae laughed aloud at that thought. The shell continued its care of Kelana as well as herself.

The shell itself was dull and faded. Its once-smooth surface was lined with tiny cracks, its golden sheen reduced to chalky gray. But it was whole and strong. Metae brought it with her to the boats.

"Why don't you leave that old thing behind?" one of the men said when she carried it aboard. "All the wealth and jewels of Komlin Keep are waiting for you at home."

Metae smiled. "The most beautiful jewels are not always the most precious," she replied. She balanced the shell on her scarred palm and held it up to catch the winter sunlight.

\* \* \*

## Afterword

*Witch World has provided the setting for many strong and colorful characters and some wondrously dark and malevolent creatures. So, when I decided to write this story, I began with the idea of creating a protagonist who must face the very darkest of Witch World evil. Metae, however, turned out to be just as stubborn with me as she was with her uncle. First, she insisted on keeping her Micronesian name, which made it almost mandatory that I place her in a tropical setting. Witch World is not known for its abundance of tropical reefs.*

*Metae then refused to accept any magical skills and was thus forced to combat the evil with only her natural, human abilities. Even so, she didn't let me make things easy for her. I thought the story was finished after she found the shell on the reef and buried it to destroy the evil. It was her idea to dig it up again, and we were both surprised when the hermit crab appeared. That made it necessary for us to . . . Well, you know the rest. As a character, Metae was unlike any other I had met in Witch World, but thanks to her insistence, I think she fits right in.*

—CAROL SEVERANCE

# GREEN IN HIGH HALLACK
## by
### Kiel Stuart

Tymmons first came upon the beast as he foraged the woods for food.

Crops were bad this year; many things that had seemed to start blooming strong and free withered later on the vine or rotted in the ground. An odd year; first the strangers tramping through (messy people!) leaving their trash everywhere. Then the widespread crop failure. Auntie Roon had taken one of the sheep that very morning to be killed for food. A ram, he remembered. Wouldn't make sense killing a good milk ewe.

Tymmons poked a toe into a rotting log, breathing deeply the forest smell. He didn't mind foraging. The wild beasts knew where everything was that could be good to eat. All one had to do was follow.

He was always careful not to take too many berries or mushrooms or greens from one place. The little beasts needed to live, too. Everything lived in balance, had purpose.

Aha! A flash of cerulean wings and the rusted-hinge call told him that here was a blue sentinel. And where a blue sentinel was, dewberries were never very far.

If only they weren't guarded by so very many long, sharp thorns . . .

Tymmons gingerly parted the tangle to insinuate himself through the berry bush. The tiny blue sentinel would already be stuffing its crop with gleaming purple fruit. He lifted his basket, looped it over one arm, looked up, and gasped.

Oh, it was beautiful.

It was something like a horse, but not exactly. Its hide shone the color of red earth loved by painters and potters, the hue of bricks lazing in the sun. Its sleek belly was the white of goat's-cream, and from a topknot of hair on its brow sprang a curving, jewel-bright horn.

It stood before him, snorting, entangled in the bush's long runners. Blood welled from scratches on its breast.

Tymmons cast his gaze about, searching for a tool, for some help to free the beast, all the while standing quiet and talking quiet, so that it would not fear him. The bush lay in shadow, but Tymmons was close enough to see the greenish undertone in the beast's large dark eyes. He slowly put down his basket; the beast followed his movement and then looked back into his eyes. It could not be made more plain if it had spoken aloud: Well? What now?

What now, indeed? Tymmons took a deep breath, held it, released it with a whoosh that ruffled his own forelock. Then he inched closer to the big beast, moving aside the spurred branches and runners, slowly freeing first the long legs, then the two-colored body. It was tangled, mostly, and not much cut up, having only been pierced by the thorns in that one spot on its breast. It meant, Tymmons thought, the beast did not struggle or thrash once caught. It meant intelligence.

"Here. Be steady. You will have your freedom in no time," said Tymmons, moving to pry away the last clinging branches. The beast whickered gently.

"You must have a name," the boy said softly, working the thorns out of its breast. He thought a minute, licking his lips in concentration. "Your name will be . . . Camryn."

He felt Camryn's warm breath tickling the back of his

neck. The hairs around the beast's muzzle were like fine bristles.

When Camryn was free, they stood blinking at one another. "Well," said Tymmons. "Well." He peered up through the overlying branches, noting how the sun had dipped. Freeing the beast had taken up a great deal more time than it had seemed. Long past the hour to head back home.

"Come," he said to Camryn, holding away some of the more recalcitrant branches. The heavy body moving broke the woods-silence with crackling twigs underneath crimson hooves.

Tymmons picked up his basket and looked once more at the position of the sun. Only a handful of berries and some mushrooms, separated by a layer of leaves. Not much for all the time he'd spent. He would see what could be gathered on the way back. Better to skirt the deep forest, because it looked like the beast was set on following him.

Even skirting the worst and deepest of the woods, it was slow going. Camryn stopped every once in a while, twisting his long neck to lick at the thorn-wounds.

"Wait," said Tymmons, setting the basket down, and Camryn waited.

Remarkable animal, he thought, sprinting back into the woods to seek a tresayne bush. There, right under the oak. He grabbed three leaves, and stuffed them into his mouth, chewing as he dashed into the waning sun. By the time he reached Camryn again the leaves had become a nice green bitter slush. He spat it into his right palm.

"This will help," he said, slapping the healing paste onto the bi-colored breast. Camryn snorted again and looked at him with those green-dark eyes.

"We'd better get a leg up," murmured Tymmons. He led Camryn again, wondering what Auntie and Uncle would have to say when he showed up with Camryn and only a handful of food.

Someone was coming. He saw a figure heading up over a gentle rise, walking alongside the woods, just as they were. It moved slowly, as if somehow fading along with the sunlight. Then it sat on a rock, head bowed.

It did not take them very long to pull near, and as they did so the figure looked up, and Tymmons saw that it was an old old woman, yet with the (still) dark hair, gray eyes, and white skin that proclaimed her to be of the Old Ones.

Tymmons quickened his pace. Maybe it would be better not to speak to this stranger. But she spoke to them, in a voice that was yet low and steady and not cracked by age.

"Ranthan," she said, as if saying the strange word to herself. "Ah. How came he here?"

Tymmons stood, fidgeting, but Camryn at his shoulder grunted softly, flickering his ears, not shying away.

The Old One rose and approached Camryn, laying her bony hands on his head alongside the curling horn.

"Ranthan, you are a long way from home, are you not? You remind me of many things."

Ranthan, thought Tymmons. Camryn's kind?

The beast stood quiet under the stroking hands, until the old woman swayed, and would have fallen, had Tymmons not caught her and set her upon the rock again. He wondered—ghost or witch or merely tired traveler—and saw how thin she was, and thought of the wild food in his basket.

Wordless, he scooped it up and laid it in her lap. And, so she would not think him patronizing, he then asked her, "You said, 'Ranthan,' as if you had seen one of these beasts before. Tell me more, if you know more to tell."

She went slowly to work on the berries. "Yes, I have seen beasts such as this before. They come from a land far from here. As perhaps I have. But—" She stopped, looked at him curiously, put her hands out to tough his brow as she had Camryn.

"You," she murmured. "You have a power. A talent." Tymmons felt himself grow sleepy; instead of struggling to break free of the old woman, he thought of how pleasant a nap would be (heard Auntie's familiar litany: Sleepyhead!), of how surprisingly warm the air felt for so late in the day. And was not the grass so very nice and soft? As soft as the old woman's voice as she whispered to him: "Sometimes, the answers are there just for the listening."

He was riding Camryn then, his hair flowing with their speed over hill and dale. A tree rose to greet them, shouting, and Gunnora appeared on the crest of the wind, fruits spilling to the ground in her wake.

When Tymmons awoke, the old woman was gone, and the basket empty. Camryn stood over him in the dark, protective, warm, whuffling softly.

Sleepyhead! he chided himself, and hastened back home, bracing against the inevitable scolding.

"Tymmons, Tymmons. And what do you suppose we'll feed this monstrosity?" Auntie Roop shook her head, then lifted the empty basket.

He looked at his toes and drew a circle on the floor with them. Uncle Vannit had said nothing yet, and that he did not like. If asked about the Old One, he thought, no choice but the truth. But no need to volunteer information just yet. Besides, was she real or had he only dreamed her?

Then Uncle said, "Mushroom crumbs. How did they get in the basket?" and of course, he had to tell them. Uncle and Aunt listened, and then Uncle said he would see the wise woman and return to speak with them all.

When he had gone, Tymmons slipped out into the moonlight, drawing his thin shirt closer about him. He passed the naked kitchen garden and dead wheat field and looked into the sheep's pasture. He saw there the outline of Camryn, drained of color by the moon, and before he could call out, the beast came to him at a gallop, clipped fluff tail catching a stray bit of the night's light.

Camryn's breath and body warmed him, and he thought with fleeting guilt of the grass Camryn must eat which the sheep also needed. But he knew that, he knew all of that. He slipped his arms around the powerful neck, and before he realized it, they were up, and away, and this time it was not a dream.

A cloud passed over the face of the moon, and it seemed to Tymmons that the cloud took Gunnora's shape.

Gunnora! Did she look down upon the barren fields and think of the people, her children, who were going to starve this winter?

Ranthan. The old woman had called his beast—for it was beyond doubt his now—Ranthan. A strange beast from a strange land, which touching, riding, seemed to waken equally strange things within him.

Thoughts. They streamed into his head and out again, like the wind streaming past his face under the moon. The cloud that had seemed to be in the shape of Gunnora had thinned, passed the moon, was gone.

Power? Talent? What had the old woman said?

He raised his face from Camryn's neck and saw that the beast had galloped him back home again.

How long had he been away? Uncle would be there by now. Angry again. One of those days where he could do nothing right, it seemed.

But he was not yet returned. And now Auntie Roop was gone too. Tymmons slipped back outside, and took care of Camryn, rubbing him down, giving him some of the water that remained in the near-side trough, standing close while the beast drank, wondering, wondering.

When Camryn was done and had trotted off to join the sheep (every living thing, thought Tymmons, needed company), the boy returned within, and went off to his pallet to fall into a rare, dreamless sleep, he who dreamed even with open eyes.


"What you are saying then," whispered the boy, "is that Gunnora wants Camryn to die."

The wise woman said nothing.

I won't believe it, he thought. Not Gunnora. They must be wrong, all of them. They are wrong. I shall prove them wrong.

"Sometimes," the wise woman began, "we must accept things that seem unpleasant. For the greater good."

Tymmons listened to her and pretended, nodding, allowing himself to look sober, sage beyond his years. In his mind's pasture Camryn frisked free and happy.

So. They had been at conference all the night. Selkurr the wise woman and Auntie and Uncle and some of the others. The Old One had been a bad omen, the beast itself a bad omen, that strange beast that none had ever seen before. The failed crops. Of course. Of course.

Needed: One sacrifice.

It was not that they hated him. It was not that they were cruel people. He knew that, as well as he knew the children and elders would need food the coming winter. He knew it all, and still . . .

He looked up, from the faces of his aunt and uncle to the wise woman, saying nothing to them, only nodding, and slowly rose to leave the room.

He went straight to the sheep-pasture, calling silently on Camryn, and again mounted and again rode, but slowly this time.

He remembered the old ram, the day before, the gleaming knife, the blood which would be saved for a pudding. (But some held back to sprinkle on the ground, for an offering). He leaned forward, touching Camryn's bloodred horn.

And turned Camryn, to head away from home, to go deep into the forest.

They walked carefully down a well-worn path, which during the daylight hours would receive some dappled sun, and so which grew the widest assortment of green things. A rabbit scampered across their way just ahead, and unlike a horse, Camryn did not shy at the sudden movement.

Running away was wrong. That he knew. But he could *not* submit Camryn to the knife.

He stretched, listening to the insect songs and bird songs. If you cared to listen deeper you could, he thought, also hear the plant songs.

Gunnora—was she not the goddess of good, of growing things, of women, children? Tymmons shivered, knowing too that she had another part to her nature. Was not Gunnora also death?

He was not at all surprised to see the Old One coming up the path.

"Talented one," she said to him, as they drew near.

Was she calling him a witch? This could not be possible. Was it not only women who had the great power?

Yet he did not run from her, this nameless lost stranger.

She laid hands on Camryn again, as she had when first they met. Camryn lowered his tufted head and green-dark eyes to her. Camryn did not fear her. How could she be a bad omen? But had they not also said that Camryn himself was such an omen?

Then she let go Camryn's head and moved her hands to touch his own.

What is a dream? he thought. What is a dream, anyway? Is this a dream?

Gunnora riding the clouds over the moon. The bare black fields. The growing green forest and the green in Camryn's eyes.

When Tymmons came again to his senses he was lying in the path, Camryn standing over him, half in shadow, half warm, half cold.

He sat up slowly and looked at the woods around him. Looked at Camryn. Looked again. And looked within.

How he had known of the blue sentinel that led him to the berries and of the healing tresayne and how a tree wanted to be known and cared for. How he had always known.

What the crops were saying. What they needed.

Resolved, he mounted Camryn, and they galloped off toward home.

He tugged at Uncle Vannit's sleeve. "But do you not see? There is no need—"

Uncle Vannit pushed him back, away from Camryn. "Stand clear, boy, you need not watch this." The knife flashed bright at Uncle's belt.

They were pushing Camryn, docile intelligent green-eyed Camryn, into the pen where before the ram had been slain. They were going to close the gate and get inside and—

"No!" He vaulted the red roan back and clapped his heels to Camryn's sides. In a flash they galloped clear.

People protested, coming after, but he knew they could not catch him. He wheeled away some distance, then stood his ground, calling out to them.

"What must I do to convince?" Poised, poised for flight. "You do not need to spill his blood. I know the cause. I have seen it, heard it from the ground and the plants themselves. It is from the leavings of the strangers —earlier. That is what caused the crops to fail. There was that in their leavings which acted to poison the earth. It can be set right." He paused, looking down, then continued. "I listened. Camryn and the Old One—she was not evil—helped me to listen. As I have always done. Remember?" He looked at Uncle Vannit, pleading. "Remember?"

"Oh, so? Then let Gunnora herself—"

"Wait!" He galloped farther off, eyes closed. Please, give them some sign! Is this not your way? Is this not your will, that all things should be brought back into proper balance?

The Ranthan. Green-dark eyes. Touched the neck, saw the grandfather of all trees, saw the seeds not yet formed, the fruit full ripe, Gunnora guardian of them all.

"Look to the clouds!" The cry went up.

Then, forming out of the low clouds it seemed, Gunnora herself.

The hum of their wonderment rose, then hushed.

"So." The goddess's voice floated to them like ripe wheat waving. They waited, respectful children all, Uncle lowering the knife.

"So. Waste is wrong. And how sad to waste such a natural gift as Tymmons can bring to bear."

As swiftly as she had come, so was the goddess gone, leaving them staring.

Tymmons closed his eyes, and started to breathe again.

He felt hands on him, hands on Camryn, leading them both back. He heard Uncle Vannit.

"What now?" said his uncle. "What now?" His uncle's hands were gentle on him, on Camryn. Auntie Roop stood close by, and her hand came out to touch the crimson curving horn.

What now indeed? Tymmons drew in another deep breath, looked around at the faces, the fields.

Much to be done. Now to call upon himself, to listen to what the life of the plants had to tell him. The earth to be cleansed with healing herbs, the planting of late-growing crops that would yet rise, riding, riding forth, before the hand of winter fell.

\* \* \*

## Afterword

*After I'd been invited to write a story for* Tales of the Witch World, *I got a very clear picture that I couldn't shake. It was a strong image like a painting: a Ranthan far from home, stuck in the bushes—and some danger lurking nearby.*

*So I decided to follow the Ranthan around for a while. "Green in High Hallack" is what happened to him.*

—Kiel Stuart

# THE ROAD OF DREAMS AND DEATH

## by

## Robert E. Vardeman

The awful words rang over and over in Luanna's head until she wanted to place her hands over her ears. But this would not stay the command given her by her father, the Lord Eoin, ruler of Rozdale.

Luanna stood on the keep's low battlement and peered into the distance as if she could see where her lover awaited her. Anscom of Arvon was but a farmer gone to market in Quayth when they had met. Luanna had held herself apart from the market barter, as was fitting for a woman of her station.

Anscom's quick wit and quicker smile had drawn her irresistibly into the bargaining and Luanna had pushed aside her faithful companion, Oletha, to carry on the dickering personally. Anscom had prevailed. And Luanna cared not. She had fallen under the rugged young man's spell.

So had begun their love the better part of a year ago. Many times they had met in other places, in assignations made all the sweeter by the forbidden nature of their love. Luanna had examined her heart and discovered that she loved Anscom truly, that the blossoming bud of her love had not been nurtured in simple rebellion against her strict father.

"To make him realize," Luanna moaned. She rested her hands on the rough stone battlements and let the breeze from the distant sea catch the soft brown strands of her hair and whip it away from her face. Luanna shrugged her shoulders and pulled close the fine cloak given her on her last name day. "Why must Father be so obstinate?"

This time she did put her hands to her ears. Luanna relived the horrible meeting with her father when she had proclaimed her love for Anscom.

"By the Nine Words of Min!" Eoin had roared. "No daughter of mine will marry a common farmer! 'Tis not enough that your sister, Kathenia, exchanges Cup and Flame vows with a *merchant*. No, that's not enough shame heaped upon this noble house."

Luanna had tried to withstand the waves of dark anger radiating from her father as the sun gives off renewing warmth. She had tried. She had failed. Even her love for Anscom paled beside the man's wrath. Kathenia, her older sister, had been given reluctantly by Eoin to a merchant in Quayth, but never again had the ruler of Rozdale allowed Kathenia within the keep to share hearth and bread. The match had been one of love and respect. Luanna thought her sister's husband too staid and dull, but the marriage suited both parties well. Luanna knew that hers with Anscom would be as filled with love—and much more excitement. Anscom's farm bordered the Waste and often, he boasted, strange creatures came from the depths of that sundered land, some peacefully, some not so peacefully, as they traveled the roads to the sea and the Gray Towers.

Luanna had tried to reason with her father, to convince him that none of the neighboring Dales held a man matching her age and station. Even letting this single thought flutter across her troubled mind now brought a shudder to Luanna. Although Eoin had not spoken of such a thing, she feared that he negotiated her betrothal to Lord Wexo, whom she had loathed since her youngest days. Wexo, twenty years her elder, laughed as if choking on broken glass, carried a stench that perfumes failed to mask and had the disgusting habit of spitting large black gobbets of *minz* weed into a linen handkerchief that he kept in a stained coat pocket.

A sudden flash of lightning in the direction of the Waste brought Luanna up to her full height. She thrust back her shoulders and silently dared the elements to do their worst. She was strong and young; she could overcome any obstacle—even her father and his desire to see his sole remaining daughter joined in wedlock with another noble.

Brown eyes focused firmly on the distant mountains now wracked with the spring storm. Resolve stiffened within her breast. She loved her father dearly and respected his desire to see her well married, but she loved Anscom the more and knew that with no other man could she find such happiness. She might give up the servants—dear Oletha! —and the fine garments and food for a simpler life, but she was no delicate flower carefully nurtured. The war that had flowed and ebbed through the Dales had proven that.

The life of a farm wife might not rival that of a lord's court, but Luanna cared not. With her love for Anscom burning warmly, she turned from the wind's slashing cold and went inside, circling down the stone staircase and finding her quarters, neat and well tended. A small, sad smile crossed her full lips. She would miss Oletha and her devotion to even the tiniest of needs bespoken by her mistress.

For a moment, Luanna considered asking Oletha to accompany her. Then all such madness left and cold logic replaced it. Oletha would instantly fly to Eoin, thinking this a service to her mistress. Oletha had been born a peasant and hungered for the station afforded nobility. Luanna and she had spoken many a long night, and

Luanna knew that Oletha would think it wrong what must be done and that she would be acting in Luanna's best interests to stop any escape from Rozdale.

Luanna lingered for a while over a note to her father, trying to console and yet seem firm against any attempt to stop her flight into Anscom's arms. She finished the brief letter and sealed the parchment with wax and the impression of a small signet ring.

She held the ring for a moment, staring at the shining golden surface of the crest. With hand atremble, she laid the signet on the note. In Arvon she would have no need of such a ring.

She hastily prepared a trail pack from her wardrobe, taking only those items which would prove warm and durable against the spring rains pelting down on the mountains between her and Anscom.

With great force of will, she kept herself from looking back in longing as she left the bed chambers that had been hers since birth some eighteen summers ago. Luanna knew that if she hesitated now, even for a quick glance, that she would lose nerve and be lost.

An hour later, her cloaked figure hunched over the neck of a strong gelding as she rode toward Arvon and her love.

"You don't understand!" protested Luanna. "I *must* go."

The innkeeper shook a graying head, then ran thick fingers through his hair. He frowned as he told Luanna, "'Tis not possible. The storms are too fierce. Even for this time of year, seldom have we seen their like."

As if the gods accentuated the innkeeper's words, a timber-rattling barrage of thunder drowned out the din of the heavily falling rain. The whiteness from the lightning blast lent all within the room an eerie aspect.

"I must reach Arvon," Luanna said firmly. "I *must*."

"There's naught but death on the roads this eve," said the innkeeper. "Even if the storm abates, 'tis folly to venture forth through the Waste." He shuddered, his heavy shoulders rippling beneath his stained and worn shirt. "Only death, only death awaits," he said, turning and leaving Luanna beside the massive fireplace.

She turned and peered into the dancing flames, her mind achurn with frustration. The storms had been severe; rumors of the Gray Ones abounded. Worst of all, Luanna felt the pressure of time weighing heavily upon her. She had thought to ride directly for Anscom's farm, little knowing—or caring about—the dangers between Rozdale and her love. Her horse had tired in the mountains, but she had reached the edge of the Waste, only to find a vast, desolate plain of destroyed lands that would require a guide to cross.

None in this small village would guide her. All spoke of the dangers. Luanna fumed at the delay caused by the storm and bordered on tears at the thought of skirting the Waste, possibly going the entire distance to the coast, then entering Arvon. Such a route would add weeks to her journey.

How she missed Anscom!

"I won't," she said firmly. No matter that the Waste presented little shelter against the battering storms, no matter that were-creatures prowled in the area. "I will find Anscom and enter into sworn troth."

A sudden gust of wind and rain pelted through the opened door. For a moment, Luanna's heart caught in her throat. She thought a Gray One had entered. The silhouette left by a dazzling lightning bolt showed only a hunched and inhuman figure. She relaxed when the door swung shut against the storm and firelight revealed a wizened old man, bent by the weight of a heavy pack.

"To the giver of the feast, fair thanks," the old man said. "For the welcome of the gate, gratitude. To the ruler of the house fair fortune and a bright sun on morrow morn."

"We can all use a bright sun," agreed the innkeeper.

"Welcome to you, Pearr. How was the hunting?"

"Good, very good," the old man said. He shuffled toward the fire and warmed his hands. From the corner of a watery eye he studied Luanna. She primly pulled her cloak more tightly around her and tried not to stare. Seldom in the Dales did she see one such as this. Pearr wore no cloak but depended on many layers of tattered shirts and jerkins to keep warm and dry against the storm. His feet were bound as if they carried myriad wounds, but only age slowed him, Luanna realized.

"What brings a fine lady like you to this small inn?" Pearr asked. He did not turn to look squarely at Luanna. He shuffled to one side, his glance still sidelong.

"Such impudence!" Luanna said, unused to those so obviously lower in station addressing her familiarly.

"There's something you seek, I can tell it from your face," Pearr said.

"Leave her be, Pearr."

"I can lead you through the Waste, if that be what you seek," Pearr said.

"By the Favor of the Likerwolf, Pearr, don't go leading her on like this." The innkeeper turned to Luanna and said, "Don't believe a word of his rantings. Pearr's been out in the Waste overlong collecting his debris."

"Debris, is it?" barked Pearr. "I get top price for the scraps of metal I find. Only I know the best places to find the metal of the Old Ones." He cackled and settled down, his feet thrust toward the warming fire.

Luanna looked to the old man's pack and shivered at the sight. Pale blue radiance danced like witchfire about it. He had found valuable metal, but it had cost the man his mind.

"No, Pearr's not crazy, don't you believe it, fair lady," the old man said, as if reading her mind. "I was a soldier, one of the finest that ever swung a sword."

"Not that story again," groaned the innkeeper. The man

left, a gesture to Luanna indicating that she ought to retire for the night or be bored by Pearr's recitation. But Luanna found herself strangely drawn to this solitary scavenger in the Waste. If he could lead her through, she would be but a few day's ride from Anscom's farm on the far side of Gatekeep.

"You need to get to the other side of the Waste, is that it?" Pearr asked.

"It is. Would you guide me?"

"Hasn't he told you of the Gray Ones?" Pearr inclined his head toward the innkeeper.

"He did," admitted Luanna, "but my business in Arvon is important."

"What's his name?"

"Anscom," Luanna said, the name slipping free before she could check it. "How do you know?"

"Just because I'm old and crazy from scouring the Waste for the Old Ones' leftovers doesn't mean I am stupid." In a voice almost too low for Luanna to hear, Pearr added, "Or what it is like to be young."

"You consent to guiding me through?" she pressed.

"What are you willing to offer as a fee?"

Luanna pulled her cloak so tightly around herself that her upper arms began to tingle from lack of circulation.

"Nay, fair lady, 'tis not your fine body I seek, though you remind me greatly of one long lost. I require only enough coin to spend another season searching the Waste."

"Searching for what? More scraps of the Old Ones' metal?"

"Aye, there is that, but it is a windfall for me. No, fair lady, I seek the Road of Dreams."

Luanna frowned. "I have never heard of such a road."

"Few have." Pearr glanced around, almost guiltily. "None here admit to believing in its existence, but I do. And one fine day I shall find it!" He fumbled within the onion-layers of his clothing and pulled out a parchment

turned amber with age and brittle with many foldings. As if
touching a religious relic of the Lady Gunnora, he spread
out the sheet for Luanna.

She peered at the rune characters and blinked, thinking
that the occasional lightning flash confused her eyes. But
the characters did glow with a green light of their own.

"A map," Pearr said eagerly, almost pathetic in his
attempt to instill his vision in her. "It shows the path
leading to the Road."

"And at the end of this road?"

Pearr looked around to be sure no one overheard. "This
I have told but a few," he confided. "At the end of the Road
of Dreams is . . . life eternal!"

Pearr remained silent. She had heard dozens of fables as
a child, all promising immortality or resurrection of the
dead. The war had chilled such thoughts and turned them
to ice in her mind.

"I see it in your expression. You think old Pearr a fool,
too. But that matters naught! I *know* the Road exists
somewhere out in the Waste. 'Twas built by the Old Ones
and carries the full import of their magics. All I need do is
tread the pathway of dreams and the years will fall from
me like a discarded cloak."

"We won't have to hunt for the Road of Dreams, will
we?" asked Luanna. She saw that Pearr, of all those in this
village, would know the Waste the best because of his long
years of hunting through it. But she did not want to tarry,
going off on silly excursions to nowhere seeking a fable.

"This Anscom, he's special to you?"

"Very," she said, softening in mood. The mere mention
of Anscom stirred longing within her. Each moment they
were apart turned into an eternity.

"Methinks I have heard of him. A farmer in Arvon, isn't
he? Quite a successful one. Rich, with dozens of servants
and field hands to aid him."

Luanna blinked in surprise. She had no idea that Anscom was rich. He had said that his farm spanned two valleys. This had seemed grand and exotic to a woman of the Dales where all was compressed into a small area, but rich? She had fallen in love with him for himself, not his wealth.

"This Anscom might pay a goodly bonus for a speedy reunion?"

"He might be inclined to do so," said Luanna.

"We leave in the morning, weather willing," said Pearr. "If that's all right with you, fair lady."

It was.

The days had passed too slowly for Luanna. Pearr had guided her well through the Waste, of that she had no doubt, but the dangers of this twisted, ruined land vaulted past her reckoning. Twice they had ridden off their course to avoid the Gray Ones. The were-creatures indeed stirred and roamed the land. And Pearr had insisted on waiting a full day without travel, such to her anger, to avoid a fierce storm.

The evidence of flash floods as they passed once dry riverbeds the following day had convinced her that Pearr knew this land and its dangers better than she. In spite of further delays that caused her to worry, she remained silent. The creatures caught in the flash floods had been strange beyond all reason.

"Spoor of the werewolves," said Pearr, dismounting from his swayback horse and peering myopically at the ground. Like an animal, he dropped to all fours and sniffed vigorously. "Recent, to boot. We might have to range farther west to avoid them."

"Must we?"

Pearr craned his head about and peered up at her with his sidelong gaze. "The Gray Ones are not to be taken lightly. Even when I was a soldier and in my prime, I'd consider twice before swinging a sword at them. Fierce they are, and fighters second to none. And when a shape-changer shifts to another form, it's doubly hard to strike. Blade cuts thin air and harms them not."

"That's a myth," Luanna scoffed. But she worried that it might not be from the look that Pearr shot her.

They rode the remainder of the day, riding directly into the setting sun, crossing several storm-erased tracks. Pearr began stirring nervously, his head moving like a sea bird's, swiveling about restlessly. Once, he stopped and for more than an hour, studied the rising land and the small range of hills ahead.

Luanna did not question his strange behavior. He had proven too accurate in his warnings. She had dismounted and walked about, studying the ground.

"Do you see it?" Pearr asked, startling her. She looked up, guilty.

"What?" she asked.

"The spoor. Evidence of a lone human's passage. Came from Arvon, unless I miss my guess."

Pearr shook her head, a soft brown halo of hair forming as she did so.

"Silver cinch buckle here." Pearr tossed it to her. She caught it deftly, then dropped it as if it had turned molten. Luanna fell to her knees and immediately retrieved it. Her eyes welled with tears.

"When did you find this?"

"When we stopped. Markings familiar?"

"Anscom has marked many of his belongings with this chop."

"Lone rider from Arvon, coming from the north even as we come from the south."

"No," Luanna said, words choking in her throat. She could say no more. Anscom wouldn't have ridden south toward the Dales for her. He had said the crop planting would take weeks. She had intended to arrive as he finished, a surprise. But what if he, like her, had been unable to stand the pain of separation and had ridden to find her in Rozdale?

"Might be one of his servants. Heard tell that Anscom's business ranges far and wide."

Pearr stared at the silver buckle. What servant rode with such fine trappings?

"Must be a servant," Pearr repeated. "Your Anscom wouldn't be so foolish as to get himself boxed in like that."

"What are you saying?"

"The Gray Ones herded the rider toward those hills, possibly into a box canyon. This part of the Waste is new to me. Been exploring deeper in and to the east."

"What can we do? It . . . it can't be Anscom, but if it's one of his servants, as you say, we must help him. We can't let anyone fall prey to the Gray Ones!"

"Precious little to fight with," said Pearr. "Haven't used a sword in years. Prefer to use this." He tapped this side of his head. "Kept me alive ever since . . ." His voice trailed off. He heaved a deep breath and straightened. Luanna watched him curiously. A definite change had come over the old man. He seemed stronger, quicker of step, taller.

"Since what?" he asked.

"Since my lovely Evona died," he said, his voice distant. Pearr might have been speaking to himself. "So beautiful, so very beautiful. The sun itself envied her brightness."

"What happened to her?"

"She died, at the onset of the war." Pearr straightened even more. "I fought as if driven, and perhaps I was. Perhaps I sought death to ease the sorrow of my loss."

"It didn't happen, did it?"

"My death?" Pearr laughed harshly. "No. I fought too well. I have medals heavy enough to stagger a pack animal. At the war's end it occurred to me that I might walk the Road of Dreams and bring back fair Evona. As the years wore on, I sought the Road only to recover my youth. There can never be another Evona, but with youth once again mine, I may find a woman of wit and charm and beauty to share life anew." He looked squarely at Luanna for the first time. "A woman such as yourself."

Luanna did not know how to react to this odd compliment.

"We cannot deal with the Gray Ones, you realize this? Nor can we fight them. But we can follow and hope that whoever fled their viciousness has survived. Only then can we be of any aid."

Luanna felt torn between pressing on to Arvon and finding if they could help against the werewolves. She looked out over the storm-wracked land, saw the destruction left ages ago, the palely glowing blue patches, the deep pits and sudden hills.

"The rider requires assistance," she said. "We dare not abandon him."

"Aye," said Pearr. "And there is more."

"The Gray Ones?" Luanna swung about, seeking the savage creatures.

"Nay, fair lady. This." Pearr pulled his parchment map from the depths of his clothing and carefully unfolded it. His fingers silently traced the contours. It took Luanna several seconds to realize that she looked at a map of this very land.

"The Road of Dreams lies in those hills?" she asked.

"Mayhap. Many's the time I have found similar formations and been deluded, but this time." Pearr shook his head. "A feeling grows within me." He flashed her a broken smile. "Mayhap you bring me luck!"

"Let's hope the luck extends to the rider," she said.

They rode less than an hour into the twilight before savage storms prevented further travel. Rather than allowing Luanna time to reflect and control her emotions, the idle time drove her crazy with worry. If Pearr felt it deep within his breast that he'd finally discovered his Road of Dreams, Luanna felt that they followed Anscom's path. It hardly seemed possible, but she *knew* that their separation had worn on her lover as it had on her. He had journeyed forth to join her even as she set her path from the Dales and toward Arvon.

What fate had befallen Anscom? She fell into troubled sleep, visions of werewolf fangs flashing and rending human flesh in an unholy feast.

"Faster, Pearr, we must go faster!"

"Stay your concern, fair lady," said the old man. "The rider lives. He has stopped much of the blood flow and rides on, weakly to be sure, but live he does!"

They had found the battleground where the solitary rider from Arvon had fought no fewer than three of the Gray Ones. For a swordsman to kill a werewolf required magics far beyond most human's command, but a combination of storm and luck—and skill, Luanna thought —had allowed the rider to escape. The copious flow of blood had marked part of the trail; rains had washed away much of the spoor. But the trail led deeper into the hills and Luanna felt magics adance around her.

Again, as if reading her thoughts, Pearr said, "It's that very magic that prevented the Gray Ones from following our unseen friend. Truly, I think this is the Road I seek. I feel years younger just from riding between the markers along the path!"

Stone pillars engraved with the same curious runes that had caught fire and burned on Pearr's map lent credence to his belief. Although Luanna felt no change in her well-being, she saw new strength in the old man.

"There!" Pearr called. "Upslope, in the mouth of the cave. See him?"

"Anscom!" cried Luanna, once she saw the fallen figure. Even at this distance she recognized her lover. Her heels brutalized her gelding's flanks. The horse strained to reach the side of the fallen man. Luanna flew from the saddle even before her faithful horse could dig in all four hooves and come to a halt.

Luanna tumbled forward, skidding in the mud on her knees. She took Anscom's head and cradled it in her arms.

"My love, your wounds!" Luanna weaved with dizziness at the sight of such injuries. The Gray Ones had ripped away at Anscom's flesh, taking huge, bloody chunks from thigh and torso.

"Luanna?" came the man's weak voice. "How? You could not have known."

She laughed and cried as she clutched him to her breast. "I rode to join you, even as you sought me."

"I'm so cold, even in the circle of your warm arms," Anscom said. "I fought the werewolves the best I could, but I am no warrior."

"You drove them off, you live, we're together." Luanna's words gushed like a freshet born after a storm. "That is all that matters. We will never be apart again."

She felt hands on her shoulder. Pearr knelt beside her and said, "Let me tend his injuries. They are serious ones. He had lost much blood. See the paleness in his face?"

"He will live. He must!"

"He is sorely injured. I saw many in better condition during the war who died. And their wounds came not from werewolves but from mortal steel. There's no telling what damage their magical fangs might cause."

"I'll tend him," Luanna said, pushing Pearr away. She took a deep, steadying breath and began working to save the man she loved.

Pearr built a small, warming fire, then left her with Anscom and her misery. The man fell into a coma, thrashing about weakly at first, then showing no sign of life.

Luanna's concern mounted. She bent down and pressed fingers into Anscom's throat. Only cold flesh and no pulse met her frantic probings. "Pearr!" she shouted. "Come quickly!"

Minutes later, the old man came from the depths of the cave. He saw the frightened expression on her face, then placed his hand in front of Anscom's nostrils.

Sidelong, Pearr looked at the woman and shook his head. "He is dead, fair lady. The werewolves' teeth left marks deeper than his wounds, and those are serious enough."

Luanna sank down, stunned, staring at Anscom and seeing nothing.

Gentle hands shook her from the trance of sorrow. "There might be a way," said Pearr, his voice clogged with emotion. "I have translated the runes on the cavern walls."

"What?" she demanded. "What are you saying? Even the Lady Gunorra cannot bring the dead back to life."

"The Old Ones were powerful, oh so powerful," Pearr said softly. "This cavern is the destination of the Road of Dreams. Within the cave lies a chance for Anscom. Will you risk it?"

"Risk what? He is dead."

"We know naught of the effects. His soul might be forfeit to evil because of the Gray Ones and the wounds they inflicted."

"You're saying Anscom might return to life but be . . . one of them?"

"I know so little. I have had no time to examine fully the runes."

Luanna looked at her slain lover and made the decision with her heart. "To be with him again is all that I seek in life."

"No matter what?"

"Even if my life be forfeit, I wish only for him to live again."

Pearr nodded. "I thought as much. Here, help me with

him. We must take him deep into the cavern, to an altar I found."

Together, they wrestled Anscom erect and carried the dead man into the dark cavern. The deeper inside they walked, however, the lighter it became. The dull blue glow so prevalent in pieces of the Old Ones' metals blazed and illuminated a large chamber. For a moment, Luanna stopped and simply stared, mouth agape.

Machines of strange and alien design lined the walls. Many glowed blue, some gleamed with a green light unlike anything she had seen before. But what caught and held her attention was the granite altar in the center of the chamber. More a trough filled with water than a traditional altar, Luanna still knew its purpose—and the risk she took.

"Anscom *will* be all right?" she asked.

Pearr only shook his head. It was as Luanna feared. They called on powers beyond human ken.

"The Road of Dreams," Pearr muttered, "ends here."

They got Anscom's corpse to the water-filled trough. Runes shone brightly on the stone sides of the trough and high above on the vault of the cavern burned a simple red cross, its reflection dancing in the water.

"No hesitation, no doubts," ordered Pearr. With a surge of muscle, he heaved Anscom up and into the water.

Luanna gasped. She had thought Anscom would sink. He floated—and the water began to sizzle and boil around him. As if evaporating, the water vanished until he lay in the dry trough.

"Anscom?" she called hesitantly. No response. She turned and buried her face in Pearr's shoulder, hot, bitter tears soaking into his filthy shirts. "How long?" she sobbed out. "When can we try again?"

"Not for long years," said Pearr. "The runes said that the trough must again fill before use. Only a drop every year is added, a single drop of the magical moisture."

Luanna pushed back and stared at the old man. "You mean that—"

"Yes," Pearr said gently. "My chance at youth is gone, but it was a noble attempt."

"You gave up so much just to resurrect Anscom? But why?"

Pearr's smile carried no sadness, just longing. "How you remind me of Evona. For her I would risk anything."

Before Luanna could speak, a rustling sound brought her around in the circle of Pearr's arms. Her brown eyes shot open and tears ran down her cheeks. In the trough Anscom stirred.

"Luanna?" he said in a weak voice. "What has happened? I remember being so cold. Then came odd dreams."

She helped him to sit. She felt the familiar flow of his muscles as strength returned. He slipped from the gelid, dry stone of the trough and stood on shaky legs.

"You're alive," she cried, weeping unabashedly now.

"I'm only alive when I am with you," he said. Anscom reached over, lifted her chin and kissed her gently on the lips.

Luanna broke off. "Pearr sacrificed so much. Anscom, he . . ." Luanna looked around the chamber populated with its strange metal machines and echoes from times long past. Pearr had vanished.

"Perhaps he has left the cave," suggested Anscom.

"Yes, let's find him. And then hurry back to your farm. It is planting season and we shouldn't be gone long."

Arms around one another, they left the chamber of the Old Ones. But they did not find Pearr. He crouched behind a blue-glowing machine long after the lovers had departed. Through weak eyes he watched as four droplets formed at each end of the cross on the ceiling, drifted slowly to the center, and coalesced into a single large drop. Its weight eventually caused it to break free of the red cross and fall downward, splashing in the bottom of the trough.

How many years would it take before the trough again overflowed with the life-giving magical fluid of the Old Ones?

Pearr didn't know. What he did know was that he would be long dead when it occurred. He had walked the Road of Dreams and found life—but it had not been his own that he'd restored.

He bustled about the cavern, gathering small bits of metal. Somehow his loss did not seem too great when he saw Luanna and Anscom together. Dreams cannot die.

* * *

## Afterword

*The magic of Estcarp and the plight of Simon Tregarth captivated my imagination from the first pages of* Witch World *when I read it almost twenty-five years ago. I followed subsequent forays into this world and my imagination began to reach beyond the words and ideas and characters Andre Norton had penned; I started making up small stories of my own. Of all the odd niches in the Witch World, the desolation of the war-ruined deserts appealed to me the most. The notion of men—and beasts and magical creatures—prowling the wastes looking for scraps of old metal conjured up the most potent pictures.*

*What else lay in those wastes? Odd bits of inspiration intrude from other sources and in this case it was the Jefferson Starship's song "Winds of Change." Somehow, the pieces from the song about winds of change blowing through a person's life and the life a scavenger might lead in the deserts of the Witch World came together. From this basic mix I added the ultimates in a person's life: love, hope and . . . death.*

—ROBERT E. VARDEMAN

# BIOGRAPHICAL NOTES

**Belden, Wilanne Schneider**

Wilanne Belden has long been closely connected with schools and a children's playhouse. Now retired, she has turned to the writing of such stories as she needed for her gifted pupils but could not find. *Mind Call* was published in 1981, to be followed by *The Rescue of Ranor* in 1983. Three more such books are now under contract with options on others. "Fenneca" is her first published short story.

She is a busy person with dance, music, travel, sailing, photography, animated filmmaking, and the like added to her writing.

**Bloch, Robert**

He has written novels, stories, articles, verse, essays, criticism, advertising copy, political campaign material, radio scripts, teleplays, and screenplays. In his fiction he has at times imitated H.P. Lovecraft, Thorne Smith, A.B. Guthries, Stuart Cloete, Hemingway, James Joyce, and others. He completed a last unfinished story by Edgar Allan Poe. But the tale in this volume represents the first time he has imitated Andre Norton, whom he greatly admires, and the first time he has written anything in drag. (Bio courtesy of Mr. Bloch.)

**Crispin, A.C.**

Ann Crispin is the author of the Star Trek novel *Yesterday's Son* and *V* (novelization of the TV miniseries) as well as the novelization of *Sylvester* (a horse story for young adults). She is currently finishing a novel of her own, *Sun Castle,* and she is a former visitor to Witch World, having collaborated on *Gryphon's Eyrie*. There are plans for a second such collaboration in the future. She lives in Mayland with her husband, son, three cats, and two horses, and enjoys writing about everything except herself.

**de Lint, Charles**

He was born in the Netherlands but is now a citizen of Canada where he is a full-time musician and writer. He is also the proprietor/editor of Triskell Press, a small house that specializes in the publication of fantasy chapbooks, and *Dragonfields,* a magazine of fantasy stories.

**Dunn, Marylois**

She is new to the fantasy field, though she has written extensively in the genres of mysteries and books for young readers. Living in Texas, she is a lover of the outdoors, a planter and harvester of herbs and miniature roses. She also practices photography and needle art. Her latest book is a collaboration with Ardath Mayhar.

**Griffin, Pauline**

She began writing in early childhood and is the author of the forthcoming *Star Commando* series, the first two books of which are in current production. She lives in Brooklyn, New York, with her parents, brother, and her cat.

**Heidbrink, James**

He is a newcomer to the fantasy field although he has written everything from poetry to self-defense articles for martial arts magazines. When not slaving over his next piece of writing, he may be found entertaining customers in the restaurant-lounge he owns.

### Inks, Clara

Graduated Clarion West in 1984. Has sold two stories to fantasy anthologies and is the creator of a shared world fantasy anthology now in preparation. Works also on games, puzzles, designs, and creates plush animals with Marilyn McMillan. Lives with her family of three in California.

### Lackey, Mercedes

Though her present occupation is a computer programmer for American Airlines she has found time to write stories for several anthologies and her own trilogy is now under consideration. She has also written some lyrics which have been set to music by a number of people. *Off Centaur* has done a tape of some of them—*Murder, Mystery and Magic.*

### Mayhar, Ardath

Out of the wide plains of Texas to misty lands of her own devising, Ardath Mayhar makes a remarkable transition, aided by the fact that she was and is a poet. She is able to enter into another writer's dreams as she did Beam Piper's in *Golden Dream.* Then there are the many worlds of her own in which a reader can lose oneself.

### Miller, Sasha (Georgia)

She has been a professional writer for some fifteen years since the sale of a novel to Doubleday, writing historical fiction and novelizations of TV Western books. She is the winner of the Tepee Award from the Oklahoma Writer's Federation and the Award of Merit from Friends of American Writers. She is a member of the Authors' Guild, SFWA, and is a Clarion survivor.

### Scarborough, Elizabeth

Though originally from Kansas City, Elizabeth Scarborough has lived in Fairbanks, Alaska, for the last twelve years. She served in Vietnam as a member of the Army Nurse Corps, and later in the now-defunct Indian Health Society. Author of six outstanding fantasy novels, she is assisted in her work by three professional paperweight felines.

### Schaub, Mary H.

A college-trained mathematician, she worked as a corporation bookkeeper until 1971. She has had stories published in *Analog* and *Galileo* as well as in anthologies. Her reading ranges from the *Wall Street Journal* to historical and mystery novels and she says that her own book collection weighs down the house against any blows that may be delivered by North Carolina hurricanes.

### Severance, Carol

She is a Hawaii-based writer with a background in art and journalism. Her knowledge of coral reefs and hermit crabs comes from actual years spent on the remote atolls of Micronesia. She attended Clarion West in 1984, has sold stories since to anthologies, and is currently at work on two novels.

### Stuart, Kiel

She considers herself a full-fledged generalist, having written mainstream fiction, humor, science fiction, fantasy, and health fitness articles, as well as regular science news columns. She is a portrait painter as well. Professional memberships include the Oil Pastel Association, Pen and Brush Inc., and the American Portrait Society, as well as the Authors' Guild and Science Fiction Writers of America.

### Tarr, Judith

Born in Maine; degrees from Mount Holyoke College, Cambridge University, and Yale. Now completing a Ph.D in Medieval Studies at Yale. Author of, to date, two fantasy trilogies: the historical fantasies called together *The Hound and The Falcon: The Isle of Glass, The Golden Horn,* and *The Hounds of God;* and the high fantasy series, *Avaryan Rising: The Hall of the Mountain King, The Lady of Han-Gilen,* and *A Fall of Princes. Isle of Glass* was a finalist for the Compton Crook/Stephen Tall Award for Best Sf-Fantasy First Novel of 1985. Shorter works include stories in *Moonsinger's Friends* (Bluejay) and *Isaac Asimov's Science Fiction Magazine.* On a more personal note, she is the owner of the statutory two cats with the statutory unusual names (Catiline and Abelard) and is an avid horsewoman currently training an Arabian in classic dressage.

### Vardeman, Robert

He is the author of more than twenty fantasy and science-fiction novels, including the very popular Cenotaph Road series, two Star Trek books, and the recently published *Echoes of Chaos.* The past vice-president of the Science Fiction Writers of America, he lives in Alberquerque, New Mexico.

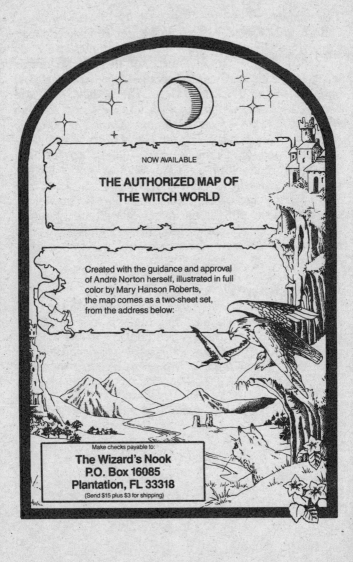